I0628968

The Brothers Angelus

In the hollowed icy cavern lay a peculiar and ancient looking ship preserved under the mountain's permafrost. It was sleek and somewhat arched in design, looking like an alien space ship from a sci-fi movie. Its nose resembled an arrowhead leading into the neck and aft form which widened to a broader triangular shape of the hull.

From its widening and bulbous aft section came downward-swept wings ending in sharp winglets. Out from its backside sprouted four triangular stabilizers, similar to the slanted vertical stabilizers of several military jets I'd seen.

Finally, jutting out from its back end, were four massive cylindrical engines. It was an incredible sight to behold, neither of us had ever seen anything like it, not in our wildest imaginations.

Jonos pointed to the exposed area of the hull we faced, flashing his Link-light over it and guiding my sight to a specific bit of what appeared to be writing. I looked at it and wondered in fascination when I read what appeared to be our own alphabet. The lettering had a slight variation but the resemblance was uncanny. The script read simply one word:

ZANZABAR

"ZANZABAR?" I said aloud. "I wonder what that means."

"Let's go find out." My twin brother Jonos said, smiling.

"Right with you."

Look out for these future titles in the omnibus:

Book Two: Secrets of the Arcos
Book Three: Angel's Demise

ANGELUS OMNIBUS:

The Brothers Angelus

Book One

Stephen Anthony Floro

Copyright ©2014 Stephen Floro
All rights reserved.

ISBN: 978-0-9991324-0-1

For the Kojima Kids,
Always looking for our own little slice of heaven.

TABLE OF CONTENTS

Note to the Reader,

Writing this story was without a doubt, a massive undertaking. From creating worlds and languages, to drawing out complex story lines, to trying to keep track of all these invented names, places, and events. I don't know how "The Greats" do it; but to make your life easier, the following pages contain a comprehensive character list for your reference, as well as notes on phonetic pronunciations for certain "Alien" languages.

But enough about *my* undertaking, The Brothers Angelus is now *your* undertaking and I sincerely thank you for making it so! Enjoy!

Stephen Anthony Floro
April 2017

Dramatis Personae
& Notes on Phonetics

Angelus Family

- ❖ **Arcus** – "Ark-us" father, engineer, astrophysicist, and project lead on UTF Operation Galaxia
- ❖ **Davriel** – "Dav-ree-el" oldest Angelus brother, Corporal in UTF Marine Corps
- ❖ **Jonos** – "Jon-os" older Angelus twin, private pilot / flight instructor
- ❖ **Savos** – "Sav-os" younger Angelus twin, unemployed college graduate
- ❖ **Cephus** – "See-fus" youngest Angelus brother, Lieutenant JG in UTF Naval Guard
- ⚓ **Brina** – Arcus' wife and best friend
- ⚓ **Valena Empallo**– Arcus' first true friend and former lover, mother to Davriel
- ⚓ **Lora Smyth** – Arcus' one-time lover, mother to Cephus

Terran

Basic Terran language, or *Terran Standard* as it is referred to, follows the same linguistic mechanics of modern English with its draws from Latin and Germanic based roots. Read it just like you would "normal" English.

Angelus Relations / Contacts / Friends

- ➢ **Ayla Varnatelli** – "Ay-la" Jonos' fiancée and successful marketing analyst
- ➢ **Tytus Hyaeger** – Savos and Jonos' long-time friend, public works
- ➢ **Shelyse Hyaeger** – "Shell-ees" Tytus' wife and registered nurse
- ➢ **Jimian Aryen** – "Jim-ee-an" long-time friend of Jonos

- ➤ **Ander Ollen** – Secondary friend of Savos, medical student
- ➤ **Pria Zaldeon** – Secondary friend of Savos and Jonos, mechanical engineer
- ➤ **Kaitoh O'Balin** – "Ky-toh" long-time friend of Jonos
- ➤ **Devian Teego** – "Dev-ee-an" Secondary friend of Savos
- ➤ **Lizia Ruels** – "Liz-ee-uh" Secondary friend of Savos, aspiring pilot
- • **Dr. Franzi Dorfmund** – Arcus' partner, former UTF astrophysicist and engineer
- • **Rennai** – owner of Shendale Locality Airfield

United Terran Federation (UTF) Officials
- ➤ **Chancellor Hulioberto Pelantius** – Supreme Magistrate and political leader of the UTF
- ➤ **Chief Commerce Minister Dekkun Pikus** – Chief Magistrate, Ministry of Finance and Commerce
- ➤ **Chief Defense Minister Luca de Gulliss** – Chief Magistrate, UTF Military Commander in Chief
- ➤ **Chief Correspondence Minister Kelanna Chavion** – Chief Magistrate, Ministry of Media

UTF Officers
- ➤ **Admiral Li Kyphese** – UTF Cybian Battalion admiral, operations commander of Joint Orbital Base Khorneus
- ➤ **Admiral Donas Willison** – UTF Amassian Admiral

Crew and Passengers of Skyhawk Delta 451
- ➤ **Lieutenant Commander Ramos Marco "Army" Elnezzi** – Skyhawk Pilot
- ➤ **Lieutenant Rahvan Delantos** – Skyhawk Flight Officer / co-pilot

- ➤ **Ensigns Dio Leheura** and **Jun Araffi**– Skyhawk gunners
- ➤ **Corporal Deonte "D-Train" Trane** – Davriel's friend and companion, mechanic

Fort Kane Battalion Officers

- ➤ **Lieutenant Commander Sha Yun Lii** – Litehawk pilot
- ➤ **Commander Hirojma Khan** – Commanding officer at Fort Kane

Crew of Naval Guard Cutteran WHEC 723 EAGLE

- ➤ **Captain Darellon Baldsmith** – ship captain
- ➤ **Ensign Lizany Nagost** – bridge officer
- ➤ **Petty Officer Mohamadi "Kash" Kashvin** – deck officer
- ➤ **Seaman Mikathon "Mike" Delhunt** – watchman
- ➤ **Lieutenant-Commander Numen** – Seahawk "Big Bird" pilot
- ➤ **Lieutenant Jansen** – Seahawk "Big Bird" co-pilot
- ➤ **Lieutenant Junior Grade Zaneil Banim** – Seahawk "Big Bird" Flight Officer, best friend of Cephus
- ➤ **Ensigns Kustig, Baumerodden "Baumer"** and **O'Bannoch** – Seahawk "Big Bird" dive team
- ➤ **Chief Petty Officer Vasic** and **Petty Officers Dalls, Granera, Simund** – boarding team "Bucs"
- ➤ **Corpsman Trasker** – medical officer

Arcos "Ark-os"

Unless otherwise noted, Arcos speech is written in Standard Terran (English) for reader understanding.

- ❖ **Andros** – "And-ros" nephew of Arcus
- ❖ **Arter** – "Ar-tur" father of Arcus
- ❖ **Brendenel** – Andros' best friend
- ❖ **Haleb** – Keeper of Andros and Brendenel

Gaïos "Ga-ee-os"

The Gaïos language follows similar rules to English, with most vowel sounds retaining their natural sounds. There are some differences however. The frequently used I with an umlaut, "ï" makes an "ee" sound like the word **tree**. An upward accented E, "é" gives an "ay" sound as in **ray**, while the downward accented E, "è" gives an "eh" sound as in **pet**. The "**u**" prior to a surname always takes the "oo" sound as in **cool**.

- **Evï u'Neréas** – "Ev-ee oo-Ner-ay-as" Prime'ïos and historian
- **Réa u'Neréas** – "Rey-ah oo-Ner-ay-as" Prïm'ella and heiress
- **Brandu Bracaras** – "Bran-doo Brah-kahr-us" Gaïos Emissariat, former surface dweller
- **Laurales e'Yazela** – "Lor-al-es eh-Ya-zel-ah" Gaïos Emissariat
- **Karïséa** – "Kar-ee-sey-ah" Galasari warrior, Gaïos Citadel guardian
- **Kadïm** – "Ka-deem" Galantir warrior, Gaïos Citadel guardian
- **Barïm** – "Ba-reem" Gaïos warrior, surface dweller
- **Roxara** – "Rok-zhar-ah" Gaïos warrior, surface dweller

v

Malïos "Mal-ee-os"

Malïos language follows the same basic rules of the
Gaïos language though their skewed sensibilities
often manifest themselves in over-pronunciation of
their "S" sounds. Phonetically they follow basic
Gaïos language rules where the "Ï" has an *ee* sound
and the "**ai**" spelling is given the " i " sound as in
pie.

- **Tar'thak** – Malïos warrior
- **Mok'junai** – Malïos warrior
- **Mok'jaka** – Malïos warrior

Acknowledgements:

I am so very grateful for several key people in helping bring this story to life: my brothers Andrew and Ian for starting this whole fantastical journey a couple decades ago; my mother Barbara and father Christopher for being my chief editors and fans, despite this not being their proverbial cup-o-tea; my "brothers from other mothers" Gabe and Chris for being additional content contributors and editors and my very first readers; that first reading group of middle schoolers at SGL for their patience and endurance reading a Z+ level book; Ms. Evans for getting me to first put pen to paper in that moleskin notebook in 2010, and of course my lovely fiancée Abisoye who rekindled the fire of publishing after I'd lost my way.

Thank you all for helping making this possible.

Prologue: Angelus

From the audio journal of Arcus Angelus – Project Lead
United Terran Federation: Operation Galaxia
Maiden voyage of the exploratory starship XTT-001
"OUTER HEAVENS"
Mission log: Day 81. 26 October 3.2212 @23:49:53
TST (Terran Standard Time)

Begin recording:
"To anyone who may find this:
Despite the mandated protocol regarding UTF operations property, should you find yourself listening to this or reading my manuscript of research or exploration logs, they are to be returned to my family: my wife or any living sons of Angelus. This is a message for them.

Brina, boys, I am sorry. I am so very, very sorry. I never should have left. I had hesitations at first—reservations about the project even—but the prospect of learning what else was beyond Terran space and Terranity itself presented me with too great an opportunity to pass up: an opportunity to know what else was out there.

And honestly, where I fit in to it all. I knew not, but ever since my youth I was unsure of my own Terran origins. I had to know if there was something else—someone else—out there.

I did not find 'myself' or anything about my past; I look at this medallion now and still wonder about its significance…

I didn't find out anything about it. No beauty, no truths, no fascinating new secrets of my life or my fate, or about my place in the universe.

What I *did* find however, was malevolence in its purest form. Now I know all too well what is out here; what awaits me, what awaits all who dare to follow: vile madness and cruel misery."

"A strange *presence* was felt shortly after engaging the Galaxial Flux Drive (GFD) and entering the Galaxia, but we didn't see any *real* sign of it until two days into the Galaxia (the space between galactic dimensions). Somehow the drive didn't disengage as it was supposed to and we remained in the Galaxia for far longer than expected.

The space seemed to close in on us; corridors seemed narrower, rooms somehow smaller and darker even. Slowly, several members of the crew began to go missing. They simply vanished without a trace. After the extensive and thorough search of the ship they had been found, or at least what was left of them. They'd been tortured, flayed, and mutilated. The sight was horror in its purest form.

But not all of the missing crew members were accounted for.

A small portion of them remained elusive to our searches and we soon found ourselves speculating about what had happened that caused them to... change. What followed was a fierce struggle to maintain the ship and attempt to drop from the Galaxia, and somehow return home...

All hope of doing any of that has since been lost.

The *presence* grows stronger by the minute and more crew members have disappeared or fallen victim to this corruption. I feel as though I can hear something faint in the growing darkness, like a whisper.

Many have tried holing themselves in their quarters or various areas of the ship, but they've failed to see that their huddled numbers attract the corrupted enemies.

Their whimpers and frightened cries seem to bring the malevolent *presence* closer; as though it is lured by their fear and then feasts on their pain and their suffering. The taint of darkness is upon us and it must be stopped.

I feel the *presence* as I did before but somehow it has grown in intensity. It seems as though the shadow of the *presence* occupies the entire ship. As more fall, and others 'turn,' it grows. Silent murmurs have become hushed whispers, those whispers turned into quiet words, and the words have since become enticing phrases; it's been speaking to us, lulling and vexing us..."

"The number of tainted crewmen has tripled and now they control the majority of the ship. Those who haven't willingly joined their ranks have all fallen victim to their barbarity and sadistic brutality: men and women alike.

I don't know if any others remain aside from me.

I have been fighting back and surviving using what weapon-like tools and devices I could find; I am currently using a plasma torch that I altered to shoot bolts of plasma which appears to be effective against them,

but I will soon have to fall back on the wrench I've kept since the first sightings; that should prove effective as the *tainted* are still the Terran bodies of the former crewmen—flesh and bone—and are still vulnerable.

My final hope now is to make it to the engine room to overload the GFD reactor and erase us and the manifestation of this *presence* entirely. Nothing aboard should be spared. It's become the epitome of horror, the essence of undoing, malevolence in its purest form. It has to be stopped.

Again I hear the voices; they have grown in volume. They almost seem to be encouraging me to drop the ship from Galaxial travel.

Get out of my head!

I must steel myself to this task. I must destroy the ship."

"Brina, I love you; forever and always. I need not go into the myriad of ways I do, for you know them all. Boys, I am so sorry. Davriel and Cephus, I'm sorry I was never there for you two as a father, but your mothers raised you just fine without me and you were always in my heart.

Jonos, I believe you'll grow up to be twice the pilot and twice the man I ever was and I'm sorry I can't be there to see it. And finally Savos.

Savos, you must forgive me.

The stars called to me and as much as I tried, I couldn't resist their lure.

You know of what I speak; I've sensed that desire in you since your birth. It was the way you looked at them; as if they had all the answers. Perhaps one day, you'll understand why I left, and be able to forgive me. I love you all and will miss you dearly."

'*Angelusss.*'

"There, there it is; the voice again. That damned voice! I can clearly hear it now. I feel its taint all around me. I must stop it. I must stop this madness!"

End recording.

Chapter 1: Deployment

13 October, Terran Year 3.2220.
20:00 TST (05:00 Cybian Standard Time)
Somewhere over the New Morrabian Peninsula…

It was only three days after his tactical deployment officially began that Corporal Davriel Angelus found himself deep in thought aboard a United Terran Federation Marine Corps transport aircraft bound for the New Morrabian Peninsula. The surrounding area was suspected hostile territory but so far their flight had been smooth.

Careening his neck back he stared up with his almond brown eyes at the ceiling of the transport and steadily exhaled a sigh. The unrelenting vibrations throughout the VTOL (Vertical Take Off and Landing) class airship known as a Skyhawk, had lulled his vexed mind to a commonly recurring memory from almost a year before.

Angelus lost his mind in thought as he contemplated the memory of his last night at home with one of his three brothers before he left for basic training.

The images from that night came swirling back to him instantly.

He pictured the flickering flames in the fire-pit at his mother's house and remembered the crackle of the embers met with the soothing sway of the trees blowing with the winter winds. He then pictured his brother Savos.

He remembered him fully despite the low light of the fire he could vividly make out Savos' face, his olive skin tone, his hazel blue eyes, the wispy tuft of hair underneath his lower lip.

Every detail flooded back to him and felt tangible. His taste-buds then began recalling the flat rummies he and his brother drank as well as the hand rolled cigs Savos was so fond of rolling for them. He wouldn't be allowed such luxuries on this tactical deployment.

A brief lurch and directional change in the craft drew his attention, but when the pilot remained silent about it, he continued with his thoughts.

Returning to the dying embers, the flat drinks, and the lit cigs led him back to the vexation he currently faced; Savos' only thoughts on the matter.

The words echoed in his mind as he mouthed them to nobody, "Be safe, be strong, and be smart. Come back to us, we still have a great many things to do."

At the time he'd responded as he normally did with their usual 'no promises' retort, brushing it off to not have it be such a big deal.

But now he was here.

Now it was a big deal.

He thought again about Savos' words, the first of which were extraneous as they were implied by the situation of his military deployment and he fancied himself all of those things regardless.

The perplexity came with the second part of what Savos said, "We still have a great many things to do."

Corporal Angelus thought about these words numerous times since he began his transcontinental trip to his current location — 8000 meters in the air over the jungle peninsula of New Morrabia — but now more than ever he pondered their meaning with great significance and considered what "great things" he still needed to do. For a moment Corporal Angelus returned to the surroundings of the cargo hold to find Corporal Deonte Trane staring at him.

Corporal Trane was a fellow aircraft mechanic and had known Angelus since boot camp. For the past two years they'd been in the same detachment and he was the closest thing Angelus had to family.

Trane was by far the tallest and largest man aboard the transport. He had dark skin and a soft, wide face that was frequently plastered with a grin. Trane stared curiously at Angelus.

As Angelus looked back, Trane silently mouthed, 'You okay?' to which Angelus simply nodded his head before closing his eyes and returning to his thoughts.

His contemplation was immediately quelled as he felt another sudden and violent lurch throughout the Skyhawk.

Suddenly sirens were blaring and the pilot's voice broke over the Tactical Communication Network — or tac-com:

"Brace yourselves, we've got incoming high velocity contacts! Strap yourselves in tight!
It's about to get bumpy!"

The UTF Mk 44 Skyhawk was remarkable in stature; resembling a great bird with swept wings. It boasted four remarkably engineered mobile turbofan engines that supported the transport's chassis with over 80000 lbs. of thrust with an additional 60000 lbs. from primary rear-firing engines.

With its unique abilities came an unrelenting need for an abundance of repairs and service calls.

Corporal Angelus knew all about these repairs and procedures as he had been sent to carry out those mundane duties as an aircraft mechanic.

The recurring inspection of fuses and electronic systems, coupled with the constant scrutiny of the Skyhawk's four turbofan engines as well as its main thrusters, in addition to the framework and body detailing; all served up an ever expanding list of new ways to fix the Skyhawk.

The endless list Corporal Angelus had compiled raced through his mind as he hoped that this specific transport was at full operational capacity.

The Skyhawk was not an exceptionally agile craft due to its size and functionality, but due to its practical points as a VTOL aircraft, it was invaluable to the UTF.

Thankfully, the pilot was uncannily familiar with its limited maneuverability and began executing its few evasive maneuvers.

Corporal Angelus felt the transport suddenly incline to its right for a rising-bank maneuver as the pilot began what little evasive action was possible.

He thought of what hostiles might be in their pursuit and then wondered as to what the pilot might do to further avoid or engage such targets.

In the cockpit of the Skyhawk Lieutenant-Commander Ramos Marco Elnezzi, affectionately known by his brothers in arms as 'R-ME or Army' took control of the situation.

His handsome almost elegant West-Eurkasyian features never seemed to betray any hint of panic, particularly his stone black eyes. Along with Elnezzi sat his relatively new flight officer and co-pilot Lieutenant Rahvan Delantos.

Delantos was on the shorter side and rather mundane in looks. He was far too serious and always feared the worst regardless of the situation.

The other two members comprising the flight team were on station at their respective gun-turrets on either flank of the aircraft.

Although Elnezzi trusted and liked his current flight officer Delantos well enough, he couldn't help but trust to his flanking gunners and his own prowess now in order to save his crew, passengers, and cargo.

With hands stiffening, gut wrenching, and palms sweating, he drew his eyes onto his radar to get a bearing on his assailants.

Delantos' voice suddenly burst over the tac-com, "Looks like two Viper Class G-8s, these Gunrunners are real mean sons-of-bitches!"

"Confirmed," Elnezzi replied coolly.

Before fear overtook Elnezzi his instincts urged him forward and he immediately grabbed the control sticks and began a series of evasive maneuvers initiated by a high-rising right bank.

He knew he had to gain altitude to provide his turret-gunners a decent shot.

The two Gunrunners followed suit and without warning opened up with machine gun fire on the bulky transport.

The Viper G-8 "Gunrunner" was a clumsy looking aircraft but packed a wallop when it came to firepower.

Designed as a cheap, viable, air-to-air dog-fighter the G-8s packed eight 30mm Hellfire machine cannons on a crudely shaped wing platform, built around a 75mm crack-shot cannon comprising the main fuselage of the craft.

With the blistering amount of fire-power the G-8s packed, it was amazing that they could even fly.

This did however lead to its unfortunate drawbacks of being less maneuverable than the UTF's smaller and more versatile FA-2s, and the Gunrunner's lack of missiles added to its ineffectiveness in dogfights.

Never-the-less the G-8s were excellent for anti-infantry strafing runs and pursuing slower, bulkier ships such as the Skyhawk currently carrying Angelus, Elnezzi, Delantos and the others.

Elnezzi quickly recalled the specs of the G-8s and immediately realized that just two of these Gunrunners could tear his lone Skyhawk to pieces in a matter of minutes. He quickly gathered his nerves and shouted to his turret gunners, "Priority targets: two hostile fast moving Gunrunners! Take 'em out!"

"Roger that Lieutenant!" confirmed one of his gunners, Ensign Dio Leheura.

Leheura was from the Old Sipian Empire in the far east of Eurkasyia. His eagerness was only ever matched by his toothy grin and his uncanny ability to crack a joke.

He had been the most recent addition to the Skyhawk's crew, and although he was colloquially known as the FNG, they all liked him well enough.

Despite his amiable nature, his stature with the crew was now truly put to the test with their current predicament.

Elnezzi didn't really know him aside from the jokes, but certainly had to trust in his ability now.

"Copy that, engaging." said the other gunner, Ensign Jun Araffi.

Araffi had been 2 classes behind Elnezzi at the UTF Eurkasyian Academy in Frensia and was later attached to the same battalion.

He was black haired and brown skinned much like Elnezzi, and was probably Elnezzi's favorite person in the whole battalion.

Araffi often copied Elnezzi in manner and appearance, looking up to him like a younger brother to his older brother.

Elnezzi had always known him as a competent and disciplined cadet, and now considered him a good friend and brother-in-arms, and his brief and calm response bolstered Elnezzi's splintering nerves.

Leheura and Araffi began firing the explosive all-purpose rounds their turrets fired as soon as their enemies came into view.

The turrets were initially designed to provide significant ground fire during a hot landing while troops would disembark, but were essential in defending against aerial threats as well.

The explosive bolts were designed to inflict maximum damage on unarmored to lightly armored ground targets but were remarkably useful against thinner air armor.

If they could score even a few glancing hits it might be enough to fend their attackers off.

Their initial volleys sent encroaching Gunrunners into evasive maneuvers of their own.

Over the staggered staccato of machine gun fire Corporal Angelus and his fellow soldiers' nerves tightened as they hoped for the best of their situation.

Angelus was no hero, and had no real desire to be regarded as such, but always had such disdain for being unable to help or have control of his own fate.

He could not help but feel intensely motivated to do something to assuage their situation.

Angelus and the other soldiers suddenly recoiled as the craft shuddered in its evasive actions and suffered from the unrelenting fire from the Gunrunners.

Pock marks rattled the right flank as the lead G-8 scored several impacts.

Hearing these impacts, the soldiers in the cargo hold all hoped the craft's armor was thick enough and that their pilot, Army Elnezzi, was fast enough.

Corporal Angelus then felt the Skyhawk roll down, now to its left, as more impacts splintered against the ship's airframe.

"Patch us through to HQ!" Elnezzi's voice suddenly came over the open tac-com.

A moment of silence passed and then Delantos' voice could be heard, "This is Skyhawk transport Delta 4-5-1 requesting immediate back up! We are being engaged by two hostile G-8 Gunrunners and need immediate assistance! Over!"

The link to command that Delantos opened was so hastily made that he failed to realize it was open and broadcasting over the Skyhawk's open com.

As every UTF member aboard was linked to the tac-com, not only did HQ hear of the transport's assailants, so too did its previously unknowing passengers.

The new found discovery only served to further the anxiety and helplessness the passengers were already feeling, Angelus could tell.

This particular troop load was already suffering from rather intense combat jitters as its load-out of four corpsmen, and a dozen auxiliary troops was not accustomed to such hostile conditions—except for the corpsmen.

Despite the nearly unanimous feeling of helplessness, Corporal Angelus felt a compelling urgency to act.

What can I do?

He wondered if he'd even get the chance to do anything at all or if he was to be helplessly gunned down out of the twilit sky.

Not expecting his chance to arrive so soon, he almost missed when it was garishly presented.

A moment after Elnezzi radioed for assistance two tragic events occurred, as so often they do in battle.

Initially, Command's response came, "That's a negative Delta. We do not have support units in your vicinity. Repeat: no friendlies in your immediate area."

Following command's response, the leading Gunrunner reengaged the Skyhawk, and pushed it into a banking maneuver that his wingman anticipated.

The perfectly timed strafing attack that ensued brought a hail of bullets which tore straight through the left side of the Skyhawk's hull, destroying the turret and ravaging Ensign Araffi's body, killing him instantly.

"Man down!" Delantos reported, still over the tac-com, "Repeat, man down! We've lost the left side turret!"

Without delay Angelus realized his window to act, but remained perplexed on what exactly he could do.

Following the sound of impacts on the hull and Delantos' report on Araffi, he knew the strafing run had damaged the left side gun turret, rendering it useless.

He wracked his mind on what he could possibly do at that moment as they had all just become more likely to lose this unraveling dog fight.

As he was a fervent observer Angelus had paid every attention to detail—regarding things he deemed important, especially in extreme circumstances—and he quickly remembered the contents of the cargo on board this particular transport.

Despite its load of noncoms, the transport's

cargo was entirely intended for full field use. The load-out consisted of ten crates; the first was full of the UTF's new Assault Carbine AC-7 a and b assault rifles equipped with under-mounted launchers, the second full of 4 X-99 Stingray missile launchers, the third full of munitions for said launchers.

The fourth crate was full of various grenades—both for the AC-7b launchers and various throw-able grenades—and the remaining six crates were all full of rations, medical supplies, and auxiliary construction tools and equipment.

Angelus focused on the first crates for their lethality and current usefulness, but to his fortune did not completely disregard the other boxes from memory.

His mind settled specifically on the contents of the third and fourth crates, as the launchers were going to be the only effective threat against their pursuers.

Only, how to use them…

Without hesitation he unbuckled his seat's safety harness and lunged forward toward the crates.

Corporal Trane immediately saw Angelus' movement and berated him shouting, "Jus' what the hell you think you doin'?!"

The only response Angelus could summon was as transient as his own instant rationale to get up in the first place, "Something!" he shouted back.

He opened the crate of X-99 launchers and immediately seized the first box. Unfastening the latches, he opened the launcher's box.

He then unfastened the locks to the munitions box and removed several rounds for the launcher.

Removing the first from its individual cartridge he loaded it into the launcher with remarkable ease.

Even though they were noncoms, as UTF Marines they were required to have familiarity with basic infantry weaponry.

Angelus' qualification on the smaller X-66 Devilray launcher gave him the familiarity he deemed would be enough to operate this larger model.

He then opened a third box from the other crate, and grabbed half a dozen flash and krak grenades, placing them in whatever open pouches his tactical vest offered.

Stepping away from the crates he mounted the launcher to his shoulder and moved toward the aft hatch to open it and ultimately engage the Skyhawk's pursuers.

He then realized this would subject the entire passenger load and cargo to their pursuers, as well as provide a sufficient window for bullet fire to penetrate through to the cockpit.

Facing this realization Angelus turned and approached the left turret access hatch, the side that had been destroyed.

The other soldiers looked on, stupefied and bewildered as Angelus keyed in the entry code, opened the hatch, and stepped out of the main hold.

The last thing they saw was him locking in his tactical vest to the operator harness as the hatch resealed.

Stepping into the gunner's seat—or what was left of

it — and strapping into the harness Angelus realized two things, the fierce biting wind from the wide open gashes in the gun-port's armor, and that the strafing run from the gunrunner had blasted Araffi's body clean from the aircraft.

He quickly gathered his wits and remembered the task at hand: saving the transport and the crew.

Instantly he began scanning the skies for the Skyhawk's assailants.

Looking toward the Skyhawk's 8 o'clock high he saw one of the Gunrunners diving into an attack run.

Looking toward his foes estimated flight path Angelus seized one of the flash grenades from his harness, and pulling the pin, let it fly back toward the approaching craft. He shielded his eyes just before the blinding white flash of light from the grenade's detonation.

The luminous flash lit up the twilit sky like a bolt of lightning for all to see, save for those sealed within the cargo hold. Even Elnezzi and Delantos sat baffled by the flash. "What the hell was that!?" cried Delantos over the com.

"What the hell is going on back there?" Elnezzi interjected.

In response a targeting siren sounded as Angelus locked on to the first Gunrunner.

The flash grenade had worked perfectly in disorienting the Gunrunner's pilot as he blindly disengaged from his diving run.

Without hesitation Angelus had mounted the launcher, taken aim, and as soon as he heard the tar-

-get lock, fired at the approaching gunrunner. With a flash and a massive shock of recoil the X-99 Stingray fired off its computer guided missile.

The missile streaked across the waning night sky and struck the attacking gunrunner in an intense flurry of fire and metal. Angelus could practically smell the burning wreckage as the blast wave rushed towards him confirming the destruction of the leading Gunrunner.

Angelus immediately tapped into the transport's open tac-com to report the kill.

"Gunrunner One is down, try and get me another shot will ya?" he shouted over the cacophony of the situation.

Delantos' unhindered enthusiasm over the changing tide of battle burst over the tac-com, "Great job Angelus!"

Elnezzi responded with a more collected urgency, "Nice one Angelus, see what you can do about that other one before he does any more damage."

Upon the destruction of the leading Gunrunner the second G-8 pilot re-engaged the transport with increasing tenacity and not a moment after Elnezzi finished speaking, the G-8 unleashed a hail of machine gun fire.

The rounds hit with deadly accuracy on the transports right vertical stabilizer and engine-mount, decimating its maneuvering capabilities. The Skyhawk reeled in a calamitous convulsion as yet more sirens blared throughout the cockpit and cargo hold. Smoke billowed from the damaged stabilizer and the craft began to drastically lose altitude.

The enemy pilot was now out for revenge for his fallen wingman and pursued the crippled craft preparing the final killing blow to finish them off.

He positioned himself directly behind the Skyhawk on an identical trajectory and steadied his Gunrunner to make use of the crack-shot cannon mounted on its hull.

In preparing for this killing blow Angelus was able to read the pilot's telegraphed move and warn Elnezzi, "INCOMING!" was all he had time to shout before the telltale *CRACK* from the Gunrunner's main cannon rang out, hurling the 75 mm round straight toward the crippled Skyhawk.

Despite hearing and reacting to Angelus' warning, Elnezzi was not able to completely dodge the shot and felt his Skyhawk shudder as the crack-shot round impacted on its right wing-mount.

It began to shatter and break up from the impact of the round and the ensuing exterior explosions.

As the transport began to break up Angelus' thoughts turned toward the crew and their survival.

He thought perhaps they could all equip parachutes and jump to safety but then retracted that thought as he realized the remaining Gunrunner would shred them to bits with its machine gun fire before they would make it to the ground.

He tried to establish a grip on the situation and radioed the pilot, "Army, what's our status?" he yelled.

"Completely fucked!" was Elnezzi's concise response, "Stand by!"

"Mayday, mayday," Delantos rattled, "This is Skyhawk Delta 4-5-1. We are hit and losing altitude rapidly! Repeat, we are going down!"

After brief static, HQ's concise reply came, "Roger that Delta. Reinforcements are still unavailable."

"Don't give me that shit!" Elnezzi cut in, "We seriously need some blasted back up! Or at least an S&R ship for the crew and cargo of this downed bird! We are going down!"

"Rescue can be inbound in 35 minutes." responded HQ.

"We'll be lucky if we last 35 seconds!" Elnezzi quickly retorted, livid with Command's inefficiency and the UTF's general lack of urgency.

As if feeding off the panic and despair growing in the Skyhawks' hold, the Gunrunner sprayed yet another hail of machine gun fire into the right side of the laboring transport.

The shots pierced the already shattered and ruined armor and killed several of the passengers sealed in the cargo hold, as well as crippling the second turret.

Suddenly Corporal Trane broke over the tac-com, "That shit tore right through the hull. Man, we dyin' in here, get us the hell outta' here!"

"All hands," Elnezzi's voice spoke, full of defeat, "chute up and get out! I'll try and draw the bastard's fire!"

Army's right, if we stay here any longer we all

die. He's settled on the last possible option then. Abandon ship and hope that some of us survive the drop. No. It doesn't have to be like that!

"Hold that!" Angelus interjected.

Faced with the potential destruction of the transport, crew, and cargo, he did the most impulsive and rash thing he possibly could have.

Reloading the Stingray launcher, he unbuckled the operator's harness, and broadcast to Elnezzi, Delantos, and the remaining passengers in the hold, his valediction.

It came as concise and confident as any words he'd ever spoken.

"Find a good place to set down and get these men to safety Army. I'll take care of this persistent son-of-a-bitch."

None of the men expected or even saw what came next as Corporal Angelus flung himself from the Skyhawk.

Knowing his time was inexorably limited now, he immediately seized a flash grenade, removed the pin and hurled it toward the Gunrunner still in pursuit.

Again he shielded his eyes from the flash but was more susceptible to the grenade's effect as it detonated in front of him this time.

With a blur in his eyes and a deafening ring in his ears he mounted the launcher to his shoulder and took aim on the target.

Unable to clearly see his target or listen for a target lock Angelus trusted his instincts and squeezed the trigger, shooting the guided missile toward the Gunrunner.

Again he felt the immense recoil from the hefty launcher and as he had no firm ground on which to brace himself, he was sent spiraling out of control from the force of the missile launch.

He was able to reorient himself toward the missile's plume of smoke and the continuing craft just a moment before the missile impacted on the second Gunrunner, shattering it into thousands of small pieces in a flourish of fire and metal.

Just beyond the exploding Gunrunner he could see the damaged Skyhawk safely escape its pursuer, though heavily smoking and losing altitude at an alarming rate.

He watched it head for a crash landing beyond the wooded area of the river, east of their intended course and southeast of his relative position.

The sight spurred him to realize his own imminent crash landing which now came at him at an alarming rate.

With his impending doom quickly approaching, Corporal Davriel Angelus' thoughts drifted away from the crashing Skyhawk, away from Elnezzi, Delantos, Trane and the others, away from the combat zone and The United Terran Federation.

He simply escaped the reality of his plight.

His thoughts turned to the peacefully foreboding fire with Savos and he realized that saving those troopers was indeed a great thing, but unfortunately the great things of which Savos spoke that night by the fire, would have to be accomplished without him.

As the sun began to rise over the New Morrabian Peninsula Davriel now looked toward his imminent demise. He saw a river running through a wooded area he decided he would aim for—he reckoned that any impact would be painful but at least crashing in the water would provide a quicker, less painful death than crashing through the trees.

Upon looking at the river and the flowing water Davriel thought of his youngest brother Cephus, a bright and hardy naval officer patrolling the world's waters aboard a UTF Naval Guard Cutter. Davriel pictured Cephus sailing on the fierce waters of Terra as he continued to fall toward the rush of the river.

The charge of the biting wind passing his body shifted his thoughts to one of his other brothers, Jonos. The elder Angelus twin was a confident and brilliant pilot soaring through the skies with the wind in his eyes and the ground kilometers below his feet.

As he looked toward the ground that seemed to grow exponentially larger by the millisecond his thoughts returned to Savos, his last brother, a determined and steadfast source of support and kinship. Every thought and memory of Davriel's time with his brothers flashed before his eyes and he realized that he would miss them all the most out of everything he ever knew in the world.

Finally, mere meters from the river's surface his thoughts turned to that last night with Savos; the burning image of the dying fire light flickering into the night sky, the words Savos had said, and his own response, "No promises."

Before the end his body temperature flared as he pictured a fire blazing eternally, its own flames the source of its undying burning light. The heat rose in him as he faced oblivion and he let go, giving in to his fate.

Then all went dark.

Chapter 2: Homecoming

The aircraft lurched yet again continuing its descent toward the surface causing several passengers to stir restlessly in their seats, anxious as they were to be back on terra firma. The flight had been relatively smooth since take-off, save for the rather harsh turbulence recently, but the crew and all of us passengers aboard were all more than thankful for the pilot's acumen when it came to flying the ancient transport.

The sounds of the deploying wing flaps and landing gear were audible as the pilot slowed the craft, readying it for the imminent landing. The aircraft lurched once more, losing altitude as it approached the surface and yet again several passengers aboard grew evermore impatient as we readied for landing.

Looking out the window I could now see the ground approaching through the cloud cover; tiny vehicles carried microscopic people about their mundane lives while we descended over the city. I watched as countless miniscule people carried out their daily routines and duties; taxi drivers, businessmen, construction workers, police officers and so-on, all carrying out their perennial tasks.

I now wondered how I—Savos Angelus— would be fitting into this every day working routine. Everything so coordinated and firmly set in repetitive motion; stop and go, red light and green light, work and sleep, on and off.

Where do I fit into it all?

Everywhere I looked there were signs of Terranity's potential for greatness and simultaneously its mediocrity and banality.

Grandiose skyscrapers and luxury apartment buildings full of wealthy executives arrayed the city center while the surrounding areas were interspersed urban and suburban areas rife with modest housing, lowly tenant buildings, and squalid projects where people wallowed in middle-class inadequacy and hopeless destitution.

Between these busy buildings, scanty houses, and packed housing projects were the bustling streets full of countless people all engrossed in their own lives.

I now looked evermore forward to the spacious and natural surroundings of my old home outside of the city, as it would provide a much needed escape from the constraints of the hustle and bustle of big city life.

We continued over the main area of Emerald City and eventually out and over its surrounding burbs as we came ever closer to our landing. Off in the southern distance I could see a flickering trail of smoke shooting up into the sky.

The pilot then came over the intercom saying, "Ladies and gentlemen as we near our final approach, if you look out the left side of our craft you can see the trailing smoke of a space-bound shuttle. Its launch trail indicating it took off from down south near San Salam Valley. I can't be sure of its cargo or destination but…"

I missed the rest of the pilot's words as I was off in another world following the shuttle as it stead-

-ily rose into the upper atmosphere.

My mind drifted into thoughts of space and Terran space exploration, far off worlds and the idea of charting them, until it inevitably arrived through the galactic mists of space and time on the thought of my father.

Damn.

The recent mass production and development of space travel was directly linked to my father's scientific achievements and his ultimate brain child — or children rather — thus many considered him the greatest man of the century, possibly of the entire third age.

The massive shipyards and launch sites all over the globe that the UTF so vigorously constructed, the outlying space stations and retrofitting platforms orbiting the planet, the four orbiting satellite colonies nearing complete construction; these were all considered his greatest achievements and I couldn't help but think of the magnitude of it all.

There were already seventeen major space ports throughout the world with new ones sprouting up every year.

It's really too bad that Dad isn't around to enjoy all of his monumental success.

Not wishing to dwell too long on the thought of my father I readily welcomed the pilot's words announcing our final approach.

"Ladies and gentlemen, this is your captain speaking. We are now on our final approach into Emerald Sound International Airport. Please return your seats to their upright positions and ensure your seatbelts are secured and fastened. We would like to thank you for flying with Trans Amassian Airlines today and hope that you choose us for your future travels. We hope you enjoyed your flight and wish you the happiest and safest holidays this winter. We wish you continued safety on your travels and should Emerald City be your final destination, Trans Amassian would like to be the first to say, welcome home."

The pilot's last words echoed in my ears, "welcome home."

After traveling and schooling abroad for the last five years I was finally coming home. Of course I had come back and stayed for short periods of time for a few vacations and holidays, but this was the first time since I'd left home five years ago that I was back for an indefinite period of time. The thought was slightly unnerving but my attention was drawn away from my personal dilemma to the approaching ground.

Ant sized cars and trucks had become entirely discernible and soon vanished as we passed over the outlying grounds of the airfield. The running lights came into view followed by the asphalt of the runway. The ground grew closer now and with a final jolt we made contact with the earth.

Touching down, the pilots deployed the aircraft's wing flaps to their full extension to begin slowing the craft to a full stop.

The sounds of rushing winds passing over the wings created a dissonance that further unsettled those wishing to touch solid ground.

It didn't faze me in the slightest as I was

accustomed to the landing procedure after years of flying in older — cheaper — transports such as this Trans Amassian passenger ship, which lacked the Vertical Take-Off and Landing capabilities of newer and more expensive transports.

The craft finished its landing cycle and we began taxiing toward the gateway. As I heard the engines spin down I felt the general ease of the tension within many of the passengers aboard as they finally began to relax after touching down.

The pilot brought us to the gate as I checked my Wrist Link for the time and any new messages: 10:55 am. We were exactly 25 minutes late from our scheduled arrival time of 10:30.

As I realized that the turbulence was the obvious cause for our delay I received a Link message from my brother, Jonos, and hoped that he'd held true to his tendency of always being late.

LM: Thirty minutes out. See you soon.
Trans Am right?

Perfect, that gives me plenty of time to get my bag, hop on the metro and meet him at the post office where we'd have to go anyway.

Having flown home permanently from five years abroad I had accumulated a few modest possessions and baggage that I had to ship to myself rather than bring aboard the plane, that way they would be waiting for my arrival. I began composing a reply using the palm-key when we docked at the gateway and began disembarking the plane.

The captain came over the intercom yet again as restless travelers immediately took to their feet, "Again on behalf of Trans Amassian we would like to thank you for traveling with us. Welcome to Emerald City."

Awaiting my turn to disembark among the several hundred passengers I finished my message to my brother:

LM: Cool. Just landed. Have to de-board and get bags. Meet me at the SPEx on Willis St. That way you can avoid airport traffic.

SPEx specialized in large shipping, postage, and exports to foreign countries and was ideal for me to use to send all my belongings home.

LM: Roger.

He responded in his typical concise manner. I thought for a moment about my twin's idiosyncrasies and what he'd been up to all these years since I'd left home.

Since I'd left for school my fraternal twin Jonos had spent his time at home at a flight school. He had enrolled in the Amassian Northwest's premier flight school: Sound Side Aviation Academy and he'd become a certified flight instructor for many training flyers including the TF-12a—the civilian equivalent to the TF F-12 mk1 that the military used to train its fighter pilots.

I remembered the immense pride I felt when I found out he had taken on such a monumental task and passed with the highest marks; but then immediately remembered his prevailing tardiness to his friends—but more importantly me—and wondered how he'd managed to accomplish all that given his mostly detached view on most anything that involved effort.

No matter, I thought as I saw the cabin thin out as the passengers in front of me made their way off the plane.

I noticed the elderly woman across the aisle, standing with who I guessed must have been her grandson, doing her best to try to retrieve her bag from overhead.

Seeing that she could not quite manage the large bag I intervened and removed the bag from the storage bin and placed it on the aisle for her.

"Thank you kindly young man." The homely old lady said to me.

"You're quite welcome ma'am." I responded cordially, hoping that her grandson might see my courtesy beyond his handheld videogame—he'd started to play it immediately after touching down— and hoped that he might go on to one-day pass on such kindness. "Happy Endyears!" I added as the two began moving down the aisle-way and off the plane.

"Happy Endyears to you too young man!" she said over her shoulder as she walked off. I was taken by surprise when the young boy then added, "Thanks for helping Grammie, mister. Bye-bye now!" He quickly turned and darted off to catch his grandmother.

"See ya." I said with a smile on my face as he ran off.

Taking down my own bags I thought of how nice that interaction was until I was distracted by an unnerved passenger behind me as he huffed and impatiently interjected, "Great, Grammie's finally off, can we get a move on now?!"

"Calm down." I found myself sternly responding, "Have some patience will ya?"

"Oh I'm so sorry *young man*," he said sarcastically, "now could you kindly get going?!"

The passenger appeared to be some kind of UTF official; aside from his elegant black suit and pristine cut he bore a simple pin of the UTF logo that indicated his allegiance.

He was tall and thin though certainly in shape, with a cleanly shaven face, slicked jet-black hair, and a sharp nose.

His eyes were sunken into his head and made him appear older than the rest of his body and he spoke with a haughty and priggish tone.

The sarcasm he employed was biting and could have gone without what followed, "We don't have all day 'Mr. Post-grad.' Some of us aren't home to relax. Some of us have connections to make and business to attend to!"

The agitated Fed had clearly heard me exchanging pleasantries with the woman sitting next to me at the beginning of the flight, and was aggravated as he felt my civility toward the old grandmother and her grandson was currently slowing him down.

"Well excuse me for being courteous," I retorted as I dramatically stepped aside to let the impolite Fed through. He scoffed and pushed passed me in a fluster as he made his way off the plane.

"Wow…" the woman next to me said with a baffled look, shaking her head as we watched the Fed storm off, "you don't know who that is, do you?"

I shook my head.

"That's Chief Magistrate Dekkun Pikus. He's one of the Federation's 'pocket politicians;' one of their financial gurus who gets his way no matter the cost. He's somehow always been able to find ways to keep the bureaucrats in power, much as they don't deserve it; himself above all others. He's certainly someone you wouldn't want to cross."

"Whatever, I hope he makes his connection." I didn't actually, but wondered aloud, "what was he even doing on this flight anyway? Shouldn't he be on a private Federation transport?"

"He works for the government but isn't necessarily a military officer, and from what I gather they try to put guys like him with us to remind us that they're 'regular people like us,'" the woman said, "Though I am surprised that he was back here with us rather than in first-class."

I didn't care, he and I wouldn't cross paths again and I didn't want to dwell on it too long, I then turned to the woman and smiling at her cheerily said, "Happy Endyears to you and yours, it was a pleasure talking with you."

She exchanged the smile as I grabbed my bags and set off to disembark the aircraft.

I passed by the small staircase that led to the

cockpit—as it was a raised flight deck—and thanked the pilots and service staff on my way through the door to the jet-way.

Looking up into the cockpit I briefly entertained the thought of myself piloting a lumbering transport such as this but was distracted by another message from Jonos.

LM: Where is the SPEx office again?

LM: Willis St. in the market plaza.

I composed the reply as I made my way off the jet-way and through the east gateway toward the tram to the main terminal.

Upon finishing the message, I took a look around the gateway just in time to make uneasy eye contact with the rude Fed from the flight as he checked into his connecting flight. I overheard him make some kind of a fuss over first-class seating then I looked and saw that he had twenty minutes to departure and had plenty of time to board.

What a jicko. I smiled and gave an obnoxious wave. He scowled, shook his head, and proceeded down the jet-way as I turned to make my way past various news and coffee stands toward the tram.

While riding the tram I was drawn to the idea of being home evermore as I took in the familiar surroundings of the tram car and gazed wide-eyed out the window as we traveled the elevated tracks between the East Gateway and the main terminal.

Taking in the city and the seascape beyond and the Great Mountain Cascade on the other side of the sound was simply captivating and I immediately felt comforted by the words that previously perturbed me: welcome home.

The view was interrupted as the tram made its way into the main terminal and the automated message chimed, "Main terminal and baggage claim. Next stop: South Gateway."

Leaving the tram and ascending a series of escalators I immediately faced the bustling area of baggage claim. I was fortunate as I only had to travel past two baggage terminals of the eighteen to find my flight's bag drop.

Fortune favored me all the more as I approached the conveyor where my duffle and attaché case were already waiting among the other bags.

Having my backpack on me already, I grabbed and shouldered the large duffle, picked up the attaché case, and approached the exit.

Stepping out of the terminal I felt increasingly at home as I took in the freshest breath of air I had had in months.

Breathing deeply, I relaxed my mind, pushing all the nonsense with the aggressive Fed jicko from my thoughts and I was greatly comforted knowing that I was just an hour or so away from home.

Returning to the reality of my surroundings I realized that I needed to cross the street to get to the airport metro station to catch my train to the post office. I was not however thrice fortunate as I saw my train fast approaching the station.

Not wanting to be later than my notoriously late brother, I raced across the street, tapped my commuter pass at the turnstile and began vaulting the stairs to the upper platforms. I couldn't be sure but I felt as though I was somehow faster than I had ever been before.

Perhaps my city life had made me a more efficient and acrobatic commuter. My muscles flared and I leapt up the stairs in bounds of three and four steps at a time. Reaching the top, I stepped onto the train seconds before the door sealed shut.

Only after receiving an odd glance or two did I realize what just happened.

I had sprinted across the street while dodging traffic, swiped through the turnstile, leapt up the thirty some-odd steps dodging the disembarking passengers, and finally boarded the train; in all of about fifteen seconds.

Not to mention I was carrying a back pack, a large duffle bag, and my attaché with me. On top of the matter I was now furiously catching my breath and drawing attention to myself.

Calm down. Don't make a scene.

Not wishing to endure peoples' continued stares I made my way to a seat toward the rear of the train car away from the other passengers and plopped down for the ten-minute ride to my stop as I contemplated what had just occurred.

During the brief trip passengers' glances turned away while I turned my gaze to the scenery of the ride outside and found myself mesmerized by the Great Mountain Cascade like never before.

Taking in the view I unintentionally drifted

off into a deep and entirely unexpected sleep where I dreamt most vividly and strangely.

I saw myself in front of the Great Mountain Cascade, gazing up at its peak as it pierced the sky. The cooling wind blew in and cleared the wreath of clouds around the mountain and suddenly the earth shook, dropping me to my hands and knees.

As I fell I looked to the ground and realized I was now on the mountain's peak looking out over the expansive landscape.

I looked around and saw the blazing sun in the sky which seemed to glare directly down on me. Suddenly before my eyes an enchanting ember lit in a fiery blaze. The flames licked at my wind-chilled face and began melting away the snow atop the mountain peak. In a sudden rush I saw the melting snow flow from the mountains like a unilateral waterfall, becoming tidal waves of fierce strength as they blustered down the mountain.

Returning back to myself atop the mountain I realized that the fire had burnt out, the ocean of snow and water had eased away and the fierce winds ceased. All was calm on the mountain as I knelt with my palms flat on the earth.

Impulsively I clenched my hands grabbing fistfuls of dirt and bringing them up I watched as dirt slipped through my fingers becoming sand.

I felt the earth begin to shake yet again, this time far more tumultuously than before, and before I knew it the fire was burning again in a blaze more massive than before.

The fierce winds returned bringing with them tidal waves of immense proportion that impacted the sides of the mountain.

Stupefied by this ferocious clash of elements I gazed upward to find a dead white sky pierced with a malicious darkened mauve sun crackling with warped energy.

Seeing this ominous sight my body stiffened and clenched the ground as the storm of sea, wind, and fire ravaged the space all around me.

The blasting winds shot the powerful waves up every side of the mountain converging on the precipice as the blazing firestorm danced around, shooting embers straight into the sky.

Fearful of the malicious sun and bewildered by the tempest of elements my body clenched tighter and tighter until it seemed as though my muscles and limbs would burst. I sat in anxious amazement as I watched the violet sun grow and begin to engulf the sky.

Taking in the whirlwind of elements and power and tightening my body to its maximum tension I suddenly, against all of the escalating commotion, let go.

The cataclysmic storm exploded in an apex of energy and shot like a beacon up to the sky, piercing the malevolent sun with a blinding light. The result was an earsplitting explosion, louder than a supernova and brighter than 10000 suns.

Then all had gone blank and before I knew I was even dreaming I was awakened with the sun on my face and the metro operator calling out, "Willis St. please take all personal items with you upon leav-

-ing the train. Willis St."

After hearing the announcement, I jumped to my feet, grabbed my bags, and left the train.

I walked down from the platform and began the two block walk to the SPEx office, all the while thinking of the clashing tempest of elements and that insidious crackling purple sun.

Crossing the street my mind turned to the traffic and the sight of the post office. In the parking lot I could see my brother parked out front leaning against the car waiting for me. He had beaten me and broken his streak of tardiness, perhaps his flight training had included lessons on punctuality.

I approached my twin and couldn't help but feel that wholeness I always felt with my only full brother.

Reuniting with him was always such an uplifting occurrence, although it was never truly complete until we were with our other brothers Davriel and Cephus.

I looked my twin over briefly after not seeing him for just over a year; he wore jeans and black leisure shoes along with a hoodie and a winter over coat, his hair was cut short, but was just long enough to see it start to curl as ours was prone to do—mine was rather long and beginning to knot and dread.

I looked into his deep brown eyes—along with the 13-minute difference in our age we shared a few differences, one of which was eye color, his brown, and mine blue.

His eyes were smiling, as were my own and my twin and I greeted each other in our typical manner, "Sup?" we each said in unison before I drop-

-ped my bags and gave him a huge hug.

We exchanged our common brotherly banter as I dropped my bags in the trunk of the car. He drove a recent model SEV (an all-purpose vehicle), it was either last year's model or the year before, I couldn't tell, but knew that it was new for him. He asked how my travel was and I told him of my flight and the bothersome exchange with the irate Fed trying to make his connection, but all of this was erroneous compared to the metro-rail experience.

While I told my twin of the events that transpired prior to boarding the train he stood and listened, taken aback by the whole situation; though he did not seem as surprised as one might think after hearing of someone exhibiting such physical prowess.

Lacking much surprise, he simply listened and once I'd finished, he said, "That's weird."

Always brief with Jonos.

For a fleeting moment I considered it strange that after explaining the situation I should get such a quip response, but sidelined the thought as Jonos cut in saying, "How 'bout we get

your stuff? Mom's probably dying with anticipation to see you and the fiancé is expecting me after I get you home."

Fiancée: what a thought. They'd been dating for a solid four years before deciding to tie the knot. It was strange for a brief moment to think of my twin brother having a life different than mine, but realized that's what things had been now.

"How is she?" I asked.

"Great," he responded, adding, "she's having a blast with all this wedding planning."

"I'm sure," I smiled.

I didn't want to unsympathetically interject and change the subject, but I felt obligated to inform my brother of what I noticed happening behind him in the SPEx office.

During our interaction I'd noticed over my brother's shoulder, a rowdy line forming within the building. Sharing the site with him, the two of us decided to enter the store and find out the source of the calamity.

Stepping across the threshold of the store we were immediately greeted with a blasting cacophony:

"Where's my shipment?!"

"Why isn't it here?"

"What the hell happened? What do you mean everything's lost?!"

The riled customers ranted incessantly.

As we beheld the sour scene in the SPEx office, every possible clerk, teller, supervisor, errand boy, and even the suit-wearing manager, was busy with an unruly or concerned customer.

Each of them trying to inform, calm, and console them; with further cacophony provided by the mass of customers waiting rather impatiently in the line for their turns.

Approaching the rambunctious line, I tapped the shoulder of the middle aged balding man in front of me, interrupting the incessant conversation he was having on his Link, which was a newer model and attached to his ear lobe rather than the wrist like my own.

"S'cuse me sir, what's all the commotion?" I asked.

"A shipping facility was bombed by Morrabians or something, lots of packages destroyed, screwed up all of their shipping lanes!"

The man's response was brusque as he eagerly resumed his Link conversation, indignantly informing myself and the person on the other end that he'd been waiting for over 45 minutes already. I frowned as I turned to Jonos who was focused on the info ribbon spanning the ceiling over the countertops, it read:

- **Cascade Valley shipping facility suffers tragic terrorist attack. Package believed to contain explosive materials suspected to be in transit to government facility in Apacinia detonated and destroyed main depot; severe damage to the main building and ancillary facilities.**
- **Casualties were limited as 80% of the facility is automated, but 7 employees confirmed dead with 12 injured.**
- **Roughly 85% of all parcels within facility reported destroyed, including local deliveries, corporate parcels, and international shipments in transit through Cascade Valley SPEx.**

My heart immediately sank. *My shipment. My belongings.*

I'd shipped the majority of my possessions home to ease the burden of my personal luggage; including most of my personal collection of books — aside from what I carried with me — some of my notes from my studies abroad, portable entertainment electronics, the majority of my wardrobe, physical souvenirs from a dozen countries, and various odds and ends which I couldn't fit in my luggage.

It had all undoubtedly gone through Cascade Valley as it was the nearest SPEx facility.

"Wow, bummer dude." Jonos insouciantly chimed in.

I tried to look at the brighter side of the situation, but failed to see how it could have been any better than it appeared.

Staring blankly at the info ribbon as the message repeated my mind drifted away from the calamity of the SPEx, away from the angry pleas from unhappy customers and the defensive employees responsible for calming the disgruntled customers.

Unlike the seeming majority of people there, I instead tried to focus — at least for a moment — on those who perished in the unnecessary attack and how the loss their loved ones now felt was infinitely greater than any anguish we now had for our lost *stuff*.

The thought was slightly mood-lifting but somber nonetheless, and with that I turned to Jonos and said, "Well, it doesn't look like there's anything we can do about all this. Let's just get out of here and go home. I'm sure I'll be notified about the status of my shipment at some point."

I didn't believe what I had said, but as we left the SPEx I felt somewhat uplifted, as though a weight had been removed.

I realized that was because I just lost the vast majority of my possessions, but somehow I felt liberated from the whole thing, as though it was a weight off my shoulders, both figuratively and literally.

Besides that, absolutely nothing could be done to change the outcome. Resigning myself to the loss, we got into Jonos' car and made our way home.

The drive was uneventful and fairly tranquil. I took in familiar scenes of trees, lakes, and mountains between the small cities and towns that made up the varying terrain on the way home.

We talked about this and that; his fiancé Ayla, the wedding, my university trifles, his flight training, my free spirited education abroad, and other brotherly jargon, including the plethora of inside jokes and meaningless conversation typical to our interactions. It felt refreshing to be getting closer to home. The closer we got, the further the events of the day drifted from my mind.

We drove over the expansive Silver Sound Bridge as we made our way back to the Shendale Peninsula. Over the right side of the bridge I could just make out the impressive peak of the Great Mountain Cascade. I was reminded of my dream and the unparalleled sense of calamity and tranquility it exhibited.

My brother and I continued to chat up until the final few minutes of the ride.

The Brothers Angelus

We silently exited the highway and turned onto the main road. A minute later we were heading down our old road and finally down our street and driveway. It was only when we finally pulled in front of the house that Jonos broke the silence and said, "You're home."

Chapter 3: Patrol

The UTF Naval Guard Cutteran WHEC 723 *EAGLE* broke the monstrous surfs of the storm's fury, crashing through the twenty foot swells and generating huge explosions of mist.

The ship's two prows cut through wave after wave as *EAGLE* skirted the furthest torrents of the hurricane.

Standing on the forward parapet of the top tier of the *EAGLE*'s watch tower, the lookout diligently scanned the angry seas. Attempting to ignore the stinging pellets of freezing rain, Seaman Mikethon "Mike" Delahunt caught sight of the small distressed transport ship across the crest of a distant wave.

Dropping his gyro-stabilized binoculars, his shrill voice squeaked out a panicked report to the Officer of the Deck through the tac-com, "Sir, contact bearing 045, range two nautical miles. She looks DIW sir!"

The Officer of the Deck, Lieutenant Junior Grade Cephus Angelus squinted with his hazel brown eyes through the salty coated viewport clouded with the sea spray and sleet.

A moment after he spotted the vessel, a red blaze cut through the squall.

Seaman Delahunt's shrill voice came through the tac-com again, "Flare bearing 045, sir!"

"Acknowledged. Good eyes Mike." Lieutenant Angelus responded before quickly bounding across the mammoth bridge cluttered with radar and sonar consoles, navigation systems, comm-

47

-unications arrays, and numerous seamen struggling to settle their stomachs, barking out engine and rudder orders along his way.

He scooped up the Captain's direct line, still mentally piecing together his report.

"This is Captain Baldsmith." The Captain responded.

"G'morning skipper, this is the OOD." Lieutenant Angelus began, "Time on deck is 09:30. I have a small transport vessel now bearing 355, range 1.5 nautical miles. She's beam to and appears to be dead in the water. She just fired off a red distress flare, sir. Request permission to set the Rescue and Assistance bill."

"Permission granted. Are we in parameters to launch the bird?"

Lieutenant Angelus shot a look to the Quartermaster who began blasting the R&A alarm over the ship's internal communication system. "No sir," Lieutenant Angelus then replied, "Outside parameters for seas, wind, and visibility. Nothing we haven't launched in before though."

"Roger." Captain Baldsmith paused for only a moment while making his decision. "Get a relief Angelus. I want you back on the flight deck to get that bird off safely."

"Aye-aye Captain." Lieutenant Angelus hung up the phone and immediately put his watch team to work. "Quartermaster, set Flight Quarters. Then calculate a flight course and speed based off the fucking hurricane we're in. AQ, call Ensign Nagost, tell her to report to the bridge on the double to assume the watch."

Ensign Nagost showed up a few quick moments later, out of breath and a bit green, "Ensign Lizany Nagost reporting for duty."

"Are you fit to assume the watch?" Lieutenant Angelus asked with genuine concern.

"Yes sir. What've we got?" She replied, overcoming her grogginess.

After a brief pass-down Lieutenant Angelus scurried aft to the flight deck, stopping in his meager stateroom to grab his flight launch equipment. After throwing on his appropriate thermal wear — which fit a bit too snugly on his large frame — he began making his way through the corridors to the launch deck.

As he was strapping on his well-used helmet, he could feel the vibrations of one of the cutteran's launch bays opening. He was so attuned with the ship from spending countless hours aboard that he could easily tell that it was the port side launch bay opening.

He finally made it to the deck hatch and swung open the outer hatch just as the pad locked into position exposing the awaiting R&A aircraft.

Emerging from the hatch he spotted Aviation Petty Officer Mohamadi Kashvin, or "Kash" as he was known, organizing the launch equipment.

"Where are we Kash?" Lieutenant Angelus asked, hoping the safety comb of the flight deck had already been completed.

"Just finished the safety comb sir," Kash smiled, exposing his flawless toothy white grin which contrasted his dark face. Not even a storm of this magnitude could dampen Kash's spirits, "Launch pad locked in position Alpha. Flight crew manned and ready, sir."

"Good work Kash. Let's get this bird off safe, you hear?"

"You got it sir," Kash replied again grinning with his pristine smile despite the stinging rain that pelted his face.

Crewmen and launch staff scuttled to and fro, undoing mooring cables and removing engine covers completely liberating the awaiting R&A craft: a UTF Mk 33 Seahawk—a lighter variant of the Mk 44 Skyhawk—capable of operating from a ship.

The Seahawk's engines thundered to life as the last of the deck hands ran out of range and Lieutenant Angelus cleared the craft for take-off.

"Tower, R&A Seahawk Echo One," the Seahawk pilot, Lieutenant Commander Numen spoke, "Pre take-off checks complete, request for take-off to port."

Numen's green eyes darted to the deck to see Angelus as he waited for the go ahead. His pale, freckled skin was exceptionally pale at the moment, as he was not too keen on launching in the middle of a hurricane, but he knew what had to be done, and he was ready and committed to doing it.

"Roger that Echo One," Responded Lieutenant Angelus. "Big Bird you are clear for launch!"

"Very well." Numen keenly responded.

After Lieutenant Angelus gave the take-off signal, Numen pitched the controls back and the Seahawk lifted off, banking sharply to port immediately after earning a few hard-fought feet of elevation off the flight deck.

The Seahawk dipped dangerously low after clearing the flight deck, but Numen expertly wrestled the craft back to a safe attitude and raced toward the distressed ship.

The search and rescue had officially begun and all Lieutenant Angelus could do was watch in anticipation, gripping the parapet railing ever tighter.

Despite this being the last two weeks of his three-year tour of duty—and thus his mandated 6-year obligation—he realized it wasn't going to wind down as slowly as he'd hoped, it would smash to a halt like the crushing waves currently hammering the ship's double hulls.

Grabbing hold of the deck mounted visor, Lieutenant Angelus observed the R&A flight until it flew above the distressed ship.

He then turned to go, back up to the ship where he would observe the actual mission; he made his way forward on the Cutteran ultimately knowing little of how tumultuous his final two weeks of duty would be.

The Seahawk's engines roared through the fury of the hurricane winds as it sped toward the distressed vessel *Daring Nomad*.

Lieutenant Numen maneuvered the controls to get his Seahawk to the ship as quickly as possible. Numen's First Officer Lt. Jansen—a short, black-haired, scrappy fellow from a Northeast Amassian fishing town—manned the co-pilot's seat and operated auxiliary flight programs.

Only through their night-vision goggles could the two navigate the craft through the darkening whirl of the storm.

As Numen and Jansen managed the flight to the distressed ship, the remaining four crew members, Flight Officer Lt. JG Banim and the diver team comprised of Ensign Kustig, Ensign Baumerodden "Baumer" and Ensign O'Bannoch, waited in the rear compartment, ready for their part of the mission, the physical rescue.

Numen broke over the Seahawk's tac-com, "Dive team prep for deployment. Two minutes. Copy?"

"Roger sir!" Banim responded holding up two fingers to the divers.

The three immediately recognized the gesture and rechecked their harnesses, oxygen tanks, and the rest of their gear.

Their dive tanks were conveniently concealed in backpack harnesses that contained two ten minute tanks and an individual-rebreathing tank designed to allow an extra five minutes after the main tanks were emptied.

Banim first checked Baumer's, patting his back and showing thumbs-up, followed by Kustig's and O'Bannoch's repeating the gesture.

As the Seahawk continued its approach to the distressed ship, Numen and Jansen looked on as wave after wave came down on the small ship pummeling it into submission.

Jansen then cut in over the tac-com, "We're coming up on the ship. She's gettin' pounded somethin' fierce boys. Looks like you gotta' step in and rescue this distressed damsel before the sea has its way with her. We're looking at twenty footers at least. This is gonna' have to be one helluva quick op. She doesn't have much time."

"Dive team stand-by. One minute." Numen added stoically, as he maneuvered the Seahawk over the *Daring Nomad,* circling the suffering ship to take in the full view of its damage.

"*Daring Nomad* this is Naval Guard Rescue and Assistance Seahawk Big Bird," Jansen began over an open channel, "does anyone read me? *Daring Nomad* do you read me?"

"We read you B** Bird!" The ship's radioman quipped. "We're ta**** on lots of **ter. We **ed Evac now!"

"Roger that *Daring Nomad,*" Jansen responded, "we have you listed for eight crewmen, that'll take a few. We need you to make your way off the ship with what life-vests you have so our divers can ready you for pickup." The Seahawk slewed into a holding pattern as it prepared to deploy the dive team on standby in the rear compartment.

"Negative Big B**d. We *ave **leven. Repeat we have el**** that need *vac!" the radioman shouted.

"What the hell?!" Numen blustered, "Tell me that's the storm interfering with the coms! He didn't just say they had eleven, did he?!"

He knew at most his ship could only take eight in addition to his own crew of six. But eleven? Numen immediately realized there was no way they could pull off flying the weight of three extra men, especially not in this weather. They'd have to make two trips. Or summon the other Seahawk from the *Eagle*.

"Roger that *Daring Nomad*," Jansen responded while immediately cutting to the com transmission to the *Eagle*. "*Eagle* Actual, this is Big Bird. Did you catch that?"

"Roger Big Bird. We're prepping Echo Two for launch." Ensign Nagost replied.

Numen manipulated the controls of the Seahawk and stopped it dead in air as he gave the rescue team the okay:

"Rescue team you are clear for deployment!"

Immediately, Banim keyed the controls and opened the right side door of the crew compartment. Not a moment after, Baumer pulled down his thermal visor, sat precariously on the edge for three seconds as he activated his strobe light, and plunged into the ocean.

Kustig stepped forward, visor down and clicked on his strobe as he sat on the threshold. He waited for Baumer to clear the drop zone and plunged in after him leaving O'Bannoch waiting on standby for him or Baumer to secure their first survivor.

"Divers away," Banim reported as he watched the two swim for the wayward boat through the turbulent waters. As his gaze followed their path to the boat he realized the massive thirty-foot wave that was mere moments away from breaking on the side of *Daring Nomad*. "Warning! Warning!" he began, "Numen, Jansen, right side! You seein' this?!"

Looking on in bewilderment, Jansen hastily called to the ship, "Warning *Daring Nomad*, brace yourselves!"

"What?!" the radioman of *Daring Nomad* barely had time to say as the enormous wave crashed down on the ship, sending it well beyond its righting limit.

"*Daring Nomad* can you read me? Over! *Daring Nomad!* Can you read me?!" Jansen yelled.

"*EAGLE* Actual, this is Lookout." Seaman Mikathon suddenly broke over *EAGLE's* open tac-com. "*Daring Nomad* has capsized. Repeat, *Daring Nomad* has capsized."

Numen and Jansen looked on incredulously as the ship lulled hopelessly; capsized on the spot. "Get O'Bannoch in the water, double time!" Numen called over the Seahawk's tac-com, "Tell those divers they'd better hurry their asses up! They've got eleven souls to save!"

"Roger that!" Banim responded, pointing to O'Bannoch and then down to the water below. He shouted to O'Bannoch, "Change of plans. Eleven crewmen. Capsize. You're goin' in! Get who you can and get back!" O'Bannoch stepped forward, pulling down his visor and activating his strobe light. Banim slapped his shoulder and O'Bannoch anxiously leaped into the water.

Upon realizing *Daring Nomad's* capsize, Baumer and Kustig doubled their efforts. Their rescue plan involved the two of them finding floating crewman who'd abandoned ship, tagging them with high frequency strobe lights, and then send them to O'Bannoch who would hold position beneath the Seahawk.

Once the crewmen were there O'Bannoch would coordinate the crewmen's retrieval with Banim operating the Seahawk's winch, pulling them one at a time aboard the hovering craft.

That plan was still in effect, though they were instantly harried now as the ship had capsized and the crew was potentially unable to make it out of the ship.

They waited momentarily several meters from the ship; then glanced at one another, nodded, and immediately dove under and made their way into the ship.

From the cockpit of the Seahawk Numen and Jansen monitored the three divers via their strobe-light positions.

On the bridge of the *EAGLE* Ensign Nagost, and other bridge crew watched as Baumer and Kustig approached the boat. They saw them stop and then disappear underneath the swells of the waves as O'Bannoch approached the ship.

"Shit. This has gone from bad to worse." Jansen rapped off nervously on the Seahawks tac-com. He switched channels and asked for an update, "*EAGLE* Actual, what's the status on the other bird?"

"Standing by Big Bird. We need to know if it's absolutely needed before we can okay the launch." Ensign Nagost replied.

"Balls!" Jansen remarked. "Banim, what's the status of our divers?"

"O'Bannoch is deployed. No strobes yet!" Banim shouted back. He then paused for a brief moment, "Belay that! I've got O'Bannoch and two strobes detected. Prepping winch retrieval!"

Numen and Jenson both exhaled a sigh of relief, knowing there were at least two survivors made the mission that much more worthwhile given the horrendous conditions.

"Roger. Copy that *EAGLE*? We have two confirmed survivors."

Lieutenant Angelus couldn't hear all of Big Bird's response through the cacophony of waves crashing and the wind blowing, but he did hear the confirmation of two survivors, as another unrelenting wave smashed into the cutteran's two hulls.

He briefly caught himself admiring the dual-hull design of the ship, the beauty and nature of it tearing through the fiercest of the ocean's tempests. He recalled how at-home it made him feel and how deeply he admired the nomadic nature of living aboard a ship, that life suited him.

But he was quickly drawn back to the immediacy of the situation of the now capsized boat, and returned his attention to watching the rescue.

Baumer and Kustig had entered the capsized ship through its port side and were immediately able to locate two crewmen making for the ship's exits.

Baumer tagged the first with a high-frequency strobe light while Kustig tagged the other man and they quickly sent them toward O'Bannoch who approached just behind them.

As they met O'Bannoch he immediately brought them to the surface, but was so engrossed in saving them that he neglected to tell Baumer and Kustig of the additional survivors to expect.

The two instinctually proceeded through the natural surroundings of the ship and located another fleeing crewman, immediately tagging him and pointing him to the surface.

Again, they looked at each other, happy that they had already located at least three crewmen, but they weren't nearly finished.

Baumer didn't wait long to point to his watch and they both thought to themselves about the time that remained before their air ran out—but more importantly the air of the remaining crew members—as much of the ship was already submerged as it began to sink.

They continued through the network of the ship to locate the remaining five crewmen, completely unaware of the eight that were actually in need of their help.

As they proceeded through the ship they passed through the crew quarters and found the room near entirely flooded, with a mere foot left of dry ground on the floor, which was now the ceiling of the capsized ship as it slowly drifted down to its watery grave.

Passing through the crew quarters they then swam through the ship's galley which led them to a passageway to the bridge. The watertight door had been dogged down snuggly and double locked.

Kustig thought to himself about the captain sealing off the bridge in pursuit of the idea of going down with his ship.

Despite having no knowledge of the captain or how he valued his ship or cargo to support this notion, Kustig knew the traditions of the sea and how deathly serious the men who worked it took them.

Regardless, they would have to check it out, so Kustig drew a small flare-torch from his vest and began cutting through the door.

Meanwhile Baumer checked his mission timer: 10:37. They had five crewmen left and just over ten minutes to get them and return to the surface.

He caught Kustig's attention, pointed to his watch and flashed five fingers twice, then pointed a finger to the other bulkhead in the passage, another two fingers to his own eyes. He concluded pointing one finger in a circling motion up to the surface.

Kustig gave him a thumbs up and Baumer was off to find the other five. Baumer didn't want to waste any time while Kustig handled the bridge door.

Protocol dictated that they stay together, but the pencil-pushing bureaucrats who wrote the regulations rarely realized how often they contradicted doing what was necessary. He hustled off without further hesitation, eager to get the job done.

Baumer swam through the murky ship as it plunged deeper into the ocean and was grateful for his thermal visor which would point out all signs of bio-heat and indicate any warm bodied survivor in his midst.

As he passed through the next passageway Baumer found himself in another crew stateroom.

Four crew racks and various personal belongings floated in the dark water in front of him; a tin of chewing tobacco, a porno mag, a picture of someone's sweetheart — typical items for lonely deck

-hands thousands of miles from home.

He found three of the remaining survivors treading water in the uppermost corner and was surprised to see a mother and father with their pre-teenage son.

They were in the midst of taking their last breaths as the remaining air pocket in the stateroom filled. The room was completely submerged.

Their faces were quickly wrought with desperation and panic as they began choking on their last breaths.

Baumer quickly realized they didn't have much longer and unplugged his five-minute reserve oxygen tank and gave it to the son. He then removed the inflatable raft he always carried and gave it to the father.

As instructions, he pointed to the surface, then wiggled his to fingers past his hand in a swimming motion, then pointed toward the sealed raft followed by a ripping cord action—the raft had a built-in strobe light so as to alert any nearby rescuers of its position. He hoped that made enough sense to the man.

As the family shared breaths from the oxygen tank he pointed toward the exit and hurried them along, leading them back the way he came and toward the passage way that would lead to an exit.

Next, he withdrew a small echo device with three set frequencies. The first indicated a successful save while the second indicated a confirmed casualty, the third indicated distress and required immediate assistance. Baumer clicked it three times, indicating three saves.

Finally, he checked his watch, 8:05. There was still plenty of time.

While Baumer searched the ship Kustig continued to burn through the door's locking hatch with his flare-torch and had nearly finished.

With a loud *thunk* the locking hatch gave, and he deactivated his flare-torch and returned it to his vest. He then quickly kicked the dogs and wrenched the door open.

To his shock he was greeted by a lifeless blood-enshrouded, unblinking body that appeared to be the ship's captain.

He must have been injured when the boat capsized. Kustig inspected the body and found a gash in the captain's head and determined that to be the cause of death; if that didn't kill him, the ensuing flooding of the bridge surely did.

He checked his mission timer: 8:47.

It'd taken him too long to burn through the door, and as much as he pitied the deceased captain, he knew he had to move on as there were others to rescue.

He tagged the captain with a strobe light and left the cabin. His body could wait to be retrieved until after the storm.

Seeing a ladder that led further down into the ship's holding bunk, he proceeded to swim up it as the overturned boat continued to sink.

As he swam up through the passageway he found a hold that housed several large car-sized crates, as well as two panic-stricken crewmen.

One was desperately tugging at the other who had been lodged under a heavy crate of whatever it was the ship was transporting.

It was immediately apparent to Kustig that the pinned man would never make it.

The look on the crewman's face told Kustig that he was clearly taking on water and in immense pain both to the crate pinning him and his lungs filling with the harsh freezing water of the Pacinus Ocean.

Kustig immediately set to helping the crewman lift the crate off of his fellow shipmate but the two of them still proved to be ineffective.

There was no way to get purchase and the man's lungs were filling. Fast.

Suddenly the other crewman began to panic as well. He was running out of air.

Kustig removed his reserve tank and gave it to the man. The two of them set to trying to remove the crate again, but again found their efforts to be futile.

Realizing that there was nothing he could do he grabbed onto the freely floating crewman who was tugging at his fellow shipmate and despite a momentary struggle, was able to wrench him off and tag him with a strobe.

He then pulled him toward the hatch, forcing him to leave his drowned shipmate. He tagged the other body as before somberly withdrawing his echo device and clicking it twice.

Once to indicate the life saved, and a second time for the life lost.

His mission timer now read 3:52.

He'd taken far too long with those crew members. The boat had already submerged beneath the surface.

They'd confirmed the other five bodies, but then wondered about the captain. That made the total six... Were they misinformed?

Always leaving at least two and a half minutes to spare, and in this case having forfeit his reserve tank, Kustig knew there was no way to get through the ship in time to try and find out the answer.

Conscious of the survivor still with him, he decided to head back to the surface.

On his way he briefly reunited with Baumer and through the use of hand signals, informed him of the dead crewman he'd come across.

Baumer held up a plus sign with his fingers and then gestured a question with his hands. Kustig shrugged in response.

Baumer pointed to himself, two minutes to his watch, and then a circle around the ship to indicate, he would continue to search for any other remaining crew.

Kustig nodded, somewhat hesitant about his partner leaving. Resigning himself to aiding his survivor, who'd manage to use up the majority of the reserve tank, Kustig activated his own pick-up strobe, and made for the surface with the surviving crewman in tow.

"*EAGLE* Actual this is the Flight Deck!" the voice of Lieutenant Angelus boomed over *EAGLE's* open tac-com despite the onslaught of waves, wind, and rain rushing around him, "I've lost visual on *Daring*

Nomad. Repeat, *Daring Nomad* is down!"

He squinted through the storm and could still see Numen's Seahawk holding his pattern, but there was no site of the *Daring Nomad,* she'd clearly gone under.

"Lookout, can you confirm?" Captain Baldsmith asked as he entered the bridge, his six-foot-six frame commanding as much attention as his rank.

"Captain on deck!" Ensign Nagost shouted, prompting seaman and officers to quickly stand-to.

"As you were." The Captain curtly said, "Lookout can you confirm?"

"Confirmed!" Seaman Delahunt's voice cracked over the storm. "No sign of her!"

"Survivor number two aboard and secure!" Banim shot in on the ship wide tac-com, much to the relief of everyone listening in, "We've got two more on deck."

Good. Numen and Jensen both appreciated the retrieval of at least two survivors and the securing of two more, but that still left seven more unaccounted for, plus the three rescue swimmers.

Jansen looked intently down on the water searching out more strobes with his night-vision goggles. Seeing nothing at first Jansen immediately focused in just as something erupted to the surface. One of the divers' emergency floats!

"Banim, do you see that?" He asked.

"Roger that Jansen. I'm seeing it." Banim responded. I also see the three survivors clutching it for dear life. We have seven survivors accounted for!"

"*EAGLE* Actual this is Big Bird." Numen shouted, "You get that? We are reporting seven accounted for. Repeat we have seven confirmed survivors."

"Roger that. Keep us posted," Captain Baldsmith replied.

As Numen received the response from *EAGLE*, Jansen reported the sighting of Kustig's strobe light and that of another survivor. "We've got Kustig plus one. That makes eight. Banim let's get 'em up here double time!"

Aboard *EAGLE's* bridge many seamen began feeling a touch of relief as more survivors were located and brought aboard the Seahawk. "Keep it up people; we're not out of this yet." Captain Baldsmith said, seeming to judge the mood and address everyone's unspoken thoughts.

Deep beneath the hovering Seahawk and the awaiting survivors were the sinking *Daring Nomad* and the determined Baumer.

He'd already seen seven survivors, and heard about two who hadn't made it from Kustig.

There was no way that family was part of the crew. That meant that their original number of eight was incorrect. There were more survivors.

He checked his mission timer: 3:16. He only had one minute to search the rest of the ship given that he no longer had his reserve tank.

They'd already checked the bridge, the galley, the crew's quarters and the hold, which left only the engine room. Well aware it couldn't be completed in one minute, he again adopted the common mantra of men in his position: *screw protocol, I have a job to do.*

Baumer swam back through the main corridor and approached the last hatch.

He pried it open and proceeded up a small stair case and peered into the main engine room. There he saw the dismally lit untidy room. Tools littered the ceiling, while various items floated in the murk.

Baumer continued to pan the room when he came across the slightly dim presence of heat. *Simply the engine cooling, the father must have been the eighth crewman* he thought as the ship sank deeper into the frigid abyss.

No survivors.

He made a point not to look at his timer, knowing it was below 1:30. He'd stayed well past his limit; he needed to head for the surface while he still had air to do so.

Leaving the mess of the engine room he swam back through the main corridor and eventually out through the same hatch he'd entered through.

From there Baumer swam toward the surface and the cluster of strobe lights, as he saw one disappear from his ocean view.

Behind him, sinking in the cold black depth were the bodies of the pinned crewman in the hold, the captain on the bridge, and floating in the engine room among the clutter of the cooling wrecked engine, were the two lifeless blue bodies of the ship's engineers.

Anymore?" O'Bannoch shouted as Baumer finally breached the surface.

"Tapped out! Less than two minutes left on

the tanks!" Baumer yelled back, slightly confused.

"How 'bout the last two?" O'Bannoch replied; his words indistinguishable due to the hurricane around them and the Seahawk's roaring engines above.

"Down to it. No more!" Baumer quickly shouted back, giving a cut-neck motion and then pointing at them both and then up toward the Seahawk.

O'Bannoch reluctantly nodded, after falsely interpreting Baumer's words. The two of them took the winch up together swaying in the fierce winds as the other survivors before them and slowly but surely made their way up to the Seahawk as Numen maneuvered the controls to return to the ship.

"We lost the last two?" Banim asked as Baumer slumped into one of the jump seats after coming aboard the Seahawk.

"Huh?" Baumer responded. "Yeah the captain and another didn't make it."

"Yeah we know that. What about the other two?" O'Bannoch queried, "There were two more crewmen."

"Two more?" Baumer hesitantly asked, catching his breath.

"Yeah, from what the others say, they were the engineers?" Banim probed.

"The heat source in the engine room." Baumer muttered more than asked. *That's what O'Bannoch was saying before they took the winch up to the Seahawk.*

Baumer ran his wet gloved hands over his short cropped hair as he acknowledged for the first time, the compartment full of the seven survivors.

Observing the remaining four crew members of the *Daring Nomad*, cold and morose after the loss of their shipmates, Baumer looked on as the family of three huddled together, frigid and frightened after the ordeal they'd just experienced.

He tried to focus on the lives saved, rather than those lost but his mind couldn't help but drift off to thoughts of the raging sea as he contemplated the nomads lost to it as the Seahawk returned to the ship.

"*EAGLE* actual, this is Big Bird, we are coming home." Jansen reported as Numen gunned the controls and sped toward the ship.

Lieutenant Angelus focused on guiding the Seahawk to a safe landing once it returned to the ship. Despite the successful return of Big Bird in the horrendous hurricane conditions, he couldn't help but feel melancholic; as though the mighty and cruel sea had yet managed to claim some manner of victory over the rescue.

He tried to shake off the feeling, well aware that every life saved from the jaws of a cold death at sea is a victory. Still, he couldn't quell the forlorn feeling creeping up his spine that everything wasn't as it seemed.

***

From the recorded audio logs of Captain Darellon Baldsmith: Naval Guard Cutteran NG 0083 *"EAGLE"*

27 November,
3.2220

Modulator: Begin recording:

Cpt. Baldsmith: A week has passed since the search and rescue. We passed through the hurricane relatively unscathed, some bent lifelines and a few seasick seamen, but nothing that doesn't build character.

We were able to recover the bodies of the 4 remaining crew members of the *Daring Nomad* after an extensive dive once the hurricane passed.

The bodies and the survivors have been flown to Santa Bianca on the South-Pacinus coast of Amassia, thus we are currently down one of our Seahawks: Mother Goose was dispatched to split the flying hours of the flight crews. This doesn't concern me too deeply as we're only four days out from port and they'll only be gone a day.

The watches have gone well since then. The waters have calmed and it's looking as though the last week of this patrol won't be as hectic as we'd thought given that hellish hurricane.

Modulator: INCOMING TRANSMISSION.

Bridge: Captain Baldsmith, Lookout spotted a raggedy-looking freighter four Nauts' off our starboard side. Radar has confirmed. It matches the profile for Southeast Pacinu smugglers.

Cpt. Baldsmith: Acknowledged. Looks as though it'll be an interesting last few days after all. Prepare boarding party. Set Alert 1. I'm on my way.
Bridge: Confirmed. Setting Alert 1.
Modulator: End recording.

***

As lead tactical boarding officer on *EAGLE*, Lieutenant Angelus had gained immense knowledge through tough on-the-job training; boarding ships, inspecting cargo and ship manifests, thwarting drug runners, and occasionally razzing pompous yacht owners who think the ocean is theirs by inheritance.

His team of twenty Buccaneer-Commandos — Bucs, for short — was well trained and practiced; the five fire-teams of four executed superb boarding-action maneuvers and each of them was a top-notch marksman.

Furthermore, all twelve boarding parties he'd overseen on this tour were executed flawlessly.

That's probably why he now found himself a quarter of an hour into his thirteenth mission which had escalated to a full-on ship to ship firefight that left his team of Bucs, crippled, severely outnumbered, and isolated on the Pacinu freighter.

Unlucky thirteen, Lieutenant Angelus thought as he crouched behind a crate in the freighter's cargo hold as pirate-smugglers peppered his cover with bullets, keeping the remains of his squad pinned down. *Son of a bitch, I wish I had some explosives.*

"Covering fire!" Chief Petty Officer Vasic

shouted. CPO Vasic led Bravo team and was an excellent leader, inspiring confidence in all of his men through tough love.

Lieutenant Angelus was happy to have his acumen below decks with him at the moment.

Vasic had smartly positioned his men up on a wall-side catwalk behind considerable cover directly above Angelus' position.

Lieutenant Angelus jolted, alert and aware that his Alpha team—which now only consisted of himself and his lead shooter, Petty Officer Simund—now had to move from their covered position to the next one in the narrow window that Bravo team provided the covering fire.

"Moving!" Lieutenant Angelus shouted in response.

He and Simund sprinted for the cover of a heavy Exo-Loader suit that he assumed was used to carry the massive weapons crates that his team discovered strewn about the freighter's cargo hold—weapons which were now held in the hands of the freighter's crew.

Not only had the routine inspection gone horribly awry after a nasty run-in with a trigger-happy gunman eager to test out the merchandise, but he was now pinned down and cut off from any return route back to *EAGLE*.

He thought for a brief moment about the first of his team's casualties: the entirety of Charlie team. Gone in an instant—a well-placed high explosive incendiary round, ending their lives before they could even react.

But there was nothing he could do for his fall

-en comrades now as his thoughts turned to the firefight Delta and Echo teams were locked in with the enemy crew above decks, evidenced by the staccato of gunfire reverberating throughout the ship.

He further wondered what efforts were being made by *EAGLE* to neutralize the situation.

"Grenade!" A Bravo team Buc called.

Angelus immediately reacted, diving under the legs of the Exo-loader and covering as much of his body as possible.

The following thump and concussive blast indicated to Lieutenant Angelus that it was merely a concussion grenade.

Mind numbed but alive, he was grateful for the concussive blast as he realized the loader's legs didn't provide full protection from any shrapnel the grenade could have ejected.

He simultaneously realized that the loader wasn't just a standard Exo-loader. He recognized the shape of an ammunition belt fed from an ammo pack on the loader's back to a twin-barreled mini-gun on the loader's right arm. Fused onto its left arm was also a triangular shield type attachment.

These aren't your everyday smugglers. A spark popped into his mind. *Unlucky? Hell no. I make my own luck.*

Lieutenant Angelus immediately shouted to his teammate who had found cover behind the Exo-loader's power supply station, "Simund, I need cover fire!"

"Roger that." Simund responded; quip and precise as always. He blind fired his AC-7 for a mo

-ment, then stepped out of his covered position and fired off five more accurate bursts from his rifle, and hinted at a smile when he saw three of the bursts score hits.

Lieutenant Angelus didn't hesitate with the time his teammate bought him and he hurried into action as he climbed aboard the Exo-loader, seated himself in the operator's chair, and engaged the hatch's sealing mechanism.

Inside the loader the internal systems hummed to life and Cephus grabbed onto the arm controls out of instinct and activated the intuitive controls for the targeting system as he loaded and readied the dual chain-guns of the right arm.

He then broadcasted over the loader's microphone, "Simund, Bravo, consolidate and form up on the crates behind me. There's a service ladder at 8 o'clock-high beyond their lines, I'm gonna' walk you right up to it. We're blowin' this joint!"

"Roger that!" CPO Vasic responded.

"Copy that." Simund said lowly.

Lieutenant Angelus spooled up the barrels of the mini-guns and pulled the trigger as he laid down covering fire from the loader. Bullets peppered the positions of the pirate smugglers while they fled and fell alike, opening up a hole for Bravo to move through.

"You've got a clear path to that ladder!" he said as he lumbered straight past the ladder to draw off any residual enemy fire.

As he took cover from a rocket launched toward him he mistakenly clenched a nob on the left arm control stick and activated the triangular shield-like device on the loader's arm. Pincers immediately opened up on the edges of the shield mount as a beam of light shot out of the shield's open end, revealing a powerful flat laser blade.

The rocket impacted on the laser-mount and merely scorched the ground around him as he realized the laser was a shield in addition to being a blade.

In response he broke cover to draw off more fire as he launched a revitalized attack with this new found weapon and the repeated salvos from the dual mini-guns.

Simund and the remaining three members of Bravo team—Chief Petty Officer Vasic and Petty Officers Dalls and Granera—formed up on the cover behind Lieutenant Angelus in the loader.

They surveyed their surroundings and gauging it clear, they broke cover and made for the ladder.

As they reached the ladder, Simund began his ascent as Bravo team laid down additional cover fire. Slowly the members of Bravo team broke off and ascended the ladder. Dalls first, then Granera, finally followed by CPO Vasic as Lieutenant Angelus carried on with his diversion.

As they neared the top Simund saw the hatch open in front of him.

Relief flooded through his body as he saw light burst into the cargo hold and thought the cavalry had arrived to escort them back to the ship.

That relief was short lived, as bullets began raining down on Bravo team, tearing them to pieces as they perched helplessly on the ladder.

Out of the corner of the loader's peripheral vision Lieutenant Angelus was able to make out the flashes of gunfire ricocheting off the surface of the hold.

Stupefied, he turned around to a vision of horror as he watched the bodies of Bravo team fall to the floor in the hail of gunfire.

Vasic, that last one on the ladder was able to return one burst from his assault carbine as he was riddled with holes and eventually lost his grip on the ladder.

His body was the last to hit the deck as Lieutenant Angelus stood aghast in dismay at the site of his murdered Buc teams.

No.

His boarding team had been completely eradicated. Where were Delta and Echo? Were they even still alive? Was anyone coming for him? No. He was trapped and alone.

I'm not going down without a fight.

Emboldened by the deaths of Simund and the rest of Bravo, the pirate smugglers rallied and continued to exchange fire with Lieutenant Angelus in the loader.

Their spirits lifted and their courage bolstered, several of them began breaking the cover of their concealments to rain down fire on the loader — the last fighting member of the boarding party.

Stupid move.

Lieutenant Angelus rallied from the loss of his team.

Revitalized by the thoughts of his last stand, he recognized the pirates who had broken cover and readily responded by claiming those foolish enough to do so with a hail of fire from his dual barrel chaingun. Claxons blared as the mini-guns began to run out of ammo.

No matter. I'll run it dry and quench its thirst with bloody vengeance.

A death at sea now sounded all the more appealing to him and a death in service to his world, country, and shipmates, was full of valor.

Why then, did he suddenly feel depressed about it? He would die a good death. Dying at sea gave him comfort and solace, but he still felt dejected as he realized it wouldn't be complete, *not unless they were here.*

But they weren't: Davriel, Jonos, and Savos were nowhere near him. They were all over the world.

Realizing that he would die without his brothers angered him. He steeled himself as the warning alarms blared in his ears and the messages littered his vid screens: **Low ammo. Skeletal Integrity: 15 percent. Systems failing**. It would end here whether he liked it or not. So he would make it one hell of an end at sea.

If I go down, we all do.

The pirate smugglers converged on the loader's position and continued their sustained fire. They watched as the mini-gun barrels spooled empty and laughed with pure malice as they fought harder, fired until their clips rang empty and then reloaded. They wanted this man dead. And they were going to have him dead.

They all watched as the loader bowed under

fire, seemed to turn in retreat, and suddenly lurched forward and charged toward one of the ship's sides.

It smashed into the hull and the impact was felt and heard throughout the ship. Trickles of water began bursting out of small holes in the freighter's sides. Pirates looked on to the calamity down in the hold, their smiles and laughs slowly fading as they realized what was happening.

The loader lifted its left arm high above its head activating the laser blade attached to the shield's end. The pirates looked on in wonder at the yellow hue that the blade emitted.

They watched in utter disbelief as the loader drove the blade directly into the side of the ship. It removed the blade as a huge rush of water washed into the boat.

The freighter shook and seemed to ring out in pain as the loader slashed into its sides a second and third time in the shape of an "X." Pirates began turning and breaking for what exits they could, horrified as they faced the realization of what this madman was doing. He knew he was dead. He would take them all with him to his watery grave.

Lieutenant Cephus Angelus now saw the remnants of the pirate-smuggler crewmen as they broke cover and fled. He suddenly smiled.

Fools. Running won't save you from the crushing impact of the sea.

With a final lurch of the controls he crashed the loader into the ship's hull one last time, breaking through the side as the onrush of the dark waters of the deep began flooding the entire cargo hold, sinking the pirates' freighter: crew, cargo, and all.

Everything went black as the waters entombed the ship and it sank into oblivion.

***

Lieutenant Angelus woke up in *EAGLE's* infirmary with Corpsman Trasker overlooking his charts. "What the hell?" He queried as he took in his sights. His best friend on the ship Lieutenant JG Zaneil Banim was waiting by the edge of the cot exchanging a word with Trasker.

"Hey, there he is." Banim responded. "Tryin' to squeeze out on the money you owe me by punchin' the ticket on your last week huh?"

"Zane? How did I—" Lieutenant Angelus began slowly.

"Get here?" Banim broke in, "Well, after the freighter went down thanks to some madman's antics, we looked for survivors and… the bodies."

Banim paused a moment to remember those lost in the battle.

"We found a couple o' guys left from Delta and Echo in the water right after the ship went under, along with plenty of those Pacinu bastards—they were real quick to ask for help. Then as we sent down dive teams we found the rest of your guys in the ship's hold. As we recovered the last of 'em we stumbled across something strange: an Exo-loader riddled with bullets and almost entirely full of water."

Banim paused his story temporarily for effect, "We opened the thing up and imagine who we found in there." Banim was smiling and shaking his head at

Angelus, "You were smiling like you were asleep and having a funny dream or somethin'. We lugged your dead ass outta' the water and got you topside, only to find that you weren't dead at all."

Trasker then interrupted, "We're quite interested to know how that happened by the way."

"Yeah, about that." Angelus started, rather unsure of it himself.

"Don't stress it too much for now. Your body's had enough for a while." Trasker said, "The good news is you escaped mostly unscathed. No serious internal or external wounds of any kind. Almost as if the ocean healed you or something. Very peculiar indeed."

"Good news for all the ladies out there." Angelus deflected.

"I don't know about that." Trasker replied.

Banim chuckled, "But hell, anyway you look at it, you're alive, and that's enough for me man. Good to have you back! And hey, today's Thursday, we're pullin' into Apacinia tomorrow — tour's over."

"Which is why I'm letting the 'irregular' manner of your survival, slide." Trasker reported, "It'd only add to the amount of work I'd have and would delay your Matriculation ceremony. We're having a feast for the fallen tonight, and you're the guest of honor before we see you off with the ceremony tomorrow. Better get some rest Angelus." Trasker concluded as he resumed studying several patients' charts.

"So now that you're done with the Naval Guard, ships, pirates, raids, rescues, and the scurvy life at sea," Banim posed, "What are you gonna' do?"

The Brothers Angelus

"I'm gonna' go home and see my brothers."
Cephus said with finality as he leaned back in the
cot and fell into a deep restful sleep.

Chapter 4: Survival

The brisk breeze rolled through the lush trees around him and he heard the rapid rush of the river as he lay prostrate on its embankment. Without command his fingers grasped the growth and sandy earth on which he lay. And with a spark that quickly roared into a wildfire Davriel Angelus awoke.

Dumbfounded and weary he immediately recounted the events aboard the Skyhawk: the pursuit of the Gunrunners, the machine gun hits as they panged against the aircraft's hull, the anxious shouts of Elnezzi and Delantos among the worried cursing of Trane and the men in the hold.

He remembered the bold and extremely reckless decision to exit the hold after the loss of one of the ship's turret gunners. He then recalled his brief firefight with the Gunrunners, his sacrificial strike against the second foe, and lastly his fatal plummet toward the ground. Only the last part confused him. The fall wasn't fatal; he wasn't dead.

Davriel drew a blank as he willed himself upright, unsure as to what happened that brought him to his current state: alive on the bank of some river. It was as if he'd blacked out and completely forgotten that moment of his life.

Before focusing too intently on his lapse in memory he caught sight of his legs and a jolt of pain immediately shot through his body as he observed a distinctly dislocated kneecap.

He reeled in pain for a moment before the soldier in him asserted itself and his survival skills and training kicked in.

He had to reset the bone and find some sort of temporary support or brace. Looking about, Davriel located a tree line not far from the river and painstakingly hauled himself arm over arm to it. Propping himself up against a sturdy tree he prepared for what he had to do.

Finding a suitably sized branch on the ground, Davriel broke it down and placed it beside his leg. Biting down on a smaller stick he grabbed his leg at the knee and slowly began moving the kneecap back into place. He cringed in anguish throughout the process and bit down hard on the stick. Finally, with one last agonizing shock, the kneecap jolted back into place.

With his combat knife Davriel trimmed the remaining twigs and nubs of the branch and fashioned a brace using the tape and compresses from the limited supplies he found within his tactical vest; all the while thankful that despite being a non-com, regulations required him to wear basic survival gear during the deployment.

Regaining his senses now that his leg had been dealt with, Davriel assessed the rest of his body.

The rest of him appeared fairly intact, despite a few minor cuts and bruises on his arms and body. Judging himself fit enough, Davriel stood and examined his surroundings. He eased his full weight onto his injured leg and with a brief wince of pain he gathered that he was fit enough to move.

He then observed the broad river and dense tree lines on its sides. He remembered that the Skyhawk had aimed for a landing on a south-eastern trajectory that ran relatively parallel to the river.

Unfortunately, he currently had no absolute way of telling the precise direction of the Skyhawk's crash, he wasn't at a high enough elevation. He then looked straight downstream on the western bank of the river where he saw a plateau jutting out above the river.

Go for high ground to further assess the surroundings.

Before setting out he checked stock of himself and searched his tactical vest for equipment. He still had another compress pack and half the roll of medical tape to replace his bandage, several different antidotes, a tube of med-gel and smaller bandages, and finally three med-stims to suppress any pain.

Checking further he reassured himself by locating the hilt of his survival knife sheathed on his vest, a standard issue view-scope, and the full canteen at his waste: he was set for medical and survival equipment as far as he was concerned. Continuing, he quickly realized he still had one of the flash-bangs and three krak grenades in the pouches of his vest.

Those should come in handy should I find myself in a last stand situation.

Finally, Davriel checked the holster at his side; there he felt the reassuring grip of his RP-18 — the standard issue repeating pistol given to all soldiers in the UTF.

He located the four spare clips his vest allowed and removed the gun from its holster. Aware of his presence in hostile territory he removed a full clip and smoothly slid it into the gun. Pulling the hammer back, he loaded the first round into the chamber.

Conscious of the need for stealth and discretion in hostile territory however, he put the safety on and re-holstered the weapon, relying instead on his knife—silent but certainly just as deadly in close quarters.

Not wishing to linger he used one of his med-stims to sooth any residual pain from resetting his knee. Judging himself fit, he set out for the plateau on the western bank.

Setting out at a pace as fast as his injured knee would allow him, he made his way south, gaining ground as he journeyed toward the plateau.

He realized that should any enemy forces spot and engage him he would be easy pickings as a lone wounded soldier, but there was no way he was going to let that get in his way. His only focus now, beyond reaching the crashed Skyhawk, was to get out of there; all he cared about was making it out alive.

Life had given him a second chance it seemed, and based on his final thoughts before what should have been his death he realized where he needed to go, who he needed to see.

The images he saw before he hit the ground; his brothers, Jonos, Savos, and Cephus; the wind, earth, water, and the fire. Then the blackness.

It all meant something, but he wasn't quite sure what exactly. All Davriel knew was that he needed to get home to his brothers. He needed them now and he would do anything necessary to reach them.

As he made his way to higher ground, more

of his surrounding area became clear to him. He continued to journey south along the ridge of the river until he finally crested the plateau as it leveled out and looked over the river and its surrounding area.

Davriel recognized the river as the Uparatese River, the largest river in the New Morrabian Peninsula.

The river cut south and eventually led southeast, all the way from its source in the Morrabian Highlands in the north to its mouth at the Morrabian Gulf where it later met with the Cybian Ocean in the south. As he looked upon the valley in front of him Davriel was quick to spot the plume of smoke coming from the east that no doubt came from the crashed Skyhawk.

He removed his view-scope from his tactical vest and zoomed in toward the crash site.

The heavily wooded area surrounding the crash was thick, and Davriel gauged the pathway to the downed transport roughly passable, right after the jarringly steep decline from the plateau that he would soon face.

He wasn't able to see the Skyhawk itself but was at least able to spot a clearing on the other side of the river where he could start his trek to it. He realized now, that every second he wasted was another second the Morrabian insurgents had to track him down and close in on the remainder of the crew—if any of them survived the crash—and he immediately stowed the view-scope and began the harrowing decent down the steep plateau toward the river.

After what seemed like an age of slips, slides, and stumbles, Davriel finally made it to the riverbank beneath the plateau, despite his freshly relocated knee. He then had a clear sense of just how fierce the river was.

He determined that the Uparatese River had to have been about 40 meters across and going much faster than he would have liked at this particular spot. His one consolation was that it was at least a dryer season and the river had visibly descended from its previous mark.

Taking solace in the little things he immediately began calculating how far up river he'd have to go in order to reach the other side in exactly the right spot.

Again, he removed the view-scope and took account of the opposite shore. He found the spot he had eyed from above and estimated he'd have to go at least 100 meters upstream in order to hit his target: a 10-meter patch of light reeds that he'd aim for on the opposite shore that led into the dense jungle.

Stowing the view-scope he began the short hike to his desired spot. After he judged he had gone far enough he removed another med-stim from his survival kit and thrust it into his thigh.

Feeling the stim's immediate effects he turned and slowly began wading into the turbulent water to cross the river. It wasn't long before the full force of the river swept him up and the current took hold of him completely.

Davriel wasn't the strongest swimmer — no, that had always been his half-brother Cephus — but he was at least competent and more importantly, he knew the dangers of swimming in turbulent water.

Given that fact he swam as hard and as fast as his damaged body would allow and he made his way to the other shore as the current took him downstream.

He was barely able to reach the spot of reeds he targeted, and grabbing hold of large rocks on the riverbed, he was finally able to stop himself from being carried too far downriver.

Straining against the river's current, he hauled himself toward the shoreline. After pulling himself ashore and catching his breath for a minute, Davriel took to his feet yet again and set off at a renewed pace, albeit slightly slower than before due to his soaked clothing. He was grateful to be out of the water though and was anxious to get to the crash site.

It wasn't long before he reached the vicinity of the crash, and before he moved in to what could have been a trap he took cover behind a large oak tree near fifty meters out in order to get an advanced look at the site.

He climbed about half way up the tree and noticed the smoke had dissipated somewhat but he couldn't see any signs of life. He toggled between the zooms on his view-scope and gave the area a solid sweep and deemed it clear, for the moment at least. He then descended the tree and moved toward the crashed Skyhawk as stealthily as possible.

As he approached the crash site he removed his side arm and took a brief mental stock of his equipment. He had his side arm and three spare clips, one remaining flash grenade, the 3 krak grenades—which would only really help against vehicles—and what was left of his personal first aid kit.

Nearing the crashed Skyhawk, Davriel was able to see the extent of the transport's damage. The cockpit glass had shattered and the nose of the ship had crinkled to a snubbed end.

The entire right wing had been ripped off in the crash and Davriel could see much of the top and rear engine-mounts had been shredded off as well; all no doubt worsened from the strike from the Gunrunner's crack-shot cannon before the actual crash.

There were countless additional holes of various sizes that peppered the hull on much of its surface; some were clearly the signs of the Gunrunners' attacks, others resultant of the crash landing. He was relieved not to have been in the Skyhawk for its final moments.

Davriel neared the crashed aircraft looking closer at the damaged cockpit and was able to see the body of Elnezzi draped over the controls, battered and bloody, head slumped forward and lifeless. Delantos' body was nowhere to be seen.

I'm sorry I couldn't save you Army.

He continued to investigate the wrecked aircraft and as he examined the perimeter of the crash he found that along with the tail section and rear engine-mounts, a portion of the rear compartment had been obliterated as well.

The entire hatch section was gone and Davriel saw that seven seats had been lost entirely, as well as the heavy arms cargo. He realized that the crates containing the Stingray missile launchers and the Ac-7 assault rifles had been lost in the crash, but also that a number of the aircraft's passengers were now laying prostrate on the ground or slumped over lifelessly in their safety harnesses.

He holstered his weapon and searched for vitals getting through six of the bodies before finding the faintest trace of a pulse in Corporal Trane.

"D-Train can you hear me?" He began, "D-Train it's me, Davriel!"

"D-D-Dave? That you man?" Trane managed, "How'd you… m-make it?"

"I don't know." Davriel muttered, bracing Trane on the floor of the Skyhawk.

"We thought…." Trane started, but faded off.

"Stay with me D-Train!" Davriel encouraged as he held Trane's head in his arms and noticed the profuse amount of blood he was losing from the back of his head and from his back.

"We… We thought you didn't make it. B-b-but you did." Trane whispered as he coughed up blood.

"I made it D-Train," Davriel said, trying to sound reassuring, "and so will you."

"Nah, man, hehe," Trane managed to laugh between labored breathing and coughing, "I ain't comin' back from this one. You gotta…" he stopped to cough up yet more blood, "you gotta' make it. You gotta' surv… you gotta' survive…" Trane's words stopped cold as his head slumped down in Davriel's hands.

Davriel didn't cry, he didn't shout in agony, he simply sat there in stunned silence for a moment.

He closed Trane's lifeless eyes and laid his body back on the floor of the crashed transport.

He clenched his bloodied fists in anger and could feel his own blood stirring in his veins; he could feel a fire beginning to burn inside him. This feeling of loss gravely disheartened Davriel, but it simultaneously emboldened him as he realized how important it was to return home.

He was drawn from his musing when he heard a muttering from the forward section of the Skyhawk, "Ang... Angelus?" the voice creaked.

"Delantos!" Davriel exclaimed as he rushed for him. Delantos was clutching a bloodied right side and was dragging himself up onto one of the jump seats.

"How the hell did you make it, you crazy bastard?" Delantos asked in fascination.

"I guess I got lucky." Was all Davriel could manage as he embraced Delantos.

"If only Army and the others coulda' been so lucky."

"I saw," Davriel paused, "Looks like we're the only two who survived."

"Yeah, looks like it."

"Well, if we want to keep on surviving we're gonna' have to move, and fast." Davriel offered.

As he said this he made for the remaining crates of rations and medical supplies.

The crates had cracked open in the crash and the contents were strewn around the wreckage. Davriel began riffling through the contents for clean medical supplies to tend to Delantos. He used his med-gel and several bandages to seal up his side, then gave him one of the med-stims to ease his pain. He had overcome his own wounded and ailing body as soon as he realized the need to care for his comrade's.

He then returned to the supply crates and stuffed his various pockets and pouches with what rations and supplies he could, as well as Delantos' pockets. Once he had gotten all he could carry without overburdening himself, he returned to Delantos.

Now, with Delantos' right arm draped over his shoulders, he picked him up and began to make his way toward the exit.

As they made their way to the exit Davriel did what he could to ease Delantos' exit by dodging to the left and right of the various bodies strewn about the wreckage.

Suddenly, and without any kind of warning, a wiz sounded by his left ear and he felt a slight mist on the left side of his face, and then he heard the crack of the sniper rifle.

Immediately after Davriel heard it, Delantos' body fell from his arms and crumpled to the floor; a gaping hole replacing the spot that used to hold the right side of his brain.

Davriel fell to the floor a split second before the second shot came; narrowly missing his head by a mere half a meter. The enemy had found him. He'd taken too long and they had come sooner than he'd hoped.

He'd been too late again. He wasn't able to save D-Train, or Delantos, he wasn't able to save any of them. Maybe not even himself.

He realized then that he hated this situation and the stupidity of it, he hated that his transport of non-coms had been shot down for the sake of some nonsensical war; that he wasn't able to save any of his comrades. But most of all he hated that he was likely to face his own death here and now, and would ultimately fail to return to his brothers.

This feeling of failure had kindled the fire inside him and it flared as he determined he would satiate the desire to avenge his fallen comrades and not fail again.

He redrew his side arm and fired off a short burst of covering fire as he took what cover he could behind the scattered detritus and bodies that littered the compartment.

Another shot rang out and impacted in the hold. Taking cover behind the supply crates he happened upon two abandoned flash grenades and was pleased to add them to his inventory. Yet another shot rang out as it hit near the open hatch that lead to the cockpit giving Davriel an idea.

He withdrew one of the flash grenades from his vest and pulled the pin. He then tossed the grenade out the back hatch, closed his eyes, covered his ears, and waited for the flash of light and the thump to follow, *fup-bangg.*

The grenade detonated and Davriel broke cover as he rushed for the cockpit and let off another salvo of shots. He made it to the cockpit and took cover behind the pilot's seat. Using the brief moment he'd bought himself, he reloaded his weapon and gathered his wits.

Three clips remaining, doubtful that'll be enough.

He didn't have time to dwell on that as he quickly focused on what caught his eye holstered on Elnezzi's pilot chair. There in a weapon holster with three extra mags, was a pilot-issued Sc-MP2 submachine gun; the Sc-MP2 shot 8.2 mm rounds either as single shot or full auto, with a magazine capacity of 28.

Having it would drastically increase his odds of surviving this incursion and he said a brief word of thanks to the lifeless form of Elnezzi for giving him help beyond the grave.

He snatched up the new weapon, loaded it and quickly assessed his next move. The shattered remains of the cockpit left a hole wide enough to fit through and immediately he decided on his plan of action.

He would slip out through the hole in the cockpit window—hoping that the enemy wasn't flanking around his position—and attempt to sneak back to the river, where he could then swim downstream to a nearby village and commandeer transport to get the hell out of there. He decided he wouldn't use the Sc-MP2 just yet but would save it for when he truly needed it.

Not wishing to linger any longer and allow the enemy to close in on his position Davriel primed yet another flash grenade and tossed it out of the cockpit to cover his escape. *Fup-bangg* came the muffled sound of the grenade.

Davriel nodded his thanks to the lifeless form of Elnezzi, quickly scaled the control panel of the Skyhawk and then exited the ship. As he dropped down he heard the whimpers of two voices, it was in another language, but Davriel could tell it was a curse simply by the way the men grumbled.

He was instantly grateful for his previous precaution, but didn't dwell long on the fact. He removed his combat knife from his harness and lunged for the man closest to him. He grabbed him by the arm with his knife-hand, placed his leg through the enemy soldier's leg and pushed forward with his gun-hand, sending the enemy off balance.

He then brought the knife down directly into his chest.

Again he thought for a moment how grateful he was for his training — this time thanking the IPC (Immediate Proximity Combat) techniques he'd elected to learn and master in Basic Training.

His appreciation was short-lived as the other man started to wildly fire in Davriel's general direction, having heard the muffled dying scream of his comrade. Davriel heard increased shouting in the distance and immediately realized that these two men, as well as the sniper from before, had backup.

Hearing the shouting get closer Davriel dove for the cover of a fallen tree and waited for the enemy soldier to stop to reload. He still had his sidearm out, now in a joint grip with the knife, and focused intently before firing.

He heard the faint breeze in the trees around him, the voices of the approaching soldiers, felt the weight of the weapon in his hand, then suddenly he heard the dimmest click and realized the wild-firing soldier had popped out the expended clip to reload.

Davriel took advantage of the soldier's lapse and emerged from cover immediately planting a burst of three bullets in the chest of his foe.

The soldier fell dead to the ground as the voices and shouting approached. Davriel sought cover yet again and was able to get into a well suited vantage point as the others approached.

Four more soldiers came into his field of view and inspected the two dead bodies of their fallen comrades. Davriel used this distraction to his advantage.

He primed his last flash grenade and tossed it.

Again the dull thump of the detonation was heard and Davriel looked out from his cover to see the four newly arrived soldiers reel in discomfort and distortion.

He'd decided now to use the Sc-MP2 to engage these new enemies and immediately opened fire. He was able to down three of the enemy soldiers, but the fourth was able to find cover quickly enough to avoid being hit.

Using the last moments of this distraction Davriel set off into the jungle cover back toward the river at a dead sprint—his mind too preoccupied with survival to even think about his previously dislocated knee.

As he ran he could hear yet another group of voices approaching the crash site. He was glad to be heading away from it but was still anxious as he was not yet out of the woods.

After a few minutes of a dead sprint Davriel made it to the river, although not where he had been before. Somehow he had gone much farther north than intended and stood on an embankment a solid 15 meters above the rushing river below. He stopped once he reached the precipice and thought of his options.

Hearing more voices converging on his position and seeing no better alternative, Davriel turned around and unloaded the remainder of the Sc-MP2's clip into the jungle behind him.

As the clip sounded empty he triggered the clip-release and let the gun fall to his side on its strap. He primed a krak grenade and tossed it into the jungle.

The grenade would have minimal effect against personnel as it was designed for use against vehicles but it would at least serve to slow down his pursuers.

He then reloaded the submachine gun with remarkable ease and fired another prolonged burst into the brush as the grenade detonated.

Judging the resounding thump of the grenade and his subsequent hail of gunfire to be enough to hold off the enemy's advance—at least for the moment—Davriel turned, and without hesitation, jumped into the river.

The strong current was enough to take him out of sight by the time his pursuers got to the embankment and they soon decided to turn back and focus on salvaging the equipment and utilities from the crash rather than continue pursuing a lone soldier.

Eventually the river led Davriel past several small villages but none that had adequate transport. Most had been simple, bucolic five to ten family communities that subsisted by the land. None of them had reliable enough transportation to get him where he needed to finally go; not a single reliable motor vehicle among them.

On one occasion he did stop to rest, eat, get some fresh water, and change his bandage again. Additionally, he had fashioned a make-shift raft with the help of a father and son in the village; repaying them with rations and medical equipment. He wasn't long before setting off again down river, hoping to chance upon some kind of suitable way back.

Where was 'back' anyway?

He realized that up until now he'd been fighting for his UTF companions.

But they were all dead now, in a transport crash in which he would technically be listed as MPD: missing, presumed dead.

Additionally, he recalled, the UTF had stood idly by as it happened. They hadn't sent any aid during the dogfight, they hadn't sent a rescue, hadn't even tried to establish contact with him.

He hadn't seen or heard a single UTF aircraft, soldier, or transmission since he'd started downriver and was positive that they'd occupied portions of the territory in which he now found himself.

He spent much time floating on the raft downriver wondering why he hadn't come across any UTF forces until late on the third night after the crash.

That night he'd come across a small detachment of Morrabian insurgents posted on a small dock along the river. Davriel broke up the raft and slowly got into the water while holding onto some of its remnants and slid past the camp unnoticed, appearing like just another piece of flot

-sam floating downriver.

After passing their encampment Davriel made his way ashore and began sneaking through their camp.

Due to their sloppy sightlines and lax patrol routines, Davriel had stealthily snuck through their camp, careful not to alert any guards to his presence.

He'd used the cover of night to his advantage and was able to successfully commandeer a small dinghy docked a ways down from the boat they had been guarding.

The dinghy wasn't much, it had room for four at most, but it had oars and a motor and would allow him to make far better time downriver—though he planned on saving the motor for when he'd made it beyond insurgent controlled territory, out to open water.

He carefully untied the mooring ropes that kept the dinghy docked and pushed off, using one of the oars to navigate his way back into the open river.

After getting a safe enough distance away he took account of the items aboard the dinghy. He noticed a small radio aboard and immediately decided to do some audio recon to get a more informed grasp on his situation.

Over the radio he listened in on guerilla broadcasts and picked up what sounded like confusion.

He couldn't have been sure, but he thought he'd heard the Morrab words for "gone" "leaving" and definitely heard the word "Feds" and sat in bewilderment as he pondered the meaning of such words.

He turned the radio off and decided to focus his mind elsewhere and began rowing to aid in his departure from this place.

As he continued downstream he eventually made his way to the mouth of the Uparatese. There he utilized the dinghy's motor and finally reached open water.

From there he could take the boat to Elpris, a small independent and neutral country from which he could surely charter a way home.

Before he set out to the island, which was clearly visible against the day-breaking sky, he scanned the radio once more and was able to find what he believed were Federal broadcasts describing some sort of mass scale consolidation.

What the hell could that be?

He also heard the Mandali UTF Head Quarters in Cybia referred to several times and wondered if that was where everyone was heading.

Finally, after cycling through the channels he picked up on a secure and explicit UTF transmission, "...ctive .... field forces are to return to base and report for relocation. Repeat: all active UTF Cybian field forces are to return to base and report for relocation."

The transmission kept repeating and Davriel decided he'd heard enough and turned the radio off to think on what he'd heard.

All UTF forces in the area were to head to Mandali HQ for relocation. They were leaving. After everything he'd just gone through Davriel contemplated why he should report for relocation.

Why should I report in when they didn't help me? They didn't help Army, D-Train, and Elnezzi, any of them. They didn't help us. They left us for dead. For all they know I went down in the crash and am as dead as the rest of them.

Then something dawned on him; he'd had enough of the UTF and their bureaucratic nonsense, the pointless sacrifices it demanded, the ultimate futility of it. He decided to be finished with it.

He would use his presumed death as a means to escape it and return to what really mattered.

With a firm constitution Davriel resolved not to return to the UTF, but in fact, to make his way to Elpris and find a way home, to what mattered most: his family; his brothers.

United Terran Federation Communique to Admiral Li Kyphese (Commander of New Morrabian Detachment – Cybian Battalion) From the Office of UTF Chief Defense Minister Luca de Gulliss,
16 October, 3.2220 @ 06:10:05 TST

Admiral,

As you already know, for the past eight years the UTF Physics Engineering and Scientific Application Program has continued its research on intergalactic space travel, despite the failures of Arcus Angelus and the detrimental departure of his partner Dr. Dorfmund.

Even with the SAE's best efforts we currently do not have a successfully tested product. Notwithstanding these setbacks the United Terran Federation Space Force has continued to construct the makings of our first intergalactic fleets.

The UTFSF is currently putting final touches on its deep space *Javelin, Saber, Broadsword,* and *Anlace* class starships. Upon completion and successful testing of the Galaxial-Flux Drive based on the original Arcus Angelus design, these ships will be retrofitted and prepared for departure. They are currently undergoing construction at Orbital Shipyards Araxia and Benthion.

As the forerunner to Terran exploration and dominion, the UTFSF is responsible to utilize the vast resources available to us to spread out beyond the stars.

Our dominion will grow and prosper once these monumental vessels are complete. They are however, unprepared to begin the mighty manifestation of our destiny.

They require crews: pilots, physicists, engineers, navigators, marines, doctors, and the like; able men and women.

These will be no ordinary men and women, no ordinary crews; no, these crews will be comprised of the very best crop the UTF — and the Great Dominion of Terra — has to offer. Dedicated and passionate men and women, who through their beliefs would lay down their lives for the unification, glorification, and destined dominion of Terrans.

Battalions across the territorial borders of our world are being relocated to reinforce and augment our already burgeoning fleets. Three of the five fleets' forces are already accounted for and are already hard at work with preparations.

The remaining forces will assemble at designated launch zones and prepare for the journey to Luna. On the surface of the moon they will perform intensive low gravity and zero gravity exercises and training to prepare the UTF Space Forces for the expansion and ultimate Dominion of Terra.

Your Cybian Mandali Battalion is being requisitioned at this time. You are to cease all primary and ancillary activity in the area. Any non-priority missions currently underway are to be scrubbed. All non-essential personnel, primary assets, and resources are to be recalled to UTF Mandali HQ in Cybia, to be prepped for imminent Lunar departure.

The United Terran Federation thanks you for your compliance.

Chief Defense Minister Luca de Gulliss,
UTF Chairman

Chapter 5: ZANZABAR

Home. I was home. My mother greeted me on the pathway leading to the house with joyous tears flowing from the dark brown eyes that sat behind her wireframe glasses and an overjoyed smile on her round face.

She seemed shorter than last I saw her and was slightly skinnier too; perhaps age was beginning to catch up to her. She also had a few more gray hairs amid her shoulder length auburn brown hair, but her loving embrace was still as heartfelt and warm as ever and I was uplifted upon seeing her.

"Hi mom." I said.

"Hi Savos. It's good to have you home." She smiled as tears welled in her eyes.

Despite the joy I felt at seeing my mother, there was a slightly hollow feeling that I couldn't help but experience when seeing her, as if something were missing. Granted there was the case of my missing — presumed destroyed — possessions, which my mother immediately picked up on.

"Oh geez, where are all of your things? You didn't send them through SPEx did you? I've been following the attack on the news. Oh no, you did, didn't you!" She had immediately deducing what happened to my things, amid her tears of joy.

But I couldn't help but think the emptiness I felt was the result of something other than my possessions. I caught sight of my dad's old office window on the front side of our house and immediately knew what it was.

He's not here.

He hadn't been there for years.

It'd been just over eight years since that day he left. August 3.2212. We had all just resumed school the week before he left. Jonos and I were local celebrities and people couldn't get enough of us over it—until he never came back.

We had both known about Davriel for a couple of years, but nobody else did; and no one except Cephus knew about his parentage until he told us that same fateful day.

The day I lost a father and gained a brother, all those years ago.

His absence was the source of the emptiness I felt upon my return—granted, he hadn't been there any of the times I'd come back to visit—but now his presence seemed more significant.

I didn't let myself get caught up in feeling such depressing thoughts and I diverted my attention to what baggage I still had.

"Never mind all that stuff Mom," I finally said, "it's just good to be home. Let's go inside."

Jonos helped me with my bags as we walked up the pathway and stepped onto the porch. It was just as old and worn as I'd remembered. The wood was cracking in many places and the fading paint was beginning to chip from the house's trim, but it felt so reassuring, so pleasant, it was home.

I'm finally home.

Mom opened the door and we all walked in. Jonos immediately elected to leave my bags at the door and dropped them where he stood before proceeding straight toward the hallway bathroom.

I walked toward the kitchen table with Mom,

explaining the trip home, "The flight was fine, although I had to deal with this very indignant Fed officer who found my courtesy to be in the way of his prerogative."

"Well, you know how demanding their lives can get. I'm sure he had some big shot to see and somewhere to be." She responded.

She was clearly alluding to my nonexistent father who'd gone into the UTF Officer Program for the Physics Engineering and Scientific Application Program, and was always traveling and meeting new important people. Again I was forced to think of him and how the UTF slowly and painfully took him away. But again I pushed the dampening thoughts from my mind, focusing instead on a far more pressing matter, my empty stomach.

As if on cue, my twin walked out of the bathroom and walked through the dining room right to the kitchen. He then began to take out the necessary food to make himself a sandwich.

"Want to make me one?" I asked.

"Not really."

"Come on."

"Make your own."

"Dude, *come on*. I've had nothing but crummy airline snacks since this morning."

"No, make your own."

"Oh, just make your brother a sandwich," Mom cut in, "He's been gone for so long and I'm sure he's tired from all of his travel. Show him how nice it is to have him back and make him the darn sandwich."

I hated when Mom stepped in to our brotherly

squabbles; mostly because my twin brother — being a whopping thirteen minutes older than me — felt that I got preferential treatment because I was the 'baby.'

He had been born eleven minutes to midnight on the last day of March and I, needing another thirteen minutes of laborious effort, was born two minutes after midnight on the first of April. He loved to use that to his advantage whenever he could, which was quite often while growing up, but also always hated whenever Mom stepped in.

We preferred to resolve our differences ourselves, often physically, which she certainly didn't care for too much. But we believed the various punches, kicks, arm-bars, head-locks, and everything in between ultimately served to bring us closer to one another.

And usually any backlash from such fights wouldn't last more than a few hours and then all would be right as it was before the fight. Although most of the time we just bickered until one of us simply didn't feel like continuing.

This time however, he submitted rather effortlessly, "Fine. What do you want?"

"Umm, whatever you're having." I said, completely confident that any sandwich he would make would be more than supremely delicious as both of us were quite the sandwich connoisseurs.

I then thought about what Mom said about me being gone so long.

How long had it been now?

Nearly a whole year had gone by since I'd seen my mother, my twin, or either of our brothers. I had tried to come home about twice a year — usually every five or six months or so — but I hadn't had any chances this year as I'd been abroad in Eurkasyia.

But I was back now so all of that didn't seem to matter anymore.

Jonos ended up making us all toasted ham, salami and cheese sandwiches with a pesto-basil spread, spinach, and tomato.

The sandwiches were simply spectacular and an uplifting taste of home. Still hungry after finishing, I decided to make a second sandwich; though it wasn't nearly as gourmet as Jonos' was. He wasn't too thrilled when he saw I was making one.

"Oh, so *now* you can make a sandwich?"

"What, I'm still hungry. I figured you wouldn't want to make me another one."

He scoffed and we all shared a chortle amid our mouthfuls of the delicious sandwiches. After finishing our meal, we talked for several long hours, well into the evening.

We spoke about Jonos' upcoming wedding and his flying career, my schooling and traveling abroad and ultimately my future work and career plans — neither of which I had set in stone.

After some time Jonos stood up and said, "Well it's been great catching up, but I should get back to Ayla. I've definitely kept her waiting too long."

"Alright then," Mom responded stifling a yawn, clearly tired from the hours of conversation. "When will you be by next?"

"Oh, we'll come by this weekend. I'm sure Ayla will want to see Savos now that he's back," he replied. "Hey, I know that you'll want to take some time to unwind now that you're home, but if you're ever looking for something to do, come by the airfield. I'm sure I could find something for you to do. Come by tomorrow morning, if you're interested."

"Sure," I replied, almost in a daze, surprised as I was to hear the offer, "Will do."

After he left, Mom and I cleaned up the dishes and I lugged my belongings upstairs to my old room which was sparse, yet cozy, and exactly as I'd left it when I moved out all those years before.

As I plopped my bags down I immediately lurched forward a few paces and crashed onto my soft and inviting bed and instantly fell asleep. I slept a deep, fit sleep unlike any sleep I'd ever slept. I was home.

***

The next morning, I awoke to find my mother already gone to work and the house empty and cold. I didn't dwell on that too long and decided to take advantage of the fully stocked pantry and refrigerator — my favorite perks about being home. I made myself a hearty breakfast of scrambled eggs, toast with home jarred apple-butter, bacon, and a tall glass of fresh squeezed orange juice.

After gorging myself on breakfast I cleaned up in my old bathroom; cutting my hair, showering, and shaving, though I left the tuft of hair under my lower lip as I'd grown quite fond of it — and it distinguished me from my brother.

Everything in the bathroom was just as it was

before I left home, although it appeared that Mom had bought some new towels which I certainly appreciated given that mine were the same ones I'd been using for the past few years and had grown rather raggedy.

Having hastily and rather lazily unpacked my bags, I took out what I deemed acceptable clothing to go pay Jonos a visit at the airfield on a cold December day.

I pulled on a pair of decent blue jeans, a plain gray tee-shirt, and donned a heavy-lined zip up hoodie over top of that. I placed my Link on my wrist and descended the stairs.

Once downstairs I pulled on a pair of old work boots that still fit perfectly and put on my pea-coat, conscious of the near freezing temperatures outside. Before leaving the house I grabbed my wallet and keys, then opened the door and took a whiff of fresh winter air. I stepped outside and locked the door behind me.

Outside I walked down the pathway to the garage where my old car sat parked in hibernation patiently awaiting my return. The car was an eight-year-old 2212 Candali Qaterro.

I hadn't driven the super-charged 407 horsepower coupe in nearly a year and at that moment I thought to myself how much I'd truly missed it. I remembered the reckless times I'd had flying down open country roads—going twice the speed limit as I would catch the eye of the few privileged girls who'd ever accompany me, while I would pretend not to feel my nerves splinter and fray as we courted deathly high speed danger.

I had also remembered the countless times my brother Cephus and I nearly killed us driving it on the winding roads of Shendale Locality as we would often disable the car's traction control in favor of reckless daring. I recalled how we'd always talked so fondly about the idea of one day racing our Qaterros against each-other, though never actually got the chance.

He'd been the one to first show me the redesigned 2212 Qaterro in all its bad-ass glory, but thanks to our well-to-do father—who'd left my mother with quite a considerable legacy—and my earlier 17th birthday, I'd been the one to get it first.

Cephus later got his through the substantial salary he received from the Naval Guard, but we unfortunately never did get to race them as we both went rather separate ways after graduating from Secondary; he having his with him on the other side of the country at the academy, and mine sitting in storage while I wandered around the world.

All those memories drifted away as I thrust open the door and gazed on in childlike wonder. My car sat covered, quiet and still in the garage—wrapped up rather like an Endyears present awaiting a happy child to open it.

It'd been years since I'd last received an Endyears present as it was a custom traditionally held for young children, but this seemed like present enough though, and I couldn't help myself from relishing the situation.

I approached the car and saw a note atop the hood. I opened it and read, 'She's all dressed up with nowhere to go.' I smiled as I recognized my brother's handwriting.

I gently removed the covering from the car and found a pleasant surprise. My Qaterro was sitting there in the pale light, glimmering with a fresh waxed glean I had not expected.

The metallic gray paint was magnificent and shiny and the bold black racing stipe down the middle gleamed so robustly I found myself mesmerized by it and the reflection it created.

I walked around the car inspecting the surfaces and curves and with a satisfying grin, clicked the unlock key. Letting myself in I felt the familiar comfort of the soft leather on the driver's seat and quietly whispered a hello to my car as I keyed the ignition.

The car roared out in a controlled fury as I revved the engine into life. I smiled, remembering my juvenile fascination with her — enough that I named her after a teen crush — and it became apparent to me that Jonos had kept a good eye on her and made routine inspections and drove her around a bit to keep the engine in good operating condition, despite my being gone for so long.

I was quite happy that he'd been keeping maintenance on it as I knew our mother certainly wouldn't as she never much cared for the car, and certainly never drove it.

I made my final checks and eventually put the car into gear, easing off the clutch ever so slightly to remember the feel for it. I let on the gas a bit and coasted out of the driveway. I slowly turned onto the main neighborhood street and returned the car to neutral as I sat idling in the street's relative emptiness. I looked left, right, behind, and finally in front of the car.

Judging the coast clear, I flew off the clutch, simultaneously hammering down on the gas and heard Silvia's roar and the tires squeal as I peeled out and erupted down the street as I had done so many times in my past.

I'd almost forgotten the rush I loved so much from such a quick and jarring acceleration but my body remembered it and immediately wanted more.

I approached the end of the street and turned onto the main road and gunned the accelerator again, feeling all 407 horses of exhilarating power as I raced my way to the airfield, completely oblivious of the harrowing experience that lay in wait for my brother and me.

When I got to the airfield I quickly pulled into the parking lot and killed the engine. My exhilarating ride was over, but my blood was still pumping in excitement from the drive.

I hadn't sped too much, but the extreme acceleration offered by the car's amazing horsepower always made it seem like you were going twice as fast as you actually were.

Sighing from my elation I stepped out, locked the doors, and proceeded to the main annex to find Jonos.

I entered the annex and greeted the receptionist, "Hi there, I was wondering if you could tell me where I might find Jonos Angelus." The petite brunette behind the counter looked at me quizzically for a moment. I could tell that she was baffled at the sight of me, so I thought to clarify, "I'm his twin brother, Savos."

"Oh I see," She exclaimed, "I thought you were trying to play a joke on me. I wouldn't put that past Jon."

Jon? I thought, slightly perturbed at the nickname. I guess they didn't address him by his full name as I always had.

"I think he's in one of the hangars doing maintenance work," she continued, "He and the owner Rennai are inspecting one of the new planes we recently acquired."

"Which hangar would that be?" I asked, enticed at the mention of new planes.

"Let me check for you. Just a moment." She then checked a wireless Link she'd had at her desk. "They're in hangar 18. You'll need this to get through our security." She handed me a lanyard with a security pass on it.

Security? What security?

I'd been to the airfield on two occasions before and hadn't ever had to deal with any kind of security. I wondered if it had anything to do with the new planes they'd just acquired or was simply a recent addition.

"Thanks," I said to the receptionist as I headed for the rear door of the annex toward the actual airstrip and hangars.

"No problem Jon—I mean *Savos*. Sorry. You just look so much like him. Have a nice day."

"You too." I smiled and left, thinking of all the ways Jonos and I *didn't* look alike.

As I walked outside I was immediately greeted with the cool fresh air and the blast of a plane landing on the airstrip.

It was a rather cold December morning, though it was supposed to warm up slightly throughout the day, but a chill ran down my spine as soon as I heard the rush of the landing aircraft and felt the wind on my face.

The plane landed and taxied to a stop before shutting down its engines. A relative calm settled over the airfield and I suddenly felt the winds change dramatically. A feeling of apprehension passed over me but I pushed the thoughts aside and continued toward the hangar.

I found my brother in hangar 18 just as the receptionist had told me I would, and to my astonishment, I had to present the security badge to a guard just outside the hangar door.

The guard shared the same quizzical look the receptionist had as he saw me enter—clearly he'd recognized my face though it took a second to process my identity. I presented my own personal ID alongside the badge and was recognized as Jonos' brother and permitted to enter the main hangar area.

Inside, I noticed Jonos and his boss Rennai; they were both completely mesmerized by something that I couldn't fully see. As I approached them I caught sight of what they were so intently looking at. There in hangar 18, were two new Macdonus FA-2 supersonic jets.

The FA-2 was the premier supersonic fighter used by UTF forces; its speed and maneuverability were unparalleled by most any fighter in the various insurgent factions that opposed the UTF, and two of them were now sitting in a hangar at my brother's airfield, just waiting to be flown.

As I walked closer I noticed their sleek fuselage and wedge-wing-like design and realized the two were slightly different from the standard single-seat FA-2 I'd previously seen.

Both of them displayed longer and wider fuselages and rather than a single seat bubble-canopy cockpit like the UTF fighter jets had, they each had a windshield style cockpit like on an airliner—which clearly designated space for a second seat for a co-pilot which I found quite interesting. I let out a low whistle as I stepped up to my brother and his boss.

"Sup?" My twin greeted.

"Well hello Savos." Rennai said, sounding rather welcoming.

Rennai was taller than Jonos and me by a couple of inches, had dark brown skin, dreadlocked hair pulled into a ponytail, hazel eyes, and a remarkably beautiful face.

Jonos had told me she'd started the flying company as a small crop-dusting business nearly 20 years ago but through various side-projects including; opening a flying school, a shipping business, a sight-seeing agency, and a freelance search and rescue team, she'd turned that crop-dusting business into a fully functional airfield.

Presently, it looked like she'd added UTF contracting and testing to her résumé.

"How in the world did you guys get those?" I blurted rather unceremoniously.

"They're civilian prototypes of a modified FA-

2 from a private Macdonus contractor," Rennai answered frankly. "We have good connections." She smiled and winked at me.

"Clearly."

"This is your lucky day Savos." Jonos said to me with a mischievous smirk on his face. "I've been given the opportunity for the first flight with my choice in a copilot. You interested?"

I'd only ever flown small subsonic civilian models before. My father had first taken Jonos and me flying when we were twelve, but we were only able to build up about forty hours of actual flight time over the few years leading up to his departure.

Since we graduated Secondary, Jonos had taken up flying full time and was currently an esteemed instructor at the airfield's flight school, but I chose a different path in academics and self-searching.

A lot of good that did.

Despite the fact that I hadn't been flying in nearly ten years, I was always a natural at it. I wasn't nearly as gifted or as practiced as Jonos—who seemed more at home in the air than he did on his two feet—but I always had solid reflexes and a great feel for aircraft control, and I certainly relished the idea of flying something faster. Not wanting to decline such a monumental offer I graciously accepted.

"Hell yes!" I then remembered Rennai's presence, "If that's ok with you, Rennai?"

"Sure." She said confidently, "Anyone Jonos trusts as a CP, I can trust. Just remember, you break it you *buy* it. And from what your brother tells me about your job status, I suggest you bring it back in one piece."

I mulled over a response to her jab at my unemployment but decided against it.

"Alright then," Jonos offered, "Let's suit up."

The powerful engines roared to life and shook my entire body; the tremors ran down my spine and had every one of my nerves tensing. Jonos pushed the throttle forward and my body immediately sank into the back of the seat.

My ride to the airfield in Silvia was exhilarating but the FA-2's acceleration put Silvia's 407 horsepower to shame.

"It's got a kick!" He said over the person-to-person headsets we were wearing.

"It's awesome!" I simply returned.

We sped down the runway faster than I'd ever gone in my life. Jonos pulled back on the control yoke and we immediately ascended into the sky.

Higher and higher we began to soar, traveling faster and faster. It was incredible. Enthralled as I was by the remarkable craft and the pure adrenaline that was running through my veins, I couldn't ignore a sneaking suspicion that this was too good to last.

We leveled out at 4000 meters and Jonos quickly pointed out a storm that was growing on the eastern horizon, "Check it out: huge storm front coming in from our 2 o'clock."

The clouds beyond were an ominous shade of gray and unnerved me. Within the gray I thought I could see flashes of violent purple lightning.

"Did you see that?" I gasped.

"See what?" Jonos said, slightly distracted by the displays and controls.

Gazing at the brewing storm I felt a shiver down my spine but was drawn away from it when Jonos followed up on the com, "No worries. We're heading that way."

He took a hand from off the control yolk and pointed off in the area of our 10 o'clock, off toward the Great Mountain Cascade. "But not before I show you what this thing can do first."

Before Jonos launched us into a roller-coaster-like thrill ride of immense proportions, I looked at the mountain and was immediately drawn toward its presence and forgot about the thoughts of danger and foreboding.

I stared at the mountain and for a brief moment, slipped into a trance like state of recall as I remembered the dream I'd had on the train when I'd arrived just the day before. Oddly though, the dream felt as if I'd known it for ages, as if it'd been a recurring dream.

I came to with a jolt as a wave seemed to rattle the plane. "What the hell happened to you?" Jonos was shouting.

"What?"

"You just passed out or something. You weren't responding."

"What do you mean?"

"I said your name like ten times!" he continued, "I didn't think the maneuvers were *that* bad."

"Uh, I don't know. What just happened?" I shouted, "Did something hit us?"

"No, just some turbulence." he responded, "Systems are holding up just fine."

It had been unlike any turbulence I'd ever felt, but I didn't have time to comment on that as there was another massive jolt; this time accompanied by a vibrant, violaceous white flash that seemed to be part of the impact. The craft lurched and several of its systems began to short-circuit.

"Shit!" Jonos exclaimed as he began battling with the controls while trying to stabilize the systems.

"What the hell is going on?" I said, suppressing my urge to panic.

"I don't know but if we can't stabilize we're going down. We're going down hard!"

"What can I do?"

"Deploy the flaps to full extension, and then lock in our position with the tower." I briefly hesitated as I repeated the instructions, but was distracted by yet a third strike.

The craft pitched downward in altitude and we began to jet toward the earth.

Our descent was fueled by our natural gravity, but also the engines which were still functioning and adding to our acceleration toward the ground.

More systems began failing and I was immediately made aware of the ground as it became our only view. But it wasn't the ground I was noticing, it was the side of the Great Mountain Cascade, we'd neared it and were clearly going to get even closer.

Jonos pulled me back to reality as he shouted, "Are you with me? I need you to cut back full on the throttle then pull the green-tipped levers just above the throttle on the right. Then turn the black dial next to them all the way. That'll fully deploy the flaps."

I immediately pulled the throttle back, then pulled the levers and rotated the dial all the way, and felt the ship slow.

We were still falling but we'd at least recovered a slight measure of control. Jonos continued to wrestle with the controls trying to keep our descent to a minimum and pulled it back evermore to negate our fall.

"As soon as I tell you to, I want you to retract the flaps and give me half throttle." He ordered.

"You want me to what?"

"Just do it. On my mark."

I knew better than to question my brother when it came to flying, but the moment got the better of me. He was far more skilled in it in every way and I trusted him with my life, so I followed his order. He pulled the control stick back and I could easily imagine the level of strain and focus he imbued.

"Come on dammit!" He yelled to the jet. Jonos managed to pull up significantly on the control stick and had nearly managed to pull the nose of the ship level with the horizon before yelling, "Now!"

I reinserted the levers which retracted the flaps and immediately felt the increase in acceleration. Afterward I grabbed the throttle and pushed it forward to half power and again felt the strain of the forceful acceleration.

As I did this, Jonos had adjusted our orient

-ation and attitude and suddenly I realized that he was inverting the jet using the boost in speed in order to roll and pitch us into a position to fully accelerate out of our dive.

Gravity now pulled us headfirst toward Terra and I couldn't help but glance around at our surroundings and saw the storm from before looming closer.

It had changed direction and was now approaching the mountain.

Additional klaxons started blaring as I felt another rupture in the craft. Several gauges had surged to max position and then flat-lined. Our propulsion was suddenly gone. Our fall had yet again become an uncontrollable nosedive.

"Jonos! Help!" I said frantically.

I turned my head to look at him and saw that his head had drooped down and to the left. I gasped in shock. He was out cold. He'd passed out or something.

Shit.

"Jonos. Jonos!" I desperately tried to revive him. "Jonos we are going to die!"

No response.

I desperately grabbed at the control stick in front of the co-pilot's seat as we continued plummeting to the surface, trying to pull us out of the dive.

I saw yet another flash of fierce lightning; this time however, I praised the fact that it hadn't hit us. The flash hit the mountain beneath us and immediately the storm let loose its full fury. The wind intensified, the clouds swelled and a hail of razor-like rain began to fall.

Returning to our perilous plummet to the earth I intensified my efforts and desperately tried to level out our fall. Recalling what Jonos had been attempting before passing out, I completed the roll that he'd started and deployed the flaps yet again, barely slowing us down.

Immediately after doing so I pulled back on the control stick, while simultaneously throttling the engines all the way forward to level us out as much as possible before crashing. Nothing happened.

Suddenly the jet lurched yet again as we were struck by lightning and a new set of alarms sounded. The engines had maxed out and detonated from the strike, sending us into a flat spin downward.

There was absolutely nothing I could do now but stare through the windshield as the world passed me by and we approached the mountainside.

Eject eject eject! I panicked as I searched for the right control. *Doesn't this thing have eject?*

We plummeted the remaining few-hundred meters in a matter of seconds. I closed my eyes and thought it the end.

"At least it's with you." I said to my unconscious twin, resigning myself to our tragic end.

"HuuuuUUUAAAARRRGGGH!"

Jonos suddenly roared to life from his unconscious state and suddenly the storm seized up around us.

We felt weightless for a few moments as if frozen in midair, and I wondered what could have possibly happened. We then dropped as suddenly as we'd stopped, falling the remaining dozen or so met-

-ers with a deafening and bone-chilling crunch.

For a brief moment I sat immobile in the cockpit next to my prostrate brother. My vision was failing and I felt blood dripping down my forehead. I listened as the storm resumed, much calmer now. I heard the wind and pattering rain against the ruined husk of our craft and lost consciousness.

I awoke to find myself in a dimly lit and hastily dug refuge in the ice. Jonos was looking over my prostrate body. I groggily greeted him as I sat up.

"Hey, take it easy little brother. How are you?" he replied.

"I've been better, but I'll live." I responded coming out of my daze. "How are you holding up?"

"Good. And also good." He followed up.

"How are we alive?" I asked, baffled that we somehow survived and trying to recall what happened, "Wait a second, what the *hell* happened to you?"

"Honestly, I have no clue. It's all a blur to me. What I know is that we *are* alive and we're safe in here. Search and rescue chopper should be here in 20 to 30 minutes. But in the meantime you're gonna' want to see this."

"See what?" I questioned.

I took a moment and looked about me and realized that the shelter we were in must have been dug out by my brother.

He must have regained consciousness and gotten us both out of the wrecked jet and then in here to safety. We sat within the cave with a small lantern casting light in the shelter as I regained my wits.

Looking around our hastily dug shelter I took notice of a smaller hole within it. It was an old tunnel made of ice. The hole was large enough to fit a man through and went back a solid 10 meters before fading into darkness.

"I already checked it out." Jonos said grinning with satisfaction, "You've *got* to see what's back there."

I got to my feet and shook off any remaining lethargy and approached the hole. I hunched over then got on my hands and knees, and turning on my flashlight on my wrist Link, I began the journey through the tunnel with Jonos at my rear.

As I passed through the other end of the tunnel I found myself cold and wet in a humongous and well-lit cavern.

A cavern that wasn't empty.

In the hollowed icy cavern lay a peculiar and ancient looking ship preserved under the mountain's permafrost. It was sleek and somewhat arched in design, looking like an alien space ship from a sci-fi movie. Its nose resembled an arrowhead leading into the neck and aft form which widened to a broader triangular shape of the hull. From its widening and bulbous aft section came downward-swept wings ending in sharp winglets.

Out from its backside sprouted four triangular stabilizers, similar to the slanted vertical stabilizers of several military jets I'd seen.

Finally, jutting out from its back end, were four massive cylindrical engines. It was an incredible sight to behold, neither of us had ever seen anything like it, not in our wildest imaginations.

Jonos pointed to the exposed area of the hull we faced, flashing his Link-light over it and guiding my sight to a specific bit of what appeared to be writing. I looked at it and wondered in fascination when I read what appeared to be our own alphabet. The lettering had a slight variation but the resemblance was uncanny. The script read simply one word:

ZANZABAR

"*ZANZABAR?*" I said aloud. "I wonder what that means."

"Let's go find out." Jonos said, smiling.

"Right with you."

Chapter 6: Reunion

Aboard the mysterious ship ZANZABAR we found things I could never have imagined in my most extravagant thoughts.

We entered through the only visible hatch, which was about a third of the way back on the fuselage from the front. The door had been left open—how, neither of us knew—but burning with curiosity, we both entered the ship, eager to find out its secrets.

What we found was astounding. The ship almost looked Terran but demonstrated a knowledge and technology that far surpassed ours as a race.

The consoles, the displays, everything was frozen over to some degree or another but we could still appreciate the immensity of it all.

Remarkable marvels aside, it wasn't long before we found the first remains of the unfortunate crew aboard the ship.

As Jonos and I walked through the main corridor we saw a frozen body lying limp on its side. We approached the figure in apprehension and saw that it was a female, frozen in death.

Around her was a small pool of blood which had clearly seeped out and frozen solid shortly after death.

Looking at the figure closely we could discern a female face that somehow looked familiar in the strangest way possible, like she could have been a relation in another lifetime.

Despite the figure's frozen rigidity we could

make out a slim and beautiful visage with full lips and dark eyes; the immense cold had clearly frozen the body before decomposition could seriously begin, thus preserving it in remarkable fashion.

"What a way to go, huh?" I stammered out.

"Yeah..." Jonos said, this time I could see that his brevity was entirely legitimate and he was clearly as dumbfounded as I was.

"What do you suppose happened?" I asked, "You think it was a ship from the First or Second Age or something? Maybe it crashed in one of the earlier wars?"

Jonos didn't skip a beat as he continued to examine the ship, "No way dude, this is *far* too advanced for anything Terran made. Even in the previous ages."

"But that woman..." was all I'd managed to say as I was at a loss for words.

Either way my words had fallen on deaf ears as Jonos continued through the ship's main corridor. I hesitated, looked at the frozen body one last time, and finally proceeded on to catch up with him. We continued on toward what we soon found to be the ship's bridge.

I let out a low whistle as I crossed the threshold, "This is nuts."

"This is... awesome." He said. "Could you imagine flying something like this?"

That was the sky-kid talking. My brother always had his head in the clouds. From as far back as I could remember he was thinking about flying and I always thought he felt more at home while in the air than he did on the ground.

It came as no surprise when we got onto the bridge, that Jonos immediately thought about flying the mysterious ship rather than how it'd gotten here, or who our newfound dead friend was, or who else we had yet to find, and ultimately *who had flown it here.*

As we searched the ship we found several more markings much like the glyphs used on the exterior of the ship.

They greatly resembled the Terran Standard alphabet but had some slight variations here and there, and usually didn't form words we knew despite being able to read some of them. Beyond the similarities between the two alphabets I couldn't help but feel as though these letters spoke to me.

"Do these letters seem—"

"More than familiar?" Jonos finished my thought, "Yeah."

"Good. Just wanted to make sure it wasn't just me." I responded as I felt my heartbeat quicken. Something was waiting to be uncovered here and we were getting closer to finding it out.

We began to dust off and wipe away bits of ice and powder from various surfaces as we looked around; searching for anything that might lead us to find out anything about the ship, its crew, or furthermore, its point of origin.

"Check this out," I caught my twin's attention and pointed at another word spelled with the glyphs as before, again it read ZANZABAR.

The writing was on an arm-sized plaque, mounted on a counter-like railing in front of the captain's chair and the bridge's main dais, centered between the two main control consoles.

I continued to wipe away the ice and powder and began to see more writing beneath the already exposed glyphs. It read:

"ADVENT CLASS ANG-07 / ARCOS SHIPMASTER ARTER ANGELUS."

"No way," I whispered in astonishment as I deciphered the lettering and the weight of the situation truly began to sink in. "*No way.*"

"You think that's crazy, check this out..." Jonos produced a small palm-sized device he'd found in the hand of a dead man who lay prone behind one of the bridge consoles with a gash in his forehead, frozen in time exactly like the woman.

The device had several buttons on it but one stood out from the others, and glowed a luminescent blue color. I anxiously watched as Jonos pressed the button.

A light shone out from the device, producing a fuzzy, irresolute hologram of a handsome, yet fierce looking man in armor before it wavered and disappeared entirely, leaving only sound. The cold unforgiving freeze of the ship's interior seemed to project the voice and I almost thought I could hear our father's voice whispering in the eerie atmosphere of the ship.

The recording was in a slightly different language, but every now and then we heard words that sounded familiar, floating on the edge of our comprehension.

Despite not understanding it fully, there were many words we ended up hearing multiple times; 'Arcon' and 'Ara' were the two that topped the list.

More foreboding than that however, was hearing the words, "Arcus, avenge us all," right before the recording ended.

Just after hearing that the speaker signed off, "Arter Angelus, Arcos Aldfather and ZANZABAR Shipmaster."

A still silence ominously descended over us.

Did he really say, 'Arcus, avenge us all'?

"Look here." Jonos said, turning the device over in his hands.

After playing the message, Jonos and I took a closer look at the device and discerned a shape on its surface that he and I had both seen before in our past. It looked roughly like an "A" with two inward slanting arcs for the sides and a very low crossbar, within the "A" were what always seemed like a random series of crisscrossing arcs and lines, but now as we both studied it the image became clearer.

Upon seeing these alien glyphs repeated all throughout the ship the text within the "A" had now become discernible; within the "A" we now saw the word "Arcos."

We looked at one another and our eyes immediately went wide with wonder and fascination as we both put the pieces together. We had both known that image for our entire lives, but up until now never knew what it meant.

Our father used to wear a necklace with a small medallion with that exact same image and lettering, with the word Arcos imbedded in it, it was the only thing he'd had since his childhood.

Yet we had never known what it meant; until now.

Our father, the great Arcus Angelus: the pinnacle of the Terran race, the inattentive bastard-rearing father, and now the lost space traveler; had come from another world. He was Arcos... and that meant; so were we...

Despite the monumental truth we had just discovered, Jonos and I both knew that we had limited time left in the ship.

We knew the airfield's search and rescue team was bound to be here soon, but we also knew that this find had to be kept a secret — at least to outsiders. I pulled out the GPS I had brought in the pocket of my flight harness and marked the coordinates before we readied ourselves to leave.

"Good call." Jonos said as he immediately read what I was doing and shoved the alien device into his pocket. "We'd better get a move on."

"Yeah." I said, ultimately too astounded by the discovery we'd just made to say anything more.

I followed and caught up to him as we made our way back down the main corridor of the ship, back toward the original hatch we'd entered through.

As we stepped to the door we both looked down the direction we hadn't gone, the aft section of the ship remained entirely a mystery to us.

"We'll come ba—"

"Just a quick peak." I blurted out as Jonos started to speak.

Jonos honestly looked torn between the prospects, "The SAR will be out here any minute." He began. "If we're in here they won't find us. Or they *will* find us and then find *this*." He gestured at the ship.

"So go stand look out then. I'll only be a few minutes." I replied.

"A few?" He countered.

I grinned and shrugged, "It'd take less time if two people were to do it. You know, cover twice the ground in half the time?"

"Ugh." He sighed, "Fine, but seriously; no more than two minutes, just get the layout. Then we're outta' here."

"No promises!" I said with a broad smile as I turned and sprinted down the other end of the main corridor, with Jonos flinching and then starting right on my tail.

We explored the rest of the ship for about two and a half minutes before turning back, returning to the main hatch and leaving.

Those few minutes were not nearly long enough and only after Jonos pestered me to leave did I finally turn back.

What we did manage to see in those few short minutes was incredible and certainly warranted many future looks for closer inspections.

Along the corridor were small man sized hatches indented in the walls, but we didn't waste our limited time to go down each ladder that each hatch indicated.

We continued on and had gotten to a fork in the main corridor where there were two steep staircases, one up and one down, and the remainder of the corridor that continued aft of the ship. Jonos had gone up the ladder while I went down.

We only took in a few momentary glances in the dwindling time, but ultimately Jonos knew best as not a second after we'd scrambled back up and down the stairs, and returned to the main corridor hatch to leave we heard the garbled sound of the SAR on our radio.

Before we left the tunnel that led to the ship we dug into the cave walls to loosen up enough snow to bury the entrance and not a moment too soon as Jonos spotted the red and blue signal lights of the rescue craft amid the evening snow flurries.

He waited until I had completely covered up the entrance before removing a signal flare and lighting it as the aircraft came closer into view.

It was the airfield's own rescue craft and looked like a prototype or older model of the more recent Skyhawks I'd seen the UTF military forces use; but obviously a civilian model as it had no armament whatsoever and was privately owned and operated.

"What's downstairs?" Jonos shouted as the aircraft hovered above.

"Huge hangar." I replied, "What about upstairs?"

"Flight deck." Jonos grinned.

"Not a word to anyone." I said.

"Not a word." He said.

We were eventually hoisted up into the craft through its winch recovery system and we were immediately flown back toward civilization along with the main hulk of the ruined FA-2—carried beneath by a secondary winch system.

As the view of the Great Mountain Cascade began to diminish I was again reminded of the dream I'd had and the incredible discovery we'd just made, and deliberated what it all meant for my future.

The ride back was fairly short and after the SAR emergency crew had looked us over during the flight they deemed we wouldn't need to go to an official medical facility but still needed to be checked out by the airfield's physician before leaving to go anywhere.

After we'd landed back at the airfield we briefly met with the physician before being cleared and then facing Jonos' boss Rennai.

She was grateful for our survival, but seriously torqued off at the loss of her new craft. After a couple long hours of unfavorable debriefing, going over the sequence of events time after time, the blank-slated stares of insurance agents, and a final *private* word with Jonos, Rennai, and the lead claims agent—which left Jonos a bit edgy to say the least— we finally had a moment of respite.

"Think it'll be ok?" I asked, "Maybe dad's UTF accountants can help us with this one."

"It's already taken care of." Jonos responded frankly

An awkward pause descended over us. I briefly wondered what they might have discussed before Jonos spoke again.

"I have a few things to sort out here before I can leave. You go on home."

"I can wait..." I started.

"Nah, I'll just catch up with you later tonight. We definitely need to talk." He said sternly.

"Alright, bye. Don't go getting all weird on me now." I submitted.

"No promises." He followed up less enthusiastically. We'd used that as our own 'goodbye' for as long as I could remember but never had it been so somber coming from him.

I turned and walked slowly toward my car still pondering the discovery and now Jonos' dismissive demeanor. As I got into Silvia and drove home, not a thought was wasted on anything other than our discovery.

"ZANZABAR," I kept saying over and over. Thinking about my father and his father before him, and who the Arcos were, and why they came here, and what happened to them after the crash.

I was so lost in thought that I hardly even noticed when I had pulled into my driveway, gotten out of my car, and had plopped down on the porch chair I always used to sit in.

A couple of hours passed and eventually Jonos came by the house. Mom had already come home and was busy cooking dinner when Jonos and his fiancé Ayla came in the door.

I was surprised to see her since it wasn't a planned dinner but I immediately deduced why he'd brought her.

Our mother was a conversational enthusiast and no doubt she'd want to hear all kinds of new details about their wedding plans, which would give Jonos and me the perfect window to leave and have a conversation of our own.

I nodded ever so slightly to him as they entered before greeting my future sister-in-law, "Ayla, it's so good to see you! How are you? It's been what, almost a year?"

Ayla was the sweetest girl I'd known and an

angel for putting up with Jonos. She was a full head shorter than him with pale skin, wavy strawberry blond hair, brown eyes, a button nose and a smile bigger than her heart.

"Hi Savos!" She said, hugging me as she returned my greeting. "It's good to have you home. It's been too long."

After our greetings and pleasantries, we sat down for a nice dinner. Mom had baked a large Salmon filet with a sweet Cadian glaze she'd learned ages ago when visiting Dad's home village near the Great Mountain Cascade—which Jonos and I now knew was only an adoptive one—and served it up with a large pot of rice and steamed buttered green beans.

We were just about to sit down to begin eating dinner and break the news about the day's events, but before we could all take a seat and begin there was a distinct knocking on the door. It was seven straight knocks.

Only two people ever consciously knock like that at our door... and to my knowledge both of them are out of the country.

I stood up and approached the door with perplexed hesitation. It was dark outside the window and I couldn't quite see out the small windows atop the door but before opening the door saw through one of the side windows, the distinct glean of black paint on a Candali Qaterro glow in the blackness of night.

My mind raced in thought to one conclusion and as I opened the door, I stood with a look of sincere happiness.

"Sup?" Cephus said grinning ear to ear.

Standing in the doorway was the bulky figure of my younger brother Cephus.

Despite being the youngest, Cephus was certainly the biggest of the four of us, though that wasn't always the case—his recent time in the Naval Guard no doubt influenced his brawly physique. He stood a few inches taller than me and looked proud and strong.

Beneath his buzzed hair his hazel eyes beamed with gladness and he smiled a broad smile with his clean-shaven jaw to match his excitement.

"Dude!" I exclaimed, baffled by his presence, "You're back!"

"Yeah. Just got in today." He replied as we both hugged.

"Come on in! You hungry?" I asked, knowing that he certainly was, "We're just sitting down to dinner."

"Sure." He said excitedly and walked right in greeting the rest of the family. "Hello Mrs. Angelus! Hey Jonos! Hi Ayla! How is everyone?"

"Hello Cephus!" My mom shouted back, bolting up to hug and kiss him. Although he was our half-brother and not our mother's son, Mom sure did treat him like he was. "How in the world are you?"

The rest of dinner took a rather different turn as we talked of Cephus' return and his last few months in the Naval Guard.

He took care to omit certain details regarding his final week, preferring to save my Mother from some harsh truths; favoring instead to tell my brother and me at a later time.

We merrily ate, drank, and talked; telling recent stories and reminiscing about past adventures. Finally, dinner ended, and the three of us excused ourselves from the table to talk brotherly business.

"We've got some crazy news for you Cephus." Jonos said as we headed for the door.

"Let's take a walk." I said.

As Ayla and Mom moved into the living room and talked wedding plans and life in general, the three of us left the house.

We decided we would head to the old cabin on the edge of our property that we'd frequented as teenagers to further reminisce and discuss matters of great importance.

First we stopped in the garage where Jonos grabbed a case of cold-brewed rummies while I pocketed an old matchbook and a two-year-old pack of my hand-rolled cigs. After grabbing what we needed for our brotherly talk we left the garage and headed up the street and into the woods at the edge of the property and up toward the old cabin.

We trekked to its location at the edge of the woods and finally reached the cabin, looking on in familiar fashion to the dilapidated structure.

The cabin was practically falling apart, the years of disuse clearly showing, but each of us looked on in fond nostalgic memory as we remembered the countless good times we'd had in it.

It had been our childhood home away from home, our place of carefree fun, shenanigans and tomfoolery; it was our magic tree-house, our boys club, our own *Outer Heaven*. But that seemed a lifetime ago.

I stepped up to the door and noticed the latch was undone and the door cracked open. *That's odd.* I pointed it out to my brothers who both shrugged and motioned for me to continue.

"Check it out." Jonos said.

I activated the flashlight function on my wrist Link, opened the door, and pointed it into the cabin as I walked in slowly.

The cabin was a rather small two floor structure with a common room, a kitchenette, a bathroom downstairs, and a small lofted bedroom upstairs.

As I entered I heard the distinct sound of water dripping; *must be the outdated pipes in here.* Surveying the bottom floor, I saw clear signs of recent occupation and further questioned the scene.

There were various articles of clothes on the floor, none of which I could readily discern but at that point Jonos and Cephus had followed me in and stood in the entrance taking in the scene.

"Dude, I think you have squatters." Cephus exclaimed, reaching down to examine the clothing.

"Yeah, I don't remember leaving this place in such a mess." Jonos added as he set down the case of drinks.

We were then alerted by a creak at the top of the stairs. We looked above and saw a shadow begin to move slowly down the steps.

I pointed the light up toward the shadow as it came down the steps one at a time but the figure produced a hand that blocked us from seeing its face.

Slowly the shape came down the steps and into the dim light and we saw the image of a wet, shirtless man, sporting tattered camouflaged pants over bare feet.

Jonos then turned on his own Link's flashlight and pointed it to the ceiling, illuminating more of the room. As our eyes adjusted to the new light, the shape came into focus.

Standing before the three of us was the dripping wet, unshaven, bedraggled form of our oldest brother Davriel.

"No way..." I barely managed, breaking the stunned silence.

"Brothers... it's been too long." Davriel said.

My day had taken its final beguiling turn after a crash landing, a mysterious discovery of an alien spaceship, the truth of our alien heritage, the random—but welcomed—return of my brother Cephus, and now the mysterious—and equally welcomed—reappearance of my oldest brother Davriel. *What a day indeed.* We were finally all together though. We were reunited after years of intermittent separation.

After we got over the initial shock of the situation and saw to Davriel's unkempt and slightly malnourished condition we took to the table in the common-room.

Jonos had run back to the house to grab a towel and some food for Davriel and to tell Ayla he'd stay at Mom's for the night.

While he did so the rest of us took to lighting the cabin with the lanterns we'd stowed in there, as well as fixing some of the old insulation and window fixtures as much as possible and setting out folding chairs around the table.

Once Jonos returned we all sat down, cracked open a fresh rummy apiece, and lit up a few of my hand rolled cigs.

Jonos and I listened as Cephus and Davriel took turns detailing their times in the UTF military and told of their narrow escapes and final weeks in the service.

Cephus' story about the boarding party and the loader was immensely enthralling and had us questioning how he'd survived at all given the harrowing conditions.

Davriel then proceeded to tell of his own death-defiance and quest for survival in the jungles of New Morrabia, his abandonment by his UTF forces and his eventual departure from that life and return to Amassia.

Apparently he'd stowed away aboard a series of barges and transport ships until ultimately reaching the Southwestern coast of Amassia where he then drifted up the coast, hitchhiking and walking his way home.

We listened in silence until both stories had been told, and despite the innumerable things we'd wanted to say, we couldn't, we were simply too captivated in the physical presence of our brothers.

I noticed a brief sense of aversion from Cephus, when Davriel explained that he'd essentially deserted, but it didn't last long and we continued to enjoy being together once again.

Eventually Jonos looked intently at me and I nodded back at him in understanding, and we began to tell them our own story and the amazing discovery we'd made.

He told them of the civilian model FA-2 the airfield had gotten, the test flight, the bizarre weather occurrence before the crash, and the eventual finding of *ZANZABAR*.

"You wouldn't believe the things we saw on there," I interjected, "All over the ship there was this alien language, but the weird thing was, it wasn't that different. It looked kind of like the Terran Standard alphabet, just with some minor differences."

"That's not even the craziest part." Jonos blurted.

"The craziest thing about it though: our father used to wear a medallion on his neck with the exact same lettering on it! He'd had it since his childhood and it was the only thing he'd had since his birth, or rather, adoption."

"Seriously?" Cephus questioned.

At this point Jonos produced the device we'd found aboard the ship and activated it once more so that Davriel and Cephus could hear the message for themselves.

"So he's…" Davriel started.

"An alien." I finished.

"He's Arcos." Jonos provided, "And that means so are we. All four of us."

"Only half though." I added, "As all of our mothers are Terran."

"What's that part about Ara and Arcons?" Cephus questioned again.

"That part has us stumped." Jonos said.

I had begun to theorize about what Ara could

have been but wasn't sure enough and therefore kept the thoughts to myself.

After hearing Davriel's account of his elemental visions during his plummet, Cephus' mysterious recovery after sinking the smuggler ship, and returning to my own dreams about the elemental tempest around the mountain, I reconsidered Jonos' surge before we crashed on the actual mountain and was beginning to piece together a working hypothesis about this 'Ara.'

But there was no way I could prove that to any sort of legitimacy and I hadn't the slightest clue about what all was actually said, so I kept quiet.

After a long silence Davriel finally said, "So when do we get to see it?"

***

The next day Davriel finally returned to his mother and he explained his "discharge" from the service, though omitting the exact details of his survival and eventual return to Amassia.

Cephus went back to his respective family as well and spent time with his mother, step-father and two step-sisters — given their different parentage, Cephus was the only one to share true kinship with them.

Jonos returned to his and Ayla's apartment, and I remained at my mother's house contemplating our next course of action. My curiosity and wonder for the ship was growing by the second and I finally called up my brothers two days after our initial reunion to plan our return to ZANZABAR.

That night we met up again in the cabin about an hour before midnight. We brought along the regular necessities; drinks, smokes, snacks, and games; enough to last the whole night.

After an hour or so of playing a card game called Bamunto, several celebratory 'reunion' drinks, and our usual exchanging of inside jokes and mindless jargon — all of which were far too complex and nonsensical to explain to others — we finally set down to the topic of the night: *ZANZABAR*.

"Lllet's go tomorrow." I slurred after folding my cards in resignation of the current game of Bamunto.

It had been dragging along for the past hour as Davriel, Jonos, and Cephus had each presented one of the four boon cards of the game and kept it going on three separate occasions, plus we'd already shuffled and flipped the deck over twice; I felt the game needed to finish.

"Nah dude, I gotta go into work tomorrow." Jonos responded.

"Just call in sick." Davriel added in.

"Ya dude. Call in sick." Cephus finally added after we'd looked to him and waited for a number of seconds for his response.

I continued before he could answer, "Come on. I mean, I'm gainfully unemployed, Cephus is a retired man, and Davriel's now technically a known fugitive. You could take *one day* off work and go check out the ridiculously awesome spaceship from our distant and unknown Arcos home-planet. Don't you think?"

"Fiiine." He finally said. "But how do you

plan on getting us there, Mr. Bigpants?"

"Well since you asked, I should probably tell you: we need another plane."

"Dude, no way!" He immediately responded, "Are you serious? I'd be calling in sick and then going to the very same place!? Also, do you honestly think Rennai would be okay with that after what happened last time?"

"Don't worry. This time we're not gonna' be flying the plane. This time we're just passengers and we're gonna' be jumping out of it while it's in air."

"Parachuting?" Davriel asked.

"Absolutely." I said resoundingly after taking a swig of my rummy.

"I'm in." Cephus said.

"I suppose another free-fall couldn't *hurt*. I'm down." Davriel added ironically.

"How do you expect me to seriously pull that off after what happened last time?" Jonos kept at it. "Rennai is still hesitant about even putting me in a plane."

"Because this time, *we* won't be flying, and we can pay."

I'd already talked over the last bit with Cephus and Davriel earlier while Jonos had stepped out to call Ayla.

They were both already in, no matter the cost; Cephus had been able to make some more-than-decent money over the past three years as an officer in the Naval Guard, and Davriel was wise enough to keep most of his earnings in cash-reserves and private banks rather than UTF controlled ones, and they both had enough to spend.

"Alright, but how exactly do you expect me to convince a pilot to let us parachute onto a mountain, in the winter?" He offered his final protest.

"Just tell 'em we're into extreme mountain climbing and want to do some brotherly bonding." I said as I smiled smugly, flipping over the fourth and final boon card from my overturned hand before lighting up my last cig.

I had taken the previous day to figure out our cover-story so to not have any holes in our plan. We'd say we were parachuting onto the mountain to camp and do a bit of brotherly bonding.

Technically that was all true, but we would be doing it in an alien spacecraft that was directly linked to our father and us—that part nobody needed to know.

We would pack for extreme winter conditions and pack whatever we'd need into a couple large duffle bags and toss them out with us.

What they also didn't need to know—and what I didn't let Davriel or Cephus onto just yet—was that inside the individual duffle bag I would pack, would be old star charts my father had kept and all his backup notes on his concept of Intergalaxian travel.

I had deduced that the only way that ship could have gotten to Terra was through such a means.

Maybe he had had some subconscious knowledge of it—and his true ancestry—*and that was why he had dedicated his life to the purpose of learning the truth.* It just so happened, that that meant missing out on most of his sons' lives in order to learn it.

But we were going to find it out, and find him in the process.

We were going to use *ZANZABAR* to do it.

On the derelict Arco moon-base Lunos-Opteran, Arcos wave to wave transmission:

BRENDENEL –

GREAT NEWS – THE BEACON THAT WE FIRST DETECTED IN THE SOUTHERN PLANES OF LUNOS BELONGS TO ONE OF OUR ALCORI CONSTRUCTS / IT REMAINS IN TACT AT THE LUNOS FACILITY – DESPITE IT BEING ABANDONED / SOMEHOW THE BODY HAS ACTIVATED AND BEGUN TRANSMITTING ITS SIGNAL / THE ALCORI HAS A LIVE LINK TO HER SHIP / SHE'S BROADCASTING / THIS IS GREAT CAUSE FOR HOPE – THERE MAY YET BE OTHER SURVIVORS OUT THERE /

HALEB AND I HAVE COMPLETED THE RECOVERY AND THE VESSEL IS SECURE / WE WILL BRING HER BACK TO THE WATCHTOWER / PREPARE THE PROPER FACILITIES FOR HER / WE MUST PROTECT HER AT ALL COSTS AND KEEP HER SIGNAL ACTIVE /

MAY FATHER ARCAZ GIVE YOU STRENGTH AND HONOR – WISDOM AND RESOLVE/

ANDROS ANGELUS // TIASALPA SHIPMASTER/

Chapter 7: Flight

We awoke groggy and lethargic the next morning around 9:00 after a rather late night of reminiscing and amusement. We wanted to start our journey far earlier in the morning, but due to the stiff drinks we'd been having as well as our lack of preparations, we used the majority of the morning to sober up and then make the necessary provisions.

Our rejuvenation was aided by a spectacular breakfast that Mom prepared; consisting of a cheesy pepper and onion frittata, homemade waffles, bacon, sausage, and copious amounts of orange juice and coffee.

Afterward, feeling revitalized and able to start our journey, we split into twos to arrange everything we needed for the visit to *ZANZABAR*. We'd all returned to our respective homes — except myself as I was already home — to each pack individual bags and explain the impromptu brotherly outing to our loved ones.

Jonos and Davriel then went to the airfield to secure a plane, pilot, and the necessary flight gear for the jump, while Cephus and I rummaged through our own houses for anything and everything we could find for 'winter camping in the mountains.'

We were able to rummage through both his family's and my mom's storage for the basics: parkas, lanterns, mini space heaters, and blankets; but we ended up having to purchase a couple of water jugs, non-perishable rations, medical equipment and whatever else we needed from a local outdoors store.

We planned to meet at the airfield at 14:00 to gather up everything, take the hour long safety course, and make our last minute preparations before taking off at 16:00.

Due to the fact that neither Cephus nor I had much cargo space in our cars—as most of the space was taken up by the Qaterro's massive engine—we'd borrowed his step-dad's AUV Aspect. The Aspect was an all-purpose activity/utility vehicle which had plenty of room for all of the equipment we'd gathered, and borrowing it fit our camping cover story rather well.

After loading it up we were ready to head to the airfield and had 45 minutes to make the half-hour drive there.

On our way up to the airfield, which was located on the western side of the Shendale Peninsula, we had to stop and get a few last minute supplies for the trip. Cephus drove us about half way out past the principal city Sevura before stopping at a hick-town fuel-station.

As we pulled up to the fuel pumps, he killed the engine, handed me his Cred-key and said, "Fill 'er up, would ya? Premium Ethlofuel."

"Okay." I sighed.

He then walked into the gas station as I got out and began pumping the fuel. His step-dad's Aspect was a newer car and ran on cleaner Ethlohyrdramine—a water based compound that was the product of a recent advancement in clean energy produced by the UTF Physics Engineering and Scientific Application Program.

I found myself perplexed as the thoughts of

the fuel and the UTF PESA Project led me to think of my father as I stood silently and pumped the gas.

I contemplated his life and our discovery of ZANZABAR, and life on other worlds and — not for the first time — found myself trapped in a sea of consternation and wonder. I'd almost entirely tuned out the minutia of the world before my thoughts were distracted by someone addressing me.

"Well I'll be damned," The familiar voice came, drawing me from my brief reverie. "Savos Angelus! What the hell are you doin' here?"

"Huh?" I drew my head up and saw the familiar face of an old friend approaching from another vehicle in the station. "Tytus Hyaeger."

I grinned from ear to ear as I watched my longtime friend approach. He was an inch or two taller than me with short-cropped brown hair, kind brown eyes, a week-old beard and light skin.

He had the slightest of gaps in his front teeth but it gave him character and he never bothered to have it fixed. He wore tan work boots, work-stained jeans, a raggedy gray sweatshirt, and an old baseball cap. As he approached I immediately hugged him, patting him twice on the back as he patted mine; our traditional form of greeting since Secondary.

"Dude, I haven't seen you in ages, how long has it been?" I said.

"I dunno! Couple'a years. How long you been in town?" Tytus asked as we released our grip.

"A little less than a week," I began, "I was gonna' let you know after I'd settled back in. I'm here indefinitely; at least for the time being." I said as I thought in the back of my mind about the star-charts and notes I had in the car, my long-lost father, and *ZANZABAR*.

"Well hey, now I know. You and me ought to grab a brew with your brother and catch-up." He replied.

"Which one?" Cephus interjected as he approached from the station-store.

He was carrying a small bag of Caffeine-shooters, chewing tobacco, and a case of rummies. I learned these were the main staples of Naval Guardsmen, used to pass the time over an 8-hour watch on the ship—except the rummies of course which were strictly for off-duty hours.

"Hawhawhaw. No way!? You too?" Tytus laughed as he greeted Cephus in the same hugging manner.

"Yeah dude. Got back a few days ago. Also here for the long haul. I'm a free man now." Cephus said smilingly.

"Well obviously we all gotta' have a brew together. Though at this point we might have to make a party out of it and throw back a few more than just one." Tytus returned the grin.

"Absolutely." I said as the fuel pump clicked off indicating that the car's tank was full.

I immediately thought about Davriel and Jonos who were no-doubt waiting for us at the airfield already.

I checked my wrist Link and realized that we only had eighteen more minutes to get there for the hour long preflight class before our scheduled take-off.

"Oh shit," I said, "as much as we'd love to stay

and catch-up right now, we actually have somewhere to be."

"What, you suddenly got a plane to catch or something?" Tytus jokingly remarked.

"Actually yes," Cephus replied getting into the car.

"I feel like a jicko for having to leave like this," I said as I removed the fuel pump and began to get into the car, "But listen, we will definitely catch up, Davriel's also back and we all need to hang. We have some seriously crazy news to fill you in on, but not just yet. I'll be in touch in the next few days."

I closed the door and held my fist out of the open window, which he slowly pounded.

"Ok man, you guys don't go gettin' into any trouble before we get a chance to hang, you hear?" Tytus jested.

"No promises." Cephus grinned shiftily.

"Look at that face," I said pointing to Cephus, "Of course we won't. We're responsible *adults*."

As Cephus started the car Tytus took a step back and smiled as we began to pull away. I waved out the window and he returned the gesture. I then looked to my wrist Link and saw that it was now ten minutes to 14:00 and we were at least 15 minutes away from the airfield.

"Gonna' have to gun it man." I said to Cephus.

"Nah man, we'll be fine." He simply smiled and maintained the speed limit, "Besides, this is the Pop's car. Not chancing anything dumb in it. Plus, Jonos is always late, right? It'll work."

We arrived at the airfield at 14:07 to an impartial Davriel and an impatient Jonos. Evidently they'd been there for a solid half hour and passed the time by going over a *pre*-preflight check with the pilot, in addition to any additional groveling Jonos had to do to his boss Rennai.

It appeared that my twin's notorious tardiness and carefree nature had disappeared altogether, and I briefly thought about how much he'd changed since I'd been gone before he began berating us about unloading the car and getting everything ready to be chuted-up and loaded into the plane.

After unloading the Aspect and getting everything re-loaded into the plane it was 15:18 and we were ready for the safety course and last minute preparations.

We were then questioned about the nature of our trip and our experience in sky-diving and parachuting.

Upon receiving adequate answers from Davriel, Cephus, and Jonos—all of whom had actually jumped out of an airplane—the pilot and jump instructor explained the take-off, cruising, and jump procedures, showing us the full extent of the emergency devices within the parachutes' harnesses we were employing.

Those included the main chutes and oxygen tanks, as well as the extra emergency chutes, the emergency oxygen tanks, the emergency transponder beacons, and the release button for the entire harness; though we were explicitly instructed to wait until we were on the ground to use that.

Following the preflight jump course and our final equipment check we boarded the plane, taking our seats in the slightly cramped compartment among the 6 duffle bags we were taking.

Before we taxied onto the runway the pilot began his final instrument check and I looked at my Link and checked the time: 16:18. Not bad. I looked at my brothers and we all exchanged an anxious look.

We weren't exactly nervous in the fearful sense, but were uncertain and excited about what the future – and *ZANZABAR* – held in store for us. Jonos and I had already seen it of course, but only for a few moments, and Davriel and Cephus were noticeably excited to see it for their first time and teemed in anticipation.

I looked at my brothers and smiled wide-eyed to Cephus, then looked toward Davriel and nodded, and finally toward my twin Jonos. He looked back at me and even though he didn't physically do it, I could tell that he was smiling inside and certainly matched the rest of our enthusiasm.

He gave me the slightest of discernible nods then turned his attention to the pilot who'd just broken in over the radio com.

"You guys all set?" The pilot's voice shouted over the building roar of the engines.

Jonos gave the pilot a simple thumbs-up and we were ready for takeoff.

"Don't break my plane Angelus. *Any* of you." Rennai's voice came over the com.

No promises. I mouthed the words to my brothers.

"Roger that." Jonos replied.

"Aircraft Victor-Tango-three-one-niner you are cleared for takeoff." Rennai gave the clearance from the tower, "Safe flying."

***

It was 16:37 and the wind raced against my body as I plummeted toward the mountain having just jumped out of the plane at an altitude of 8000 meters. Typically, skydivers jumped from 2000 to 4000 meters above ground level, but since we were jumping onto a ground level of roughly 4500 meters we had to make up the difference to allow us ample time for the actual dive.

In my outstretched arms I guided my bag bundled together with one of our two communal bags and Jonos' bag opposite; he too was holding onto his as we plummeted toward the mountain. Through our helmet visors we could see Davriel and Cephus slightly below us holding their bags in a similar fashion.

We continued our free-fall, plummeting straight down toward the Great Mountain Cascade, but I felt myself drawn to the setting sun off in the western distance. Despite it being winter it was a clear day and the sun was just beginning to dip below the horizon.

It offered a warm radiance which calmed me despite the rushing squalls around me and the heightened sounds of my breathing heard throughout my helmet.

My attention was drawn away from the sunset as Jonos signaled me and then pointed to Davriel and Cephus' first chutes. The bags were each equipped with their own separate parachutes that were all connected so that as two jumpers pulled the ripcords for their own bag, the bags separated and deployed the last chute on the third bag.

Shortly after seeing the first three parachutes deploy we saw Davriel and Cephus' chutes deploy. I wondered how Davriel felt at that very moment; if memories from his previous earthbound plummet arose.

He's probably just grateful for having a parachute this time around.

But my attention was drawn from my thoughts as Jonos signaled me a second time for our own preliminary parachute deployment. He nodded and even through his helmet visor and respirator I could tell that he had a massive grin on his face.

Despite his love of flying airplanes and our own previous fall in the FA-2, he seemed to be thoroughly enjoying this controlled fall and seemed to be as accustomed to it as birds are with flying.

For a split second before releasing our parachutes the setting sun seemed to reflect off of something and caught in the corner of my eye but I was immediately distracted as Jonos held up a fist and opened it, indicating he was ready to deploy the parachutes.

Jonos and I nodded at one another and pulled the ripcords, pushing off our bags as the parachutes deployed. The parachutes on the bags were significantly smaller than ours, allowing for a controlled gap between their landing and ours. Seconds later each of us pulled our own ripcords and with a jostling lurch our parachutes deployed, slowing our plunge down to the mountain.

After a somewhat soft and snowy landing, gathering up our parachutes, removing all of our jumping gear, and collecting our bags; Jonos and I ventured to meet up with Davriel and Cephus who we could see about 60 meters off to our left.

"That was awesome." Jonos said grinning widely as we walked over to them.

"Definitely." I exhaled, staring at the ground we'd just landed on and taking in the surrounding area. "Is it just me or does it seem different than last time?"

"What are you talking about?" He asked.

"I dunno, I can't place it, but something's different." I wondered aloud.

"So ZANZABAR... where is it?" Davriel asked over the beginning nightly gusts from the east.

"Yeah let's see this awesome alien spaceship we've heard so much about." Cephus added.

I removed the GPS from my harness and immediately saw the Nav-marker I'd previously set for the location.

I looked up from the screen and in doing so noticed the sun had nearly diminished in the distance and again I'd caught the gleam of light I'd seen before. The shining glint was coming from the same direction where the Nav-marker pointed.

As I looked closely I questioned what I saw, though I continued to wonder about the change in the mountain I thought I'd noticed when landing.

I continued to gaze, slightly stupefied, until it dawned on me like a bus hitting a parked car at full speed and I realized what I was looking at. It was the tips of the slanting V-tails of ZANZABAR.

The difference I'd noticed on the mountain was that there was less snow than before; it had been slowly melting away around the ship. The bulbous shape of ZANZABAR's body was slightly discernible beneath a thinning layer of snow.

We had much less time than we'd all hoped for.

"We have to move. Fast." I said as I picked up my bag and darted off in the direction of ZANZABAR as fast as I could, trudging through the snow with all of my equipment.

The snow was melting, exposing the ship's outer surfaces and soon the entire thing would be visible to anyone flying over the mountain or looking down on it from satellites above, and the last thing we needed was for some satellite analyst to pick it up and eventually report the finding to some UTF official who would come along and claim yet another of my father's incredible finds, and thus our own legacy.

The four of us trudged through the snow as quickly as possible as we made for the initial tunnel Jonos had dug out when he and I crashed on the mountain only days earlier.

I was grateful for having saved the coordinates in my GPS as any sign of our presence had already been eliminated.

We approached the marker on the GPS and I saw a depression in the snow marking the hole Jonos and I had covered up. It had also seen signs of melting.

"Quickly now, we gotta' move." Jonos said.

We dropped our bags and began shoveling snow aside to make an entrance. It wasn't long before the four of us cleared out a hole big enough to hunch through. We then picked up our bags and disappeared into the mountain one at a time starting with Jonos, then Cephus and Davriel.

I kept up the rear taking a final glance around the mountain and up to the sky, suspicious of what secret eyes might be watching.

I crawled into the familiar cavern to see my brothers standing in very slushy snow. "Looks like the tunnel's a bit flooded." Cephus said.

"What the hell?" I questioned no one in particular, "Why is all the snow melting?"

"Don't know, but we don't have much time." Jonos urged.

Without further delay the four of us crawled through the inner tunnel and into the chamber where *ZANZABAR* lay dormant and waiting. This time I crawled through first, followed by Cephus, Davriel, and finally Jonos. Having previously seen the ship I didn't expect to be taken by surprise when I saw it again, but immediately found myself awe-struck when I laid eyes on it for the second time.

"By the maker..." I started.

"Whoa..." Cephus said as Davriel let out a low whistle.

Cephus and Davriel were mesmerized by the initial sight of *ZANZABAR*, but what they didn't know was that its metallic gray hull was far more luminescent than before, the ship no longer appeared battered and damaged from the crash, the glyphs on its flank reading '*ZANZABAR*' were far bolder than before and everywhere we looked showed signs of restoration. I looked at Jonos and he looked back at me expressing the same bewilderment I now felt.

ZANZABAR was no longer dormant. We initially thought we had plenty of time, then we thought we were pressed for time, we now realized we had no time at all.

ZANZABAR was somehow *awake*.

As we stepped toward the hatch I immediately noticed that it was closed, however just as we approached it, the doorway opened. Crossing the threshold, we immediately felt the warmth of the ship.

My breath wasn't visible as it had been the first time aboard and I realized that the frost that had previously coated the surfaces of the ship was gone. The four of us dropped our bags and began shedding some of the layers we'd worn for the cold weather.

"Guys," I quietly said to Cephus and Davriel, "This was all frozen over last time we were here."

Before I had the chance of hearing a response there was an audible chime aboard the ship. We looked about us in confusion and were further surprised when a female voice addressed us.

"Wenito zurack Shipmaster Angelus..."

"What the hell?" Davriel muttered as we all stood stupefied.

"Who said that?" Cephus added.

"Esto tro lange Arc—" The voice cut off mid-sentence and suddenly a blue light flashed down before us presenting the image of a naked and pale tattooed woman with long black hair draping down over her body.

"Wait a minute, you're not him." She suddenly said in perfect Standard Terran.

Jonos was the first to respond, "Not who? Arcus?"

The woman before us quietly beheld each of us individually.

We could see the flickering image of her body as it walked around each of us, disappearing partially as she walked behind us. All the while she whispered, though entirely to herself and in her alien language.

After looking us over she returned to her initial position and regarding us all, spoke the exact same Terran Standard we spoke, "My bio-scans show your bodies partially match that of Arcus Angelus, but none of you are him. Who are you?"

For some reason, something felt trustworthy about this woman and I had no reservation about responding, "I am Savos. This is Jonos, my twin. The one with the dark hair is Davriel, and the big one is Cephus. We're brothers. We're the sons of Arcus Angelus."

"Sons?" The image of the woman standing before us flickered as she responded, though it seemed she spoke mainly to herself, "How can that be? Arcus is merely a child. He could not possibly have sons, unless... has it been longer than I thought? Tell me, where is he? Where is Arcus? Where is the last son of Arco?"

"Hold on a second, we told you who we are," Jonos chimed in, "Now, how 'bout you tell us who you are."

"Who *I* am?" The image of the woman looked bewildered for a moment after hearing the question and flickered yet again. "I suppose there isn't any harm in telling you as your bio-scans are partial matches to that of Arcus Angelus and therefore I am at your service; you are Arcosan after all.

The four of us exchanged wide-eyed glances after hearing her words, 'you are Arcosan.' It was true, we were part Arcos.

"Very well. I am Zanza-carina-lalilu-losana-arcana-barabar." She said with a smile.

We waited in stunned silence before Davriel finally broke in saying, "Well that's a mouthful."

"You may call me something shorter if you so choose." She added, clearly realizing our bewilderment regarding her name.

"We so choose." Cephus confirmed in comedic fashion. "How 'bout Zan?"

"So *Zan*, who *are* you?" I persisted. "And how do you speak our language?"

"I am ZANZABAR, and ZANZABAR is me. I am the breath ZANZABAR breathes. I am its Ara and it is the vessel through which I live. I am an Arcosan Alcori-Construct designed to give ZANZABAR life."

We stood in silence for yet another moment before she continued, "And many of your Terran languages are quite similar in structure to my own, I have learned your primary 'Terran Standard' by accessing telecommunications around your world."

She paused for a moment to let that sink in, "I have told you who I am; now you must tell me, where is Arcus Angelus?"

I knew full well that she intended to ask about our father's whereabouts again, but couldn't help but frown in disappointment after hearing her inquiry.

The thought of my father always brought ab-

-out such melancholic thoughts. My brothers and I shared several uneasy looks with each other before Zan persisted, "Will none of you sons-of-Angelus tell me the fate of the last Arcon?"

"He's..." I started.

"He's gone." Cephus bluntly stated. "He built a ship and left."

"But Arcus was merely a child..." Zan stammered out.

"Well he grew up, and he moved on." I said, "Presumably to find these Arcos we've been hearing so much about.

"Oh... that is most unfortunate." She said in a dejected manner leading to a moment of silent sadness. Finally, she broke her silence, "Tell me; what do you know of the Arcos?"

Jonos answered saying, "Just what we've been able to piece together over the past few days since we discov—" Jonos was suddenly cut off.

The cacophony of warning sirens cut in before he could finish.

"What the hell?" Davriel exclaimed.

The flickering image of Zan disappeared before reappearing a moment later in a sudden daze. "Proximity alert. Multiple contacts." She said in agitation. "Are there others with you?"

"What?" Cephus blurted out.

"Oh shit." Jonos cursed, "Did someone find us?"

My mind reeled in paranoid thought for a brief moment as I contemplated what would happen if it was the Feds who were coming.

If they were able to get their hands on the ship, on Zan, on any hope I had of finding my father, everything would be over. I couldn't come so close to being able to find him only to have them rip him away from me again.

"We can't let them get their hands on Zan or the ship," I yelled, "Zan, can this thing fly?"

Zan's image flickered again in thought before she answered, "Yes, but none of my control systems are at full operational capacity, I won't be able to boot up and manage all of *ZANZABAR*'s systems and fly at the same time."

I immediately turned to Jonos as he turned to me. We nodded in unison before he shouted, "Worry about the power, I'll handle the flying!"

The four of us frantically rushed toward the bridge, as Zan's image dissipated before us. We were determined to elude our newfound company.

As we ran down the corridor I couldn't help but notice the body of the dead man from our previous visit was no longer there, but I had little time to question the thought or even think twice about it before we arrived on the bridge.

"Ok Zan, we're here, now what?" I shouted upwards unsure of where she was exactly.

"Jonos," Zan started after she appeared on a small dais on the main bridge console, this time in a much deeper blue image. "The pilot's console and controls are at the foremost point on the bridge. I'm powering up the core and spooling up the engines as we speak; you should have flight control in a moment."

As Jonos sat down in the pilot's chair I again noticed the frost that had previously covered the ship had disappeared entirely; an outcome of Zan's awakened presence no doubt.

The proximity warning rang out again and Zan's voice was commanding as it resounded throughout the ship, "Proximity contact. Range 2.5 taramels."

"What's a taramel?" Cephus asked.

As he spoke we felt a sudden rush throughout the ship accompanied by a thunderous rumble.

"Impulse power active Jonos. You have vertical repulsors, lateral winglet thrusters, and 20% main engine power at your command. For your information Cephus, a taramel is roughly equivalent to two of your Terran kilometers."

As Zan spoke I looked through the main viewport to see a cascade of flowing slush and snow and wondered how she would know so much about our society but did not have time to fully address the thought as I began to see through the windshield.

Through the cascading snow-water I could just about make out two gray shapes in the distance.

"They're Feds alright." Davriel said flatly, confirming my worst fears. "Looks like two Mark 22 Litehawks. They're variants of the Skyhawk, smaller, outfitted for recon."

Shit.

I didn't question Davriel given his UTF background and his familiarity with the Skyhawk, nor did I have time to take a closer look before Jonos activated the vertical repulsors and thrust ZANZABAR out of its frozen entombment like the long-extinct gargantuan whales breaching ocean water. We all promptly grabbed whatever support we could.

The ship continued to rise steadily. Snow fell off and broke away in massive chunks and we could hear, and feel, the ship groaning as it woke from its slumber and slowly emerged from its frozen encasement.

We hovered up into the sky slowly gaining altitude as Jonos familiarized himself with ZANZABAR's controls.

He truly was a natural at flying and I believed that our new found Arcosan ancestry helped him somehow or another, as though piloting the ship was embedded in his genes.

"Do take care." Zan said much like a mother would as we heard more and more groans throughout the ship. "It's been a while."

"Trust him Zan, he's a natural." Cephus chimed in.

I knew Jonos heard the comment and didn't have to see his face to know that it was alight with a toothy grin from ear to ear as he sat at ZANZABAR's controls.

I had previously thought—and planned on the fact—that he would be flying ZANZABAR off the mountain, but was certainly still surprised at the circumstances we now faced.

"We now have 27% main engine power." Zan stated as we leveled out and sat hovering in the air facing the two approaching Litehawks. She continued, "The approaching contacts are broadcast-

-ing a signal. They're hailing us. Patching them through now."

"Unidentified vessel: this is Lt. Commander Sha Yun Lii with the UTF Air Corps, Fort Kane Battalion. You are ordered by UTF mandate to stand down and follow us to the closest UTF airfield for inspection and classification. Comply or we will be forced to take action. Do you copy?"

"Inspection and classification, huh?" Davriel said, "More like, detainment and confiscation."

"Shall I patch us through for a response?" Zan asked.

"No." I said, *we are not giving this up.* "Jonos, show 'em our response."

"Don't mind if I do." He said with a huge grin.

"You might want to hold on." Zan added, clearly anticipating Jonos' move.

Davriel, Cephus, and I grabbed onto whatever we could just as Jonos gunned the throttle and blasted us straight toward the approaching Litehawks. We accelerated toward them at an incredible velocity—far faster than Jonos and I had gone in the FA-2—and passed straight between them as we began our escape.

The sheer power that ZANZABAR exuded was unfathomable and I found my body straining to deal with it and could see Cephus and Davriel responding similarly.

This was clearly something none of us ever could have imagined in our wildest dreams.

The Litehawks immediately slewed and changed their course to pursue but were only matching our direction when Jonos pulled the con-

-trol yolk back and pitched us up toward the sky, putting all of our bodies in an even more strenuous position.

We couldn't see our pursuers after the maneuver, but they followed at an even pace, though I imagined they were having a rather tough time keeping up with ZANZABAR.

"Jonos, be careful," Zan advised in a concerned voice, "We can't break atmosphere too soon. I need time to run the proper diagnostics and atmospheric spin-up cycles."

"I'm just seeing what she has to offer!" Jonos yelled over the roar of the ship.

"Well remember, *she* is *me*, and *I* don't have that much to offer yet." Zan said sternly, "By all means get us out of here, but not that way. I understand the need to go where your pursuers cannot follow and I might have a solution. I need one of you at the console on the left to activate the E-scrambler, and another one of you to head down to the engine room to help me boost main-engine power."

"Unidentified aircraft," the UTF pilot continued, "you are ordered to surrender your vessel and land at the nearest UTF airfield. If you do not comply we *will* take action."

I disregarded the Fed's orders and instead wondered what the 'E-scrambler' was, but didn't waste time to figure it out.

Despite the slight speed advantage we had over our pursuers, they weren't gone just yet, and I knew that the UTF had assets everywhere and could track us down even to the smallest corner of the world.

"I'll take care of this 'E-scrambler.'" I said, "Davriel, you go down to the engine room and see what you can do. Cephus, see if you can figure out some navigation and find us somewhere secluded to land, yeah? Jonos, you just keep doing your thing."

Despite not being familiar by any means with this type of situation I found myself oddly at ease, comforted as I was by my brothers' collective presence, and reassured by Zan's presence as well.

Hearing my plan of action, Zan immediately chimed in, "Savos, on the console on the left, the three red switches on the top left will power up the display, the blue one on the far right will activate countermeasure systems; after that you can activate the primer button for the E-scrambler. It's the large blue one. That will need to charge for a moment before you can fire it. Cephus, the console on the right is for 'navigation' as you call it. Davriel, follow the main corridor all the way to its end and you will find the engine room, I will join you as soon as you get there."

Right after Davriel left the bridge Cephus sat at the navigation console and began searching for viable destinations, "You know I'm much more familiar with navigating waters, right?" He said.

"Then try and find a hidden alcove or crevasse or something, I don't know. Just work some magic." I said as I waited for the primer to power up. "Jonos, how's it going?"

"How do you think it's going? This is incredible!" He replied. "I'm taking us east toward the Cadian Mountains; that should give us some extra cover and make it a bit tougher for our company."

"Who, by the way," Cephus interjected, "are still keeping pace. We need to lose them."

Zan cut in, "Savos, as soon as the primer for the E-scrambler is charged, fire it. That will emit a targeted electromagnetic pulse that will scramble and disable our assailants' electronic systems. Davriel is getting to the engine room now, I will be back momentarily."

"Wait!" I started though she had already gone. "Won't an EMP blast cause them to crash?" I questioned to my brothers. "I don't want to kill any of these guys, just take the wind out of their sails, you know?"

Jonos turned his head back and Cephus looked away from the nav screen for a moment and we exchanged a look of confusion and uncertainty.

"Uhh." Jonos started.

"Every EMP that I've seen completely cripples the target." Cephus answered. "Though maybe this super advanced alien ship has a different one?"

I hesitated for a few moments before Zan reappeared, "Jonos, you now have 45% main engine power, and Savos, I understand your concern; wait a moment to fire the scrambler and I will reprogram its function to target specific systems; communication for now. However, they will have more time to call for reinforcements if we delay any longer."

I initially breathed a heavy sigh of relief as I had no desire to make enemies with the Feds by killing any of them, I simply wanted to outrun them;

but then considered the second bit of what Zan had said.

Unfortunately, my sympathies got the better of me. Little did I know how much trouble was soon to follow after that moment of hesitation.

Our dilemma was suddenly interrupted by a warning claxon and a brief flash across our front, "What the hell was that?" Cephus shouted.

Zan responded with renewed urgency, "That was weapons fire, though it only seemed to be a warning as it was a clear miss. Apparently our pursuers aren't happy that we ignored their warning."

"Those jickos!" Cephus exclaimed.

"Well I guess we'll just have to give them a bit more to chase after then." Jonos boasted as he grabbed the throttle and pulled back. Let's see what 45% power can offer."

Again we lurched back as *ZANZABAR* blasted off at faster speeds than we'd previously gone, all the while Jonos grinned enthusiastically, as the rest of us held on for dear life.

We immediately began to pull away from the pursuing UTF Litehawks and I returned to my thoughts of the fully charged E-scrambler that was waiting to be fired, "Zan, how's that reprograming coming?" I desperately asked.

"Nearly finished, I have to lock onto the specific signal emission for their communication and tracking. Furuck! They're transmitting!"

"What?" I gasped.

"They're sending a signal!" Zan yelled back.

Just then Davriel returned to the bridge slightly winded, "What'd I miss?" He was short for breath and had clearly sprinted back after helping Zan boost the engine power.

I briefly wondered how much of it was due to his mechanical knowledge or Zan's instruction but the thought lasted for less than a second as I returned to our plight at hand.

"We're pullin' away from the L-Hawks." Cephus said. "But we're no doubt being tracked by Fed satellites now. They definitely made a transmission."

Davriel wasted no time before answering, "Fire that E-scrambler thing now! The emergency systems on those should recover enough power to at least allow them to slow and control their fall. If they catch us we're finished!"

I waited another split second before Zan urgently chimed in, "It's ready."

Upon hearing her acknowledgement, I immediately flipped the safety catch on the E-scrambler and pressed the switch. We then heard a low bass-like sound from the top side of *ZANZABAR* as the weapon fired.

"Firing successful," Zan continued, "I don't detect any communication activity from the pursuing ships. Zero detectable signals in orbit. Jonos, kindly bring us up to 60 taramels, sorry, level out at 12000 *meters*. Once there I will initiate a high density particle shroud emission that will effectively conceal the ship from radar; unfortunately, the engines run too hot and will neutralize the effect, so

I'll need you to power down to impulse power once you hit 12000 meters for the remainder of our escape."

"Sure thing." Jonos replied, tilting the controls back and launching us ever higher into the clouds.

"Contacts are withdrawing." Zan said after a short while, "Cephus, have you located an adequate location for us to land and recuperate?"

"Yeah. There's a broken plateau twenty klicks north of our current heading. There's a bunch of cracks and crevices in it, so we should find somewhere to set her—*you*—down out of sight."

Cephus was clearly hesitant about how to address Zan and *ZANZABAR*, "The surrounding area is made up of fissures, so should provide solid seclusion from aerial observers."

"Perfect." Zan said, "Jonos, I've marked the position Cephus selected on your nav display. Do take care in getting us there."

"No promises." Jonos said smilingly.

Shortly after our aerial escape from the Litehawks we returned to the surface and Jonos exercised his expertise and maneuverability as he slipped *ZANZABAR* into a rather tight fissure to conceal us from any Feds who were no doubt now scouring the entire Amassian Northwest for a never-before-seen ship that outran and crippled two of its reconnaissance aircrafts.

At least they don't know who we are, was all I kept thinking, along with what our next step was going to be.

***

"If we're going to do this, we have to do it right." Jonos said after we convened in ZANZABAR's empty galley.

Since landing we had taken several hours to recuperate and explore the ship. We checked out the crew quarters that Jonos and I hadn't seen on the previous visit, each claiming our own and dropping off our bags before exploring more.

Zan toured us around the ship, showing the rest of us the engine room, the hangar — which I had only glimpsed on the previous visit — and the launch deck; which held the escape shuttle and about a half-dozen, one-man defender ships Zan explained were designed to engage enemy fighters in ship to ship battles.

After finishing our tour, we felt quite famished and found ourselves in the galley, enjoying crisp cold rummies, and what various snacks we'd packed.

We sat around the main table — which was clearly meant for more than just the four of us — eating and drinking and contemplated our next step.

"There's certainly a lot here." Davriel said after a sip of his rummy.

"Yeah, ships rarely work without at least some form of a workable crew." Cephus added.

"Not to mention handling everything aboard ZANZABAR amidst trying to find Dad." Jonos added.

I thought about ZANZABAR and my father for a moment; how large the ship was, how infinitely large space was, and where he would possibly be.

I thought about how pressing it was to manage the escape from two Fed Litehawks with just the four of us.

I thought about what mysterious beings and forces would be out in the galaxy waiting for us, waiting to challenge us.

I then thought about how we were only four against all the odds in the galaxy.

"Well then, I guess we'll need a crew."

**United Terran Federation Classified Communique
to all Commanding Officers
From the Office of UTF Chief Defense Minister
Luca de Gulliss,**
19 December, 3.2220 @ 20:16:25 TST

Commanders,

At 17:35 Pacinus Time UTF satellites detected an unidentified power source on Mt. Cascade in Northwestern Amassia. The battalion at Fort Kane dispatched two Litehawks to investigate. The Litehawks discovered an unidentified, never-before-seen aerial object. Upon arrival the commanding officer of the recon mission, Lieutenant Commander Sha Yun Lii, attempted contact with the unidentified vessel. The vessel did not return Lt. Cmdr. Lii's hail and instead turned tail.

Lt. Cmdr. Lii followed UTF protocol firing a warning shot to obtain compliance, but the ship continued its escape. In continuing their pursuit our Litehawks were able to profile the ship, capturing several images.

It is a design never before seen by Terran eyes and clearly of an advanced origin. Attached are the images they captured. The unidentified ship ultimately deployed a targeted Electro Magnetic Pulse and crippled the Litehawks pursuit efforts. The ship continued its escape heading toward the Cadian mountain range where our satellites lost its signal.

This unidentified ship is an absolute priority target for capture, inspection, and classification. The ship's crew is considered fugitive from the law and should be arrested on sight for resisting UTF mandate. If neither can be successfully captured, termination is only permitted as a last-possible option.

If any contact is made with this unidentified ship you are to immediately inform the chain of command and the appropriate reinforcements will be dispatched.

The United Terran Federation thanks you for your compliance.

Chief Defense Minister Luca de Gulliss,
UTF Chairman

Chapter 8: Recruiting

Tytus Hyaeger was our first potential recruit. Jonos and I had actually known him for longer than we'd known Davriel and Cephus and he was as close to being a brother as one can get without actually being related.

In addition to our strong and long-lasting friendship, and the fateful encounter with him on the way to the airfield which served to put him at the front of our minds, Tytus offered many skills that would prove helpful on our intended search.

First and foremost, he was a skilled repairman and plumber—he'd been involved in his family's business since we were in Secondary—and would be a certain asset to our crew with his knowledge and maintenance experience.

On top of that Tytus was an avid hunter, an excellent shooter, and was generally experienced when it came to the outdoors and survival. Not knowing what we were to encounter out in the wild unknown of the galaxy we figured we could inevitably use his knowledge and skill.

Jonos, Cephus, Davriel, and I were unanimous in our decision about Tytus. We certainly all wanted him on board but there was one apparent reservation in our minds: he was married.

We doubted and debated over how and what to tell his wife until Jonos provided his thoughts on the matter as he said, "Just tell her the truth and invite her to come along. That's what I told Ayla."

Cephus, Davriel, and I sat dumbfounded at

the table.

"You told Ayla?" I exclaimed in surprise.

"Well yeah, she's the woman I love. And I'm about to venture out on a perilous quest into the vastly unknown galaxy in search for my long lost father, and no offense to you guys—I love you and all—but you're not the only faces I want to see for the entirety of this trek."

"Fair enough." Cephus said plainly.

"So what exactly is she gonna' do?" I asked. "And what about Shelyse? What would she do?"

"Well Ayla would be more than happy to help in any way. For starters she can take care of the expenses aspect of all this. After all it's certainly not going to be cheap. She can handle our finances—we are planning on reimbursing our crew right?—she is a wiz in math after all. And she's got all kinds of other skills to contribute that four guys together don't have. She'd be more than happy to be the ship 'mom.' All this wedding planning has her all kinds of eager for a family and a house. The family will be the crew, and the house will be *ZANZABAR*."

"I'd like to think that I'm 'maternal' enough for my own ship." Zan interrupted. She'd kept quiet for the discussion so far but clearly had something to say about Jonos' ideas.

"Of course you are Zan," Jonos was covering his tracks now, "She'd just be the physical mom, the one to cook and handout our allowances, you know?"

"I see." Zan said flickering in consternation but remaining quiet.

"Ok." Davriel cut in, "But what about Shelyse?"

"She's a registered nurse. Or at least that's what I last heard." Jonos answered. "Her experience would be invaluable with medical issues."

"Ok, so we'll put her under medical. Awesome." I said, "Moving on?"

"Hold on." Cephus interrupted, "Just how *are* we gonna' pay whatever crew we're *recruiting* anyway? There will definitely have to be some sort of reimbursement. People just won't up and quit their lives to do this."

I knew that was coming.

"About that..." I hesitated while everyone looked to me, "I've been thinking... Since we've discovered *ZANZABAR* I've been looking at Dad's old star charts and Galaxial notes. With our collective knowledge and Zan's help we can figure out where he went wrong. We can figure out Galaxial travel and..." I hesitated again, "and give it to the people."

"You mean sell it to the government." Jonos said rather than asked as he looked at me sternly.

"Cephus and Davriel forked over a lot of money for the trip up here, and trying to fund the rest of this would just be way too much to ask of them. I wouldn't ask you and Ayla to foot this either what with your wedding and all. Plus, I doubt we'd even be able to pay a crew without real funds, so unless anyone has any better ideas..."

I waited for a response but none came.

"I have the contact info for Dad's old research partner, Dr. Dorfmund. The doctor is in the private sector now and has cut ties with the UTF after what happened with Dad. I think that's our best prospect for a buyer. What do you guys think?"

Silence.

Jonos hesitated before replying, "Well I guess if we need the money to get—and keep—us flying, and there's no other option..."

"That's fine by me." Cephus added with a shrug of his shoulders.

"Are you sure the Dr. D. has completely severed connections with the UTF?" Davriel prodded; his disdain for the UTF was ever at the forefront of his thought, leaving him permanently suspicious.

"As far as I know."

I wasn't *completely* sure, but remembered Dr. Dorfmund's reaction at our father's memorial service all those years ago. The doctor had a feeling of melancholy for the loss of a longtime partner and supreme dissatisfaction for the way the UTF handled the entire debacle. More importantly though, was the doctor's anger that I saw neatly kept in check. It was clear that all ties with the UTF had been severed and the doctor would do anything to avoid further involvement with them. It was our best option.

"Ok, well let's continue with the list before we go worrying too much about payment. We gotta' have a crew to pay in the first place." Jonos pressed.

Jimian Aryen was next on our list. We weren't quite sure what exactly he could—or would—do aboard ZANZABAR but we were all sure we'd want him aboard.

Jonos was the first one to meet and introduce

us to Jimian during Secondary and since then we'd had plenty of incredulous adventures and commonalities, and this adventure certainly required his special something and flair for all things science fiction—though fiction was slowly becoming reality.

Jonos knew Jimian wasn't thrilled with his post collegiate life and figured he'd be accepting of the opportunity to work with friends in the vast unknown adventure that was space.

"So who else do we want?" I had asked.

"Jimian Aryen." Jonos said.

"Yeah." Cephus said.

"Of course!" Davriel exclaimed.

"Good. Well that's settled easily enough."

After Jimian we began to think more pragmatically about potential crew members. Obviously we wanted people we could trust, but we also needed capable people who could serve a purpose aboard ZANZABAR. This led us to thinking about what tasks we would need to fill in order to keep ZANZABAR flying successfully.

"Hey Zan?" I started.

"Yes Savos?"

"How many crew members would we need to operate the ship at full capacity?"

"The full complement that ZANZABAR supports is twenty-four. Making full use of my advanced operating capacity it can be done with as few as six. But I must also point out one thing: my ability to govern the ship is drastically limited when the ship is in-warp—Galaxial space as you call it. While in-warp my operating capacity will have to be directed entirely to maintaining ZANZABAR's warp field regulators; the shield that protects *ZANZABAR* from anything from the warporal realm — or Galaxial — meaning, anything not of this realm."

She paused for a moment to let the information sink in before continuing what was the first of many in-depth explanations Zan would provide for us.

"Given this unfortunate drawback and your uh... inexperience, I'd recommend not constraining yourselves to so small a crew." She curtly replied before adding, "Though it goes without saying that a secret such as this is best kept to those you trust intimately.

"Thanks." I said flatly, "So who else are we thinking guys?"

"Might I make a recommendation?" Zan interrupted.

"Of course."

"Given the fact that your bodies — despite their improved Arcosan genes — are like all flesh and bone bodies and are susceptible to injury, you might consider recruiting someone proficient in Terran medical science and practice in addition to this Shelyse person. Perhaps a friend with surgical skills?"

"Are we anticipating losing limbs?" I asked.

"No, but it is far better to be prepared for such an event." She responded.

"Good point." Jonos added.

We sat silently in thought once again before Davriel made a suggestion, "What about Ander Ollen?"

"Yeah." Cephus chimed in, "Isn't he in an IMS

program?"

"He was," Jonos continued, "He finished the Medical Study part but was wait-listed for the 'Integration' part and hasn't yet been placed."

"Well it sounds like we'd have a placement for him." I said, "provided he's even interested…"

"So, we're in agreement?" Davriel asked.

We all nodded our consent and moved on.

"We're also gonna' need someone who knows a thing or two about engineering and advanced propulsion systems." I said, knowing full well that maintaining ZANZABAR would be just as crucial as our own health.

"Yeah," Davriel echoed, "I can only do so much with the engine systems here given my limited understanding of it. I hate to admit it, but I don't know much about engineering in general; it's mostly just the ins and outs of fixing Skyhawks. You know, what button to push, what wires to fuse, that sort of thing. From what I've seen so far, Zan's gonna' need someone with a bit more expertise than me in the engine room."

"I concur. Not that Davriel is inept; we simply need someone with high-aptitude for physics and engineering." Zan popped in again, "My systems are highly advanced and certainly not for anyone but the most skilled engineer. I can absolutely teach anyone you recruit their intricacies, but whomever you chose must already have substantial knowledge, and be willing and able to learn new systems. And quickly I might add."

Zan's prerequisites were certainly demand-

-ing, but they absolutely had to be met.

There was no way we would bring anyone on board who wasn't the best, but more importantly, there was no way we would bring anyone on board who we didn't trust.

We sat for another minute thinking in silence. Davriel lit up a cig and began smoking it. Jonos and Cephus both looked blankly off into nothingness, and I cracked open another rummy.

"What about Pria?" Jonos finally asked. "Right, that's her name?"

"Pria who?" Cephus wondered.

"Pria Zaldeon? Is she around?" I followed up.

"She's around and quite unhappily employed last I heard." Jonos answered, "I saw her a while back while I was out with Mom and Ayla. She's been working at a design firm over in Emerald City, and isn't too thrilled about it."

"Can we trust her?" Davriel asked, voicing concern.

"You've both met her," I began, "she lived with Jimian for a few years at University and graduated top of her class with a degree in mechanical engineering. Jonos and I have known her for years. I'd say yes."

"But can we trust her? I mean this isn't your usual secret." Davriel pressed.

"Absolutely," Jonos said confidently, "plus she loves space and this kind of sci-fi stuff."

"Man, it's a good thing everyone conveniently hates their jobs." Cephus jested.

"Hey man, nobody's said yes yet. Anyway, I trust Pria as a far as Cephus could throw her. And he could throw her pretty far." I joked, adding, "She'd make a great addition to the crew. And honestly, I don't know or trust anyone who knows more about engineering than her."

"Ok." Davriel finally conceded, "I'll take your word for it."

"So we're all in favor of inviting Pria along?" I asked.

"Yeah." Cephus and Jonos said with finality as Davriel nodded.

"So far that's ten." Jonos said, "Anyone else?"

We all sat in prolonged silence yet again.

It seemed as though we'd hit a wall in thinking of possible crew members and jobs before Davriel dropped an empty rummy can on the floor.

The noise of the can hitting the floor echoed slightly prompting me to remember something Dad had taught us back when we were younger.

Jonos and I had been about 7 years old and Dad had time off from his duties at the UTF Research Command and had taken us to Oridiany — a territory in the Southeast of Amassia — for a family vacation. We had been snorkeling in the barrier reefs of the Akaradian Sea and Dad had found something he wanted to point out to us.

At the time, Jonos and I were preoccupied with the schools of fish and incredible wildlife of the reefs and he couldn't catch our attention.

What he had found was a relic from ages past: a well preserved model of a wooden ship in a bottle. I remembered that in order to get our attention he had chimed his Arcos medallion against the bottle to create an audible clicking sound which we both heard and immediately searched out.

After bringing the bottle to the surface and examining it further he began to tell us facts about ships and how he caught our attention.

He explained to us that it was called echolocation; a method that worked by emitting a small sound — his clicking — and measuring how long it took to return to the source to determine how far away something was, it also served to catch attention when sight wasn't possible.

He further told us that the ancient whales from the previous ages used this method to determine where their mates and pods were.

Finally, he had told us that submarines, ships, and spaceships used sonar — a mechanized form of echolocation — in addition to radar and ladar to locate other friends and foes in their vicinity.

Memories such as this, where we were able to learn from our father and enjoy time with him, were some of the only positive thoughts I still had about him.

"Sonar." I finally said to my brothers after I finished reminiscing. "We'll need to have it in space to detect our surroundings — well, not sonar exactly, since sound doesn't carry in space — but we'll need someone who can interpret radio waves. Someone with excellent aural and acoustic understanding to operate whatever coms systems Zan has."

"Good point." Jonos seconded, "Couldn't hurt to have someone skilled in that regard for when we transition between galaxies and Zan is preoccupied."

"Also couldn't hurt to just have another deck-hand on board." Cephus added.

"But who?" Davriel chimed in, "It has to be someone we know who can do the job."

"Kaitoh." Jonos said, "He's got the best ears of anyone I know, he could hear a song one time and be able to pick out every instrument and vocal in it, as well as be able to play it back for you. He could hear a pin drop in a hail storm. He got an advanced degree in audio engineering from Northwest Technical Institute. He's our guy."

I knew Kaitoh — or Kai — from Secondary, much like I did most of the people we'd decided to recruit.

We'd interacted fairly regularly but he was always more of Jonos' friend than mine, which was odd since we were twins and basically had the same friends; but I never doubted Jonos' judgments about people, so gave my assent to Kai as a prospect.

"Yeah, I remember him." Cephus then added, "I was on the wrestling team with him in Secondary. I vote yes."

"Davriel?" Jonos prodded him, waiting for his answer.

"Sure." Davriel simply nodded and we settled that we'd invite Kai and moved on.

"Anybody have anyone else in mind you'd want aboard?" Jonos asked.

"What about DT?" Cephus asked.

"Who?" Davriel asked

"Devian Teego." I answered. He was someone Cephus, Jonos, and I had known throughout Secondary. He was a good friend but I wasn't quite sure how he'd fit in aboard ZANZABAR, "Why him?"

"He's trustworthy, reliable, handy, and good in a pinch. He knows how to shoot, fight, and survive and he could be useful in a dire situation. I'm pretty sure he's been working a series of random dead end jobs since finishing University. He'd certainly be a solid addition to the crew." Cephus concluded.

"Anyone have any objections to that?" I asked, mulling the thought over in my head and not finding any real reason to naysay.

"None on my part." Jonos said.

"Me neith'." Davriel added shaking his head.

"So we'll offer him a spot." I concluded, "Anyone else?"

Zan cut in at this point, "Might I make another suggestion? You do recall the launch deck I showed to all of you, correct?"

"Yeah," we responded unanimously.

"You should consider looking into other crew members with flight experience to operate the support craft. I understand that all of you have some kind of flight experience but you will most certainly require additional crewmen with aptitude in flying. I can teach anyone the specifics of the crafts, but it will be considerably easier to teach those with pre-existing flight experience."

"Good point." I said.

I certainly didn't know of anyone who could fly, aside from my twin. I looked at Davriel and then at Cephus and thought about who they might know who could fit the bill and concluded that they probably knew plenty of people who could, but none outside the UTF who would be willing to forsake their connections to join our cause.

"I think I might know someone who can help us out with that." Jonos provided.

"Yeah? Who?" Cephus asked.

"Believe it or not, Lizia Ruels has been around the airfield taking flight lessons." Jonos continued, "She's been flying with my boss Rennai, but I've been up with her a couple of times and she's good. She's quite the natural really. And you guys know her, she's always gotta' be the best at everything so she's got the right sense of mind for aviation."

Everyone was silent for a moment, clearly thinking over the prospect of having Lizia aboard.

Cephus and I shared brief eye contact. We were both thinking the same thing; would that be such a great idea?

Cephus had dated Lizia in Secondary and I'd had complicated feelings for her that had since diminished — mostly.

After their break up things eventually smoothed out between them and being away from each other for University certainly helped, but there always seemed as though there was a lingering connection. I had gotten over my teenage crush but I'd also only seen her on a handful of occasions since Secondary so I had no idea what might resurface upon bringing her aboard.

"I know what you're thinking," Jonos interrupted, clearly sensing what we were contemplating. "Honestly she's the best I know, who's also crazy enough to do something like this. Plus, you know she'd do anything to help us out, especially with something like this, don't forget she knew Dad too."

Good point.

I'd completely failed to realize that aspect of this recruiting process. The entire time I was thinking about people to fulfill jobs on the ship, people we could trust with its importance.

The entire time I'd neglected to realize that every single person we had selected so far knew our father.

Every one of them had interacted with him. Every one of them cared for him in their own way.

Despite our father being extremely busy with official UTF business, he had made efforts to at least be part of our friends' lives.

Dad had coached Jonos and I, as well as Tytus, Kai, and Lizia in primary school soccer; he met Jimian, Ander, and Devian as our friends during our years of Secondary, and he knew Pria through Youth Career Training Corps with the UTF Engineering Division.

All of them had known our father in one way or another and as much as he wasn't always the greatest father to his sons, he was a nice guy and did so much for our community that they had to have appreciated him.

"Yeah," I finally responded to Jonos, "they all did."

"I think that's probably good for now." Cephus said, "We don't want to get too many cooks into this kitchen."

"Cephus is right, the less people we have in on this the easier it'll be to keep under wraps." Davriel said.

"Plus, we do have to figure out how we're going to sell this idea to everyone and actually get them to drop what it is they're doing and join in our cause—which I might remind you, is pretty far-fetched." Jonos added.

"So we'll have to devise some kind of ingenious plan." I responded.

"Like skydiving and then camping on a mountain?" Cephus said, causing us all to burst into laughter.

Our list was complete and we were ready to actually bring them in, the trouble was now to find them all and convince them to leave this world behind in search of others. In search of the Arcos. In search of the last Arcon. In search of our father.

"When can we expect to depart?" Zan asked in anticipation.

"As soon as we have our crew."

***

The sun was shining bright through the main crack of the fissure the next morning when we opened the primary hatch of ZANZABAR's main hold. The hold opened up on the underside of the ship and could fit a couple dozen or so cars within, though it was currently empty save for the four of us.

We had decided that we would leave ZANZABAR in the fissure to insure its concealment and proceed home by other means.

"We'll hitch a ride back to civilization and then come back when we've got our crew. And then we'll be off and destined for *great things*." Jonos said.

I thought about the 'great things' Jonos spoke of as Cephus acknowledged his idea, "Let's do it."

"You'll keep home locked up nice and tight for us won't you Zan?" I asked.

"I'll even leave the heat on." Zan joked as we walked down the large loading ramp.

We'd concluded our meeting and set out to recruit for our grand adventure and whatever great things lay before us.

We arrived back on the Shendale peninsula from our maiden flight with ZANZABAR later that night.

After an arduous climb up the steep walls of the fissure and a subsequent ten kilometer walk across frosted planes, we found a moderately used highway where we were able to hitch a ride to a Transit station.

Exhausted and utterly drained, we all went back to Jonos' apartment to maintain our cover story of being gone.

After the previous days of excitement and adventure, the four of us toasted a single drink before promptly falling asleep before 22:00.

The next morning, we set out from Jonos' apartment to begin recruiting. The four of us and Ayla — who had already confirmed coming with us — first decided to meet with Tytus and his wife Shelyse. Before we left however, I couldn't help but notice that Ayla had already packed up several plasti-crates worth of supplies for ZANZABAR, and was apparen--tly ready to move right on in. Her preparation skill was already evident.

We drove in two cars to Tytus' house and when we arrived, had to dodge movers and a large truck before we could even get to his front door.

He met us on the driveway to the garage, "What's up you jickos?" he jokingly greeted us, "Hey Ayla, how are you?" he followed up, smiling at her.

"Hey man, what's goin' on?" Jonos started as he hugged him and patted him twice on the back as they always did. The rest of us greeted him in turn.

"Just movin' a buncha' stuff into storage." He said, "Our lease expires at the end of the month so we're getting out."

Tytus and Shelyse's place wasn't the nicest of houses, but it had a homey charm to it, and we did have a few fun memories to recall from our good times spent there. I looked at the house and thought of some of those fun times and then watched as the movers continued to haul crates, boxes, and furniture off to the truck.

"Where are you guys gonna' live?" Davriel asked.

"Well, we got out bid on two of the three houses we were looking at, but the plan is to hold out for number three, and if that falls through we'll stay with her folks until we can get something concrete."

"About that..." I began, "Do you have a minute?"

"Sure." Tytus responded, as he turned and led us into the garage.

He sat down on an overturned bucket and opened a case full of traditional beer. Grabbing one for himself he cracked off the top and took a swig, then offered us some with his eyes.

"Okay." Davriel said as he grabbed one, popped it open, propped himself against an empty shelf and began drinking.

Tytus burped after a long gulp, "So what's up?" he asked.

"We wanna' ask you something." Cephus interjected.

"But before that, we have to tell you something." Jonos added.

We all sat, leaned, or found various places of comfort to relax and proceeded to tell Tytus everything we'd learned about our father, the Arcos, and finally *ZANZABAR*.

We fully explained our plan to look for answers to his disappearance, for him, for something. He sat listening intently as we told our tale, from discovery to flight; all the while he nodded, drank his beer and, muttered the occasional, "wow."

We showed him the device and the symbol from *ZANZABAR*'s bridge and explained that it was the same emblem our dad used to wear around his neck. Tytus nodded, and I could sense that he remembered seeing it at least once in the past during our time playing soccer. We concluded our story and let silence descend for a moment

"We want you to come with us." I finally said after a while.

"We know you had a connection to our dad, and we hope you'll believe that and our friendship would be reason enough to come with us." Jonos entreated.

"We would want Shelyse to come too." Ayla

added. "And you'd be paid for any services rendered."

"Wow guys. That's... That's some serious business." He stroked his beard in thought, "I'd have to talk to Shel about it, you know? She's just all about gettin' outta this place right now, but I don't know if that means gettin' *that* far out... Listen, we'll be at this for most of the day but let me get back to you on that."

"Yeah, no problem. No rush, we understand it's a huge ask. We'll get out of your hair." I answered, "Just think about it and get back to us later."

"Will do."

"Just remember what he meant to us man, what he meant to you." Jonos added.

"Yeah man, I will." Tytus said.

Davriel dropped his empty beer can in the trash and grabbed a second one for the road as we all got up and said our goodbyes. We then departed to continue our recruiting efforts.

Twenty minutes down the road, on our way to meet Jimian, Tytus sent me a Link message and said he was in. And Shelyse would come too. He always had a way of charming his wife. I never did understand it.

We'd found out that our second potential recruit Jimian Aryen was in town for the Endyears Holidays and so later in the afternoon we met up with him to try to convince him to leave this world behind in search of our long lost father and worlds beyond.

In the end, we told him the same story we told

Tytus, but had barely even asked him to join us before he interrupted.

"So when are we going?" he asked, confirming his interest.

He later explained that he'd recently quit his job and was looking for something to do to start fresh for the new year and believed the best thing to do was to go on an unfathomably amazing adventure with us across the stars.

We quickly realized that recruiting was going to be a hassle if all five of us visited each person one by one and we set a plan to visit the rest of our prospects; we would split up to cover more ground, and try to meet more than one person at a time.

The fortuitous beauty of our recruiting plan was that the timing lined up perfectly with the Endyears Holidays and as we soon found out, all of our old friends were home for the holidays which made locating them far easier.

First on our list after Jimian, Cephus and I visited our good friend Ander Ollen while Davriel and Jonos went to speak to Kaitoh.

Ayla went home to make more preparations for actually hiring these new crewmates as she was uncannily skilled with numbers and had agreed to handle the monetary and contractual aspects for our adventure given the rest of our rather inept abilities in business finance.

Ander and Kaitoh eventually agreed to our invitation though both took a rather arduous level of convincing. Ander had just finished his Integrated Medical Study program and was currently on a never-ending wait list for his official placement.

Cephus and I had to convince him to abandon his hopes of that for the sake of his friends and new, unknown horizons; it was rather tough and required a bit more persuasion than I initially wanted, but we needed to have him aboard for his medical expertise and we were more than happy when he finally agreed.

Kaitoh on the other hand was even tougher to convince and Davriel later told me that Tytus had to get involved as well to help convince Kai to even come and hear out the full offer, as the two of them had been quite close in Secondary.

I privately hoped that Tytus would be able to work more of his persuasive magic on his good friend.

Afterward, the four of us met up for an early evening meal at Davriel's mom's home.

She insisted on seeing all of us since we were back and we figured it would be good to put in the time since we were about to head out for an undetermined amount of time, possibly never to return; all while looking for her one-time lover and father to her son.

Filled to our eyes on her famous chili-meat-pies, whipped garlic potatoes, green beans, and corncakes, we sluggishly set out again for an evening of more of the 'job interviews' we were conducting.

In the evening Jonos and Davriel met up with Jimian and "interviewed" Pria, who was more than happy to abandon her current engineering job as it lacked any great financial bearing or serious interest.

She was a tester for a safety company and was

apparently looking for something more lucrative or at least more interesting. Jonos later told me that she'd graciously accepted the offer with the same ease and enthusiasm that Jimian expressed.

Meanwhile, Ander, Cephus, and I went to see our mutual friend Devian Teego. I had questioned his involvement as he was always a bit of rabble-rouser.

He was always outspoken and sometimes seemed radical, but he was good company and could certainly handle himself in a fight.

He had been open to the idea but didn't seem too sure about the prospect of the actual adventure since he didn't have the same profound relationship others had with our father.

The financial aspect of things didn't help convince him either. He did however relish the idea to explore other worlds and ultimately agreed to hear out our plan despite the unusual nature of our 'job-offer.'

When our meetings had concluded, Cephus and I called it a night and he dropped me off at Mom's house. After he left and my mother went to sleep I sat out on the front porch deep in thought.

This all seems too convenient… How weird is it that everyone is in a transitional phase or hates their job? Fate is mostly real, but come on, this is like clandestine to happen. No, something is going to happen and they won't all go. Well they especially won't go if they won't get paid, which reminds me…

I opened my Link and began composing an encoded message.

***

The next morning, we sent everyone Link messages with a time to meet at the airfield to discuss the matters of the journey more in depth:

MLM: T: 1030.
Shendale Locality Airfield.
Hanger 26. More on offer.
Wear good travel clothes.

We met everyone around 11:00 in the morning and chatted for an hour or so before actually getting started. Tytus caught up with Kaitoh, while Ayla and Shelyse discussed their concerns over the imminent departure.

Cephus, Davriel, Ander, Devian, and Lizia — who Jonos and I also invited to the meeting despite not meeting with her earlier — all reminisced of days passed and questioned our offer; deciding whether or not they would drop what they were doing and come with us. Meanwhile Jimian and Pria joked about the similarities our current situation had to different sci-fi Flix they'd loved.

Eventually Jonos and I quieted everyone and explained everything in full. To ask them to blindly follow us into the unknown was an unfair request to say the least, and we gave them all a guarantee.

One year.

We wouldn't be gone for more than one year. Even if we didn't find him, we would come back in one year and they would get paid — quite handsomely if everything went according to plan. Half upfront and half on return.

We only asked for one year of their time and

dedication to look for our father and whatever else the wide unknown had to offer. We'd already heard tentative "yeses" from everyone and after a while, even Lizia agreed to come with us due to the immense impact our father had on her life — an impact I was apparently quite unfamiliar with.

"We're willing to lay down our lives here," I said, "we don't expect you to, and if you feel like this is too much, you're always free to walk out. We can't guarantee we're going to find him; we can't guarantee we'll find *anything*. But for those who stay, we do offer this agreement: for the next year we commit our lives to this thrilling and possibly life-threatening search, and to those who choose to follow in it."

Silence.

After a few tense moments Tytus spoke up, "You know we're in."

We shook hands and hugged as he and Shelyse stood forward. They were in.

Jimian came next and so too did each person present; Pria, Ander, Lizia, Devian, and finally Kaitoh, all shaking our hands or hugging or just giving a nod of the head. Each embrace was another symbol of our new bonds.

ZANZABAR was sitting pretty with a standing crew of thirteen.

"But maybe you guys should wait to decide…" Jonos added.

Everyone looked at him in bewilderment.

"That is, wait 'til you see her fly."

In the early afternoon we took Mass Transit services to the Norhatchee station where Davriel, Jonos, Cephus and I had come from during our previous return from *ZANZABAR*. Norhatchee was an Amassian sub-territory northeast of the Cadian Mountains and the Great Mountain Cascade, characterized by dry plains and immense cracks and fissures that lay deep within the lands.

Since we were heading back to *ZANZABAR* we didn't want to risk any chance of the UTF or local authorities tracking us through our vehicles and therefore relied on public transportation.

After getting off at the Norhatchee station we hiked the same path that the four of us had made on our trip back.

It was a long and arduous hike given the time of year and the terrain, but thankfully there wasn't too much snow on the ground.

There were some mumbled complaints along the way, but we pressed on as we wanted everyone to see *ZANZABAR* for themselves.

It had to be done. Norhatchee's vast plateaus and intricate series of fissures were the secret location of *ZANZABAR* and we had to traverse them to get back to it since we couldn't risk bringing it back out in the open skies for too long.

Several hours later, when we finally arrived at the fissure where *ZANZABAR* was hidden, we carefully stepped up to the precipice and all peered over the edge.

Kaitoh let out a low whistle in amazement. It was ultimate darkness. Evening was setting on and all light seemed lost in the gloomy depths, "*Real impressive.*" He joked, "So how are we getting down?"

"I'll bring her up." Jonos said.

As he did so he effortlessly jumped off the cliff and for a moment everyone's heart stopped. They resumed with a sigh of relief after they saw him deploy the wing-chute he was wearing on his back to control his fall as he disappeared down into the shrouded crevasse.

"I wouldn't be worried," I smiled, "He's been getting really good at falling lately."

Hardly had a minute passed when we began to hear a rumbling from the depths of the fissure. A dissonant sound emerged from the cracks and rocks began shaking as the ground began to tremble. This was the first time I was actually witnessing *ZANZABAR* take off from the outside and I was rather astonished by the jarring nature of it, it really was quite impressive.

"What the??" I heard someone shout over the cacophony of *ZANZABAR*'s launch.

"It's okay." Cephus urged.

"Stand back!" Davriel thundered over the noise.

Moments later the tips of *ZANZABAR*'s tail-wings could be seen rising from the dust, followed by the massive arching top, and finally the full splendor of its entirety emerged from the shadows. Everyone stood in bewilderment as they gazed upon *ZANZABAR*: the alien ship from our ancestry, the ticket to finding our father.

Jonos seamlessly maneuvered *ZANZABAR*

onto the plateau, deploying the landing struts and opening the cargo bay door simultaneously — though I figured Zan was giving him a hand with that, or perhaps maybe it was in his blood to just know how to work the ship.

After landing near 20 meters away, ZANZABAR sat perched, exposed and inviting for our crew to observe and scrutinize.

People were stunned silent.

"Well shall we?" I calmly asked.

I walked toward ZANZABAR, followed slowly by 11 of my favorite and most trusted people.

As the last person entered the main hold, a life-size hologram of Zan flickered to life in front of us. "Hello everyone," she began, "my name is Zan. I'm pleased to have you all aboard."

They stood astonished and smiled at the excitement of it all. Everyone aboard had committed to our cause. Shortly thereafter we took everyone for the ride of their lives — or rather the beginning of the ride of their lives.

**United Terran Federation Classified Communique
to all Amassian Commanding Officers
From the Office of UTF Chief Defense Minister
Luca de Gulliss,**
21 December, 3.2220 @22:53:09 TST

Commanders,

At 19:45 hours Pacinus Time, UTF satellites detected a spike of a previously unidentified power source in the Norhatchee Plateau region. The signal was only active for seven seconds before it disappeared.

It appears to be a match of the previously confirmed UAO (Unidentified Aerial Object) sighting by the Fort Kane Battalion. Upon registering the signal reading, the battalion at Fort Kane dispatched reconnaissance ships to investigate. Two FA-2 Falcon wings and two Litehawk recon vessels conducted the search of the surrounding area to no immediate avail.

A small detachment of 'Ghosts' were also deployed to search the fissures and found a large gathering of tracks in one specific area over the series of cracks—the tracks were deemed to have come from the Norhatchee MT station. We are currently reviewing their surveillance footage for any leads.

While exploring the region beneath the cracked surface, the Ghosts discovered clear signs from thruster burns resulting from a vertical take-off of a large ship. From these findings we can establish that there is a sizeable company — approximately 10-15 judging by the number of tracks — who know of this mysterious ship previously detailed.

We may assume that they are all in league and are now all fugitives considering the previous classified incident. They are hereby charged as threats of our great United Terran Federation for their collaboration with fugitives during the first sighting, and must be detained for questioning; anyone who has come into contact with these unidentified persons is also to be brought in for immediate processing.

Amassian commanders, you are ordered to increase your combat readiness levels to Gamma 2 and post recon and fast-response squadrons during all operational hours.

All commanders are to begin 24-hour surveillance scans for unidentified electronic signals and unusual power readings in your regions: you will receive a complete diagnostic on the UAO's recorded power signature for cross referencing purposes.

Furthermore, you are ordered to post long range lookouts outfitted for thermal scans throughout your controlling sectors.

This vessel is a Level 1 priority and is to be detained at any cost. If any contact is made with this UAO you are to immediately inform the chain of command and the appropriate reinforcements will be dispatched.

The United Terran Federation thanks you for your compliance.

Chief Defense Minister Luca de Gulliss,
UTF Chairman

Chapter 9: Endyears

One week had passed since our first flight with the crew, but we were still waiting for our official launch. December of the 2220th year of the Third Age of Terranity was coming to a close which meant that Endyears was drawing ever closer, and January and the beginning of the 2221st year were all rapidly approaching. We decided to set out on the third and final day of Newyears: Trentia.

Before the full group left ZANZABAR we had all toured the ship, exploring its entirety. We visited the bridge, the galley, a few of the crew quarters, the hangar bay, the med bay, the engine room, and finally the launch bay that contained ZANZABAR's smaller ships, before we reconvened in the galley. I thought everyone had been particularly impressed with the small contingent of ships we now commanded with the fighter jets Jonos and I dubbed 'Interceptors' and 'Valkyries' and the bulkier shuttle we called the *Corsair*.

We then assigned quarters and duties, and everyone signed hardcopy agreements and verbally recorded official pledges with Ayla and Zan—for contractual purposes of payment and our own life-insurance policies.

After that, everyone dispersed and had been given the time to enjoy the Endyears and Newyears holidays with their loved ones, and explain their departures in their own ways. Some *actually* told the truth while others tactfully avoided it.

Ultimately everyone enjoyed the holiday cheer. Everything seemed to be coming together, save for one nagging truth: we still couldn't fund this epic and imminent interstellar search for our long lost father.

On Endyears Eve — the second to last day of the year — after a rather warm-felt day inside with my mother, brother, and Ayla, spent celebrating the holidays with food and gifts, and gifts of food, I finally heard some good news regarding our imminent voyage.

There were many delicious holiday sweets and delicacies that day and all took part in the cooking and the baking, but more importantly the eating.

Content with our meal, we sat down and explained everything to our mother. She patiently listened and experienced a full range of emotions as she remembered her husband and considered what we had proposed.

I wasn't sure how she would respond, though certainly did anticipate the tears, but when she finally did speak I was taken quite aback.

Despite her constant teary eyes, she kept her thoughts rather succinct, yet sincere and loving, "You boys find him. Find him and bring him back. Be careful and be safe. Always look out for one another, and go with Jorah's blessings. I love you both."

She also spoke to Ayla, "You watch out for these boys, they need a good prodding and handling from time to time. I know in my heart that you'll all come back and I won't have to wait for too much longer for that daughter I always wanted. Look out for yourself and remember that a little bit of love goes a long way."

She smiled as she softly kissed her check and hugged her.

She then hugged Jonos and me together and each of us kissed her cheeks, "Take care of each other."

"We will Mom, we will."

Despite Mom's religious nature neither my brother nor I were practicing Jorahthic — I never knew exactly where Jonos' beliefs lay, but I always believed in equilibrium and the balance of life and whatever cosmic force brought it about — but we accepted her words and blessings, readily and graciously.

Afterward we retired to the living room to enjoy the fire and the soft falling of the snow out the window. Mom had stopped crying and was asking Ayla more about her ideas on everything while Jonos and I cleaned the dishes and cookware.

I was drying off my hands when my Link went off and I left everyone for a minute to check the E-Link I'd received:

> **Sender**: EFS_68737&&:#FD_mund/llc:
> **Subject:****LIMITED HOLIDAY OFFER**
> (@(786asdjhY35asfdhsbq=687)@)
> Message: WANT A FREE LINK!!??!! OFFER EXPIRES ON ENDYEARS DAY! WIN LINKS IMMEDIATELY! MUST ACT NOW! Trade in yOur old MOdel and with pRoof of puRchase, be selected tO Win big!

Participants And members, You'll autoMatically bE eligible for additioNal prizes and producTs, like the latest and greatest, tkx 7.1 i-Link! WHAT A DEAL!!! RESPOND NOW and yoU could Potentially receive a cash card fOr use oN any parTnEr tkx group merchandiSe or producTs!!!
ACT NOW! Don't miss out on deals like i-Link S40 earpieces, ordinarily 30.00 notes, now for just N13.60 OR 4 i-Readers for the price of 3!!! No down payments on neW tkx 7.1 customers, only N29.95 per month for the first year! That's right you get all .12 months for the price of 7!!! ACT NOW! Offer ends @ 24:00 on ENDYEARS: 31 December 3.2220!!!

Looking at the message I very nearly deleted but something told me to stop. I was expecting something like this.

I read through the message again and seeing it a second time, I began to notice its truer meaning. I looked at the sender and realized the "FD_mund" and concluded that the sender was undoubtedly Dr. Franzi Dorfmund whom I'd previously contacted using an encoded message; which the doctor must have gotten and subsequently responded to.

In the subject I saw the numerical depiction for yes in the 'number-language' known as Numlang: Y35. YES. The doctor was interested in my offer.

From there the message wasn't too difficult to decipher, it was likely enough to fool the auto-censors and filters the UTF used to monitor possible hostile messages in order to have been sent, but was not a highly elaborate encryption.

The doctor had simply chosen the words wisely and emphasized certain letters and numbers.

I slowly pieced the message together and read the encoded message: 'Tomorrow. Payment upon test.'

The sales deals at the end of the message hid numerical values for GPS coordinates and a time: N43.603 - W125.127 @2400. Apparently the doctor wanted to meet.

Dr. Dorfmund was interested, it was my move.

After reading the message I enjoyed the remainder of the night with my mother, brother, and Ayla but couldn't help but dwell on the possibility of the upcoming meeting with Dr. Dorfmund.

Later in the night, after they had left, I lay awake in bed wondering what the meeting would bring, if I could eventually convince the doctor and get us paid, and how many people would actually commit if I couldn't. My thoughts drifted off into space, distant stars and planets, and the far reaches of reality and eventually I fell into a deep sleep.

In my dreams I dreamt of a bright and beautiful world, marked by glorious views of nature as well as civilization.

Beautiful mountains and grasslands were neighbored by large striking and visually stunning buildings that challenged basic architectural principles.

It was stupendous and uplifting to gaze on such a scene until my ears were caught by a floating melody. A serendipitous sound of the most beautiful voice imaginable strayed into my mind and my senses were immediately enticed and soothed by the wonder of the sound.

But it was not to last, the sound slowly faded and as it did, so too the lush landscape and vibrant colors of the world began to crack and fade. The sun grew hot and purple flairs began to spark from it. The world as I had known it suddenly and violently died as the planet cracked asunder, engulfing nature and civilization into its deepest recesses.

But the planet did not explode as I thought it would, it merely cracked into gargantuan pieces through a shuddering earthquake that was felt down to its very core.

The world became dark and the sun shown no more through the dust that had arisen from the tumult. The ground was desolate and everything in sight seemed demented.

The few buildings that still stood were dark and shadowy and figures could be seen shifting within the gloom. I soon heard a frantic scream followed by an almost haunted beating noise.

My body took me closer to the sounds, as horrible as they were, and suddenly and unexpectedly I found myself peering over a balcony on top of the dying world.

I had no idea how I'd gotten there, or where there even was. From over the edge I could fully witness the extent of the planet's horrific death.

Enormous fissures patterned the lands and colossal peaks jutted up through the planet's craggy surface; the dust around had persisted and become vast gray clouds blotting out the sky where one could see the insidious and sudden flashes of malicious mauve lightning.

A velvety voice crept up behind me, salacious and cunning. It cooed my name, "Savos......"

I turned around to notice, a beautifully cruel face shrouded in shadow that somehow reflected what greyish light still remained.

Her face was stern and malicious and her eyes and hair were the blackest I'd ever seen but somehow I was transfixed; despite her malevolent appearance she enticed me. I had no time at all to comprehend her presence before her eyes flared a fiery orange and she shoved me in the chest, pushing me right over the balcony.

I fell for what seemed like an eternity — and was later surprised that the fall didn't wake me up from this chilling dream — until I landed harshly on a dirt floor.

I could feel my body shatter on impact and felt an immense pain afterward as I coughed and spit up my own blood, gasping for air.

Then the woman from up on the ledge suddenly appeared in my hazed and bloodied vision. Again her body was shrouded in darkness yet was clearly shining in the night as it reflected the remaining light.

My mind reeled in confusion trying to comprehend any of this before I finally heard her mutter something under her breath as she lifted her shadow-lit boot up and smashed it down into my face.

I immediately awoke and jolted upright. I sat perplexed for a moment before I subconsciously remembered the music I'd heard in the dream, the sweet and serene sound it made and the sensory appeal it had.

I focused on the music, its melody, the sights and images and feelings it inspired and forgot everything that happened afterward in the dream and immediately fell back into a restful sleep.

***

The next morning was Endyears Day; the last day of the year. I was to meet Dr. Dorfmund that night and attempt to secure the means of beginning our adventure. I woke up with a very happy demeanor though I didn't know why, and afterward I ventured downstairs to see my mother sitting quietly at the dining room table, with an old fashioned book and her breakfast.

"Hey Mom. How are you this morning?" I said, entering the kitchen.

Initially she did not respond.

After a few moments without a reply I asked if she was okay.

She was neither reading her book, nor eating her breakfast. In fact, her book was closed and her food was almost entirely untouched.

"Savos..." She weakly spoke.

I looked at her in sincere fashion. She was about to burst into tears.

Then it hit me: eight years ago she'd lost her husband; the love of her life, and now she was about to lose her two sons—her only remaining physical presence of him, the only loves that could rival his importance or her love for him.

For a moment I stood frozen and bewildered. She looked melancholic and forlorn.

I noticed her hands were folded together on the table. I could tell by the necklace loop coming from under them that she held something underneath.

I immediately went to her and embraced her as she began to cry, "Oh Mom, it'll be ok. I promise."

"I know, I know. I'll just miss you boys so much."

"It'll be just like when I went to university, no big deal. We'll come back. And we'll come back with more than we left, okay?" At this point I looked in her eyes and began wiping the tears away from her face. "We'll come back Mom. I promise you that."

She simply smiled amidst wiping away the tears, "I want you to have this." She held out her hand.

My eyes moved to her hand and so too did my hand. As I cupped it beneath her own, she dropped a coin sized object in my hand. It was a medallion. And it looked exactly like the one our father used to wear.

"He gave it to me the day he left. To remember him. He wanted me to have it so I would always have a piece of him. But I think you should have it."

I hesitated.

"Mom… I'm grateful, but I can't accept that. He gave it to you. And you're the one he meant to have it."

I took the medallion in my hands, and threaded the thin chain around her neck, clasping it about the back.

"It's yours Mom, and you should keep it."

This brought her to more tears and she hugged me fully. "I love you Savos. Go with Jorah's blessings and come back to me in one piece."

"I will Mom. I will."

Eventually her tears dissipated and she calmed down. "Do you want me to reheat this for you?" I said, pointing to her breakfast.

"No, that's ok. I'm not too hungry right now. I'll just eat it later."

"Ok, I'll hold you to that though. After all, you can't start your day without eating breakfast." I said while smiling, trying to lighten the mood.

I took her plate away and went to wrap it in baking foil when she sat up from the table and walked toward the living room. There she sat in a chair facing the window and watched as a light snow began to fall.

I went in after her, hugged her and kissed her on the cheek, "I love you Mom."

"I love you too Savos."

After finishing breakfast of my own, I hugged my Mom once again before setting to my day of making my own final preparations for leaving in the following days.

I finished packing—which was partially easier since I didn't actually have much to pack, since most of my possessions had recently been destroyed—but still had one major preparation to make.

Throughout the day after my mother's des

-pondency I anxiously looked at my Link checking for any new messages to distract my thoughts, but saw none.

In the afternoon after a brief doze in which I thought I dreamt of a vast ocean of emptiness and a very peculiar mammalian creature, I awoke to see something I'd never seen before in a strange blue light flashing on the screen of my Link.

I looked at it for a moment before grabbing my Link and putting it on my wrist.

It flickered to life and suddenly a finger-sized body appeared hovering slightly above my wrist. It was Zan.

"What the hell?"

"Hello Savos." She said smilingly. "You're no doubt wondering how I'm here. Let me tell you."

"Yeah…" I barely muttered.

"The last time you were aboard the ship I took the opportunity of analyzing the communication components of the "Links" you and your crew all wear. From there I inspected the communication networks they all use and hacked into them, drawing on their preexisting coverage and utilizing this planet's intricate satellite system to bounce the signal off of a few hundred satellites to negate any possibility of a trace. Then I merely altered the keyboard display micro-camera on your Link to display my own image instead of the keyboard. It's all quite simple really."

"Sure it is…" I barely made out in my freshly awakened stupor.

I had no idea how one would go about doing such things but since she was an alien AI of immense intelligence I didn't question her ability to do something of that nature.

"So was there something you wanted to tell me or is this just a friendly wake-up call?"

"Yes actually. I have been spending my time monitoring this planet's satellite traffic and in doing so, I have picked up increased discussion on military channels about some mysterious ship in the Northwestern Amassian area."

She paused a moment as I realized we'd failed at keeping a low profile as intended, then continued:

"That would no doubt be due to our recent activities and previous encounter with the UTF. I must voice my concern that by further delaying our departure and search for Arcus we increase the chances of them finding and detaining us, as they are being ordered to do, based on the communiqués I've intercepted from a certain Chief Defense Minister Luca de Gulliss. This planet isn't exactly the friendliest to its visitors."

"I know I know. Believe me; I want to get out sooner rather than later too. And we will be leaving in the next day or two if I can make a deal with an old acquaintance. Which actually, you can help me with... Do the Interceptors aboard the ship have Galaxial capabilities?"

"You mean the Azintras?" She corrected me using the Arcosan name, "They do not, nor do the larger Avalkas, but the Zieru possesses that capability. Why do ask?"

"Two things Zan: getting used to 'Arcos' names and words is gonna' take me some time so please be patient," I began, "for now I might just stick to 'Interceptor,' 'Valkyrie,' and *'Corsair'* if you don't mind. But secondly, and more importantly, can you remotely fly one?"

"Of course I can. I am quite capable of..."

"Good," I cut her off before she could go on, "I need you to fly it to a specific set of coordinates."

"Ahh, you mean the ones from your latest e-Link? For the 'test' for your meeting with Dr. Dorfmund?"

"What? How did you... you can read my messages!?"

"Mmm, of course you can..." I said realizing the futility of questioning it, "Listen, we need to make this deal happen so we can afford to leave. The crew is made of family and loyal friends, but they won't all work for friendship alone, we need some form of payment beyond shallow promises."

"Yes I see." She said, not at all regretful of the invasion of my privacy, "I would be happy to help you in this regard if it means expediting our departure process. The smaller craft aboard this ship do possess some stealth ability that can mask their presence, so shouldn't raise too much suspicion; provided the UTF isn't paying minute attention to every individual engine emission—as Arcosan technology clearly has different ones than those of anything on this planet."

I wondered about the likelihood of the UTF's eyes being that refined before she continued.

"Additionally, *ZANZABAR*'s new location and the location of your meeting are outside of our previously known grid of activity so we shouldn't have to worry too much about the UTF tracking our activities. When shall I have it at the proposed destination?"

"I'll let you know once I get there, but I'm sure you'll know when I arrive." I said, hoping that Zan's new hiding place — an obscure harbor in the waters of the Emerald Sound — was concealed enough from the prying eyes of the UTF.

"Very well. When shall I be seeing you and the crew again?"

"Why? Getting lonely?"

"Merely growing restless. Despite the vast details, facts, specifics, and general minutiae of your race's three ages of history, it hasn't taken much time or effort to learn it all. Though, learning of the second age's technological revolution was quite engaging."

Again she paused for a moment in hesitant thought.

"However, I must admit I much prefer the company of real beings from which to learn and grow. Meeting, spending time with, and understanding sentient life and its experiences are how one truly learns about the mysteries of life itself."

"I see..."

I felt somewhat perplexed about Zan's response, it was strange to hear an artificial being speak so fondly of biological and emotional beings and experiences. It seemed as though she wished to be closer to them, perhaps closer to being one herself.

"Well then, I will see you soon Savos. You can contact me by simply tapping the blue light on your Link's screen when you are ready. Do drive safely."

"Okay," I said, "thanks Zan."

"You're welcome."

"One more thing Zan..."

"Yes?"

"Stop reading my messages."

"No promises." With that, Zan smiled and her image disappeared.

I smiled afterward, thinking about how quickly she had adopted a common expression I used among my brothers and how much she desired real personal contact and interaction.

Strange. It's like she wants to be alive or something.

I couldn't give it much more thought as I realized I needed to depart shortly in order to make my meeting with Dr. Dorfmund. I had quite the drive ahead of me.

After eating a half-hearted dinner of leftover pastries from the day before, I opened the garage, got into my car Silvia, input the coordinates Dr. Dorfmund had sent me into the GPS, and set out for our meeting.

The coordinates led to an old ranch near 140 kilometers southeast of the Great Mountain Cascade in a lush green and somewhat forested country. I arrived near a half hour early for our 24:00 meeting and took in the surroundings.

The ranch looked abandoned from the main road. I decided to park my car about a kilometer out to avoid being detected on my way toward the property. After scanning the area, I decided to begin my approach on foot.

I inspected the grounds as I approached and noticed there was no trace of Dr. Dorfmund's vehicle, whatever it was. I carefully walked toward the house and approached to see the front door ajar and no lights on inside.

I decided to go inside and search the decrepit structure for any sign of the doctor. After searching the house to no avail I walked toward the barn and moved to open its large doors but stopped suddenly as I heard the distinct click and cocking of a shotgun behind my back.

A honeyed female voice spoke from behind me as a spotlight appeared around my figure, "Back away from the door and turn around slowly."

I slowly put my hands up and turned around to face my assailant.

Once I'd finished turning, I faced a slender figure in muddied jeans, old cattle boots, a flannel shirt, a black thermal vest and an old fashioned cowboy hat.

But I couldn't make out the face that was hidden underneath the black brim of the hat due to the light shining on me. The shotgun was difficult to make out as the flashlight seemed to be emanating from it.

"What the hell are you doing on my property?" She voiced sternly as she approached.

As the figure slowly drew closer I blocked the light with my hand and my eyes adjusted and began to realize who I saw in front of me. I began to make out a beautifully aged female face, with piercing brown eyes and cheeks full of freckles, framed with long blonde hair and showing a stern look.

"Dr.... Dorfmund?" I questioned.

It had been several years since I last saw her

but she somehow looked spirited and more vivacious — perhaps that was due to the fact that she was crying and more or less enraged the last time I saw her at my father's memorial service. She lowered the gun and took a closer look at me.

"My word…" she said, "Savos, you've certainly grown up. You got my message then?"

"Yes ma'am." I said as I lowered my arms, "I'm glad we could arrange this meeting."

"Come on, let's get inside." She said looking all around and up above. Despite her lively demeanor she seemed rather paranoid that someone was watching.

She opened the barn doors and as soon as we were inside and the door was shut and barred a hole appeared in the floor as a door opened and exposed a hidden stair case and passageway.

"Follow me." She said.

As we descended several flights of stairs I tried making conversation as we walked, "So you and my dad worked together for a long time huh? From what I can piece together he was kind of a ladi—"

"We never slept together, if that's what you're getting at." The doctor said severely.

I shut my mouth and immediately tensed up as I was surprised at how quickly the conversation led to that, and I immediately regretted trying to make conversation in the first place.

"I'm joking." She smiled, "But really, my relationship with your father was strictly work related. I do believe he learned his lesson after the unexpected outcome of his last work fling."

She was clearly hinting at my brother Cephus—few people knew of his begetting—and his mother Lora, who'd worked with my father on the Terran Physicist Initiative's space-drive project a shocking nine months before Cephus' birth.

I wasn't sure but I almost detected a hint of jealousy in the doctor's hasty response but was entirely distracted as we arrived at the bottom of the stairs. She activated a series of light switches and the subterranean setting was illuminated.

Down underneath the barn was a sizable underground lab that must have housed the entirety of Dr. Dorfmund's research.

She had been quite industrious when she was working with my father for the UTF SAE Division and their labs were top of the line, but leaving the UTF also meant leaving their funding, but it seemed as though she still managed to conduct a prolific operation in this secluded lab, albeit on a much smaller scale.

There were huge whiteboards and Intelli-screens containing equations and many different formulae, star-charts with hundreds of different mapped out coordinates, telescopic and satellite images, planetary, solar system, and galaxy maps, complex engines and devices I knew very little about.

It was entirely overwhelming to walk into and observe, but the doctor seemed entirely focused and immediately got down to business.

"So, you have working proof of inter-dimensional 'Galaxial' travel. Show me."

I pushed my incredulity aside and tapped the blue button on my wrist-Link and Zan popped up smilingly. Oddly enough she was suddenly clothed in a fine business suit and lab coat.

"Hello Savos."

"What the?" Dr. Dorfmund started.

"Ahh, you must be preeminent physicist and astronomer Dr. Franzi Mishaya Dorfmund. Arcus Angelus' former research partner, yes?"

"Why yes, yes I am. And you are?"

"My name is Zan and I am an associate of Savos and of the late Arcus Angelus. That is all you need to know."

Dr. Dorfmund beheld her somewhat quizzically but nodded along as Zan continued:

"I have taken the liberty of sending you a heavily encrypted e-Link with the formulae that you seek. *I* will have to open the message for you to activate the proper encoder, and then after you've seen it, I must require that you destroy the message. You'll find that everything is correct and that your current power sources are in fact adequate for Arcus' Galaxial Flux Drive when used in the correct arrangement."

Dr. Dorfmund blinked incredulously, perhaps amazed or dumbstruck that she'd had the potential in front of her all this time, just not the sequence.

Zan continued, "I have taken the liberties of identifying and correcting yours and Arcus' mistakes in your original formulae and through these corrections you should find it well within your capacity to duplicate the process successfully. You are no doubt wondering how I have procured the original blueprints, theorems, and equations; I assure you they were given to me by Savos of his own ac

-cord and I have neither reproduced nor distributed them to anyone. In regards to the proof and test you requested I would like you to begin monitoring the unidentified High Frequency Wave signal that will be popping up directly above your location in a moment."

Not a second passed when a blip appeared on a nearby display. It was some kind of radar monitor that previously registered nothing, but now registered a blip just as Zan dictated.

"That would be the test craft." Zan stated. "Lock onto its High Frequency Wave signal if you would please."

Dr. Dorfmund approached the display, tapped a few screen controls and I saw a second marking appear around the original. It was locked in, we were tracking.

The doctor then turned to another display and activated it. On the screen there appeared eight different video displays of the entire ranch property. She began maneuvering several cameras on the spot to no doubt glimpse the craft hovering above.

It took her a moment to find it as its shape was difficult to discern to the naked eye as well as for the night vision her cameras employed, it wasn't until she flipped her cameras to a thermal view that she identified the craft by sight.

There, hovering about thirty meters above the roof of the barn was ZANZABAR's shuttle, the *Corsair*. Its full figure was slightly obscured by the night sky and since we were looking from beneath, we could only make out its basic kite shape framed by its acute back wings.

"Lock onto the craft's power signature and observe the warp drive's mass-production fluctuation — the same readings you would get from your GFD technology." Zan continued, "Upon hitting the correct frequency the craft's warp drive activates, simultaneously establishing the dimensional rift in space and propelling the craft into the dimensional warp — the Galaxia as you call it — pushing it through space and time faster than light.

"Judging by your equipment you should still be able to measure the craft's warp drive signature from the closest star system, Proxima Soltari — approximately 5.2 light years away — albeit however faint, after it returns to normal space."

She paused for a moment before continuing, "To double-check its position you will also be able to track the HFW signal. I should be able to boost your power through a wireless reroute of the nearest power-plant for the few moments the *Corsair* remains in normal space."

At this point I noticed Dr. Dorfmund's pure and utter bewildered excitement. She was no doubt making the connections in her mind and was beginning to be overcome with the thrill of knowing the right answer and achieving her goal in life.

I also couldn't help but notice my own anticipation.

I had had a similar experience like this so many years ago; Dr. Dorfmund, my family, billions of Terrans around the world, and I witnessed my father depart from this world forever in such a similar fashion.

I now stood anxious and stupefied as the doctor and I watched the *Corsair* begin its ascent.

"I'll fly the craft beyond the thermosphere and then activate its warp drive," Zan said, "do monitor your displays as we continue."

"Yes, of course." Dr. Dorfmund barely managed, still fixated on the *Corsair* and Zan's continued procedural voice.

"Beginning spin-up sequence in ten seconds; watch closely now."

The *Corsair* began to soar up into the sky and very quickly became lost to normal vision and the ranch cameras; though we could still follow its signal through the High Frequency Wave signal we were tracking.

Zan had already activated the ship's stealth functions to avoid any attention we would no doubt have received from unwanted onlookers.

I sure do hope that nobody's watching this...

"Countdown commencing. Warp jump in 5... 4... 3... 2... 1."

Neither the doctor nor I were able to see the *Corsair* disappear in what I later learned to be an instant flash of the most vibrant colors imaginable; the deepest purples and brightest blues surrounded by sunburst oranges and piercing yellows, and everywhere stars, more stars than the mind can count, disappearing as quickly as the image appeared.

The doctor and I saw none of the majesty that was interstellar travel, all we could see was the signal being tracked until it suddenly disappeared from the screen. The doctor turned her attention to the other monitor that was tuned to the High Frequency Wave signal waiting to see it.

Once again I found myself on the brink. That moment right before the fall. That breath you take between the jump and the landing.

It worked, right? It has to!

"It will be some time before the signal reappears given the nature of space and travel across such vast distances. Despite the ship traveling faster than light, it does take some time to transition."

I couldn't help but feel the same pangs of loss and failure as I once had. I began to feel the same emptiness I'd felt when my father left all those years ago.

Dr. Dorfmund and I sat in relative silence as she busied herself with checking and rechecking many of her instruments and regularly glancing at the mission timer she hastily set up before launch.

I watched on, curious as to where exactly in the infinite expanse of space—and the 'other side' of it—the *Corsair* currently was and just how long it would take for the ship to get there.

"I'll go ahead and boost your power output now." Zan said after some time, breaking the silence. "Dr. Dorfmund, if you'd be so kind as to max out your instruments' capacities."

Dr. Dorfmund then flipped several switches and turned several knobs before looking back to the monitors. Suddenly the High Frequency Wave signal reappeared and registered ever so minimally on the doctor's monitors.

Holy shit it made it!

"Signal... confirmed!" Dr. Dorfmund said astonished, gazing at the mission timer and seeing a mere twenty-seven minutes had passed.

The *Corsair's* HFW was active again and clearly reading across trillions of miles.

"How? How is that possible?" Dr. Dorfmund's bewilderment betrayed her profession.

"The physics are without a doubt beyond anything you or any Terran have ever known." Zan replied, "until now."

"This... will change Terranity... forever." Dr. Dorfmund stammered out.

"Yes it will." I echoed, unsure exactly if that was for the best.

"Beginning the return cycle." Zan's procedural voice continued, "Countdown commencing. Return jump in 5... 4... 3... 2... 1."

Dr. Dorfmund and I seemed to hold our breath for the twenty-seven minutes of the return trip until the *Corsair* finally reappeared in our solar system, its signal noticeably stronger than before.

"Unbelievable." She stammered out. "It works. By Jorah, it works!"

"I didn't figure you for a religious woman, doctor." I smiled wide eyed and mystified.

It worked.

Galaxial travel was possible and I had the means to do it. I could find my father. Our adventure was on.

After the *Corsair's* return to normal space, Zan completed the spin-down cycle and flew the ship back toward Terra; mere moments later the doctor's cameras refocused on a small object returning in our atmosphere.

It flashed and burned as it reentered our atmosphere. As it raced closer to the barn its image expanded until it slowed drastically and came to a sudden stop near fifty meters above the barn before descending straight down ever so slowly.

Dr. Dorfmund could hardly contain herself and she ran up the stairs back to the barn entrance. I quickly followed.

She threw open the doors and burst outside to gawk at the *Corsair* hovering, now just a few meters off the ground.

"Test cycle complete." I heard Zan say from my wrist Link as I gazed on in pure adrenaline-fueled excitement. "Now if you'll excuse me, I must be returning this before it attracts any unwanted attention. I trust this will be enough for the doctor?"

"Could I just run a few tests on..." she began.

"I'm sorry doctor, but I really must be going. The e-Link has been sent and opened for you. I assure you, you now have the instructions and ability to recreate the process yourself."

"But just a few diagnostics...." She persisted.

"I am sorry." Zan stated flatly.

"Very well then," the doctor submitted, the fire in her eyes quelling for a brief moment.

"I will be in touch soon Savos. Doctor Dorfmund, it's been a pleasure." Zan finished with a smile and a brief bow.

With that the *Corsair* soared off into the night sky to return to Zan's secluded hiding place and the blue silhouette on my Link disappeared as she ended the connection.

"I don't mean to be a prig Dr. Dorfmund," I began after a long moment of silence, "but I believe there was an agreement for payment to be made upon a successful test and transfer of the formulae?"

"Yes, of course." She said staring up at the stars, "Let us go back down to the lab, shall we? I believe I have something for you."

That night after leaving the doctor's ranch, I drove my car into the next morning.

I stared up into the star-speckled midnight sky as I drove into the New Year thinking about the upcoming adventure.

As the colors mixed at the horizon I saw beautiful opportunity. I suddenly saw the means to a new life, a new purpose.

I drove until the horizon looked like a clandestine oasis in my own perception of reality; until I found myself in one of the remote wildernesses of this world; until the dark blue of the night sky lightened and was bordered by the light purples and pinks that precipitated the sunrise.

At that point I stopped.

I stepped out of the car and looked up to the heavens, looking somewhere between the depths of the sky and the expanse of the earth, somewhere between this world and the next, I realized how confident I was.

I was ready for anything from that point on. That moment marked the beginning of the rest of my life. For the rest of the night I laid on the hood of my car in peaceful, serenity. As a cool breeze glided throughout the night I gazed into the starry sky and saw my future.

***

The first thing I did Newyear's Day was drive home to my Mom's house and wish her a happy New Year with a massive hug and kiss.

After eating a hearty breakfast of blueberries and yogurt, scrambled eggs, and ham, I drove over to Jonos and Ayla's apartment with a briefcase that weighed at least half of my own weight. It was filled with untraceable Peliatonium bricks which were quite valuable if you knew anything about construction of anything space-faring and durable.

They were valuable on any market and would give us the means to begin our journey and pay our crew. On my way I sent a voice Link to Cephus and Davriel telling them to meet me over at Jonos and Ayla's so we could begin making our final preparations.

"I got it." I told Ayla as I let myself in the front door of her and Jonos' apartment.

Jonos hadn't yet returned from the airfield where he was no doubt explaining to Rennai that he found a new 'job' and was leaving, or perhaps that he was having trouble working there after the crash in the Fa-2.

I was somewhat surprised that my brother was one of the dissemblers when justifying or explaining our departure, but then again I realized that I too, probably would have told a fabricated story if I had a boss or someone of importance other than my mother to tell it to.

"Got what?" Ayla said, somewhat surprised as I stepped in and removed my coat.

"What we're going to use to *fund* this adventure." I responded somewhat out of breath, "I met with dad's old partner, the famous physicist and astronomer Dr. Franzi Dorfmund. Have you heard of her?"

"Yeah I remember hearing her name. She kind of disappeared after your dad did."

"She's the one who helped him implement his Galaxial Flux Drive on the Outer Heaven project. She helped him develop, design, and build it, though she wasn't aboard when it launched. Instead, she was on the supervisory ground crew."

I had taken a block of the Peliatonium out to examine it as I spoke.

"She was running the observation the day he disappeared, but wasn't allowed to continue the research or try to find him afterward as the UTF viewed her as a failure and decided to simply cut their losses. Anyway, I was able to meet with her and with Zan's help, I secured us a way out the door."

"Great! How do you want to handle that now? I think it best that we go ahead with the signing bonus, but give it all to them now. That way they can do whatever they want with it while they still can."

"Well they'll get their bonus now, but I'll keep some for the 'policies' we established. Don't want anyone thinking they can take the money and run. We *do* need to meet up with everyone as soon as possible though; we're running short on time."

"Should we plan to go back to ZANZABAR?"

"No not yet. I don't want to risk giving away the location until we're ready to leave. The next time we go to the ship it has to be the last time. What are the chances we could all meet here?"

"Sure, we can do that." She said. "It'll be a little cramped, but we can manage."

Just then Jonos walked in the door and I told both of them the full story of my meeting with Dr. Dorfmund, the ranch, the doctor holding me at gunpoint, and the test; everything that led up to the case full of Peliatonium bricks that was now on their dining room table.

Around the end of my story, Cephus and Davriel arrived which prompted me to retell my meeting with Dr. Dorfmund.

I also repeated the news of Zan's newfound ability to hack and communicate using our Links; which I briefly showed them, tapping the blue light on my Link and spawning Zan's image.

She said hello and wished us all 'Happy Newyears' then returned to her own business and preparations for our imminent departure.

After describing the events to everyone, we turned the discussion toward the next step; the five of us then determined how we would meet up with everyone on Trentia at Zan's concealed location and begin our journey.

First and foremost, we began planning our Newyears Launch party; our last party on Terra.

***

Secundia soon arrived, it was the second day of the New Year and a clear and sunny day; though with a bit of a chill. We were to leave the next morning. We met at Ayla and Jonos' apartment for an early cook-off and celebration to begin our final night on Terra.

Everyone arrived in the afternoon and brought over a delicious dish or a brewed beverage and all were merry and amused throughout the afternoon.

As the afternoon soon became evening Jonos and I drew everyone close for a few words.

Jonos began by saying, "We're extremely grateful that all of you guys are aboard with this—both figuratively and literally, get it?"

"Oh you're a pun-ny guy Jonos." Ander said, drawing quite a few laughs.

I smiled and Jonos couldn't help but chuckle after the comment.

"Ha, what a great pun-chline!" Davriel added.

The laughter subsided and Jonos continued, "Seriously guys, thanks for coming out, tonight and tomorrow morning and for the next year. This is gonna' be great."

"What is 'this' exactly?" Jimian jested to his own entertainment, "An arduous journey? A dangerous quest? Or maybe a secret mission? Perhaps a daring expedition?"

"Actually I'm officially going with adventure." I said, playing along with his joke, "I know we're asking a lot from you guys, but believe me, we couldn't wish for better company to share this with."

At that point Cephus raised his drink, calling for a toast, "Raise your glasses everyone, not just as crewmen and friends, but as family."

"To *ZANZABAR!*" Jonos and I bellowed.

"TO *ZANZABAR!*" Everyone shouted in response.

The whole gathering participated in the joint cheers and everyone smiled. We continued our celebration laughing and reminiscing about past occurrences as we speculated about what lay ahead on our imminent adventure.

As the evening progressed, people gradually left the party to go and celebrate with their families. Each of us left Jonos and Ayla's to go and spend our last night on Terra in the manner we best saw fit.

After saying goodnight to my three brothers, Ayla, and Jimian as they were the last people there, I caught a bus back to the Shendale station and walked the 30-minute walk to my mom's house in quiet serenity.

Along the way I could hear the occasional firework crack or the bassy beat of a party off in the distance, reminding me of the rest of the world's normal revelry.

I walked into the house and found my mom sitting in the front room. I stood silently in the doorway and watched as she looked through a very old photo album; the kind with printed pictures rather than digital ones.

I sat down next to her, not saying a word. She was looking at pictures of her wedding and honeymoon, Jonos' and my birth, our infant years, birthdays, camping trips, vacations, parties, first days of school; everything from a life that now seemed to be ending. Her husband had left, and now her sons were about to leave. I felt terrible leaving her.

I pulled her close to me, hugged her gently, and whispered that I loved her dearly. She held me tightly and wept quietly into my sleeves.

Eventually she stopped crying and I went to the kitchen to make her some tea. After returning with the tea I sat down with her and we talked late into the night. She eventually got up and moved toward me.

She kissed me on the forehead and told me, "You've got a big day ahead of you. Be careful my son, keep your brother safe and he will keep you safe. Find your father and bring him home. Jorah bless you and keep you."

With that she left me and retired to bed.

I sat on the couch wondering how everyone else's nights were going until I drifted off into a restful sleep where I dreamt of my father, Jonos, and me kicking a soccer ball across an open field on a sunny summer day.

We were children in the dream, only 7 or 8 and we watched in amazement as he would kick the ball high up into the air and then as it fell he would effortlessly settle the ball at his feet.

He was teaching us how to do the same thing, though neither of us could ever kick it as high as he could.

On one occasion he kicked the ball so high up in the air that Jonos and I lost sight of it in the bright sunlight. We saw it again as it fell back down to the ground, though this time our father was not there to settle it. He was nowhere to be seen.

Jonos approached the ball and as I looked at him he was much older. He rolled the ball under his feet and then flicked it up into the air toward me. I moved my foot to settle it as our father had and noticed it was much larger than before, I too had grown in size. I flicked the ball back to Jonos a little higher than he had for me and he settled it at his feet.

He looked toward me and said with a confident grin on his face, "Now it's our turn."

As he said this he flicked the ball up and kicking with all his might, he blasted it up into the air. I traced the ball into the sky and once again lost it in the bright sunlight.

I awoke calmly and realized it was morning. It was Trentia and we were about to set off to find our father.

ZANZABAR awaits, now it's our turn.

United Terran Federation Communique to UTF Chief Defense Minister Luca de Gulliss Forwarded from the Office of UTF Admiral Donas Willison, Commander of NW Amassian Detachment — Pacinus Battalion (via Commander Hirojma Kahn — Station Commander, Fort Kane) 1 January, 3.2221 @05:08:35 TST

Admiral,

At 00:03 hours Pacinus Standard Time on 31 December, 3.2220, an energy spike was registered in the thermosphere above the Amassian Northwest. The reading was recorded and traced to a ranch belonging to Dr. Franzi Mishaya Dorfmund. The energy spike was recorded soon after Dr. Dorfmund received a visitor. The reading was unlike any before detected and was well beyond the capacities of most of our sensors, several monitors red-lined as soon as they picked it up.

Fifty-four minutes later at 00:57 the same energy spike was recorded near to the first. The power readings were again recorded and analyzed. Based on the readings and the initial spikes, it is believed to be a GFD signal; we can safely assume that the doctor has been experimenting with Galaxial Flux Drive technology outside of our protocols and it appears that this mysterious visitor has helped her out.

The local power supply station also reported a massive diversion of power during the period of the signal's activity.

We are investigating this further but believe it to be a remote hack initiated by Dr. Dorfmund. The visitor eluded our tracking and we are currently pursuing all avenues of his identification and capture.

We will continue to monitor the doctor's activities.

Request orders and message forward to Chief Defense Minister.

UTF Commander Hirojma Kahn,
Station Commander, Amassian Pacinus: Fort Kane

United Terran Federation Communique to Admiral Donas Willison and all NW Amassian Station Commanders
From the Office of UTF Chief Defense Minister Luca de Gulliss,
2 January, 3.2221 @08:11:37 TST

Admiral,

Find out what the doctor knows. Track and identify the 'visitor' at all costs. Use of force is permissible.

Chief Defense Minister Luca de Gulliss,
UTF Chairman

Chapter 10: Gaïa

Trentia, the third day of the New Year and the final day of the holiday celebration: our departure day. We were to meet at 13:00 that afternoon in a supermarket parking lot in town. Mom had driven Davriel and me to a vehicle rental dealership where we met with Jonos and Ayla.

There we said our goodbyes before renting the two vans we were going to drive to the parking lot to pick everyone up before continuing on to ZANZABAR.

Our goodbyes were grim and sincere and Mom hugged and kissed each of us, except Davriel whom she only hugged, and wished us the best of luck.

She stayed strong and it wasn't until we'd said goodbye and had gotten into the vans that she finally cried. I only saw a single tear fall from her eyes as I reversed out of the lot and pulled away, waving my hand out the window.

After the four of us drove to the supermarket and pulled the vans into the lot, Cephus was the first of the others to arrive.

He was dropped off by his step dad Dauntlas Jimian, or 'DJ' as everyone called him.

Despite our father Arcus Angelus being Cephus' biological father, DJ was definitely Cephus' Dad and I always envied the adult relationship he had with him.

Although I had to remind myself that it was all relative since Davriel didn't even get a real *child*

-*hood* relationship with our dad.

My thoughts on our whole paternal situation immediately dissipated as I helped Cephus with his bags and exchanged a brief hello with DJ.

He was always concise with his words and always got to the point, perhaps that was because he was a retired UTF Naval Guard Captain; but our conversation was brief and amiable.

Despite my own dismissive views of the UTF, DJ was cool in my books. He always demonstrated the finest qualities of not just a military man, but any man. It was clear where Cephus had gotten his sense of duty and valor, and why he made the decision to go to the Naval Guard Academy.

After my exchange with DJ I briefly wondered what Cephus told him and how he would have felt if he knew that Cephus and I—as well as everyone else present—were considered fugitives from the law and enemies of the UTF, but I pushed the thought aside as more people began to arrive.

Pria and Jimian were the next to arrive and stepped off a local bus, each with a duffel bag and additional smaller travel bags and smiles on their faces. They were deep in the midst of some discussion about a B-list celebrity's exploits in some sci-fi show.

Immediately after them Tytus, Shelyse, and Kaitoh arrived in an over-sized truck that almost looked like a small military troop carrier. Tytus' father was driving it, but I knew it belonged to Tytus.

It was the same truck he used to take when we would all go out shooting in the boonies during our final years of Secondary.

The rumble of its engine was a blast from the past and reminded me of adventures from days gone by, but spurred me to think of future days when the rumble of *ZANZABAR*'s engines would lead us into new adventures.

We greeted all of them in turn and helped them offload and reload their bags as Tytus and Shelyse said their last goodbyes to Tytus' father.

At that point I wondered as to what types of stories or truths people had told their loved ones before leaving. But I barely had any time to consider that before more of our group arrived.

Ander and Devian were dropped off shortly after by Ander's father, both carrying backpacks and duffel bags, while Ander carried two additional medical bags and a crate with a large red cross on it.

Regarding everyone's bags, I hoped that people packed well enough for themselves. Not knowing exactly what to bring on an adventure into the far reaches of the galaxy I mostly thought to bring survival gear and a durable wardrobe, but most importantly a good pair of shoes; boots actually.

That was one thing both of my brothers who'd been in the service told me about survival instances or anything of a similar regard, *the shoes you wear can make all the difference.*

I hoped that everyone had packed everything they needed — there wouldn't be any chance of coming back to get something.

By 14:05 we had 12 out of the 13 possible crewmates present. I was beginning to worry about our last member Lizia, and whether or not she was going to make it. We'd already given out the Peliato-

-nium bricks and essentially paid everyone their first shares, but I still wasn't entirely convinced of her involvement on this whole thing.

How much was it all worth to her? Was her connection with our father enough to warrant such a leap of faith?

Were we close enough friends that she would risk everything for us and our cause?

Suddenly I realized the full weight of the situation: it was real, it was *actually* happening. We were about to leave our world to go blindly into the depths of the unknown to search for our long-lost father; a microscopic needle in the colossal haystack that was the universe. Well at least we had Zan to help guide us. That thought did comfort me, but I couldn't shake my unease.

Oh hell, what am I doing? Asking all of these people to just give up their lives to come with me?

I looked all around me. My brothers and closest friends were smiling and embracing, stowing away their belongings and beginning to take their seats in the vans, anxious as they were to depart.

A gut wrenching feeling was beginning to take hold of me and I could feel my body tense up. The world around me slowed and I could sense the tension in the air.

A hand very coolly and calmly set itself on my shoulder from behind, giving a reassuring squeeze.

"I'm not too late am I?" Lizia said.

I turned around to face her, her crystal blue eyes locked with my own. I noticed that her hair was lighter than I'd seen it last—at least before I saw her recently at the airfield. It was her original russet brown color, pulled back in a ponytail with long slender bangs on either side framing her face.

She was carrying a large hiking pack on her back and a duffle bag to her side, and she was smiling from ear to ear.

Everything around me seemed to stop for a moment as I considered the enormity of what her arrival meant; what we were about to embark on.

The two of us stood there for a moment, locked in a trance, before she lunged as if to start a punching match and playfully hit my stomach and shoulder.

"Come on. Are we doing this or what?"

I came out of my daze as she locked her arm in mine and pulled me toward everyone and the vans as Cephus and Devian came over to help her with her bags.

"Yeah, we're doing this." I said, mostly to myself.

After everyone had arrived and we packed up the vans — it was a tight squeeze with 6 people in one van and 7 in the other, plus all of our gear, many people even had bags on top of them for the 3-hour ride — we started out for the harbor where Zan had secluded the ship.

Zan had sent me a general set of coordinates to head to that were west of the local principal city of Sevura. Once we'd passed beyond the city limits she would send additional directions, bit by bit, indicating where to go, as her current location was one that was just as concealed from us as it was to anyone we were trying to dupe.

We arrived at the rather isolated bay in the neighboring locality of Baltirond, after following Zan's sporadic directions for nearly 3 hours.

The dock was in rather dismal conditions—as was most of Baltirond locality in general, given its general neglect—but was large enough to fit small freighters in.

It clearly used to be a major port but was now entirely vacant, save for one rickety motorized jalopy.

Both sides of the dock's "U" shape were clear as was the space between them, except for the jalopy which lay anchored at the base of the dock. We parked the vans in adjacent spots and then set to unloading while waiting for Zan's final confirmation and coordinates.

Shortly after disembarking and completely unloading the vans my Link flickered on with the same blue as before that indicated Zan was there.

I looked at the light and tapped it, but was surprised when I didn't see her figure but instead saw a brief message that read:

LM: Two by two out on the blue,
Outside the cove where ships did rove,
Under trees you'll find your ease,
Above the tide, you'll board your ride.

A riddle?

I realized that at this point we couldn't leave anything up to chance and we had to play it smart until we were safely off planet—really from that point on.

The UTF knew that we were somewhere in the area and if they had somehow managed to track us we still needed to maintain a low profile.

I thought again about the message and quickly realized that two by two we were to ride that rickety beat-up jalopy out past the cove of the harbor to find ZANZABAR.

'Under trees' must mean underneath the overhanging trees that frame the banks of the cove.

The last part slightly confused me though as I figured that if ZANZABAR was above the tide, we should easily have been able to see it, but that was not the case.

I decided the last part could be deciphered once we were actually out beneath the trees. It was to be quite the process as we soon discovered.

Jonos, Davriel, and I — having forsaken the two by two part of Zan's message — were the first to make our way out past the inlet to ZANZABAR; which we soon found delicately hidden in the shallows of this backwater region of the peninsula. Covered by dense foliage, ZANZABAR was well concealed to any onlookers.

As we arrived we found that the topside was exposed enough so that we could enter through the dorsal launch tubes which currently sat empty and were at just the right height in the water for us to board with minimal difficulty — *above the tide, you'll board your ride.*

Each of us took the first few minutes aboard to secure our quarters which we'd already claimed from our previous visits. To save time nobody unpacked just yet, and Jonos and Davriel quickly set out to readying ZANZABAR for our immediate departure.

Though I had no doubt that Zan had already made the necessary preparations and was well capable of carrying them out better than any of us.

I then returned to the dock in the jalopy to transport the next of the crew. Cephus and Ayla were the next two to come, as they were clearly next in our order of succession.

Upon arriving they settled into their rooms, Cephus had selected the second bunk beneath the main corridor—between mine and Davriel's—and Ayla already had her room set with Jonos in the first officer's room.

In addition to the main crew quarters along the neck of ZANZABAR there were two other levels of quarters; above the main corridor there were staterooms for the captain—or shipmaster— and the first officer, as well as honored guests and dignitaries; below the deck there were additional double and quadruple bunks for the pilots of the support crafts.

Upon bringing Cephus and Ayla aboard I quickly realized that I was to play ferryman throughout the entire boarding process.

And so I ferried back and forth between the dock and ZANZABAR for nearly an hour, bringing her crew members aboard. Tytus and Shelyse came next, followed by Kaitoh and Ander, Devian and Lizia, and finally Pria and Jimian.

Despite the building nerves, excitement, and

anxiety as we approached our departure time my mind was entirely fixated on the last moments of my time on this world before venturing off into the wild unknown.

Each time I ferried someone I felt as though they thought and felt the same. This resulted in rather somber and quiet rides for the majority of the hour, until Jimian and Pria came along with their rambunctious banter and uplifting nature.

"So which of you two is the captain?" Jimian asked with a smile.

"What?" I distractedly replied.

"Which one of you gets to be Captain Angelus?" Pria clarified. "Who gets to sit in the Captain's chair?"

"Yeah, who gets the Captain's quarters?" Jimian persisted.

"Uh…" I stammered out, "Well Arcos ships don't have captains, they have Shipmasters, but I guess… I guess it'd have to be Zan? She's kind of the one in charge."

They both chuckled before Jimian proceeded to say, "Well at least it's a good thing the ship has *two moms* to go with its *two dads*, how would that one have worked out if not?"

Pria and I laughed and I was enjoyably distracted up until we got to the topside launch tubes for the last time.

Jimian and Pria hauled up their bags and climbed through the opening end of the left tube hatch, proceeding down the length of the tube to the aft ladder, then down to the main deck and all the way forward toward the quarters and the bridge.

Watching them proceed down the dimly lit tube I turned back toward the shore and the dock and beheld our vans. After renting them we'd arranged for a same day pickup and someone would be here to retrieve them soon. We wouldn't get the security deposit we made back but I didn't worry too much.

Instead I looked back with a sense of foreboding before our departure; this was the first step before the giant leap.

Catching my breath, I returned to the moment and turned the jalopy around to where it could easily catch the tide and find its way ashore, hopefully.

After that I climbed over and nearly all the way into the open tube hatch. I then kicked off the jalopy sending it on its way toward the shore as I climbed aboard ZANZABAR. Making my way down the empty launch tube I found Pria and Jimian being helped by Cephus, Devian, and Ander down on the main deck.

I sealed the launch tube before descending the ladder to the lower deck.

Before the hatches sealed completely I watched as the jalopy drifted toward the shore and took in the last naked view of my home world.

The hatches sealed shut and a secondary blast covering sealed shut afterward with a definitive clamor, solidifying this new enclosure.

Ship life had officially begun.

As I walked down the main deck corridor I heard quite the hustle and bustle of people settling in, and tasks being tended to. All around bunks and quarters were secured, packs were stowed, and people got settled in.

I made my way toward the bridge where I found Jonos, Cephus, Kai, and Tytus. Jonos was already settled into the pilot's chair and tinkering with something, and Cephus was at the navigation post, while Kai manned and familiarized himself with the communications array. Tytus was busy stowing a rather indiscreet gun-locker in the storage racks available in ZANZABAR's bridge.

"Plan on running into trouble?" Kai asked.

"Y'never know, always good to be prepared." Tytus answered back.

"Hopefully we don't have to worry about it coming to that though." I added.

"Always better to have it and not need it, than to need it and not have it." Cephus chimed in, before adding in the ancient Latenos, "Sampor paratos."

"Tell me Zan," I changed the subject after a short silence, "Are we ready to depart?"

"Yes Savos. We're awaiting the go-ahead to launch."

"Jonos," I said to my brother, "You ready?"

"I was born ready! Oh sorry, you wouldn't know that, 'cause I was born before you!" He grinned like a madman as he made his final preflight adjustments; he was clearly in a very good mood.

"I suppose you should probably say something…" Cephus said to me, "You know, pre-castoff speech, or something like that."

I hesitated for a moment as Cephus had addressed me.

Was he insinuating that I was somehow the captain? Was that how he saw it? Was that how everyone saw it?

I hadn't quite thought of it in that way up until that moment. Jonos and I had discovered *ZANZABAR* together and I didn't feel right claiming myself to be captain, or shipmaster, over him.

I admittedly did feel responsibility for things though, as I was one of the lead catalysts for our current situation. But again, it was always Jonos and me who'd started this.

I hadn't really thought about it though; as between my brothers, none of us was ever an all-out leader.

Sure, we had leadership qualities and led in certain instances, but nobody ever commanded anyone in that type of manner.

Furthermore, I did not wish to come across as arrogant or selfish. This adventure, this voyage, it was meant for them as much as it was for me.

I looked at Jonos, who was slightly lower than I was due to the bridge arrangement on *ZANZABAR*, and he looked back and he nodded.

I realized I was thinking on it too long when Cephus called to me again, "Hey! You gonna' say something or what?"

"Oh yeah, uh…, Zan? Can you patch me through to the whole ship?"

"Yes Savos. Go ahead."

"Ladies and gentlemen, friends and family, this is your cap—this is *Savos* speaking. Once again I want to thank you all for dedicating yourselves to this task—*adventure*." I paused, reflective on the word choice but lacking anything better in the moment, continued on:

"This probably won't be easy, but we'll be

here for each other—for all it's worth—to see it through. One year is all we ask of you, but should you find that you cannot continue or would not continue, we would understand and do not hold you to stay any longer than you are willing or able."

Again I paused, giving weight to the gravity of the precipice on which we now stood.

"We now go forth to explore the far unknown reaches of this galaxy and of space beyond, in search of life, in search of hope, in search of a man so near and dear to all of us, that we will risk the vast unknown of space to find him. If any of you have any reservations, now's your last chance."

I paused for a long moment of silence that seemed to echo throughout every corner of the ship.

A moment passed.

Then another.

Finally, after no one responded in any way I continued on, "We're about to leave Terra with a course set for the planet Arco; the planet of our ancestors, and the first place on our hopeful search for our father. Before we launch however we're gonna' need everyone to take a seat and get settled for the ride. Those of you not at key operational posts during flight are to convene in the galley and strap in for flight."

I then turned my attention to Zan, "Zan, where are we with the warp drive?"

"The drive is currently charged and ready to execute Savos. I currently have an ECM shroud concealing its power signature."

"Excellent. Jonos, we're all yours."

Jonos then keyed a few controls and through-

-out the ship there was a rumbling like a giant turbine powering on and spinning up. Jonos manipulated the controls and immediately we lurched up a few feet and I grabbed onto the handrail of the center dais.

From our submerged position in the bridge we could slowly see water rushing down in front of us off the viewport.

Jonos had activated the first of ZANZABAR's thrusters and we were taking off.

I made my way to the Shipmaster's chair though didn't necessarily feel that I fulfilled the qualifications to sit there, but hastily strapped myself in before we'd fully launched. Everyone else took their seats throughout the ship.

There was a final lurch as ZANZABAR completely breached the water's surface and lifted into the air. We hovered mere meters above the water for a few moments before Jonos then adjusted the power on the maneuvering thrusters and gave us more rear power thrust from the main engines and we began our ascent.

"Everyone, now would be a very good time to take a seat, strap in, and hold on to something." Jonos shouted over the calamity of takeoff.

Waiting just a few more moments, he then gunned the controls and shot us on an immediate space bound trajectory.

I nervously hoped that everyone had enough time to get seated and strap in, and that all their gear was safely stowed before Jonos' antics.

"Jonos, we need to pass through the exosphere before engaging the warp drive. Two-

-hundred-fifty Taramels ought to be far enough. Do take care getting us there." Zan's voice was still audible above the calamity of ZANZABAR's takeoff.

"No promises." He jested back.

Suddenly I was fixated on the view racing past my eyes in the viewport. The sky roared past us instantaneously as clouds and air began to rush by.

We launched higher and higher into the atmosphere, watching our entire world pass by.

My heart raced as the light blues and wisps of white clouds in the sky slowly dimmed and darkened to the midnight blue and black of space.

Specs of white then dominated the viewports as the vast starry void of space was all we could see.

The timing was ephemeral; we'd cleared the thermosphere and now approached the highest reaches of the exosphere in what seemed like mere seconds. ZANZABAR was incredible, and Jonos was clearly going to enjoy flying and testing her limits, though ultimately Zan still handled much of the ship's happenings.

No doubt they'll have plenty of time to test each other.

Before we fully embarked on our intergalactic voyage I thought to address the crew once more, "Alright everyone, this is it; we're activating the trans-dimensional drive in T-minus 15 seconds. If you're religious, you might consider saying a prayer to Jorah."

I then turned my attention to Zan, "Zan, finalize jump procedures and input coordinates."

"Coordinates confirmed Savos. Warp drive spin up complete. The system is primed and ready for ignition. I will take my leave now, to administer to the warp-field regulators. I will return after our emergence from the warporal realm."

With that, Zan's image disappeared from the command dais and we were on our own.

"Ten seconds to activation." Jonos began the countdown.

"Nav systems are green." Cephus added.

"Coms are good." Kai tacked on.

"Engineering is good for a go." Pria chimed in over the com.

"Life support is solid." Tytus followed.

"All flight systems are green." Jonos finally concluded.

The room around us seemed to draw closer within and the lights dimmed as the warp drive began amassing power and taking effect. I could only imagine what the whole thing was like for anyone else in the ship, but was cut short of any thought about it as Jonos continued his countdown.

"Five seconds to activation. Four... three..."

"Alright everyone, here we go." Cephus said.

Now it's our turn.

"2... 1.... See you on the other si—."

***

In a flash and an instant our world turned upside down and inside out before returning in a jarring fashion and we entered what we could only call reality.

My senses slowly began returning to me and I realized that I was sitting in the Shipmaster's chair on the bridge of *ZANZABAR* holding on for dear life.

I realized that my brothers and friends were around me and I could hear Zan's voice, muffled but distinct above all else, as she reactivated after completing the jump.

"Galaxial jump complete. We've returned to normal space." She said in a smug voice before trailing off, "Hmm…. Something's off here…"

I then heard the stifled voices of my brothers and companions as Jonos and the others called out from their respective positions giving the all clear.

Before I fully came to my senses I beheld a far-off voice singing. Soft and tender, the voice seemed to penetrate my consciousness, enticing me.

I could feel it all throughout and I could truly understand its pure positive force and good nature. Its full and loving sound surrounded all I knew and captured my full focus.

The voice drew me toward the sight that now shown through the main viewport and there before my eyes, floated a beautiful emerald green and ocean blue planet.

Its seas and oceans looked serene and wondrous and we could see the massive milky swirl of clouds and weather systems that appeared all over the planet.

The planet's beautiful landscapes were captivating and ornamented with great lights that emanated from several spots on its surface.

Gazing at the lights I felt such bewilderment I could not fully regain my senses.

Even as Zan's voice could be heard in the background, troubled over some trivial matter, I could not fully comprehend the magnitude of what floated before us.

Suddenly I became aware of a distinct voice speaking directly to me, greeting me in kindness, *Well met, son of Arco and friend. It is good of you to come. Long has it been since last we heard from the Arcos. How is it you have come here? What news would you have of Arco and its peoples?*

What?

Who are you that approach? Of what Arcosan family do you belong? It has been several generations since last we had any contact from the Arcos; we feared they were all lost.

My name is Savos... son of Arcus Angelus. With me are my brothers; Jonos, Davriel, and Cephus. We come from Terra but are Arcosan by heritage. Our companions however, are all Terran. Who are you?

My name is Evï u'Neréas. I am the Prime'ïos. The keeper of this planetary realm called Gaïa: the life of the Solara system. Welcome.

Thank y— I had begun thinking before my head suddenly pounded and my ears popped as I seemed to lose focus with the voice and regained focus on my current surrounding. I now distinctly heard Jonos' voice stating that we'd completed our spin down cycle and we were ready to make planet fall.

"Successful jump. Spin down cycle completed," Jonos repeated, "Kai, begin scanning for planetary transmissions and welcomes. Cephus, let's figure out someplace to land."

"Roger."

You are more than welcome to land at Dal'Sera, The High Citadel; the Capitol city of Gaïa. The voice returned, *We would be well pleased to host a visitor of the Arcos and to hear of your tale and your people. I will inform our emissaries of your arrival.*

The voice was so welcoming and genuine that I had no doubt of its goodness or intent.

I then heard Kai's voice suddenly over the excitement, "Contact from the surface. They're speaking Terran standard! I'm patching it through now."

"Welcome, unknown Arcosan vessel, hail and good tidings! On behalf of Prime'ïos Evï u'Neréas and the Gaïos people, we welcome you to Gaïa." A foreign sounding, yet clearly discernible and amiable voice welcomed us.

"Wait what? Gaïa?" Davriel blurted, from one of the jump-seats behind me.

"Follow them down." I said, "The Gaïos will have answers for us. They aren't Arcos, but we ought to check them out."

"Okay." Jonos said, sounding somewhat hesitant.

We then felt Jonos maneuver ZANZABAR on an approach vector toward the planet. Gaïa loomed in front of us and grew in the viewport as we descended down to the first uncharted territory of our existence; another unknown, intelligent—and somehow telepathic—race existed.

And we were about to see it live.

Thank you. I told the voice.

AÏA wills all to do for the good of all. The voice responded, before disappearing again.

"So wait," Cephus began, "where are we?"

"That's what I've been trying to tell every-

-one," Zan blurted out indignantly, "We're at Gaïa. Not Arco. Something went wrong with the jump. These are the appropriate Galaxial coordinates for Arco but we somehow entered normal space at Gaïa. I'm trying to figure it out as we speak. However," her mood suddenly changed, "as Savos surmised, they will most assuredly have answers. Gaïa is the home of the Gaïos. They are the sibling race to the Arcos."

She continued on in an encyclopedic tone, informing us of what she knew about the planet and its people.

"Arcosan and Gaïan legend has it that the Great Light birthed the two races in its image to populate its worlds, love one another, and to proliferate in its celestial body. Each race was given its own planet to govern and cultivate. The two species have lived in prosperity for millennia. It is most strange and disturbing that they haven't heard from the Arcos in *generations*. Hopefully that isn't a sign of ill tidings on Arco..."

"Hmm... well this should be quite the interesting meeting then." I smiled as I looked forward to our imminent meeting with the Gaïan Prime'ïos, and any possible answers into our heritage and maybe even our father's whereabouts.

As we entered the atmosphere we noted similar elements that occur during atmospheric reentry back on Terra. The space around us and the surface of the ship glowed in intense fiery oranges and reds, the ship rumbled ever so slightly throughout reentry and I looked around the bridge as we entered the atmosphere; everyone looked on with apprehension as it was all of our first atmosph-

-eric entry and we were landing on an unknown world full of mystery and wonder.

We all held on intensely as Jonos brought us down.

Everyone remained quiet and tentative as we made our approach.

Even Zan remained quite save for the intermittent updates she would give us; no doubt she was perplexed and intent on figuring out what happened during the jump that put us off course.

We finally broke through the last layers of the atmosphere and found ourselves flying through a gorgeous sunset decorated with large puffy orange clouds. A soft pastel of fuchsia, magenta, and vermillion coated the sky as the sun set and the violet twilight sky began to edge up on the horizon.

Zan broke everyone's captivation as we continued our descent toward the planet, "The High Citadel is approximately 300 taramels west of our current location. I'm marking its position on your nav display now.

"Keep it steady Jonos," I said.

"Yeah. *I know*."

I then briefly addressed the rest of the crew who up until now had been strapped in and seated in the galley, "We've broken through this planet's atmosphere and the view is quite stunning. Seeing as we've cleared atmosphere and are within a safe gravitational environment you are free to move about the ship. Any of you who are interested in seeing another world, now's your chance..."

"Imminent Arcosan guests," the Gaïos voice broke over the ship's intercom once more, "As you approach *Dal'Sera* you will see a path of azure and jade lights illuminate before you; follow these lights as they will guide you to the landing dais we have delegated for you."

"Thank you." Kai replied.

Suddenly, I again became conscious of the singing I'd heard before. This time it had a much clearer sound and I almost felt as though I could exit *ZANZABAR* and follow its luscious sound to its source.

The singer was beautiful, tonal, and harmonious. I looked around and wondered if anyone else present could hear it; but then the clouds cleared and suddenly, before our eyes, one of the most breathtaking objects any of us had ever beheld, appeared.

Dal'Sera, The High Citadel, floated in the sky before us, shining golden with the final reflections of the setting sun. Comprised of two enormous concentric circles, its interior circle's curved surfaces had only just begun reflecting the dim pinks and purples that crept through the sky.

Its lights gleamed brighter than the purest gems imaginable and were tantalizing to behold.

The inner circle consisted of larger structures and had the appearance of a protected city center with an impassibly curved surface wall, while its outer circle appeared to be lower rising, outlying domestic areas that must have housed the natives.

A vast array of colors and lights adorned the immensity of the floating city's outer circle; the small spires, obelisks, and pylons occupying its surface were lit up as beautifully as the city's epicenter. It greatly resembled a Terran neighborhood lit up for Endyears, though the lights here were far more brilliant and far more magnificent.

Right before our eyes we began to see another set of lights appear.

Just as we were told, azure blue lights, coupled with jade green ones hung motionless and baseless in the night sky, leading us to our destination.

No one saw where the lights came from or what caused them and our bewilderment was suddenly intensified as more people entered the bridge to witness this splendor.

Everyone on the bridge immediately noticed the sudden presence of all 13 of our crew members as the rest joined us to observe our descent into this mysterious and magnificent civilization. People sat on laps or leaned over railings and stations to see what lay before us and there was scarcely room to see through ZANZABAR's viewports.

"Impressive."

"That really is somethin' else."

"That's gorgeous."

"Whoa…"

"Incredible!"

"Holy mother of Jorah."

Everyone looked on with their own fascination and wonder as we approached the floating city; but one thing was certain, other sentient life was out there, and we were moments away from meeting it.

***

The landing dais the lights led us to was well within the Inner Circle and was above many of the other structures around. Much like everything else around, it was adorned with lights.

As it was just past sunset the speckled lights added to the magnificence of the scene.

As Jonos maneuvered the ship to land we noticed several figures waiting on the dais. They appeared Terran in stature and presence though their garb was far different from our own.

Everyone on the bridge held on to something or someone and had a look of anxiety or excitement on their face as Jonos maneuvered ZANZABAR directly over the dais and landed the ship with a satisfying and solid thump.

"Well, shall we go meet these so called Guyos?" Cephus broke the silence.

"Yeah." I said with a smile.

"Let's do it." Jonos echoed and we all began gathering ourselves and making our way to the hangar door as it was the lowest access point.

"Hold on a second. Shouldn't we find out if it's safe? I don't want to step outside and realize I can't breathe or something." Jimian said, only half-arguing, before continuing in his usual jests, "I don't want to have a *Full Remembrance* kind of moment and have my eyes swell up and pop out of my head while my skin burns to a crisp."

Jimian was ever the kidder, bringing up yet another sci-fi movie we'd all watched as teenagers.

Not a bad idea though...

"We clearly entered some kind of atmosphere

when we made planet-fall." Davriel said.

"Zan," Jonos started, "What's it like out there? Can we breathe?"

"Of course. The atmosphere is comprised of 73% nitrogen, 26% oxygen, and trace percentages of other gases. The Gaïos and the Arcos are quite similar to Terrans, not only do they look much alike, they also function quite alike as well."

I wonder just how much alike we all are...

"So yes," Zan continued, "you can breathe, Jimian won't have to worry about his eyes exploding out of his head like the... *Full Remembrance* moment. What is that by the way? Despite scouring nearly all Terran history I don't recall hearing of any *Full Remembrance*? Also, the temperature here is comparable to that of Terra so you should not need to worry about its climate conditions and freezing or burning to death either."

"It's this movie where this guy is on Ma..." Jimian started before being cut off.

"Don't worry about it." Cephus jibed. "He can tell you all about it later."

"I look forward to it." She countered.

"Thanks Zan." I said, "The ship's yours while we're away. Well everyone, shall we?"

"I believe it's mine while you're here too." She joked as we began leaving the bridge. "Jimian, I really would like to hear all about *Full Remembrance* later, so do *remember* to tell me."

"Okay!" I heard Jimian holler as I made my way past the bunk hatches to everyone's quarters and down to the main hold, followed by my brothers and friends.

We anxiously made our way through the ship's corridor and down the various ladders and staircases before coming to the ship's hold, which stowed many of our main supplies for the journey.

We made our way past the heavily packed cases and toward the front hatch.

I keyed the door switch and anxiously awaited as it depressurized, then one by one the safety latches slid open and I opened the smaller door-hatch and was the first to exit our ship; the first to step on a completely different planet, far away from home, with nothing but faith and hope leading us on.

One by one we crossed over the threshold; Jonos came after me, Cephus and Davriel next, followed by everyone else one at a time, coming into a new world.

As I took in my surroundings I realized that the night was waxing and the moon of the planet was coming up over the horizon, large and prevalent in the starry night sky.

Despite the darkness coming on, it still remained light. Stars could be seen in the night sky and the rising moon provided another light that was calm and cool.

"This place is beautiful." Ayla said as she looked at her surroundings in awe.

"Incredible. Absolutely incredible." Jonos followed.

"I don't mean to detract from the splendor of this, but can we get back to how they speak our language?" Kai asked.

"Who knows," Ander answered, "but I'm sure

we'll find out."

I had heard what Kai said but was far too distracted by the moon I saw coming over the horizon, "That moon is massive."

"Seriously though, it's *way* bigger than ours." Shelyse added.

"Guys, what if it's not a moon at all, what if it's a giant space station?" Jimian, referencing yet another sci-fi franchise from our youth and inciting a few snickers; though we immediately resumed our gaze, as if entranced by the splendor of the moon.

"It sure is gorgeous." Lizia added.

"It sure is." I concluded as we all stared up into the sky.

"It is called Lunarïo," a soft female voice called out as it approached, "it is the light of the night-star, the father of Gaïa; he gives us watchful light and protects us from the encroaching darkness while Solara, the mother of Gaïa, sleeps. Greetings and glad tidings Arcos and Terrans; I am Laurales e'Yazela and this is Brandu Bracaras, we are the High Citadel's Emissariat. We will escort you to meet the Prime'ïos."

As we looked on at our new hosts I noticed just how different their raiment was to our own. There were twelve of them in total, six males and six females.

The two leading the party, Laurales and Brandu, stood in front of the other ten, all of whom smiled yet remained motionless.

The females wore crisp blues and greens, and soft purples; their flowing gowns clung tightly to the skin on the torso before cascading off in perfectly balanced furls down the length of their gowns.

As it was growing dark out and the moon was almost fully out and shinning, I could see that their clothes were darkened but they were somehow reflecting what light there was, causing their clothes to shine like glass and glitter much like the lights of the buildings all around us.

Additionally, they wore elegant headpieces and delicate ornaments on their wrists and necks, bangles and jeweled necklaces that brilliantly reflected the light from above while emanating their own light from beautifully colored gems.

The males wore form fitting tunics of matte colors, bright grays, dusky reds, and deep greens, and were also adorned with jewelry, in the form of rings and elegantly jeweled collars that hung from the neck; additionally, each male carried an ornate staff. They all varied in height, but seemed comparable to Terrans, though taller and slenderer.

All of their skin tones differed with pigments similar to our own, but no matter what, they all seemed to be somehow lighter, near glowing, as if they were almost made of light.

"Greetings," I finally replied, "I am Savos. These are my brothers, Jonos, Davriel, and Cephus."

Jonos then added, "We are sons of Arco, of the family Angelus — though our mothers are all Terran.

We have ventured from Terra with 9 other friends; Ayla, Tytus, Shelyse, Kaitoh, Jimian, Ander, Pria, Devian, and Lizia. We've come in search of our father, Arcus Angelus. We're very pleased to be here in your midst. Thank you for receiving us."

"I assure you, the pleasure is ours." Laurales replied with a beautiful smile and a bow.

She was among the shortest of the Gaïos welcoming party with a beautiful olive-colored face and long dark hair with several layers of auburn and goldenrod highlights. She had an air of genuine appreciation and interest about her; as did the other Gaïos present.

The one named Brandu had sleek white hair and was taller and darker than the rest then spoke, "If you would please follow me, we can go and meet the Prime'ïos, he is expecting you."

He gestured to a staircase that appeared off to the side of the landing platform.

"Thank you." I replied to him before turning to everyone and gesturing for us to follow.

Brandu and Laurales led us down a winding staircase that seemed to magically levitate and light up as each step was walked upon. We walked through beautiful rooftop gardens with inordinate amounts of plants, flowers, and jewels of light; everywhere we looked there seemed to be some sort of ornament reflecting the light of the moon and stars.

As we walked Laurales told us about *Dal'Sera* and about the Gaïos people; she explained that it was the capitol city of Gaïa and contained the majority of its people.

"There are few communities that live on the planet's surface in the various livable terrains it offers, but many of us have chosen to live here, amidst the clouds, to be closer to the light of Lunarïo and Solara when they grace the sky, so too to be clos-

-er to the heavenly sound of the cosmos."

Brandu then continued saying, "All Gaïos hear the Music of AÏA through the light of the Cosmos. The stars sing to us, speak to us, and guide us. We strive always to be in their presence."

"AÏA? What's that?" Ander asked.

"Sounds more like *who's* that." Devian followed up.

"Yes, who is AÏA?" Pria echoed.

"AÏA is the Light, AÏA is the Creator, the one from whom all life comes." Brandu replied.

"Interesting," Cephus replied, "so he's like your god?"

"You misunderstand." Laurales replied with a charming smile and snicker, "AÏA is not a man, nor is it a person in the sense that you understand. AÏA is a presence, a being of omnipotence, ubiquitous in all realms of being. AÏA is love. AÏA is life."

"Oh." Cephus said, suddenly moved to silence.

"Your interest is virtuous, friends and travelers, but save your quandaries for the Prime'ïos, he will have all the answers you seek, and more beyond." Brandu said.

"One more thing though," Kai persisted, "how is it that you speak our language?"

"Yet another excellent question; Terran inquisitive nature is simply astounding," Brandu answered, or rather didn't answer.

"But that is yet another question that the Prime'ïos will answer when you meet him. All in due time Terran and Arcosan friends."

As Brandu spoke the stairs we'd been walking

on ended at a grand chamber door. At some point they had turned upward and I realized that we were higher up than we had been when we landed. I took a look around and again noticed the grandiose view of *Dal'Sera*, the High Citadel. Its majesty was paralleled by its foreign design and the giant moon making its way up into the night sky, and still we couldn't help but marvel at what we beheld.

Laurales and Brandu then drew our attention to the door in front of us.

It had beautiful runes in it that somewhat resembled the Arcosan runes we'd encountered on *ZANZABAR* but with a more subdued look. The runes glowed with the starlight and changed colors through the spectrum and looked somewhat similar to our own written language but were far too ornate to decipher.

"The Prime'ïos resides beyond this door." Brandu stated as he tapped one of the runes causing it to change color. "He will be most thrilled to meet you."

"This is where we take our leave, though we will surely see you again for the welcome feast tomorrow. It will be truly spectacular as it has been some time since we have entertained visitors, not to mention the First Born and the Ordained Children." Laurales added.

"A feast huh? I like the sound of that." Tytus chimed in as most of our group agreed.

"Ordained Children?" Ayla asked quizzically.

"Go now, and seek your answers, sons of Angelus and Terran friends, the Prime'ïos awaits you."

With that, Laurales and Brandu bowed and began descending the steps with their entourage—who'd all remained perfectly silent throughout our walk from the landing dais. We all stood motionless as they continued their descent without hesitation or further word, before the lights on the door captured our attention.

Before us, the lights changed and shone in unison and the door cracked open from a seam that appeared out of nowhere.

An immense light burst through the opening doors and all of us recoiled, pulling arms and hands up to block the intense light. Before our eyes could adjust though, we were suddenly engulfed in darkness. For a moment I panicked.

Is this a trap? Did the Gaïos just betray us?

Suddenly all around us the room lit up and in an instant we could see and what we saw was truly remarkable.

The vastness of the room was occupied with stars, planets, nebulae, and all things celestial. Massive gas giants floating around supergiant suns appeared and rotated around the immense room.

Comets could be seen trailing from one end of the room to another, nebulae floated in nascent beginnings, and amidst it all was the light of stars; countless stars of brilliant light specked the room.

From where we stood it seemed as though there was no door to the room and that we entered in the dead center of the chamber.

Despite being in the middle, there was no way to tell where the room ended and where it began. The floor beneath us looked no different than the ceiling overhead; everywhere we looked there was the vast beauty and splendor of the cosmos. We stood there, bewildered in wonder for what felt like a lifetime before a smooth and sagacious voice spoke up:

"Welcome intrepid visitors, Arco sons of Angelus, and Terran progeny. Long has it been since last we saw any of your kind. I am Evï u'Neréas; Chronicler of the Solus Hexus, Emissary of the Light, High Seer of the Gaïos, and the Prime'ïos of Gaïa. Welcome, Ordained Children of AÏA."

Chapter 11: Chronicles

"You are no doubt bemused and have many questions," The Prime'ïos began, "and all of them shall be answered in due time. But for now, we will start with the most important one: Ayla, would you please speak your quandary for all to hear."

What?

I was absolutely dumbstruck.

What question is more important than my own? What's more important than finding out what happened to our father? After all, isn't that why we're here in the first place?

My borderline indignation was noticed by some of my companions as well as the Prime'ïos — who no doubt didn't need to read my facial expression to know what I was thinking as he could very clearly read our minds, based on knowing what Ayla wanted to ask.

"Do not fret, son of Angelus, your questions will be answered in due time, but first you must understand where your father's absence and your arrival here on Gaïa fit into the grand symphony of the cosmos."

The Prime'ïos gestured to the space around us with arms raised; again pointing out how positively vast and widespread the cosmos were.

"Ayla, if you will…"

"Yes, thank you Lord Prime'ïos," Ayla said, stepping forward.

At this point my focus shifted and I legitimately considered what question Ayla had that was so imperative.

"Laurales mentioned the *Ordained Children* before we entered your chamber, and you did once more just now. But you were clearly referring to all of us, not just Jonos and his Arcosan brothers, but those of us who are full-blooded Terran as well. Who *are* the Ordained Children?"

Of course!

I suddenly realized my haste and determination to find my father had clouded my usual curiosity.

"Yes, who are they indeed," The Prime'ïos started, "to answer your question Ayla, we must travel back in time, before the universe began, before time, before life, before AÏA..."

What happened next was utterly extraordinary and visually surpassed everything we'd seen of Gaïa, ZANZABAR, Terra, and anything else.

The room suddenly went black. Blacker than the asphalt of Terran roads, blacker than the hulls of UTF stealth fighters, blacker than the depths of the deepest Terran ocean, blacker than the darkest midnight sky. Not a flicker of light could be seen anywhere and for an instant I wondered if we'd all died and this is what came after life. The Prime'ïos' voice had disappeared with the light, as did my companions' presence, and it seemed as though I was alone.

Suddenly, a small dot of light appeared in the infinite blackness.

It was miniscule and was hardly noticeable but it began to grow and intensify.

As the light grew in size and intensity it began radiating heat.

It was a warm and tender heat, like that of a mother-bird incubating her eggs, but eventually the light stopped growing and its heat subsided.

The light began to slowly pulsate with increasing intensity; once, then twice, then a third time. On the third time there was a massive glow, almost like a bomb exploding—though far brighter and more powerful than any bomb imaginable.

After the light subsided and my eyes adjusted I saw more lights appear. These lights were stretched out as far as I could see and amidst them were smeared colors. Vivid oranges and neon greens were interspersed with lush reds and vibrant purples, and all the while there were pinpoints of light. They were the stars, planets, and nebulae of the universe.

I was staring at the beginning of the universe.

Recognizing that, I further regained my senses and noticed that my brothers and companions were all staring in bewilderment alongside me; we all watched as the cosmos began their millennia long movements. Planetary bodies within solar systems inside galaxies contained in clusters floated around the universe which all seemed to center on the original light.

The light had calmed and settled from its brightest color to a warm orangey-yellow hue and all seemed fine in existence.

But the warmth and happiness was not to last, just as abruptly as things began, they rapidly started to change. The light began to dim and shrink away from existence.

Just before going out, the light drastically changed and heated once more.

This time it was violent in its heating and it burned with an intensity we had not yet seen. Despite heating up the light still seemed to sink from its former position eventually stopping its descent as it landed on a nearby star.

Suddenly it began to pulsate, far more intensely however, and this time its pulses lashed out against the surrounding space around the star. Again it pulsated three times and each time I could feel the space around me waver and crack. The light then began to superheat and turned white-hot before suddenly and cataclysmically erupting in a shower of sparks; shedding its light throughout the entirety of the cosmos, and completely decimating the surrounding galaxy in the process.

The light had died but still the universe remained. Planets and stars continued their habitual orbit around the former center of the universe in the dimly lit space that still remained.

Then before us, out of the remnants of the explosion and the shattered galaxy a figure appeared.

It was massive and beautiful to behold, like a phoenix rising from the ashes of its own fiery eruption. It was more colorful than the most vibrant rainbow and looked out at all around it with a smile.

It looked anthropomorphic, but only in its basic appearance. It had a slender body with two arms and two legs, but its hands and feet had only three fingers and three toes, and its face was far different than any I'd seen on any Terran, Gaïos, Arc-

-os or anything else, and instead of hair it seemed to have a large fiery headpiece of vivacious colors that beamed with brightness.

The figure then uttered one word, "AÏA," and it echoed throughout the cosmos.

It then set out amid the decimation of the former galaxy, conjuring a new star and creating new planets to accompany it.

Above, below, and to its sides, it created new planets, each time traversing the vastness of space then descending to the planets themselves to create more life on them. Wherever it went, it created life, and whatever life it created, it loved.

It was life. It was love. It was AÏA.

"What you just witnessed was the creation of our universe," The Prime'ïos' voice broke into our visions and revived us from the trance we had endured, "specifically the creation of our *universal realm*, and within that, the Ïandus galaxy. The figure you saw was AÏA, The Creator and parent of all life."

We found ourselves back in the Prime'ïos' chamber, though it was no longer entirely occupied by the image of the cosmos. We now sat on a slate-tile floor, on velvet-pillowed seats in a half circle surrounding the Prime'ïos who sat on a larger red pillowed seat, sewn with gold seams and embroidered with large images of bursting novae.

The ceiling above us retained the image of the cosmos and continued to move slightly as we conversed.

"So Terra was one of those planets he created, right?" Kai asked.

"Yes, but you must understand, AÏA does not have a gender. Despite the beliefs of many races and religions, the Creator was neither male, nor female. It simply had the power to create within itself and gave that power to its creations, though split it between what you know to be two sexes. And Terra, Gaïa, and Arco were merely three planets within the trillions AÏA created — but yes, they were of the six remade planets after The Cataclysm."

"But that doesn't answer Ayla's question." Lizia chimed in. "Who are the Ordained Children?"

"Ahh, yes," The Prime'ïos continued, "I did not wish to overwhelm you with the intense visualizations of the entire chronology of our galaxy's beginnings, for fear of it being too much for your senses — and that it is considerably long and spans many millennia — so I will now tell you the rest in the original fashion of our peoples:

"AÏA's first step in repairing the damaged galaxy was to create worlds to fill the void left by Its previous explosion. AÏA created the first two planets Ossïah and Shakrah, above and beneath the repaired sun It called Solus; these were the first two planets to comprise the Solus Hexus — the unique planetary system that houses our worlds. To these planets AÏA gave the first elements; earth, water, wind, and fire.

"Ossïah was a planet composed of vast magnificent oceans that stretched all across its expansive surface save for a single small landmass. It was host to all manner of aquatic life; largest of all were the Cetesïa; colossal creatures that swam the depths and governed the seas.

"Conversely, Shakrah was a planet made of

land comprised mostly of forest and mountainous regions riddled with volcanic formations.

"Because of the rough terrain, Shakrah's skies became the primary environs of its inhabitants. Shakrah was home to many airborne species; its mountain peaks and massive forest canopies were the homes of its birdlike denizens; the Shakroosari being the highest order and sovereigns of its skies.

"AÏA loved these planets and the life It created on them, but still had much to do to repair the Ïandus galaxy and complete the Solus Hexus, and so created shepherds to monitor and govern their life in its absence.

"So AÏA then created the ÏOS and the SHÏK, to protect, marshal, and educate the species of Ossïah and Shakrah respectively. After creating them, AÏA left them to their ordained tasks and continued the restoration of the Ïandus Galaxy by regenerating the remainder of the Solus Hexus. The two governed their worlds as they saw fit and for a time all was good as AÏA continued with The Restoration.

"Filled with new inspiration, AÏA created two new planets to surpass the splendor and life of Ossïah and Shakrah. These two worlds were to harbor new life, life that was capable of a feat that Ossïanï and Shakïrï life did not possess, the ability to create.

"The Ossïanï and Shakïrï could certainly create in the sense of reproduction, but none of their species was able to create beyond that. They lacked a certain *intuition*. AÏA wished to observe the creations of other beings and in order to do that, other beings had to be able to create. Thus AÏA reached out to Its sides and created two worlds: Gaïa and Arco, your ancestral worlds."

"Wait, worlds? With an 's', as in plural?" Shelyse probed.

"I thought you guys said your dad was from Arco?" Tytus added.

"Yeah, he was..." I began, though I now had questioned that information.

Was he somehow Gaïan too?

"Indeed Arcus Angelus was from Arco, and was pureblooded Arcos," the Prime'ïos explained, "Your Arcosan ancestry was not the only thing I was referring to, but your Terran lineage as well..."

We all looked to each other quizzically before looking back to the Prime'ïos.

He smiled, nodded his head, and continued his story, "When AÏA had completed the magnificent planets Gaïa and Arco It introduced new life into the universe. Thus the Gaïos and the Arcos emerged with newfound thoughts and abilities, with the capacity to create and to love, AÏA's favorite things in this life.

"Both peoples lived in autonomy, pursuing their own loves and desires for creation. The Gaïos favored emotive creation; music was their main form of expression and they excelled in expressive and artistic forms. The Arcos on the other hand, favored technological endeavors; creating efficient tools and utensils to advance their species.

"Despite their differences, both always remembered their own creator and always created in Its image and for the *good* of existence. Having to continue The Restoration, AÏA again created shep-

-herds for these people; the Prïm'el Gaïane for the Gaïos and the Supreme Arcon for the Arcos.

"These shepherds led and guarded their respective species in many glorious generations living and loving, creating in their image and in that of their creator AÏA, but their joy and prosperity was very soon challenged..."

"Challenged?" Jonos interrupted, "by whom, or rather, what?"

"To explain that we must return to what the Gaïos refer to as The Cataclysm," The Prime'ïos replied, "Prior to the emergence of AÏA, the presence you witnessed, The Light, the Supreme Being you saw was called AÏZ. AÏZ was responsible for The Creation and is the original source of life in the cosmos. But ultimately AÏZ was consumed by self-affliction and inner conflict, the outcome of which was The Cataclysm.

"What emerged afterward was AÏA, the being of light and goodness. However, AÏA was not alone. In the far reaches of the cosmos, a dark presence emerged. Fueled by spite and consumed with rage and malice, another being emerged from The Cataclysm. ZÏZ.

"Darker than the void and callous beyond measure, ZÏZ was the opposite of AÏA. The two had formerly comprised one being, but their opposing force severed its existence and split the universe forever in two."

"So wait, they're light and dark?" Ander asked pragmatically, "Like good and bad?"

"For all intents and purposes, yes," The Prime'ïos answered.

"That seems too easy." Devian skeptically responded, voicing a thought I was wondering myself, though was perhaps more accepting of.

"The universe can't be that easily defined or based." Devian continued, "I mean, seriously? There isn't more to it than that, really?"

"Why not? Everything you see and experience is a combination of good and evil, hot and cold, light and dark. Duality is the basis of existence. And should you have been there when there was nothingness, the concept of duality would have seemed quite monumental indeed.

"The only reason you consider this exact truth of life to be so primitive is because you have witnessed a life far beyond its simplicity, far beyond its intrinsic value; occupied with time and space, the complexities of scientific achievement and emotion; a world so convoluted with trifles that the basic principles of life have become lost to all. Living this calamitous and often abrasive life, you automatically consider anything elementary to be banal or inconsequential."

"Come on man, it's all relative." Cephus said to Devian, accepting the Prime'ïos' answers quite matter-of-factly.

"Indeed, life is relative." The Prime'ïos concluded smiling at Cephus, "such profound yet *simple* words."

"All universal truths aside," Jonos shifted the conversation, "what about this ZÏZ character?"

"Yes of course," The Prime'ïos continued, "ZÏZ awoke in the void fueled by hatred, and was compelled to undo everything that AÏA was doing and had done; after all, the two were counterparts and AÏA's joy and creation brought misery and disdain to ZÏZ, leading to the inevitable conflict between the two.

"As life continued to thrive on the first four planets of the Solus Hexus ZÏZ began sowing the seeds of dissent among AÏA's creations.

"It started on Shakrah. As AÏA busied itself with designs for its newest creations, ZÏZ used a unique and powerful Ara — what you would know as magic — to show the SHÏK what life was like on Ossïah; the vast oceans prosperous with sea life and the lush tropical paradise it boasted were unreal to the SHÏK, and it began to feel a sense of longing.

"ZÏZ hinted that if the SHÏK wanted to live in such a serene and attractive place, it should. ZÏZ suggested that the SHÏK take it for itself, and thus ZÏZ imprinted the ideas of envy and desire in the realm.

"The SHÏK quickly became jealous and unknowingly had become ZÏZ's pawn in a grand scheme to destroy all life. It began coercing its fellow Shakïrï subjects to its perverse cause and created much discord among its populace, resulting in a large scale civil conflict that saw the elimination of many of its species.

"Additionally ZÏZ had set its sight on the other planets of the Solus Hexus; Gaïa and Arco. In a similar fashion, ZÏZ whispered thoughts and lies into the minds of the Gaïos and the Arcos, tempting them with lures of power and governance. The Arcos were strong willed and their constitution could not be broken and ZÏZ saw no success there. But here on

Gaïa, ZÏZ saw a much different outcome..."

At this point the Prime'ïos suddenly stopped. His melancholic and reminiscent feelings were immediately clear to us; despite his capacity to control his thoughts and feelings, his discomfort was apparent.

Your pain... I found myself thinking to him.

It is the pain of my people...

It's so immense. Insufferable even.

You no doubt can deduce now why Laurales and Brandu said there are so few of us left...

How can you bear it?

AÏA's light comforts all darkness in this world, no matter its severity. And despite this travesty, there is still much good to counter the evil. AÏA's will feeds our own and gives us strength.

I quickly noticed that everyone seemed to hold their breath for the moment the Prime'ïos paused his story.

He noticed and promptly resumed his story, "The Gaïos that ZÏZ convinced to betray their race lost all of their sensibility and became slaves to its will. They inherited its spite, its jealousy, and its anger and they became forever lost to our people. Ever after they were known as Malïos and were slaves to the darkness.

"While ZÏZ and the SHÏK plotted their attack on The Creation, AÏA had been consumed with the planning for the third and final pairing of planets to complete the Solus Hexus: Macra and your home-world, Terra.

"Just as before AÏA created two lush planets, beautiful in design, and splendid to behold; vast blue oceans and massive green, brown, and white continents marked these planets with land.

"This time around, these planets were to incorporate all walks of life that AÏA had previously created. Creatures of the sea, the air, and the land were to exist in one environ, in blissful harmony. These were to be AÏA's greatest and final works of the Solus Hexus.

"Unfortunately, so absorbed was AÏA with the ideal plans for these new planets, these ultimate creations, that ZÏZ's perverse and malicious actions nearly destroyed everything before their completion; had it not been for Ossïah's guardian, the ÏOS, and the watchful eye it kept on the realm.

"The ÏOS had taken great interest in AÏA's creations and thus took to watching them from afar. Since its creation, the ÏOS had learned many things from AÏA and through its own experience.

"The greatest of all these feats was its ability to psychically project itself through the cosmos; a feat it used to save all of existence. Before the SHÏK and ZÏZ completely organized and attacked the realm the ÏOS was able to warn AÏA.

"With the warning the ÏOS gave to AÏA the two were able to organize an alliance to fend off ZÏZ's onslaught against creation. The alliance was comprised of the Cetesïa and the varying Ossïanï who could fight, myself and the remaining Gaïos who were willing to fight for the preservation of life, and finally the Arcos—led by the Supreme Arcon, Arcaz Arnathi.

"When the time came to fight, many Arcos answered the call to arms and dedicated themselves to fighting for AÏA using their great technological expertise; unfortunately, their will and arrogance were not then realized, and later contributed to their ill-omened fate."

For a moment I became lost in thought about the Supreme Arcon, the Arcos fighting expertise, and moreover, what ill-omened fate the Prime'ïos spoke of, but didn't have time enough to fully consider it before he continued his story.

"The resulting conflict—The Contention—saw the first war the universe had ever seen. A war that stretched across the various planets of the Solus Hexus and involved all of its peoples. On one side AÏA and the Alliance of Light fought against ZÏZ and the encroaching darkness.

"The conflict stretched beyond the reach of each planet and thus, its combatants required a means to traverse these distances.

"The ÏOS and AÏA then devised a means of passage between the various planetary realms of the Solus Hexus, given their transcendental abilities—this became the first form of interdimensional galactic space travel. The ÏOS then taught this method of transit to the Cetesïa who would serve as the galactic transports throughout the conflict.

"They ferried the warriors of the Alliance of Light to and from each planet where conflict erupted, and were forever known as the masters of the Warporal Realm.

"The ensuing war lasted for a millennium and saw victories and defeats on both sides until the battle prowess of the Arcos ultimately proved superior and led the Alliance of Light to the doorstep of the enemy.

"On Shak'usar, the highest peak of the planet

Shakrah, AÏA and ZÏZ—both of whom had taken their true physical forms for the first and only time during the conflict—fought the final battle of The Contention.

"As the combined forces of the Arcos, Gaïos, and Ossïanï fought the Malïos and Shakïrï, the giant forms of AÏA and ZÏZ clashed above all else, making everything else insignificant.

"Each blow they landed was as an earthquake that shook the foundations of Shakrah and devastated its terrain down to its very core.

"Despite the successes of the Arcos in combat and the tide of battle flowing in the Alliance's favor, AÏA realized that the battle was impossible to win. AÏA realized that ZÏZ was too formidable an enemy to fall in combat.

"Its rage gave It insurmountable strength and endurance which meant that ZÏZ could fight forever, despite the loss of Its army.

"Realizing this doom AÏA had but one choice. Gathering all of Its might and drawing strength from the warriors present, from those that remained detached from the fight, from the Solus Hexus, the Ïandus Galaxy, and the universe beyond; AÏA drew forth an energy the likes of which had never been seen.

"AÏA harnessed this power in a great sphere of energy and took it into Its hands, absorbing it directly into itself. At this point the planet began to crumble. AÏA bade for the ÏOS and the Cetesïa to transport all of the Arcos and Gaïos off the planet and return them to their respective worlds. Additionally, AÏA commanded them to fulfill their legacy; AÏA's legacy.

"As the planet began to split and the ground erupted in a calamitous storm of earth and fire, AÏA grappled with ZÏZ. Restraining ZÏZ, AÏA began to unleash the energy It had previously harnessed directly into ZÏZ's body.

"In doing so, the planet cracked down to its very core, causing large fissures to open and momentarily incapacitating ZÏZ. AÏA seized the moment and grabbed ZÏZ.

"Hefting ZÏZ and itself up into the air, AÏA plunged them both into the depths of the planet as It clung onto ZÏZ.

"After the two of them plummeted into the chasm an earsplitting explosion could be heard all across the planet, sending a wave out to the farthest reaches of the Ïandus Galaxy and every corner of the Solus Hexus.

"Just before hitting the core AÏA released the full force of the energy it'd harnessed and in a catastrophic implosion, removed itself and ZÏZ from this realm; thus ending The Contention in Its ultimate sacrifice."

***

For a long moment we all sat dumbfounded with the story we'd just heard. No one dared speak or comment. Each of us sat in introspective silence and waited for someone to break the ice, though it seemed as though no one was going to.

I had just opened my mouth to say something

before the Prime'ïos continued, "But this still does not yet answer Ayla's question... AÏA's legacy remained after the conflict. Its legacy was..."

"The Ordained Children." Ayla concluded.

"The Ordained Children." The Prime'ïos nodded and continued, "Before the battle to combat the darkness of ZÏZ, AÏA formed a contingency plan to complete the restoration of the Solus Hexus. The Restoration would be completed by what remained of AÏA's Firstborn Children after the conflict on Shakrah.

AÏA charged the surviving Arcos and Gaïos with completing its designs by populating the worlds of Macra and Terra with their intended peoples: the Ordained Children.

"After AÏA's sacrifice, the ÏOS inherited the duty of Guardian of the Solus Hexus and thus it was the ÏOS who oversaw the Arcos' and the Gaïos' enactment of AÏA's legacy. The two races received their instructions and set out to create AÏA's Ordained Children: the Macran and the Terran.

"The ÏOS resumed its post as Guardian of the Solus Hexus, and took it upon itself to figure out a way to free AÏA from Its self-imposed imprisonment. Meanwhile, the Gaïos and Arcos set out with full alacrity to fulfill AÏA's plans. The Arcos set out to birth the Macran, while we Gaïos tasked ourselves with creating you: Terrans.

"In giving life to your first generations, we taught you our best skills, gave you our finest attributes, and loved you above all else just as AÏA intended; and for a time all was good. But as we soon discovered, AÏA's sacrifice did not achieve a lasting victory and the fate of all people of the Solus Hexus was forever changed."

At that point, a portal opened up on the far side of the Prime'ïos' chamber, and in walked Laurales. She did not walk far before reaching the Prime'ïos and I then realized that the room was not as large as it once seemed.

It now felt as though we were in a much cozier setting, slightly smaller than ZANZABAR's main hold. Laurales smiled at us as she approached the Prime'ïos.

I expected her to have a message for him and for her to whisper it into his ear, but quickly remembered that the Prime'ïos was a telepath and was not surprised when I neither saw nor heard any actual contact between the two of them.

After a moment of silence, in which I could only presume that they were having a telepathic conversation much like the one I'd had with him, the Prime'ïos stood and addressed us:

"My friends, the hour grows late, and you are no doubt weary from your travels and my extensive story. We shall adjourn for the night and resume tomorrow after the welcome feast. Laurales will escort you to the quarters we have apportioned for you; there you may change your clothes, eat, and rest, for tomorrow we shall celebrate the Second Coming of the Ordained Children."

"But what about—" I protested.

"Do not fret son of Arcus, you have only just arrived and already you have learned so much. You still have many questions to ask and there will be plenty of time for more answers; for now, take your rest. Tomorrow will be quite the day indeed."

He gestured toward the door, encouraging us to follow Laurales out onto the foyer outside his chamber. Following the others, I got up and walked out behind my companions, somewhat dejected at not receiving the answers I'd come so far to hear.

"Don't worry," I looked up from the floor as I heard Jonos' voice come from beside me, "the Prime'ïos is right, we've learned so much already. Way more than we came looking for. We've waited all this time to start finding answers, what's one more day?"

"Yeah man." Cephus followed up, "Besides, the night will give us the time we need to process the whole history of the universe we just learned. That was a lot to take in."

The Prime'ïos opined on the matter as we approached the door, "Indeed, I am quite surprised you were all able to follow as well as you did. Your minds are far stronger than ever we could have expected.

It seems that time has been good to the Terran people and the offspring of Angelus. I look forward to our next meeting, but I must leave you now, though I will meet you again tomorrow morning. Laurales will attend to you for the remainder of the night. Good night."

"If you would all follow me please," Laurales said smilingly as the same floating staircase from before began to appear, leading us down from the Prime'ïos' chamber.

As the moon rose high and massive above our heads Laurales led us along the same path we'd previously taken back to *ZANZABAR* where we got what belongings we needed for the night—which wasn't much—and said a quick hello to Zan before making our way to our designated lodgings for the night.

On the way back Laurales had explained the linguistic mystery Kai and all of us were so interested in. The Gaïos knew our language and could speak it back to us perfectly.

Laurales had said that when the Gaïos had created and imparted their gifts on the Terran, they'd passed on the gift of language and communication.

She'd added that throughout Terranity's years, those Gaïos still attuned with the sounds of the deep cosmos could hear us and our language as they listened to the symphony of the stars.

Laurales had further elaborated that the most skilled of the Gaïos could even speak more Terran-based languages than any of our group combined.

The Gaïos continued to mystify and baffle at every turn. Her story ended just as we'd gotten back to *ZANZABAR* where everyone quickly set to gathering their things.

Before everyone had reconvened outside the ship I had a brief exchange with Zan—who was quite excited for more than one reason.

Firstly, and *almost* disconcertingly, she'd been observing our recent exploration of Gaïa through a series of high-frequency pulse emissions, satellite relays, and sub-connections from our own wrist Links which we still wore—more out of habit than necessity—and had constructed an entire map of the space we'd explored on the High Citadel.

With this map, the signals from our wrist Links, and a few satellite probes she had launched as soon as we entered the system, she could locate and contact us almost anywhere on the planet.

She also informed me that the probes she sent out were mapping the rest of the planet for her own ship-board navigational archives.

Zan was unfathomably innovative and efficient and knew what she was doing, but that didn't stop me from thinking that she may have had a bit too much power and could have been misconstrued as borderline big-brother.

Though I was certainly grateful that she was allied with us and was more of a loving big-sister instead.

"You'd best be careful with all of that," I said, "We wouldn't want the Prime'ïos and the Gaïos thinking that we're snooping around."

"No promises." She responded, smiling.

I shook my head, baffled that after all of her techno-babble about bouncing high frequency emissions and whatnot, that she still used our Terran sayings; as if she were becoming one of us.

I sidelined the thought as I realized people were waiting for me outside the ship, "And the second thing?" I asked, trying to conclude our business and get back to my hosts.

"Oh right, I figured out the problem with the warp drive sequencing that brought us here."

She then launched into an excruciatingly technical explanation as to what the problem was, and before long noticed that I wasn't exactly following.

Despite my neophyte levels of understanding the theoretical physics behind our particular space travel, I had no such knowledge of *ZANZABAR's* systems and how they worked.

She frowned for a moment before summarizing, "Basically, the drive was incorrectly wired at some point, who knows why, or perhaps it was damaged in a previous jump, but ultimately it inverted the coordinates. The final coordinate inputs I entered before jumping should have been correct for a jump to Arco, except the last coordinate was the incorrect value, as it should have…"

"Been inverted," I finished her thought, "because Gaïa and Arco are at opposite ends on the same axis in the Solus Hexus. Their coordinates are the same except for the fact that one is positive and the other negative, right?"

"Indeed. Though it's not exactly *that* simple." Zan replied, dumbstruck that I had come up with the answer after understanding little of her scientific explanation.

I was inwardly grateful for the Prime'ïos' history lesson on the creation of the galaxy earlier in the night.

"How did you know?" she asked.

"Zan, I'm surprised. I would have thought that with all the snooping you've been doing you would know how I know."

"Hmph." She frowned as her blue image glinted a slight reddish hue before it disappeared, leaving her natural blue color. "If you are referring to the happenings in the Prime'ïos' chamber, I wouldn't know anything about that. My signal was blocked the moment you stepped in."

Zan spoke in the tone of a disappointed toddler.

"Aw, you finally found somewhere you couldn't get to huh? You poor thing." I joked and began to exit the bridge. "Anything else before I go? Do you need any help rewiring the warp drive?"

"The Tech-Mechs on board should be enough to take care of it, but an extra set of hands would certainly make the work go a lot quicker."

"Tech-Mechs?"

"Technical Mechanical Servitors; my 'hands' and physical presence on the ship when it doesn't have a crew."

"So *those* were what..."

"Removed the deceased Arcos that you and Jonos found when you first arrived on the ship." This time *she* finished *my* thought, "Yes, after my awakening, I ordered them to restore the ship to full readiness."

"Hmm..."

"Once they carry out their tasks they return to their housing compartments within the ship's machine shop and divert to standby until called upon."

"I see."

I simply stated, realizing that I hadn't seen these Tech-Mechs at all since finding ZANZABAR. I figured they weren't needed since we'd successfully found ourselves a crew.

"Alright, I'll see if Pria or Davriel can give you a hand with things here. I'm sure you could use the company too." I followed up, sensing that she seem-

-ed somewhat lonely.

"Very well, enjoy tomorrow's feast Shipmas —
uh, my apologies. Enjoy tomorrow's feast *Savos*." She
said, clearly catching herself.

"Not a problem Zan." I said while
suppressing a smile. "We'll just keep that one
between us, huh?"

"That would probably be for the best."

"No promises." I said as I left the bridge to
meet my awaiting companions, "I'll be seeing you."

Shipmaster, I ran the word over and over in my
head as I exited the ship and followed along with the
group; Laurales leading us through more of the High
Citadel's beautiful gardens and architectural
wonders toward our lodgings.

No, I'm no shipmaster. I'm no captain, *I'm just…*
me.

**United Terran Federation Communique to Chief
Defense Minister Luca de Gulliss
From the Office of UTFSF Admiral Li Kyphese
(Operations Commander – Joint Orbital Base
Khorneus)**
17 January, 3.2221 @11:13:42 TST

Chairman,

For the past week Lunar Base Apollus has
been engaged in Operation Starwind. Test probes
with the upgraded Galaxial Flux Drive tech our UTF
Amassian agents procured from Dr. Franzi
Dorfmund have been sent to the far reaches of our
solar system, into the Galaxia, and the uncharted
normal space beyond.

The probes are testing the limits of the GFD
and establishing its efficacy. We've monitored the
probes using the same High Frequency Wave
tracking system Dr. Dorfmund used in her own
recent GFD test.

We've sent a total of 46 probes out and are
pleased to report 95% success rate, with 44 probes
returning to normal space in optimal condition. Of
the two probes that failed, one returned with its
Galaxial drive intact but detonated unexpectedly
prior to being retrieved by UTF units.

The second probe was lost after completing its
initial jump. Its HFW signal continued to operate
after completing its jump, but shortly after entering

normal space on the other side the probe's signal was lost, and it never made its planned return jump.

An investigation is currently being conducted to determine the cause of both failures. Since test completion, Orbital Shipyards Araxia and Benthion have been hard at work to retrofit our new ships with the upgraded GFD tech.

Exploratory Battle Fleet *Astaros* is fully fitted and currently completing shakedown prior to deployment orders; battle fleets *Typhon* and *Veriso* are 70% fitted and nearing combat readiness. The fourth and fifth fleets *Kandimar* and *Delpheon* are still undergoing major construction on 80% of their ships with both fleets' Javelin battle cruisers ready and awaiting installation of their GFDs; both fleets are currently working with skeleton staffing and are awaiting their full crew complements. Furthermore, SRF CP-0147-VC-02 is undergoing final tests and will be ready in approximately 26 hours.

Finally, Chief Magistrate Dekkun Pikus concluded his observation and report of the shipyard facilities at OS Benthion at 18:00 yesterday and will be arriving at OS Araxia at 06:00 tomorrow. Is there a particular reason the Magistrate is here now?

With our initial testing concluded, our probe recon ongoing, and our first fleets nearing their completion and departure, wouldn't it have been better suited to postpone the Magistrate's arrival and observations of our facilities and fleets until after their completion?

My sub-commanders are growing anxious as he has apparently taken to randomly questioning each of them for quite long hours, and word of his arrival has spread amongst the ranks and has set my facilities on edge.

Frankly, his presence is a distraction and is an unnecessary burden so close to our inaugural departure.

Admiral Li Kyphese,
UTF Operations Commander: Joint Orbital Base Khorneus

**United Terran Federation Communique to
Admiral Li Kyphese
From the Office of UTF Chief Defense Minister
Luca de Gulliss,**
17 January, 3.2221 @09:42:33 TST

Admiral,

Your progress is behind schedule. EBF *Typhon* and *Veriso* were to be completed and carrying out shakedown procedures alongside *Astaros* by now. Though your candor and that of your officers is appreciated I must inform you: if the presence of Chief Magistrate Dekkun Pikus is a distraction, perhaps I shall find someone to run J.O.B Khorneus who does not feel that his presence is debilitating. If your officers cannot perform under the UTF's scrutiny than I recommend you replace them. You have a schedule and I suggest you take whatever action necessary to keep to it.

Chancellor Pelantius has ordered an increase in probe deployment to the coordinates of the two lost probes. Identify any remains of the probe that detonated immediately. Its detonation could be related to the recently observed unidentified vessel from the NW Amassian sector.

Additionally, I expect a full status report of your continuing search for said vessel.

Chief Defense Minister Luca de Gulliss,

UTF Chairman

United Terran Federation Communique to Chief Defense Minister Luca de Gulliss
From the Office of UTFSF Admiral Li Kyphese
(Operations Commander – Joint Orbital Base Khorneus)
17 January, 3.2221 @10:51:26 TST

Chairman,

Our probes have not yet detected any trace of the mysterious ship. Its departure was virtually impossible to trace; but we have increased our probe dispatch count from the original 46 to 107. They are being continually sent and retrieved on regular intervals and through their explorations we have discovered several star systems with life-sustaining habitats and have marked them as primary targets for our fleets' further investigation.

As a primary directive, each probe has a recorded HFW signal reading of the source obtained from Dr. Dorfmund's tests and tracks it throughout its entire deployment, additionally they have signal readings based on those recorded by Commander Hirojma Kahn's Fort Kane Litehawks, and that of the most recent recorded data.

We are utilizing every avenue to pursue the ship. We will find it and bring the outlaws piloting it to justice.

Admiral Li Kyphese,
UTF Operations Commander: Joint Orbital Base Khorneus

**United Terran Federation Communique to
Admiral Li Kyphese
From the Office of UTF Chief Defense Minister
Luca de Gulliss,**
19 January, 3.2221 @11:16:45 TST

Admiral,

For your sake, I hope you do.

The Chief Magistrate's reports on J.O.B Khorneus' operations to date indicate that your progress has nearly doubled in the last two days, and fleets *Typhon* and *Veriso* are now initiating shakedown procedures.

My compliments on rectifying your productivity situation.

Chief Defense Minister Luca de Gulliss,
UTF Chairman

Chapter 12: Revelry

After reconvening with Laurales and my companions, she led us off to the building where we were to stay the night, which was not far from the landing dais where *ZANZABAR* resided. As I had discussed with Zan, Davriel and Pria stayed aboard the ship to help her with the modifications and repairs she needed to carry out before we could effectively navigate the warp. A few others stayed behind as well, which I was surprised to see.

Tytus and Shelyse both decided to stay aboard the ship — though I privately believed it was mainly her decision — as did Jimian, which surprised me the most as I figured he would have wanted to experience this alien culture more than the rest.

I later found out that it was out of his friendship with Pria that he stayed, noting that he didn't want her to feel left out by having to stay on the ship.

The building that Laurales took us to was relatively small compared to others we'd seen around the High Citadel, but it was elevated above the surrounding buildings on an elegant platform, much like a treehouse sits near the top of a tree.

As we ascended the building the floors began extending out beyond the main, a structural feat I couldn't help but admire. The top floor extended out far beyond the rest and looked almost like a halo surrounding the building.

Our rooms were on the top floor and had a beautiful view of the outlying residential districts to one side and the core of the city on the other.

From the balconies we could also clearly see the Prime'ïos' chamber, high above the rest of the skyline.

The view was breathtaking and its splendor captured my attention throughout the night.

Before leaving us for the night, Laurales indicated she and Brandu would be spending the night in the building as well and that we were to inform either of them if we needed anything.

Jonos and Ayla were the first to turn in for the night, saying they would see us a Terran hour after dawn. The remainder of us — Cephus, Kaitoh, Devian, Ander, Lizia, and myself — stayed up for a while on the rooftop balcony, discussing everything we'd experienced since leaving Terra; namely how the Gaïos spoke our language and could communicate telepathically.

Before long, the weariness of travel and the immensity of our newly acquired knowledge took its toll, and each of my companions slowly turned in for the night. Kai first, then Ander, followed by Devian and Lizia.

Everyone left the communal balcony space we shared for their own rooms and called it a night; leaving Cephus and me as the last two on the roof.

Despite the enormity of what we were experiencing and how crazy it all was — searching for our long lost father on a new alien planet, finding out the truth of our Terran origins, learning the history of the entirety of creation as we knew it; all of which weighed heavy on our minds and inspired us to learn more — Cephus and I talked of everyday matters just as we would have had we been talking one on one back on Terra.

We talked of the crew and how we felt about each one of them and the 'job postings' and what people thought of their own assignments aboard *ZANZABAR*.

Our conversation then turned to our current setting and the Gaïos and what we thought of them.

I expressed my admiration for them, but also a bit of apprehension as we didn't yet know them or their full intent, and noted that I felt there was something that they were not yet telling us given the number of loose ends in the Prime'ïos' story.

"Well duh," Cephus said, "we haven't heard the whole story yet."

"I know. I mean that there's more of a reason *why* they're not telling us everything yet, you know?"

"I guess..."

It was quiet for a few moments after that as we both considered what was said before Cephus broke the silence again, "How 'bout that Laurales though? She's a total babe."

I snorted in mild disapproval while shaking my head, but couldn't help but agree with him; she was quite pleasing to see. It seemed like everything on Gaïa was pleasing to see though; the lights, the architecture, the people; all of it was aesthetically pleasing.

"Would that be weird?" He continued, as we both started at the stars, "You know, 'cause I don't think it would be. I mean, we're kind of the same species, right? I mean they did make us. You think it all works the same?"

I shook my head again and couldn't help but laugh out loud.

It seemed that despite being light-years away from our old lives, Cephus still thought like his old self.

He was still the rambunctious and fervent bachelor looking for a fast girl and a fun time while ashore — which I could understand given the fact that much of his time for the last six years had been spent isolated on a boat in the middle of the ocean, with several hundred other men.

Cephus had told me there were women aboard too, but he often said that they rarely had much semblance of femininity or mental stability, and there was usually some kind of rule against fraternization anyway.

"She is quite attractive," I finally agreed, "and I'm sure that given the fact that they made us, I imagine that *it* probably works the same way. But I doubt that she'd be like the Terran women you found in the various seaports of the world. Somehow this place just seems a bit more refined."

We both laughed.

"Whatever man, I'm not looking for that type of girl anyway, I've matured since then." He said trying to keep a straight face.

Eventually our conversation turned to other subjects but was drawn short as someone approached.

A hooded figure holding a lantern walked slowly and silently up to us before making her presence known.

Both of us looked at each other in stunned surprise as Laurales pulled back her hood and spoke, "How is it you are still awake sons of Arco? Do you not tire from your journey?"

"Yeah," I said, "We're physically tired, but we can't sleep with all this information running through our heads, you know?"

"We're just trying to take it all in and make sense of it." Cephus added.

"Indeed, you have learned much today, I can only imagine what kind of feelings you must be having right now after learning what you have thus far." She said, looking directly at Cephus. "Would you care to tell me?" she asked him. *Him*, not *us*, but *him*.

"Uhh... sure." He said, clearly surprised at her request.

"Forgive me Savos, but I wish to speak with your brother a moment." Laurales said.

"Sure, no problem." I said.

"Might we walk?" She said as she offered her hand to him, "Lunarïo will be up yet a while, and the moonlight is truly relaxing and perfect for a stroll."

I simply looked on, puzzled at what was unfolding in front of my eyes, as he stood up and began walking away with her. He looked over his shoulder as they turned to go and I wagged my finger and frowned at him the same way his stepdad DJ used to whenever we borrowed his car. As Cephus walked away with Laurales he clearly mouthed 'no promises' before turning and walking around the balcony and out of view.

I got up from the chair I was sitting on and

313

moved to a reclined lounge-type chair next to it. Left alone on the balcony, I stared at the stars and the moonlight of Lunarïo and privately addressed my thoughts on the day.

"Greetings," a voice suddenly said from behind me, "you are up late, son of Angelus."

It was Brandu. He approached me and took a seat in the chair adjacent to my own and I noticed he was smoking something.

"What keeps you from your rest?" he asked.

"I uh, I'm just a bit too overwhelmed with thought, right now. You know, today was a lot to process."

"Indeed." Brandu nodded.

He then let out a controlled puff of smoke which coiled and swirled up above him before dissipating in the light of Lunarïo.

Noting my attention to the smoke, he offered me the pipe from which he smoked, "Would you care for some? It is the leaf of the Sibanna tree. It calms the nerves and relaxes the mind. There are some on the High Citadel who refrain from smoking it as they view it is a base recreation."

"Umm…"

"I, believe it to be a means to hone one's emotions and senses."

"Okay…" I said somewhat hesitantly as I reached out my hand.

"There is no need to fear. It will do you no harm and its affects will dissipate as you sleep throughout the night."

I took the pipe from his hand and examined it before putting it to my lips. It was smooth and glossy despite being made out of a material that looked like wood.

Its cylindrical shape made it look more like an instrument than a pipe, as if it were some type of clarinet or something. Here and there were decals and runes that I had not yet seen on the High Citadel, though they looked Gaïan in design.

"This is beautiful," I said as I continued to marvel at its ornate crafting.

"It is an heirloom that has lasted for many generations in my family. The symbols on the sides are the names of all who have owned it; many of which are no longer used by my people. I brought it with me as a token to remember my family when I came up to the High Citadel."

"You're from the surface?"

"Yes, but it has been several centuries since I left. Like many Gaïos, the lure of the cosmos drew me here and here is where I have found what I longed for."

"What's that exactly?" I asked as I looked for a means to light the crushed leaves within the pipe.

"The sound of serenity." Brandu responded as he looked up in longing at the stars and moon, before looking back down at me. He noticed my struggle with the pipe then said, "Simply breathe."

I put the pipe to my mouth and as I breathed in I felt as though a rush of cool, refreshing water had been poured over my mind and into my very soul.

My muscles began relaxing and I could feel my senses calming. Any and all tension immediately left my body and I began to feel a strange feeling, one of equilibrium.

"Sibanna has been used as a Gaïan remedy for eons now. Though many on the High Citadel have ceased its use, it still grows freely on the surface and provides for a natural effervescence that brings a soothing calmness to the calamities that life might bring."

A moment of silence passed for an eternity.

"Simply put," he continued, "it calms the body and quenches the mind. I use it to enhance my aural senses and to come closer to the sounds of the cosmos: the Symphony of AÏA."

I exhaled the smoke in successive rings as my brothers and I used to when back in the cabin on my mother's property and felt sublimely relaxed.

Brandu looked on, impressed at the rings and taking the pipe once more, he blew several starbursts through my rings that speckled the starlit sky beyond before disappearing.

He returned the pipe to me and I drew from it once more before blowing out a single large ring, then blowing the rest of the smoke through it, as even my facial muscles had all but relaxed completely.

"What troubles you, Savos?" He finally asked as we watched the smoke disappear.

I hesitated for a moment before slowly answering, "I guess, I'm scared. Scared that we'll fail. Scared that we won't find him."

"You speak of your father..."

"Yes. I mean, look at it all." I looked up to the stars. "There are so many of them. And now after finding out there's different dimensions and systems to them too... He could be *anywhere*."

"Do not stress yourself too much on what is

beyond your control, you will wear yourself thin. Do not overthink the melodies of the future, instead, focus on the now, and remember the harmonies of the times you had with your father; the disappointment and sadness along with the joy and the love, for there was — and is — much of it in your life. The tune of the now will lead you into the melodies of the future.

AÏA has seen fit that your life, your part in the cosmic symphony, has proceeded as it has up until now, and that is enough to be grateful for.

AÏA will guide your way, and will lead you in the part you must play."

I pondered his words for a moment and his musical metaphors and philosophies, but was drawn back away to the stars and the light of Lunarïo.

Its brilliance gave me comfort and clarity — as did the Sibanna — but beyond that, I felt a warmth on Gaïa I had not felt often in my life; a warmth of serenity.

As I gazed into the night sky I began to hear music off in the distance. There was a low vibrating sound that drove the music that lulled and comforted me. Beyond that there were sounds that seemed to emanate from the stars in the sky in addition to the main clarion sound I'd heard.

Despite my lulled state looking at the stars I noticed Brandu in my peripheral vision and was surprised to see him with the pipe to his lips, though he did not move it to exhale.

I then noticed that he was not smoking the pipe. He was playing a soothing sound from it. He was responsible for the low driving sound I'd heard.

I was further surprised at how low it was, given that the pipe was no bigger than the length of his forearm. The sound had reminded me of the long horn-like instruments played by the aboriginal tribes that still lived in some countries on the southern hemisphere of Terra.

I thought back to such peoples for a moment, but the continuous driving sound lulled me yet again.

New sounds came to life and refocused me onto the stars above, satiating my wandering mind all the more.

I began feeling drowsy and before long my eyes drooped and I fell into a deep sleep.

"Rest easy Savos Angelus, for I fear there is much unrest in your future."

***

Regardless of the calmness with which I fell asleep, that night I dreamt of chaos. I dreamt of a large battle that ravaged the entirety of a planet. I couldn't see the enemy or any of the fighting, but everywhere I looked countless people lay dead or dying.

Walking through the remnants of the battle I approached a temple of ancient design that burned in the night sky. Everywhere I looked, there were dead bodies strewn about the temple and its surrounding grounds. Here and there I began to see melancholic victors of battle standing over the bodies. They stood insipid and expressionless over their enemies' corpses and I could see that they vastly outnumbered the dead.

Looking out across the heaps of bodies in the fire light, I saw amidst the tragedy of the scene one particular individual standing out above the rest.

It was a man, bloodied and vile, holding a child by its neck. As I got closer I saw that the man looked wretched and malicious, and could see how madness consumed and contorted his figure.

In his grip was a boy, no more than a toddler.

Despite the victim's diminutive size and young age, he struck out at the vile man who held him, hitting him hard in the face and drawing fresh blood.

The demented man quickly seized the boy's arm and cracked it, then held him up for all to see before stealing the life from him as he crushed him beneath his grasp.

The man then threw the lifeless body to the ground and screamed out in barbaric rage. At seeing this sight, the victors slowly turned their backs and crept into the shadows, leaving the field of battle, leaving their victory.

The man stood staring down at the lifeless corpse he'd just tossed aside, panting and enjoying a sickening laugh before calming himself as he noticed eyes were on him; they were my own, and for a moment we locked eyes before he uttered something malicious and abhorrent.

I didn't understand what he initially said, but he then repeated it and this time I understood perfectly, "All angels must fall."

I woke up with a start as I heard knocking on the door and realized that I was in a bed. I was no longer out on the balcony where I'd fallen asleep but was in the room that had been arranged for me.

Again I heard the knocking on the door. Seven knocks.

Cephus?

I pushed myself out of bed, thinking back to what I'd witnessed in my dream and slowly made my way to the door. As I opened it I was surprised as I was greeted by Jonos and Ander.

"Yo man." Ander greeted.

"Hey," I managed, stifling a yawn.

"Wake up dude, everyone's waiting for you." Jonos said briskly.

"What?"

"The feast is set and ready; the Prime'ïos — and apparently half the population of the High Citadel — are expecting us." Jonos continued, "You were supposed to be up at dawn and to have met us an hour after, remember?"

"Yeah, sorry. Just give me a minute. I'll meet you guys downstairs." I said as I turned to get dressed.

"No, head to the balcony. Laurales has an air speeder arranged to fly us to the feast since we're gonna' be late. Why aren't you ready anyway? Were you up late drinking with Cephus or something?"

"No… Geez, you sound like mom." I replied as I put my pants on. It was then that I noticed that Jonos and Ander weren't wearing their normal clothes; instead they had on vibrant Gaïan tunics and wore robes of green and yellow over them. "What are you guys wearing?"

"They're the ceremonial robes Laurales and

Brandu set aside for us." Jonos snipped back, "Yours is hanging by the window there."

I followed the finger he was pointing to my window to see an embroidered ocean blue tunic and robe hanging neatly and swaying slightly in the morning breeze coming from the window.

"You can keep your clothes on underneath though," Ander chimed in, before opening his own robes to indicate he was still wearing his own clothes underneath, at least his own pants, shirt, and shoes.

"They gave us some kind of moccasin to wear too, but they don't fit to well. And the robes cover our feet anyway."

"Hurry up." Jonos urged, "We'll meet you on the roof."

"Okay, okay! Geez. Telling me to hurry isn't gonna' get me to go much faster."

"Whatever, just hurry." He said as he turned to go.

"We'll see you up there." Ander added on as he turned to follow Jonos.

After pulling on my boots I threw on an undershirt before delicately donning the tunic and the robe that went over it. Before leaving I looked into the mirror, grateful for my short hair which didn't need combing, and realized that I looked slightly ridiculous as my boots weren't completely covered by the robe.

I looked around for the moccasins that Ander mentioned but couldn't find them anywhere. I looked at my wrist-Link, more out of habit as I had no actual sense of what time it was on Gaïa or how late I now was, and saw a message from Zan. The me

-ssage read, "Warp drive repaired. Enjoy your feast."

I was happy to hear the good news but was immediately drawn back to the situation at hand. Realizing my increasing tardiness, I resigned myself to my foolish look and left the room to meet with my companions.

After arriving on the balcony and greeting my companions, Laurales, and Brandu—and receiving quite the bit of shaming, not only for being so late but also for my ridiculous look—I quickly noticed that the majority of my companions were wearing the moccasins, save for Ander, Cephus, and myself.

Fortunately for them, their robes covered their feet when they stood, but I didn't have time to dwell on that as moments after I greeted everyone, we all boarded the open-top air speeder that Laurales requisitioned for us and sped off toward our welcome feast.

On our way to our destination everyone engaged in conversation. The majority of them were listening to Laurales as she spoke of the Gaïan feast we were about to enjoy, while Kai and Brandu were in a private conversation of music, sound, and the varying ways of communication.

Cephus eventually broke off from the communal conversation and approached me asking how the rest of my night had gone, to which I hesitated to answer.

"I should ask you the same question." I deflected back to him, still unsure of what to make of my dream.

"You'd actually be surprised," He chimed back, smiling and confident, "I guarantee you, I did

-n't do what you think I did."

"What would I think you did?" I retorted.

He laughed before continuing, "To be honest, all we did was talk. For quite a while too."

"Seriously?" I was astonished, "What did you talk about for *a while*?" All kinds of stuff actually; we talked about Gaïa and Terra; I told her what I did back on Terra and about the UTF and how happy I am to be done with them. I told her about you and how we met and all about everyone we have with us. Then she talked about the Gaïos and what they do and all about her youth—which was ages ago; since they live considerably longer than us.

"Then she started telling me about the beliefs she was raised with and whatnot; she started to talk about the Gaïos and how they widely preach and practice pacifism ever since The Contention against ZÏZ.

"But then she started talking about how as much as she buys into the whole 'listening to the symphony of the stars' thing, it's not her favorite thing in the world, and she's been dying to express her, more adventurous side; I guess she's anxious to play her own part in it rather than always listening to it."

I was quite taken aback at what Cephus was telling me, it was strange to hear as I hadn't figured her—or anyone on Gaïa for that matter—for the *adventurous* type. I looked at her for a moment, and she back at me. She smiled and I returned the gesture before she spoke to everyone.

"We're about to land at Gallï Gaïanos, the Great Gathering Hall of AÏA." Despite the noise one would expect from an open top air speeder she did not shout and we had no problem hearing her.

"What about the others? Aren't they coming to the feast?" Ayla asked.

"Yes of course, your companions have been summoned and will meet you shortly." Laurales replied as we began our descent onto the landing dais.

I looked on in anticipation as we approached the platform, eager to not only enjoy the feast, but also to hear the rest of the story about what happened after the creation of the Terran and Macran; ultimately I wanted to know the fate of my ancestral people and my father.

Upon landing on the platform we met Davriel and the others who'd stayed the night on *ZANZABAR*. They were similarly dressed as they had also been given the Gaïan ceremonial garbs and everyone looked forward to the feast to come. I was privately grateful to see that Davriel was also wearing his boots and that his robes didn't completely cover them.

Our combined group was then led by Brandu and Laurales along the pathway toward Gallï Gaïanos, the Great Gathering Hall.

The pathway extended well above the majority of the Gaïan High Citadel; from above we could see all the way out to the exterior platforms and off to our right I could see the landing dais where *ZANZABAR* sat awaiting our eventual return.

Near the entrance to the Great Hall we could hear ethereal music coming from within. It was a kind of deep chant and seemed to resonate from the building itself, which looked like a grand domed palace.

We stopped short of the entrance as the doors opened up to us and a procession of Gaïos emerged. The two lines of the procession split and flanked us on either side. They carried banners decorated with Gaïan sigils; each was elaborate and entirely different from the last.

"Welcome, Terran and Arcosan guests." The members of the procession said in unison.

"These are the heads of twenty-one of the twenty-two Gaïan houses of the High Citadel." Brandu explained, "You have already met the twenty-second, Evï of house u'Neréas; our Prime'ïos."

Just as he finished speaking the procession lifted their banners up to the sky and in a flourish, whipped them around revealing unifying colors of blue, green, and silver beneath the family sigils. As they completed this stroke of splendor, the Prime'ïos emerged from the doorway wearing an elegant robe of jade green, ornamented with a white sash that was plaited with ornate Gaïan lettering.

"Welcome friends, to the Terran *Ordana Returallo*; the Ordained Children's welcome, the Feast of the Second Coming."

We greeted the Prime'ïos and followed him into the Great Hall with the proceeding members in front and behind us.

The inside of the hall was grandiose. It resembled a performance house with its high vaulted ceiling — which was decorated with an elaborate mural of the galaxy surrounding a beautiful depiction of AÏA's physical form, colorful and majestic.

The walls were silver with six massive pillars reaching up the entirety of the walls before meeting the dome shape of the ceiling.

Floating at various levels beneath the ceiling were sculptures of glass-like substances that lit up the whole room with a warm orangey glow.

Along the floor of the hall, which felt both larger than the Prime'ïos' chamber and more intimate at the same time, there were blue, green, and white lights that surrounded tables that were set up in a clear banquet setting.

We were led to two curved tables that faced out toward the other tables, clearly set aside for the guests of honor of this celebration.

Between the two tables we found someone awaiting us. The figure was draped with a satin-like hooded indigo robe that shined from all the light it reflected.

As we approached, the figure removed the hood and revealed a beautiful pale female face; slightly freckled with blue-gray eyes. Her slender face was framed by white hair that fell over her left shoulder in thin waves.

She smiled and bowed as we stopped in front of her, "Ga'hanjï." She said in her native tongue. "Greetings to you, AÏA's Ordained and Arcosan brethren. I am Réa Lunailï u'Neréas, daughter of Evï u'Neréas, Prïm'ella of Gaïos, Light of the moon, and voice of the Gaïan people."

I hesitated to reply as I was—without a

doubt—love-struck, but also felt as though I'd somehow known her already.

"Hello." Jonos finally responded; followed by everyone else in their own manner, save for myself.

"Réa has prepared a very special welcome for you today." The Prime'ïos said before addressing her in their native language.

After a brief exchange with her father Réa bowed again and said, "AÏA's blessings on all of you, our most gracious guests."

She then turned and walked toward a doorway to our right and disappeared. I watched as she walked away, completely infatuated by the presence she exuded; it was such a positive and reassuring aura I couldn't help but be enamored by her.

"Come my friends," the Prime'ïos said, gathering our attention and motioning us to the tables, "We are ready to begin the festivities."

We took our seats at either table, with six of us sitting at one table and seven at the other, while Brandu and Laurales joined us each at a table.

The Prime'ïos then approached the central point between our tables and the hundreds of Gaïos that had assembled for the feast.

He slowly lifted his hands and suddenly deep intonations began emanating from Gaïos in the surrounding seats and all around the hall. A bass chanting occupied the Grand Hall, yet none of the Gaïos seemed to be singing.

It seemed as though the space itself was singing. It was bizarre but ultimately entrancing. The sound faded away and the Prime'ïos then motioned to his sides and several Gaïan attendants promptly emerged from the side doors with trays of food and drink. The festivities had officially begun.

The Gaïos proved ever more gracious hosts as they continually served us plate, platter, dish, and delicacy; each looking and tasting more exotic than the last.

As all of it was foreign, we'd officially become the first Terrans ever to try cuisine from another planet.

Much of the food and drink we had was unlike anything we'd ever tasted, but some of their looks resembled those of what we ate on Terra.

There were several pastry type delicacies and some of their produce — or what would have passed as produce — resembled the fruits and vegetables we knew, but each had a new and unique flavor, some were great and some were simply too unfamiliar to be appreciated.

In addition to the varying types of food we were served, the Gaïos provided us with many delicious drinks.

Some of these were somewhat familiar much like the Gaïan produce; but again there were many surprises with the flavors, smells, and even the effects of some — those that were fermented and brought on a sort of stupor or inebriating feeling were particularly enjoyed by a few of my companions.

As we ate and drank and visited with the Prime'ïos, Brandu, and Laurales, there were many Gaïos who came either to introduce themselves, present gifts, or perform short musical numbers and emotive demonstrations for us.

Each one was beautiful to behold and every gift — food, drink, artistic creation, or musical rendition — was exceptionally presented and thoroughly enjoyed. Our pleasantries and merriment seemed to have lasted for several hours until there came another low bass-filled chant that again, seemed to emanate from the very structure where we resided.

The lights dimmed around us and the ceiling lit up in spectacular fashion. The Gaïos began taking their seats which prompted us to do the same. This change in scenery diverted all of our attention as we slowly began moving in the Hall.

I noticed our seats and tables were on separate daises raised above the floor, and were now moving slowly apart.

Between the two tables a third dais appeared from within the floor and out of some opening that didn't appear to exist a moment before, Réa emerged. She was dressed in the same indigo hood as before and emerged without moving a muscle.

In a flashing flourish the robe fell from her frame and exposed a glossy silver, form-fitted dress that cascaded down to the floor in perfect frills from the waist down. She stood proud and dignified on the slightly elevated dais and smiled to all of us and the audience of Gaïos who sat all around her.

As she glanced in my direction I could only hope that she would match my gaze and express the same kind of fascination I currently did. There was something about her that did more than intrigue me, but I couldn't quite figure it out.

Seemingly as sudden as she appeared, a sweet and entrancing music began to emanate from all around the Great Gathering Hall. The sound was ubiquitous, coming from all around and seeming to go through everything. It was soothing to the soul and shortly after beginning to hear it we heard the single most beautiful thing I'd ever heard, or would ever hear in my life.

Réa began to sing.

Softly at first, and growing in emotion and presence as she sang, her voice carried throughout the hall, throughout the entire High Citadel, it seemed throughout the whole planet.

I immediately recognized the voice and realized it was the same voice I'd heard when we first arrived in Gaïos space. It was enchanting. Immense. Elating. It was the purest and most wholesome sound I'd ever heard. It brought on a flood of positive feelings that seemed to overcome every amount of negativity there was in the world.

She was magnificent; in every sense of the word.

I did not understand the words she spoke; at least at first. But shortly after she began singing I began to hear her voice within my mind, though not the voice with which she sang. Amidst her captivating recital voice which dominated the entirety of the Great Gathering Hall I could hear her softly reciting the words to me, as though she would recite to the wind when no one was around.

We connected just like I did with the Prime'ïos when I first arrived. Hearing her voice in my head I felt that I'd known her forever. She said to me:

> *Life goes on and always finds a way.*
> *Light shines brightly through even the darkest day.*
> *Love conquers hate and courage outweighs fear.*
> *Life is always fighting, though Death is ever near.*
> *The two spiral together and existence does remain.*
> *As the stars above burn bright, burn out and burn again.*
> *AÏA ïante ZÏZ; ZÏZ ïante AÏA.*
> *Life unto Death; Death unto Life.*

After she finished singing we all sat stunned by her splendor. Entranced by her performance, I was oblivious to everything around me and it seemed as though the stars from the mural on the ceiling were swarming all around her in a dazzling flutter, as though she were at the very center of the universe, of all existence.

It was a long moment before I snapped out of my trance and noticed the ceiling suddenly start to crumble down and shatter at her feet. I heard a harsh hissing, a pinch, and then several deafening thumps.

Then I began to see blasts of orange and red, and the gray and black hue of smoke beginning to form all around me.

The room was suddenly engulfed in the fire of panic and chaos.

**United Terran Federation Communique to Chief
Defense Minister Luca de Gulliss
From the Office of UTFSF Admiral Li Kyphese
(Operations Commander – Joint Orbital Base
Khorneus)**
21 January, 3.2221 @07:14:05 TST

Chairman,

I have updates on the investigation into the destruction of two of our original 46 tests probes: ETP-016 and ETP-037. ETP-016 — the one to have completed the return jump — was deemed to have been defective. I have evidence and finalized reports detailing how several systems and hardware failed mid-Galaxial travel. The systems that failed were monitored throughout the test and have been deemed to be the cause for the disruption in equipment that led to the probe's subsequent destruction.

ETP-037 — the one that detonated shortly after completing its first jump — is a different case however. After its initial jump the probe broadcast its signal, clear, untainted and uninterrupted for 15.35 seconds before detonating. There are no spikes or irregularities in any of the probe's activity whatsoever. Moreover, after dispatching an additional 9 probes over seven separate missions to the last known position of ETP-037 we report zero successful returns.

Three of the subsequent probes (ETP-072, 078, and 080) were able to document the region before their destruction and found a spatial environment similar to our own—no gravitational or elemental anomalies, which rules out any kind of instability or caustic environmental destruction; which leads me to believe that the cause of these occurrences is that our probes have found something.

However unlikely it has seemed throughout Terranity's years of space exploration, I have reason to believe we've established contact with extraterrestrials. Furthermore, that they are hostile and do not care for our presence...

After scouring through Dr. Dorfmund's notes and recordings I've made a startling discovery about this particular incident which might substantiate my claims, but also gives cause for concern. The doctor—and her former partner Dr. Angelus—believed there to be a dimensional subsystem within our own solar system that is all together removed from the galaxy in the dimensions as we know them. This is evidenced by her repeated testing after the 'Ranch Incident,' as she continues to send her own probe throughout this apparent sub-solar-system. Apparently her notes on this planetary multi-dimensional sub-realm claim that we are one life-sustaining planet among 5 others in it and I believe this problem lies within her theoretical realm.

From the audio journal of Dr. Franzi Dorfmund – Astrophysicist

"Our solar system will never be the same. Those Angelus men are really quite spectacular and their theories are out of this world. I must admit I did underestimate the son however. The results of his test were conclusive and I've continued testing with the formulae that their contact 'Zan' gave me and have made astounding discoveries. It seems that one can not only transition via worm-hole from system to system and galaxy to galaxy, but also between dimensions. Apparently using these spatial equations, directional coordinate vectors, and a rather simple plot summary of coordinates, one can transition throughout the different star systems *and* dimensions of space — provided the dimensions work within our understanding of three dimensional space. Within the formulae I believe the first coordinate inputs to belong to a sub-dimension within our own galaxy. What follows is purely conjectural but I believe that this sub-system is located about a point of origin, (0, 0, 0) on a three-dimensional axis. About this axis, there would theoretically be multiple sub-dimensions. Should that hypothesis prove to be correct it would appear that transitioning between different realms would be as simple as varying the X, Y, and Z values for each coordinate set. For instance, if our world is located at 1, 0, 0, for example, it would theoretically be plausible that there is another world located directly in an opposing dimension across our axis at -1, 0, 0. Should that prove true other worlds at 0, 1, 0; and 0, -1, 0; and 0, 0, 1; and 0, 0, -1 would be logical assumptions. It would seem that many more tests are in order. As a scientist and an academic it seems obligatory to ask, what about all of the in-between space? Is that where every other planetary dimension is? Is that where the entire universe's other galaxies and planets come into existence? Is there a separate realm along 1, 1, 1 and -1, -1, -1? What would then exist in the space at -.7, 1, .5 or what about the space at 6, -14, and 32? Is that to say that there are infinite dimensions within the space between whole numbered axes? Does each planet in each star system contain its own sub-system of planets and dimensions? The possibilities would literally be infinite..."

The doctor's recordings are supplemented by many pages of notes but are rather conjectural and perfunctory.

However, if her notes are accurate and her theories true, the probes we've lost all traveled to one of the doctor's theoretical dimensions: the negative end of her supposed "Y" axis.

Our probes were sent out along random trajectories and ETP-037's just so happened to travel within Dr. Dorfmund's theoretical 'sub-dimension.'

Despite this possibility, I have not yet acted on these findings as they are still speculative and not yet proven. I await the Magistrates decision on the best course of action, but I believe it our duty to send a vanguard of UTF forces—I would recommend SRF CP-0147-VC-02 — to explore this particular region of space with caution.

Admiral Li Kyphese,
UTF Operations Commander: Joint Orbital Base Khorneus

OFFICIAL FLEET MOBILIZATION ORDERS 22-1-3.2221:07089-3556-1646-00301
United Terran Federation: Operation *Harbinger*–
Exploratory Battle Fleet Astaros,
To Admiral Li Kyphese
From the Terran Ministry Headquarters,
22 January, 3.2221 @03:26:40 TST

Admiral,

> ➤ You are to take charge of the full complement of UTF Exploratory Battle Fleet Astaros. Relief for your post as Operations Commander of J.O.B Khorneus will arrive within two standard cycles.
> ➤ At 06:00 Lunar Standard Time on 29 January, 3.2221 EBF Astaros will depart J.O.B Khorneus with spatial coordinates matching those of the lost test probes. Upon arrival you have two primary objectives:
> - o Subdue any hostile forces by any means necessary.
> - o Commandeer lands and assets for the growth, colonization, and manifestation of UTF forces abroad.
> ➤ Chief Magistrate Dekkun Pikus will accompany EBF Astaros on its maiden deployment. He shall oversee operations and insure our assets successfully carry out their mandates.

--CM Pikus will supersede the normal chain of command and report directly to the Chancellor—

➤ You are ordered to provide sit-reps every four hours Terran standard time.

➤ Mission time is TBD due to unique nature of objectives. Reinforcements and relief will follow upon completion of operational preparedness procedures.

The United Terran Federation thanks you for your compliance and wishes you success on your deployment.

Supreme Magistrate Hulioberto Pelantius,
UTF Chancellor

Chapter 13: Malïos

As Jonos sat in the pilot's seat on the bridge of ZANZABAR he thought about the afternoon's events as he keyed in the appropriate controls and pulled back on the control yolk, lifting ZANZABAR up off the landing dais.

He, Davriel, Ayla, Jimian, Pria, Ander, and Devian had had a trying time getting back to the dais amid the calamity of the Malïos attack, and as ZANZABAR lifted off Jonos let out a brief sigh of relief at being safely aboard the ship with at least half of his companions. He piloted the ship, remembering how they'd gotten there from the Great Gathering Hall, all-the-while grateful that he was on his way to meet up with his other brothers and the other half of their crew.

The first thing Jonos remembered from the attack was grabbing Ayla and ducking for cover after hearing the initial blasts and realizing what was happening. He remembered that prior to the explosions and chunks of roof that collapsed he had been enjoying a delicious bubbling fruit beverage with Ayla and was about to try another pastry she'd offered him. The pastry smelled delightful and resembled a glazed scone and he was moments away from indulging on its foreign tastes when the first explosion rang out.

A thunderous thud had sounded from above and debris rained down from the ceiling, followed by a dozen more thumps.

That moment, panic broke out and Jonos did

what his instincts told him to do: survive.

He grabbed hold of Ayla and wrenched her to the floor as yet more blasts could be heard. Commotion and chaos filled the air as many Gaïos shouted and ran this way and that.

Immediately after Jonos hit the floor, the others followed suit before they could be noticed and subsequently injured or killed. Amid the blasts and crackles of various weapons Jonos could hear the distress of the Gaïos people as they were being killed mercilessly; their cries of anguish filled the room where just before Réa had been singing so eloquently.

He couldn't help but wonder about his brothers and companions across the way at the other table, but he was ultimately focused on remaining undetected at the moment.

Suddenly Davriel dove down into a prone position next to him with a repeater in his hands.

"We need to get into safer cover." Davriel urged his brother, "the table would provide what we need but we'll have to flip it on its side."

"Okay!" Jonos said. "Where the hell did you get that?"

"I brought it with me." Davriel said nonchalantly. "Just in case."

"Good thing." Jonos said.

With a purpose now, Jonos began piecing together what to do. They were under attack, but by whom, he did not know. They needed to take cover, evade detection, and somehow escape back to ZANZABAR. First things first, take proper cover, just as Davriel said.

"I'll cover you. Get this table on its side and get it against the wall." Davriel barked.

"Yeah. Ander! Devian!" Jonos turned his attention to his friends around him, "Give me a hand with this! We need to get it on its side and then against the wall."

"Got it!" Devian affirmed.

"I dig." Ander added in his typical manner, relatively unfazed by the calamity of the situation.

"Be careful!" Ayla shouted as Jonos got into a squat and moved toward the edge of the table.

The three of them spread out behind the cover of the table while Ayla and the others huddled beneath it waiting to move. Davriel moved several meters beyond the table and took cover behind one of the six large pillar-like spines that had flawlessly led up to the beautiful mosaic that had been the ceiling. There he stood ready to give his friends cover.

With a heavy heft, Jonos, Ander, and Devian were able to overturn the table and duck back behind it before they proceeded to drag it over to the wall.

Suddenly, a flash lit up off to their side and hit the wall just over the table. Davriel caught a second flash out of the corner of his eye and dodged to the side as it hit the wall behind him.

A large figure appeared off to his right, it was roughly man-shaped and bounded for him in a blinding fast movement, though Davriel's instincts were sharp and he was able to quickly dodge the swipe of the assailant's weapon.

The figure was tall, heavily muscled, and lightly armored; and the wild swing of the weapon was clearly aimed at Davriel's head. He'd ducked just in time for the bladed weapon to pass over his head and embed itself in the pillar.

The attacker that held the blade then attempted to pull it loose, and did so, but was stopped as it suddenly felt several punctures in its torso.

Without a moment's hesitation Davriel had dodged the attack and shot his assailant several times in the chest.

The figure staggered back, shooting his weapon off into the ceiling in a final death-throw and then dropped.

Davriel looked on at the purple-blue blood that leaked from the attacker's wounds and realized that he looked quite like the Gaïos, though much more muscular and far less refined. The attacker's armor resembled forged metal and leather and seemed to offer little real protection, but certainly provided him with mobility.

Jonos sat just behind the table, watching how Davriel had dispatched his attacker and briefly marveled at his brother's combat prowess until he realized Jimian and his friends huddling around Devian. He looked and saw blood dripping from his head and feared he'd been shot.

"What happened?" Jonos yelled in a whisper.

"Something from the ceiling fell and hit him." Ander replied. "He's a bit dazed but he's still breathing. I can look him over now but we'll need to get back to the ship ASAP."

Jonos gave a brief sigh of relief that his brother had subdued the enemy and that his friend was okay, but was immediately distracted as he heard a blood-curdling shriek.

The sound came from above where two figures descended upon them.

As if in response to the previous attacker's death, these new assailants brandished several blade-like weapons, and advanced on Davriel, ready to exact their revenge.

These must be the Malïos. Jonos thought to himself, remembering what he'd been told by the Prime'ïos. *They look just like the Gaïos, except twisted and deranged.*

"Davriel, look out!" He started to say, but was cut short as he saw two Gaïos guards leap out from a secluded passageway beyond the pillar where the first attacker had fallen.

One of the Gaïos guards—a stunning red-haired female warrior called a Galasarï—carried a green-lit katana in each hand and was confidently ready to engage the Malïos invaders. The other Gaïos guard—a male warrior called a Galantir—was tall, silver-haired, and handsome, and carried a large two-handed weapon that looked like a halberd with long straight blades on either end. The blade glowed bright yellow and looked rather fierce.

The two of them took in their opponents, and immediately engaged them, crying out, "For AÏA!" and "For the Light!"

The Malïos attackers then shifted their attention from Davriel to their new assailants and began a fearsome duel as Jonos, Davriel, and the others looked on in wonder.

The Galantir began by swinging his lumen-

-escent halberd in a magnificent flourish before charging at the Malïos attackers, as the Galasarï inverted the grip on her short katana and charged at them.

The lead Malïos warrior was a humongous specimen — at least a full head taller than Ander who was the tallest of Jonos' friends — with a partially tattooed face and very little armor. His legs were completely covered by armor as were his forearms, though his torso was bare, exposing intermingled scars and tattoos. He wielded a massive broadsword and challenged the two Gaïos guards with an engrossed smile.

He met the approaching Galantir's strike with full force and parried it to the side before swinging his broadsword high over his head to bring it down on his foe.

The Galantir quickly dodged the downward strike and then began dodging the subsequent attacks.

Simultaneously, the Galasarï engaged the second Malïos warrior, a shorter and slimmer warrior, fuller in armor but equally gruesome and ugly in appearance. His hair was shaved on the temples and shaped into a double Mohawk on the top and his face was littered with piercings.

The Galasarï attacked with lightning fast speed and alacrity and the Malïos warrior was hard-pressed to stymie her attacks. He wielded a long sword and a long spiked shield that covered twice the width of his arm.

He used his sword and shield in combination to deflect and parry the Galasarï's quick strikes but was clearly outmatched.

Jonos and the others watched on in fascination from behind the cover of the table as the Gaïos and Malïos warriors engaged each other.

Not wanting to get too sidetracked with the spectacle, Jonos quickly assessed their situation. They had cover, but it was not completely concealing them and Jonos realized they needed more.

"Ayla," He whispered to his fiancé, "get Pria to help you collect some of that rubble and debris and fortify our position. We need to conceal ourselves."

She responded with a nod, but Jonos could tell by the look in her eyes that she was terrified. He too was rather fearful being in a combat situation on an alien world with an unknown yet brutal enemy, but he knew he had to remain strong; for her, for himself, for his brothers, and all of his friends.

He pulled her close and whispered in her ear, then looked in her eyes, and kissed her, "We'll be ok. We'll make it out of here. I promise."

Again she nodded her consent and crawled under cover to the others to help fortify their position.

"Only grab what's already behind cover." Jonos added, before turning his attention to his brother, "Davriel, take Jimian down that corridor where those two just came out. See if there's a way out of here."

Davriel nodded with confidence, and quickly moved down the hallway in search of an exit; staying low and moving as stealthily as possible with Jimian following behind matching his furtive stance.

Jonos then took another look toward the unfolding battle just as the Galasarï parried a high strike from the mohawked Malïos warrior.

She used her second sword to deflect the warrior's shield and kicked out at his chest, stunning him. He immediately reeled backward and clutched his stomach.

The Galasarï then stabbed her short katana through the Malïos warrior's left thigh which caused him to cry out in pain as he stumbled to a half kneeling position. The Galasarï then used the opening and cut off his right arm; dropping it and the sword he wielded to the ground.

Jonos heard a brief wail resound throughout the Great Gaïan Hall — amid the ever-present distressing cacophony of the situation — before it was quickly silenced as the Galasarï spun around in a beautiful flourish and seamlessly decapitated the Malïos warrior.

Everyone stopped what they were doing and watched on as the Malïos' headless body slumped to the ground.

Jonos watched in mystified wonder at the feat he'd just beheld, but his amazement quickly turned to horror as he watched as the first Malïos attacker — the one with the broadsword and tattooed face — closed in on the Galasarï after momentarily besting the Galantir.

Sneaking up on the Galasarï with a massive grin on his face, the Malïos warrior brought up his broadsword and inverting the grip, brought it down straight through her upper back.

"No." Jonos whispered.

"Karïséa no!" The Galantir shouted as he regained his feet, having previously been beaten down. Maroon blood seeped from his forehead and left side and he cried out in anguish as he watched the Galasarï fall to her knees, spew blood from her mouth, and slump to her side, lifeless.

The Galantir could only watch on as the Light began to leave his partner's body, leaving it cold and dim.

"I will avenge her!" he shouted as he picked up his halberd, and hastily charged for the mountainous Malïos warrior.

The Malïos warrior stood in defiance and waited for the Galantir's strike. He expected a stabbing motion or a low tripping swipe, and just before the Galantir stepped within striking range he jumped high in the air. He came down swiftly and powerfully with an over-the-head strike and narrowly missed the Galantir. Responding quickly, the Galantir swooped low and swiped again for a tripping blow.

Jonos continued to watch on in horror as he realized the Galantir was fighting a losing battle. He was on his last efforts and was soon to be defeated.

Arcos...

Jonos heard a voice in his mind.

Son of Angelus... come to me. I am not yet lifeless. The Light is leaving me, but I still live.

Jonos immediately realized the voice was that of the fallen Galasarï, the one called Karïséa.

Take my weapons, the weapons of Light. Fight the enemy. Defend this place from the Taint of Darkness.

Without thinking, Jonos climbed over the table and rushed toward the fallen Galasarï. Ayla and the others watched on in disbelief as Jonos did the unthinkable. As he approached he saw out of the corner of his eye, the Malïos closing in on a killing blow on the Galantir, and then looked to the near lifeless Karïséa, picking her up in his arms.

"Take them, son of Angelus," She said between her final gasps of life, "Take them and bring swift justice to that which would taint and destroy all that is good in life."

With those final words, the valiant Galasarï Kariseá passed out of this life. The Light departed from her body, leaving behind a faint, yet beautiful and noble Gaïos.

Jonos gently set aside the body of Karïséa and immediately grabbed her katanas, both of which flashed in a bright green hue when he gripped them, clearly responding to the life of their new wielder's warrior nature. Jonos' heart raged like a tempest that he could only quell with vengeance and he immediately turned his attention to the monstrous Malïos warrior and the wounded Galantir.

The Malïos warrior stood over the wounded Galantir in arrogant dominance, speaking to him in an ancient tongue. At first Jonos did not understand it, but as he got closer he realized he could not only hear what was being said, but understand it as well.

"You are just like the rest of your pathetically weak race. ZÏZ will blot out the 'light' you cling to and destroy all that you hold dear. Your woman may have bested my little brother Mok'jaka, but he was weak. She died as easily as he did. And now, so will you."

He then gently set down a large booted foot directly atop the Galantir's knee.

"Tell me, what is your name?"

"I will not give you that satisfaction." The Galantir replied in defiance.

"Yes you will." The warrior answered, stepping down in full force, shattering the Galantir's knee beneath his boot.

The Galantir cried out in agony before shouting, "Kadïm!" Hoping that in doing so, the pain would stop.

"Thank you Kadïm." The warrior said, "My blade thirsts for your soul, and now that it knows the name of yet another Gaïos victim, I can satiate its thirst, and my own."

As Jonos got closer he could see the great amount of maroon blood pouring from the Galantir. His knee was now crushed and fragmented and bled profusely, in addition to the gash on his head and the wound on his side.

Jonos then watched as the Malïos warrior brought up his broadsword once again to bring down a killing blow. With blazing speed and precision Jonos wielded the shorter of Karïséa's two katana and stabbed it right through the Malïos warrior's torso, stopping him before he could finish his downward stab.

However, Jonos quickly realized that was not enough to stop the warrior completely. The Malïos warrior turned around surprisingly fast for his size and sucker-punched Jonos in the face, knocking him back a good distance.

"Who in ZÏZ's name are you?" The mountain of a man asked as Jonos staggered back, leaving the blade in the warrior's torso. "No matter, I'll deal with you in a moment."

Turning back to Kadïm the Galantir, who now saw his doom at hand, the Malïos warrior effortlessly stabbed his broadsword through his chest, killing him instantly. Jonos watched as the Light drained from him just like it had with Karïséa. As he watched the light fade from Kadïm, he saw the Malïos' blade darken and sheen with a violent purple hue.

"That's enough!" Jonos cried out as he produced Karïséa's second katana.

"You want more, do you? Just who are you anyway?" The warrior asked.

"I'll gladly tell you my name, though I should like to know yours first." Jonos replied.

"Very well, I will grant you the satisfaction of knowing your killer. I am Mok'junai, the Mountainous, and this is *Jux'carar* the Soul Eater," he hefted up his sword.

"Your sword will not eat another soul, nor will you defile this place any longer with your malicious taint." Jonos replied, obstinately. "I am Jonos Angelus, Arcos warrior, and son of the last Arcon; and I will send you to your doom."

"Arcos?" Mok'junai asked quizzically.

Before he knew it, Jonos lashed out in a lightning fast strike. In one fluid motion Jonos darted toward Mok'junai. He switched the long katana to his left hand, slashing at the left side of Mok'junai while sidestepping behind him and removing the small katana that was still lodged in his back.

Mok'junai stumbled forward and felt his side, drawing back a wet hand, covered with his own blackened-blue blood.

"What the?" He questioned as Jonos darted back around the other side of him, slashing out with the two katana at Mok'junai's right arm. Despite his armor, his muscles flared and he felt a sharp bite as both blades struck and retracted with lightning fast speeds, drawing yet more of his dark blood.

Ayla and the others tried watching on as Jonos engaged the monstrous Malïos warrior, but they could barely follow his movements as they were so fast.

At this point Mok'junai began lashing out with slow, aggravated strokes, but Jonos was much too fast for him to hit.

"The Arcos are all dead! You are just some Gaïos abomination! This cannot be happening!"

"The Arcos live. And we will avenge all that you have harmed in this world! We will send you to oblivion, and your God ZÏZ will know that its power is not unchallenged." Jonos taunted Mok'junai now.

"No! ZÏZ is almighty! ZÏZ is power! ZÏZ will bring darkness and despair to this world and the next! Our Lady will have her prize, and ZÏZ will return to bring about the end of your precious life."

Jonos stopped his attacks after hearing the words of Mok'junai and having inflicted several cuts and wounds on his foe. He wondered what 'prize' Mok'junai spoke of.

"Hah! Why did you think we were here? You fool. You may have bested me, but the others will succeed. We will have the Prïm'ella, and we will res-

-urrect our Lord, and you will die in agony as you watch your loved ones submit to the Darkness by torture and madness! You cannot stop it!"

With these last words, Mok'junai hefted up his hulking figure, and struck out at Jonos. Jonos was able to parry the attack outward with the long katana—now in his right hand—and with the short katana in his left, he stabbed through Mok'junai's throat.

The Malïos warrior staggered backward, dropping his sword and falling to his knees with the short katana still in his throat. Blackened-blue blood spilled from his wounds and gushed from his throat and mouth as his body heaved in staggered breaths.

"Just as I assured you I would be your doom, I will assure you now; we will stop you." Jonos spoke with finality.

With a final double-move flourish Jonos removed the short katana from Mok'junai's throat, and then hacked the long katana right through it, detaching his head from his body.

He turned his back to the dead Malïos warrior, thankful that the fight was over and returned his attention to the rest of the scene at hand.

Regaining his wits, Jonos quickly realized that he needed to regroup and immediately pursue Réa and her captors. Davriel caught his attention after returning from the tunnel and confirmed that they now had a way out from where the two Gaïos warriors had come from.

Good, now we just have to regroup with Savos and the others.

Jonos looked across at the other table and saw

that it had been similarly flipped on its side, indicating survivors who were taking cover. He also noticed that the tumult within the Great Gaïan hall had died down considerably, except several small pockets of fighting and resistance here and there.

These Galantir and Galasarï sure are valiant warriors, Jonos thought to himself.

As he continued to look over the table he saw his twin Savos and was awash with happiness; he was alive and okay. Not wanting to wait any longer to see his friends, he immediately tried waving his brother over.

Savos wasn't fully attentive though and momentarily held up a finger, signaling Jonos to wait.

Hearing yet more shrieks Jonos quickly returned to the task at hand; escape.

From his advanced position he caught sight of a Malïos attack group numbering half a dozen, prompting him to remain concealed, though it appeared the Malïos attack group was preoccupied with the sadistic torture of one surviving Gaïos.

At that point Davriel again caught his eye and gave him another nod, indicating that they were good to proceed with their escape.

Davriel then moved out from the hallway and crouched behind a massive ornate chandelier that had fallen in order to provide cover for his friends.

Jonos nodded back before signaling the others to get up and follow them down the corridor.

Ayla and Pria got up—staying low to limit their profiles—and proceeded to the hallway, followed by Ander who was supporting Devian who was clearly still dazed from the knock to his head.

After they'd all safely made it to the hallway Jonos followed suit and carefully made his way to the doorway.

Once there he looked back once again at his twin and motioned again for him to come over. He watched in dismay as his twin shook his head.

He's not coming over.

Jonos then watched as Savos signaled with his hands; first he pointed to himself, then in an arcing motion around the hall, then to Jonos, finishing with an opposing arcing motion and finally he formed a Z with his thumbs and pointers.

He wants us to meet at ZANZABAR.

Jonos confirmed what Savos conveyed by nodding and slowly and rather hesitantly he turned his back and proceeded down the hallway to catch up with the rest of his friends; all the while hoping that his brothers and their companions would survive the horror of the Malïos until they could meet up again.

***

The hallway led out to an antechamber that had yet been untouched by the attackers. Davriel had safely led them to it and there they were able to regroup.

"What are we going to do about the others?" Ayla asked, "Savos and them were on the other side of the room."

"Yeah," Pria followed, "what about that shriek we heard just before leaving. We can't just leave them in there to deal with the rest of those savages."

"Savos is alive, and I can only hope the others are too." Jonos reassured everyone, "What we need to do now, is find Réa. From what that Malïos warrior told me, they want to sacrifice her to revive ZÏZ or something and bring about the end of the universe; the end of life as we know it."

Jonos' words hit the group hard and they sat for a moment waiting for him to continue.

Jonos realized at that point that they were looking to him to lead them. He quickly discerned that because this was his quest—his and his brothers—that he should be the one to lead them through this trying time. They waited for him to continue but he did not know what to say.

Davriel broke the silence at that point, "Savos can handle himself. And he's at least got Cephus and the others with him, they'll be fine."

"How can you know though?" Jimian interjected, "You have your gun, and Jonos was able to get those swords, but what weapons do they have? How can they defend themselves?"

"I don't know." Jonos answered, "But they will. And we *will* see them again. But for now we have to get back to ZANZABAR and at least get after Réa. The Malïos struck fast and hard and we can only assume that they'll be trying to leave just as quickly. Let's go."

Jonos then led the group out of the antechamber and through another hallway before coming to a split juncture in their path. The pathway continued straight, there was a turnoff to the left, and there was a staircase leading up. Running on nothing but instinct and a vague sense of his geographic location, Jonos decided to go up the stairs and the rest of his companions followed suit.

The staircase led them up two levels and eventually out onto an open platform that was directly behind the Great Gaïan Hall.

"What is this? A parking lot?" Jimian asked, clearly noticing that the vast space was occupied by many air speeders, similar to the one that took them to the feast earlier in the morning.

"Looks like it." Ander answered.

"We're gonna' use one of these to fly back to ZANZABAR." Jonos confirmed.

Just then Davriel noticed a flicker of light and instinctively shouted, "Get down, now!"

Jonos and the others immediately ducked into the recesses of the doorway and behind parking barriers that protected the entrance, narrowly dodging a volley of flashing cracks that impacted on the doorway from which they'd come. There were several Malïos on the platform, clearly expecting survivors to attempt an escape.

"Davriel, what's the sitch?" Jonos asked in a hushed tone.

"Six combatants. I count three with ranged weapons."

Jonos took this information hard. They had a greater number, but the outnumbered enemies were all experienced warriors. Davriel was the only truly tested combatant among them and despite Jonos' recent success against the Malïos warrior Mok'junai, he was doubtful that they would survive this ordeal without help.

"This doesn't look good." Jonos admitted, "Any ideas?"

"The priority is gonna' be their ranged attackers. If we can pick off their shooters we should be able to close in and do some damage." Davriel said.

"But how?" Ander asked, "You've got the only gun, and Jonos is the only other one with weapons."

"I'll draw their attention," Jonos answered, "that'll free up Davriel to take a few shots and hopefully take a couple of them down."

"And then what?" Ayla persisted, concern clear in her voice.

"I don't know," Jonos said, "we'll play it by ear."

"Play it by ear? Are you serious?" Ayla said, quite indignantly, "That kind of mentality may have worked back on Terra when figuring out where you were eating dinner, but this is life and death here! You can't just leave that up to 'playing it by ear.'"

"Once Davriel does what he can with the ranged Malïos warriors, I'll close in with my katanas and redo what I did inside." Jonos said, trying to sound confident.

"Whatever we decide to do, we'd better do it fast," Jimian cut in, "they're getting closer."

"As soon as we engage the enemy you guys head for the closest craft." Davriel ordered.

"Ready?" Jonos asked Davriel.

Davriel nodded in reply and immediately after, Jonos drew both katanas and jumped over the barrier he'd hidden behind and dashed off to the left.

Davriel promptly stood up from cover and shot several rounds from his repeater as the rest of them rushed to the closest speeder under the cover of the parking barriers.

Davriel's first round found its mark between the eyes of the lead Malïos gunman. The subsequent shots caught the second Malïos shooter in his chest, shoulder, and arm, dropping him straight to the ground; but the third gunman dropped under cover before Davriel's shots could find him.

The Malïos warriors had briefly taken the bait as Jonos continued sprinting off to the side, but the majority of them now turned their attention to Davriel, clearly realizing the ranged target as the immediate threat.

One Malïos warrior, the leader of the group — a tall female with a fiery orange ponytail, pale tattooed skin, and red eyes — remained focused on Jonos and immediately jumped to his position to engage him.

Before Jonos knew it, the lead Malïos warrior was on him. She'd drawn a fierce toothed blade from its scabbard and unleashed a flurry of attacks that Jonos was hard-pressed to defend. Despite Jonos' advantage of having a second blade, the warrior showed no sign of even acknowledging this as an advantage at all.

She struck out at him with vicious slashes, stabs, and reversing swipes; sweeping blows, overhead cuts, and faint attacks; all which Jonos was barely able to parry or narrowly avoid all together. From the beginning of the fight Jonos was losing and it was only a matter of time before he lost for good.

In the meantime, Davriel had the remaining three Malïos warriors converging on his covered position. Since he first felled the two gunners, the rest had slowly stalked Davriel; much like a pack of dogs furtively hunting a fox.

The remaining gunman intermittently let off shots around Davriel's position to keep him pinned down, while the other two approached him in flanking formations on either side.

As Davriel and Jonos' predicaments unfolded, Ayla and the others watched in tense apprehension. They had fulfilled their part of the plan and sprinted—as stealthily as possible—to the closest Gaïos air speeder and waited for Jonos and Davriel to complete their tasks; a feat that was looking less and less likely. They huddled in cover and anxiously deliberated what to do next.

"We have to do something to help them." Ayla urged.

"But what?" Jimian asked.

"Yeah, we can't attack those *things.*" Pria added, "They're too much for us."

"What's going on guys?" Devian surprised everyone as he finally spoke, still dazed but coherent enough to sense trouble.

"Jonos and Davriel are in serious tro—" Ander began to say before he was stopped mid-sentence.

A roaring sound suddenly rushed overhead and drew everyone's attention. A flashing light and a quick shadow passed above the tumult of the battle and for a brief moment friend and foe alike looked on in stunned captivation, anxious to find out the ident-

-ity of the newfound arrival.

Several shots then rang out and before anyone knew what happened, two of the Malïos warriors dropped cold.

A sudden flash of light caught everyone's attention and only the most alert saw as a flashing figure darted past the final Malïos gunman, decapitating him instantly.

Everyone questioned what had happened as they finally turned their attention to Jonos and the last remaining Malïos.

"What in ZĪZ's name?" The orange-haired Malïos shouted, "What new trickery is this?"

Jonos watched as an armored figure soared down from the sky and impaled the Malïos warrior through her shoulder.

He beheld the figure and realized it was female—based on the slender figure and the form-fitted samurai-like armor.

Her greyish-green armor covered her body entirely, but was lightweight enough to provide exceptional mobility and her head was concealed by a rather rudimentary helmet with a facial visor. She wielded a long glowing pike that was embedded in the ground as it had pierced directly through the Malïos' shoulder. The new warrior stood above her victim triumphantly before finally opening her helmet's visor, exposing a beautiful dark face with emerald green eyes framed by long white bangs.

"Malïos filth. You have no business here." She said stoically.

The orange-haired warrior responded by spitting out some of her blue-black blood, "So there are some real warriors among you after all?"

"Indeed, someone has to combat your insidious barbarity." She replied. "Now, why are you here?"

The Malïos spit yet more blood before answering, "I will not indulge your questioning. Enjoy your small victory while you can. The darkness will soon consume all. ZÏZ will destroy your world and everyth—"

The Malïos warrior was cut off as a flash of light shot out and impacted directly in her head.

The Galasarï standing before them sighed as the orange-haired Malïos slumped down on her blade. She removed it, kicked the dead Malïos off, and withdrew the lighted blade.

"Roxara, I was not yet finished with her," She addressed a second armored female who approached, "I would have liked to have known why she and the rest of her fiendish friends are here."

"Barïm, you are too wishful in thinking that you can learn anything from such abominable creatures. They should be eradicated. Every last one of them should be destroyed so that they may join the darkness they love so much and rid this world of their malevolence."

"Yes, but they have never yet attacked the High Citadel in force like this, we must find out why." The Gaïos warrior Barïm added.

"I can tell you why," Jonos began, reminding the new-comers of his presence.

"Who are you?" Roxara asked brutishly, "some Malïos underling?"

"My name is Jonos Angelus. I am of Arcosan lineage and Terran as well. I am a friend of the Prime'ïos and of the Gaïos people."

"An Ordained Child?" Barïm said, mystified.

"Arcos and Terran? How have you come to be? The Arcos are dead and we have not heard from the Ordained Children since they left this world, eons ago." Roxara persisted.

"I do not have time to fully explain," Jonos replied, "You wanted to know why the Malïos are here? They are after the Prïm'ella. I heard it myself. They want to take her for some sacrifice for ZÏZ."

"By the Creator they mustn't succeed." Barïm exclaimed.

"We're on our way to get her now." Jonos said.

"We?" Roxara asked.

"My companions and me." Jonos said, pointing out his friends by the speeder, and Davriel who was double checking the kills on the Malïos.

"But we have to go now. We're going to meet up with our other companions and our Gaïos guide Brandu. Will you come with us? We could certainly use your skill."

"Do as you must Arco son." Barïm said after a long and rather uncertain pause, "We will not stand in your way. But we must remain here and cleanse our capitol of the remaining Malïos taint."

"AÏA's blessings on you friend." Roxara added, "Go and find the Prïm'ella. Bring her back safely, and Brandu too."

"What?" Jonos started to ask before being cut off as the two began to leave.

"Go now. You have no time to lose." Barïm exclaimed.

Jonos turned to go but hesitated for a moment. He looked back at the two and nodded to their backs before heading for the air-speeder. Davriel followed suit and met him there.

"Who were those two?" Davriel asked as they boarded the craft and Jonos took the flight controls — thankful he had watched the Gaïos pilot earlier in the morning on their way to the feast and had developed a basic understanding of its controls.

"Yeah," Ayla seconded, "they certainly saved us back there."

"They were true Gaïos warriors, like the Galasarï and Galantir inside. That's all I really know. I think they might know Brandu..." Jonos hesitated before concluding, "But we've got to get a move on."

Jonos' words ended the conversation on the matter as he settled into the pilot's seat.

Everyone continued to think on their experiences as Jonos piloted the air speeder back to *ZANZABAR* with full speed.

So many thoughts raced through Jonos' mind as he worked the controls to fly the air speeder; foremost in his mind was meeting up with his brothers and friends, and getting after the Malïos who'd captured Réa.

Ultimately he began wondering where the Malïos would take her but was distracted as they quickly arrived at the docking platform where *ZANZABAR* laid waiting. So far their journey had been one of newfound and mystic learning, but now it seemed as though it was becoming far more perilous and life-threating.

Moments after landing they disembarked the air speeder, boarded *ZANZABAR* — many of them chose to remove their tattered Gaïan robes as their ceremonious value was clearly outlived — and immediately settled in to their posts. Ander and Ayla carried Devian to the medical bay to treat his head wound; while Pria immediately went to engineering to take up her post.

Fearing the worst, Jonos sent Jimian and Davriel off to the dorsal turrets in case of further Malïos attackers, and now Jonos found himself on the bridge of *ZANZABAR* clutching the flight controls and taking them airborne to find their friends.

"Welcome back Jonos." Zan said. "Everything okay?"

"Hey Zan." Jonos somberly replied. "Not really, we need to get to the others, fast."

"I've been tracking your signal for quite some time now, I've remote dispatched the *Zieru* to pick them up. I was growing concerned."

"You already sent the Corsair to get them?" Jonos said, "Good thinking."

"I've set up a nav marker with its heading on your display for our rendezvous."

"Good. Let's go find our friends."

Chapter 14: Rendezvous

The room shook all around me and smoke filled my nostrils as I lay motionless on the ground. A piercing sound occupied my ears and I struggled to open my eyes.

"Savos." I heard a muted voice cry.

"Savos!" Again it cried, more pressing and almost panicked.

"Savos! We need to get out of here!" I finally came to as Cephus jostled me out of my daze.

"What?" I yelled.

"There are hostiles all around us. We need to get the hell out of here!" Cephus replied as he ducked his head behind whatever cover he could find.

I took a moment to look around and try to get a grasp of the situation. Everywhere I looked there was chaos.

Cephus and I and a few of my companions were hunkered down between the wall and our table — where only minutes before we were enjoying a feast in our honor and a resplendent performance by Réa. The table was now on its side and had clear signs of being dragged toward the wall.

I looked again to see who was with me and found the familiar faces of Cephus, Tytus, Shelyse, Kai, and Lizia. I quickly asked them if anyone was hurt and was beyond relieved to hear that aside from a few cuts and scrapes everyone was fine and in one piece.

I then tried my best to mask my inner panic and mustered my most assertive urgency and said,

"We need to find the others and get out of here."

"No shit." Cephus replied curtly. "They're across the hall." He motioned with his finger through the table though dared not lift his head above cover and risk revealing our place of hiding.

"Hey." Tytus whispered while showing me something in his hand.

He held a small pistol that he'd taken from the locker he'd installed on ZANZABAR's bridge.

Clever. Samper... per – what'd he say? Paratos?

"Savos." Cephus drew my attention, "we have to go."

"Tytus, how many of those do you have?"

"Just the one." He replied, "Davriel has the other one I brought."

I considered the limited cover that would supply. *It's something...*

"We can't stay here." Cephus pressed.

The situation suddenly erupted around us within the confines of the Great Gathering Hall. I could hear shrieks, wails, and strange electric sounds, and vile laughter. It was a sick and twisted laughter but it was ever present and sent a shiver down my spine.

Lizia then caught all of our attention as she had found an adequate spot within our cover to look out onto the main floor and observe the situation.

"Guys, check this out." She said, waving us over.

We could see clear over to the other table, which was flipped on its side much as our own was and had several chairs stacked on one side and bits of rubble all around; a clear effort to make cover.

That meant that someone at least tried to conceal themselves over there and hopefully they'd succeeded.

I then looked toward the main entrance of the Great Hall, or what was left of it, and saw a small group of half a dozen figures holding someone hostage. Two figures held the Gaïos man while another beat him senseless. Two others stood watching in amusement and the final figure stood hooded and cloaked with its back turned.

I could hear shouts emanating from the conflict but was distracted when I caught sight of my twin across the room. I was overwhelmed with gladness when I saw him and immediately tried to communicate with him somehow.

He stood somewhat aside from the table, concealed behind some rubble, holding two glowing swords and I noticed blood on his face. He pointed toward a doorway where Davriel and Jimian crouched in waiting.

Davriel emerged from the cover of the doorway and snuck out of cover to a position farther left. He was holding the other gun Tytus had brought in and I immediately knew what was about to happen.

Davriel waved back toward the table and I then watched helplessly as Pria, Ayla, Ander, and Devian got up from behind their makeshift barricade and snuck toward the doorway with Jimian, Davriel, and Jonos covering them.

I noticed that Ander had been supporting Devian who was not walking entirely of his own will.

Jonos motioned back over to me as if he wan-

-ted us to get up and come join them, but the distance was too far and there was little to no cover, even with our two guns. I looked at him, then at my friends behind our barricade, and suddenly heard a noise behind me.

I turned back to those behind our table and found the familiar face of Brandu.

Relief washed over me momentarily, as my mind worked, I then turned once again to my twin and held up a finger, telling him to wait.

Looking back at Brandu I realized he had a gash in his forehead and was clutching his side as he crawled over to us, and suddenly I had the realization that I didn't know what had happened to the Prime'ïos, or Laurales, or *Réa*.

Many Gaïos lay dead or dying throughout the hall and I only now realized their plight. Upon coming to my senses I'd immediately worried about my own people before even considering the Gaïos, and now I grew more worrisome.

"Where is the Prime'ïos? And his daughter Réa?" Brandu asked urgently, managing, despite his wounds.

"We haven't seen them."

"We must find them!" He continued. "They are no doubt the enemy's targets."

"Whose targets?" I demanded.

"The Malïos. They are here."

By mere mention of their name I felt compelled to look back around at the group of figures and this time I could make out much more than their number.

They stood rather tall and slender, with pale

limbs and dark hair. Their raiment didn't seem practical and rarely consisted of much beyond chains and hastily forged armor that left many gaps exposing bare, uninhibited flesh; it resembled that of gladiatorial armor of the First Age.

There were male and female Malïos and each was equally fearsome, yet also provocative, and they all shared in the barbarity of the situation; directly enjoying the cruelty or watching along in sadistic enjoyment.

The group continued to beat and maul their captive but eventually their enjoyment lessened and finally, in a morbid display of cruelty they all stabbed him multiple times with their various bladed weapons, except the scarlet hooded one who'd had its back turned.

I looked away and once again Jonos caught my attention as he frantically gestured for us to join them, having just witnessed the same atrocious sight we saw.

"We can't chance that," Cephus answered my unasked question. "It's way too risky without proper covering fire. Even with Tytus' gun, we're outmatched."

"I know another way." Brandu offered, "But we must leave now, and we must find the Prime'ïos and Réa. The Malïos must not take them."

I then heard an almost feral, hair-raising shriek that came from the Malïos invaders and they began moving. I looked in the direction in which they moved and saw several Gaïos men rise from having been buried under a pile of detritus.

Despite being outnumbered two to one they

attacked the Malïos invaders with long staves that emitted blades of light, engaging them valiantly and providing the perfect opportunity to cross over to the others.

"Quickly, we're clear now, we can make it to the other side while they're preoccupied." Kai urged us to go toward Jonos and the others.

Brandu protested and urged us to use the hidden passages he spoke of. I agreed with him, as did Cephus and we quickly decided to take Brandu's hidden passageway rather than risk the open run toward Jonos and the others.

I glimpsed one final time at Jonos, who was now in the doorway, and looked on with a furrowed brow and a concerned look. He had realized that we weren't coming over. I nodded to him, then pointed behind me and in an arcing gesture tried to convey that we would meet him around the back of the hall, motioning in the same way for him. I finished with a Z sign with my fingers to indicate meeting at ZANZABAR.

He nodded back in tentative confirmation and I watched him slowly turn away and disappear down the hallway.

Looking back at Brandu who briefly nodded in approval and then squatted up a bit to check if the coast was clear. He moved low about twenty meters out of cover to a spot on the ground. Again a hole seemed to appear in the floor as it had when Réa emerged before her performance, and Brandu signaled us over.

Cephus went over first, followed by Lizia, Shelyse, Tytus, myself, and finally Kai. Kai argued the point of him going last, and not wanting to waste time arguing over who went last I yielded and went before him.

As I crouched and made my way out of cover I looked back one last time at the Gaïan warriors who'd valiantly stepped up to engage the Malïos. Right at that moment, I saw them all fall.

The first took two spears — or something like them — straight to his chest as the two Malïos whom he'd engaged bested him.

The male and female Malïos spun around and stabbed him once more in the back with small knives that they carried in their off-hands — they'd accomplished all of this in perfect unison, mirroring each other's movements as if they'd rehearsed the attack.

They looked at each other and despite being so far away, I could see the lust that reflected in their faces for their actions and each other.

The second Gaïos was caught in some kind of bola that a Malïos woman employed. It wrapped around his legs and tripped him up.

I watched as his assailant then pulled out small pickaxed knives from a harness on her chest and hack at the Gaïos man's back as he fell, spraying blood everywhere.

Upon seeing this I faltered a step and tripped over some detritus and crashed into a prone position.

Kai, who was right behind me, similarly dove into a prone position next to me to avoid attracting further attention.

The hooded figure looked up toward our direction as the third Gaïos man was surrounded by two male assailants and brutally hacked and stabbed to death.

The figure removed the hood to get a full view of the area and upon removing the hood we found that it was a female Malïos.

Her skin was gray but she was beautiful to behold, with small, sharp features, and a black Mohawk tipped with blood red before ending in a long black ponytail, and both Kai and myself caught our breath for a moment, clearly surprised at how hauntingly beautiful such a malicious being could be.

She began walking towards our hidden position. We were safely concealed behind enough rubble that she could not clearly see us, but we were still about ten meters from the secluded doorway where Brandu and the others sat hidden and needed to move and fast; before we were discovered and shared the same fate as our would-be-saviors.

Kai looked at me, really looked at me and said, "Go. I'll cover you."

I hesitated for a moment. I knew that despite Kai being humble and friendly, he was a tough and hard-hitting guy. He was burly, strong, and always ready to have a good bout and he was an excellent wrestler and could handle himself in a bar-fight or a good tussle; but this was anything but that. And I doubted what he could do to engage our foes and cover me.

"What? Are you crazy!? We'll go together."

"You'll have a better chance if you go before me, you're faster than me and I can slow them down for you."

"We're not seriously arguing about this are

we? Don't try to be a hero man. Come on! She's getting closer."

The Malïos woman was nearly ten meters away and would clearly see either of us if we tried to run now. Brandu and the others were signaling us over fervently now.

What happened next was entirely unexpected, and will never be forgotten.

"I said go!" Kai shouted.

He then grabbed me by the loose cloth of the tunic I was wearing — we'd since taken off the robes as they hindered our movement — and rising up with me, tossed me half way to the door before moving toward the approaching Malïos woman.

As I stumbled my way toward the door in the floor I turned my head once more, just in time to see the Malïos woman dart toward Kai in a flash.

She leapt from the ground in a flourish, tossing aside her robe as she did so, exposing subtle yet full body armor, luscious curves, and agile limbs wielding two pick-axed knives. She landed directly on top of Kai and imbedded the knives deep in his shoulders.

"No!" I cried, as Brandu and Cephus grabbed me from within the hidden doorway.

Kai shouted out in excruciating pain and I couldn't handle seeing him taken from us, but his pain quickly turned to anger, and he lashed out at his assailant, grabbing her, punching her square in the stomach several times and hurling her aside.

A moment later, the other Malïos attackers were surrounding him in a semicircle, waiting to strike.

None of them pursued us for a moment as we lingered over edge and watched.

Two of them began to dash at him—the two who'd struck in perfect unison before—and as quickly as they'd darted out, they fell to the floor. I barely saw it happen it was so fast.

The previously hooded Malïos assailant had responded so quickly that as soon as the two made the decision to attack Kai, she'd thrown small stilettos into their backs, putting them down instantly. The other three immediately backed down and stayed out of the fight. Kai saw an opportunity in the newly downed enemies and defiantly picked up one of their spears despite his pain.

I then heard Brandu say something in his native Gaïan tongue that sounded much like a curse before saying, "AÏA's Light no! He mustn't use their weapons!"

It was too late though. Not a moment after picking up the spear Kai dropped it, and in a paralyzing heap he dropped to his knees, clutching the hand that had just grasped the spear. The Malïos woman who'd attacked him stood in front of him, removed the previously imbedded knives from his shoulders, and re-imbedded them in his lower back.

Cephus pulled me into the doorway as Brandu closed it. Kai's brief agonizing shout was the last thing I heard before the doorway sealed completely above me.

"There is nothing you can do for him now. He is gone to us. We must go now before they find us. We must escape or his sacrifice will have been in vain!" Brandu urged.

I couldn't move. I was bewildered. Dumbstruck. Lost. *Kai... He's... gone. Just like that.*

"Savos, come on!" my friends shouted from further up the tunnel.

"Come on, we have to move, now!" Cephus said as he straightened me up, "we still gotta' find Réa and the Prime'ïos!"

Despite the loss of Kai, the prospect of finding and saving Réa and the Prime'ïos served well to distract me from what just transpired, and I was able to refocus — however slightly — on our situation. The three of us quickly caught up to Tytus, Shelyse, and Lizia at a crossway within the hidden tunnels.

As we met up with them Tytus immediately asked, "Where's Kai?"

I looked to my friend of two decades and couldn't muster a response. Out of all of us, Tytus was always the closest to Kai and I knew that it would hit him hard that Kai would no longer be with us.

Cephus followed up behind me and shook his head somberly, "Kai didn't make it. He sacrificed himself to save Savos and ensure our escape."

Tytus heard the news and wouldn't accept it at first, "Well we have to go back and help him!"

He'd had much more time with Kai throughout the years and was closer to him than any of us, and he — quite understandably — found it hard to leave him behind.

"We can't Tytus. He's gone." Cephus repeated as he grabbed his shoulders and locked eyes with him.

Tytus swallowed hard. He slowly nodded and

I could see that it hit him hard. Shelyse further consoled him, and he began to gather himself.

"We have to keep moving." Brandu said hastily. "I was able to secure the entrance to the passage with a sufficient seal on the door, but we must move. The Malïos will not be far behind. They no doubt saw us, and don't give up on prey that easily."

He pointed down the path we were to take, and swiftly entered it as the rest of us followed suit. Despite his previous debilitating wounds, he didn't miss a beat in getting us moving.

As we snuck through the hidden passageways Cephus asked aloud, "Brandu, when Kai went for the spear, you said not to use their weapons. Why?"

"Indeed, son of Arcus," Brandu replied as we continued moving through the passageways, "Never, under any circumstances should you use the weapon of the enemy; for its taint is malicious and foul. Any who wield it in violence shall suffer from it equally. Your friend Kai," he hesitated for a moment, "he wouldn't have suffered long. He wasn't their target so they would have dealt with him swiftly."

Tytus looked to say something until Lizia — who was currently leading in front of Brandu, scouting out the way as she was among the fastest of us — alerted us of something up ahead.

"Guys, look, this passageway is a dead-end." She said.

We caught up to her and finally stopped at a wall. "Maybe we took a wrong turn somewhere," Shelyse provided.

"No, we are just where we need to be." Bran-

-du made his way between us to the wall where he put up his hands and spoke some Gaïan phrase, activating the door through some enchanted method. Suddenly, the wall moved back and aside, exposing a dimly lit shaft. The shaft led up a dozen or so meters to a sealed hatch. I must go first; there is another seal at the top. Please, follow me."

"Come on guys," Cephus urged us along as Lizia, Shelyse, Tytus, and myself slowly began the climb following after Brandu.

Brandu then spoke another Gaïan phrase and the door exposing the shaft beneath us closed, pitching the whole shaft black. Immediately, dim translucent lights flashed up along the ladder we were to climb, providing significant lighting the whole way up.

"We are fortunate my friends," Brandu said on the way up, "This passageway has been used just recently, and I believe it was the Prime'ïos that passed through here."

Once at the top, Brandu opened the door using his Gaïan enchantment once again and we all filed out. The surface was quiet and we were immediately able to find a secluded place to take cover in case any other Malïos were around.

"The Malïos typically hunt in various packs of three to ten members. Sometimes animals hunt alongside them. Be mindful and as quiet as possible if you should see them. They strike quickly and with great cruelty and savagery." Brandu briefly explained to us as we sat in cover, "Now, we must hurry and find the Prime'ïos and Réa before they do."

We took in our new surroundings and I quickly realized that the streets and walkways were completely empty; the Malïos attack had clearly sent everyone into hiding and put the entire High Citadel on high alert.

Out of the corner of my eye I noticed a familiar sight on my wrist Link. It was a blue blinking light in the upper corner.

Zan!

I quickly answered it, tapping the blue light and a hologram of Zan immediately opened from my link.

It was a LiveLink, and Zan was rather tense, "Savos, finally! I've been trying to reach you for some time now. Where have you been?"

"Zan, it's good to hear from you. We've been a little preoccupied lately. Have you heard from Jonos and the others?"

"Yes, after picking up on the commotion via Gaïos transmissions and my own satellite data, I established a Link with him and heard what happened during the feast. I've advised them to return to the ship immediately. You should do the same."

"No can do just yet, we've got a rescue to mount. Any chance you can send us some kind of assistance?"

"Affirmative, wait just a moment," After a brief pause she continued, "I'm sending the *Corsair* to you. Now that you've resurfaced it will track and come to you via your Link's signal. Aboard you'll find more sufficient weapons for your own defense and any rescue mission. Do take care of yourselves."

"Good. Thanks. When Jonos gets there, track our signal and come pick us up, will ya?"

"Of course. Be careful Savos."

"No promises."

I nodded to the others, who'd all clearly listened to the LiveLink conversation I just had with Zan.

Brandu had picked up on something and addressed us all, "The Prime'ïos surely went this way, but from here I do not necessarily know where he might have gone. There should have been guards here to protect him and since there is no presence of them, he must have escaped. But we need to find where."

Brandu, Savos… you must find me.

I heard a voice suddenly address me inside my mind. It was the Prime'ïos, and he was reaching me, clearly in distress.

I am just above you… the building on your right; I've taken cover on the top floor.

I looked to the building and addressed the others, "The Prime'ïos, I hear him in my mind. He's telling me that he's hidden up there, I pointed up to a building that I simply *felt* was where the Prime'ïos was.

"Then we must hurry." Brandu said, "Quickly now!"

We all hurried into the building and rushed our way up the stairs, grateful that they were fixed stairs unlike the enchanted ones we'd taken on the way up to the chamber of the Prime'ïos.

As we ascended the stairs I briefly wondered why Brandu hadn't known he was up there since I believed Gaïos to be telepathic.

Perhaps it's a skill to be learned, or not?

Nearing the top floor, I could hear voices, they were hushed but I could tell they were Gaïan. The stairs led to a lush atrium that occupied the main area of the top floor.

Upon ascending the final steps, I noticed the Prime'ïos was lying on the ground propped against a tree-planter box.

Laurales and two other Gaïos attendants were with him, Laurales tending to the Prime'ïos with another of the Gaïos, while the third — a soldier — stood guard.

"AÏA's grace! You made it." Laurales exclaimed as we entered the atrium, smiling and furtively gazing at Cephus before looking to the rest of us.

"Indeed." Brandu responded, "How is the Prime'ïos? What is his condition?"

"He's fading. He was wounded by a Malïos poison-tipped dart. The light of AÏA is fading from him. He can't hold out much longer unless we get him to a Gaïan healer." Laurales replied.

"Bra... Brandu," The Prime'ïos managed to falter, "Where is Réa? Is she not with you?"

"No..." Brandu replied somberly. "I had hoped she was with you."

"How can we find her?" I asked.

"I fear... I fear she has been taken by the Malïos. You must... track them down and find her. We cannot let them escape with her."

"Of course." Brandu agreed.

Just then Lizia called from by the window, "Hey, something's coming this way."

I looked up and saw the profile of the *Corsair,* "That's our ride out of here. We'll meet it in the courtyard and set out after Réa."

"Go then," Laurales urged. "You must save her."

"I shall stay with you, Prime'ïos, some Sibanna herb might help slow the poison and I know some enchantments of the healers of the surface." Brandu provided.

"No Brandu. You must go with them. Guide them. Find her. Protect her from the taint." Laurales urged.

Just then we could see the *Corsair* roar over our heads through the atrium windows and descend over the exterior courtyard.

"Come on, our ride is here!" Cephus bellowed over the roar of the *Corsair,* then more calmly, "We'll find your daughter Prime'ïos."

Tytus then covered them as Cephus, Lizia, and Shelyse headed out toward the *Corsair;* Brandu and I hesitating for a moment, staying with Laurales and the Prime'ïos.

"Go, Brandu Bracaras, go with Savos… Find Réa. Save her from the fate of the Malïos." The Prime'ïos rasped.

Brandu then turned to go outside after the others, and after looking at Laurales once more — she nodded and tried to manage a smile — I followed suit. As I hurried out I could hear the Prime'ïos in my thoughts once more.

Protect her from the Taint; from the Darkness. Keep her in the Light. You will need her Light before the end. I am sorry I could not yet tell you the remainder of the Arcos' story and of your father.

Seek out the ÏOS; he will have the rest of the answers you desire. Go with the Light of AÏA, the blessings of the Gaïos, and the strength of the Arcos. Go to your destiny, Savos Angelus.

I boarded the Corsair as he communicated his last words to me and found my friends waiting to lift off.

"Lizia, you good to fly?" I asked through the crew door.

"This thing? Uh... I guess?" She stuttered but got up and moved to the pilot's seat.

"Don't worry; I'm sure Zan can give you a hand. Tytus, what do we have for weapons?"

"On it," he said solemnly, already bending down and retrieving a weapons case from beneath the seats.

"Can the equipment aboard this ship scan for high frequency energy signatures?" Brandu asked, eager to begin tracking the Malïos.

"Of course," Zan's voice came through over the com-link. "And Lizia can certainly help me fly. Regarding your question Brandu, though there are hundreds of thousands of energy signatures on this planet, I have been able to track one signature that registers higher than the rest but it is further out in Gaïan space."

"That would no doubt be a Malïos *Melfiantu*. They are marauding ships that traverse the realms pillaging and destroying whatever is in their path." Brandu explained. "But we need to find the raiding ships that it sent out, the smaller crafts that it deploys to execute its attacks. There would most likely be between two and five of them for this type of quick strike. Those are where they'll likely be taking her."

"Wait," Zan continued, "I'm registering sev-

382

-eral other signals that read larger and far more unstable than most others. They're operating beyond most normal safety parameters. Would those be the enemies' means of escape? They are currently remaining stationary."

"Good, we can still catch them." Brandu said.

"Let's get a move on then!" I urged.

Just then we lifted off as Lizia took the *Corsair's* controls with Zan guiding her through the motions and procedures. The exterior hatch automatically sealed shut behind us as we lifted into the sky and blasted off to track down the Malïos attackers.

***

As we flew up in the sky Zan's voice was heard throughout the *Corsair* guiding us to the Malïos ships she was tracking, "The three of them are spread throughout the High Citadel; two on the underside of the city and one above on the exterior platforms of the city."

"Let's aim for two birds with one stone and head below, shall we?" Cephus suggested, from up in the in the co-pilot's seat, to the right and behind the pilot's chair.

"Sounds good." I said over the hum of the ship.

"Lizia, please take us out and over the edge." Zan genially asked.

While flying over the city I couldn't help but look at the various screens within the compartment of the *Corsair;* there were navigational readings, system readouts, communications equipment, and camera shots of outside.

I looked at the images of outside, trying to get a scope of what we were seeing but couldn't quite make out the full details despite seeing smoke, fire, and destruction throughout various sections of the city.

I stood up and walked the three steps it took to get to the flight deck.

Standing next to Cephus in the co-pilot's seat I had a full view of the cockpit and the scenery beyond.

The *Corsair's* bulbous canopy allowed for a huge view of the surrounding area and I could see several smoke plumes, billowing up above the High Citadel.

It seemed as though the attacks were happening everywhere. The Malïos must have orchestrated attacks in dozens of other places in addition to the Great Gathering Hall. I took a minute to ponder the other attacks and what their strategic value may have been or if their only target was Réa and the Prime'ïos.

My thoughts were interrupted as we approached the far reaching platforms on the rim of the High Citadel. I noticed, the dwellings which shared similar architecture as those in the center of the High Citadel, were significantly smaller and spread out, much like the suburbs of any major Terran city. They were also primarily unharmed — clearly they were not targets.

"The Malïos must have known most of the population would be at *Gallï Gaïanos*, they did not target our homes, but our place of celebration." Brandu said somberly.

No one replied to what Brandu said, though all of us thought of the loss of so many of his people. Our thoughts were diverted as we passed over the final outlying dwellings and out over the edge of the High Citadel.

The view beyond was all clouds, grey and dreary, far gloomier than the previous conditions.

I took a moment to ponder the view beyond and what the surface of Gaïa could possibly have looked like, but was drawn away as we flew down and around in a wide arcing shape toward the underside of the High Citadel.

Beneath the High Citadel there were hundreds, if not thousands, of curved glowing discs embedded in the bottom of the city. They glowed bluish white and looked to be the source of what kept the city afloat.

"You'll want to avoid those exhaust ports Lizia," Zan advised, "They could very easily disrupt our airspeed and launch us into a spiraling tailspin."

"Got it." Lizia promptly responded.

As we wove our way through the exhaust ports we made our way toward the center of the High Citadel and slowly our objective came into view. In the center of the circular shape that was the High Citadel there was a spire—much like the tip of a spinning top—which had several different tiers, each with several different platforms. On the second highest level we could see the outline of two ships on two platforms: the Malïos strike vessels.

"I detect three life forms in the vicinity of the

ships." Zan replied.

"That may be true, but I do not think Réa is anywhere below." Brandu added.

"Well, best to go down and have a look anyway." I said.

"Lizia, bring us low and around into a hover just behind their position." Cephus ordered, "We'll cut under and surprise 'em. Tytus, you and Savos get ready to hop out on my mark."

"Roger." Tytus responded.

He still looked slightly broken up about the loss of Kai, but he understood that there wasn't time to mourn just yet and held himself in check. He handed me a pistol and several mags as I walked back into the passenger compartment thinking about the 'orders' Cephus had just given out.

Tytus then hefted a shotgun up from a stowaway gun-rack that was concealed under the seats of the passenger compartment and cocked it emphatically, clearly feeling comfort from its weight and familiarity.

"Ready in thirty seconds!" Cephus bellowed.

My little brother's military experience conducted his every action and even though I was thinking more about the idea of myself as a potential 'Captain' — or *Shipmaster* rather — of this voyage, I was quickly finding that I wasn't exactly the best person to lead in combat. Not for the last time was I grateful for my brothers' talents when it came to combat situations.

I checked the safety on the pistol and checked the chamber — just as Tytus taught me to when we used to go shooting. I found that there was a round in the chamber and a full magazine in the clip. I clutched the three mags that I'd hastily thrown into my pockets and for a moment I hesitated.

I briefly doubted what we were about to do before Cephus shouted again, "Saddle up boys! Stay low when you hit the ground, we'll provide air support for you."

Shelyse grabbed Tytus by his shoulder and I could see her say something but the passenger compartment of the *Corsair* wasn't at all a place conducive to hearing whispers.

They embraced each other, holding one another close and tight. They separated for a moment, but he held her hands in his own and then replied to her in a similar inaudible fashion as the two of them stared deeply into each other's eyes.

His stare seemed to bore through her soul and down to her very core, while she matched his intensity with a steely gaze that could have split an iceberg. I wasn't sure but I thought I could see her mouth the words, 'come back to me' and later on something resembling 'kick' and 'ass' but that part I wasn't so sure about.

"Fifteen seconds!"

Suddenly I felt the ship lurch down and swiftly back up again as we maneuvered underneath the platforms the Malïos ship occupied and launched back above before settling into a hover. The lighting in the passenger compartment shifted from the red hue it previously had, to a green one.

"Go go go!" Cephus shouted.

"Be on your best guard," Brandu encouraged us. "The Malïos are quite lethal and are not to be taken lightly."

"Lethal is my middle name." Tytus said confidently.

For a split second I thought about the nature of Tytus' response and remembered that his middle name was in fact Aron; but then remembered that his last name Hyaeger was actually an old Eurkasyian word for "hunter" proving that he was implicitly, by name, lethal.

Before I continued my thought Tytus pressed the release lever on the hatch, passionately kissed Shelyse, and jumped from the hatch.

"Don't do anything stupid Savos!" Cephus shouted as he turned around from the co-pilot's chair to see me off.

"No promises!" I quickly shouted back to Cephus before taking a sharp breath and following Tytus out of the hatch, making the two meter drop to the surface, tucking and rolling as I landed so as to avoid injuring myself.

Finishing the motion, I immediately dashed further into the cover of some nearby utility crates, while Tytus dove behind some kind of power docking station that looked like it could have provided power for one of the Gaïos air speeders — like the one we'd flown in to arrive at our welcome feast just several hours beforehand.

The Malïos guards were immediately onto us and moved for our position. There were two males and a female, all of which wore similar armor to what we'd seen before; sparse armor plating interspersed between hastily laced together harnesses and chains, again offering the wearers a wide degree of motion, yet little real protection—still it was more than I presently had.

Only one of these Malïos carried any type of bladed weapon however, the other two carried slender, slightly curved weapons that resembled firearms.

These were quickly discovered to be just that, as they immediately fired on the *Corsair*. Bright, darting flashes of purple streaked out at the *Corsair* which Lizia maneuvered as well as she could—especially well I'd say for it having been her first time flying it—and we immediately found ourselves in our first firefight with an alien race.

As the two Malïos with the firearms kept up their fire, the third one—one of the men of the group—jumped behind one of their craft just moments before retaliation came from the *Corsair*.

Among the cacophony of battle, I now heard the even louder whirring and clattering of rapid gun fire.

I chanced a look out from cover to see the *Corsair's* wing mounted turret pylon spraying the landing platform with a hail of projectiles. The shots quickly found their marks and before we knew it the two Malïos warriors were down.

Lizia then adjusted her approach vector and positioned the *Corsair* just beyond the platform, spinning it around to where we could see directly into the cockpit where she and Cephus sat.

Cephus then used hand signals to communicate to us as we had no direct communication link with him. He held up two fingers, then pointed them at us and then waved in an arcing fashion to one side of the platform. He then pointed at himself and did an opposite arcing gesture and then pounded his fist into his other hand to suggest we would flank the remaining warrior.

"You get that?" Tytus asked me.

"Yeah, we're gonna' flank from one side while they do the other, right?"

"Right. Be on your guard though." He continued, "This one has a blade, keep your distance. It may also be best to keep him alive for questioning so we can find out where Réa is."

"Good thinking." I exhaled as Tytus emerged from his cover and I followed suit.

He approached the Malïos air speeders with his shotgun trained on their shapes, and I mimicked his movements as we rounded the left side of the platform. I could see from the right corner of my eye that the *Corsair* was slowly making its way around the other side.

As we neared the Malïos vessels their shapes grew in clarity and I couldn't help but shudder at their hideous and malicious design.

The ships were about the same size as the air speeder we'd ridden in earlier in the morning but were far more malicious in appearance. They were dark in color, a blend of blacks, grays, and purples and their edges were sharp and severe. They were slightly bird-shaped as their fuselages resembled birds' beaks, and they had tiny rear-fixed wings that swept back like a bird's; with long sword-like tails.

There were blades and spikes coming from many places on the ships and everything about them seemed menacing; most of all the front mounted ramming pikes.

As we drew nearer I felt the air surrounding them begin to grow foul. It felt thicker and danker, and every step we took toward the crafts had an ominous feel to it. As we nearly made our way around the ships to where we saw the final Malïos warrior take cover I looked up to the *Corsair* which was now hovering in a holding position.

I wasn't sure who was to make the first move so Tytus and I waited for a moment before he looked to me and nodded, he was ready.

At that moment, he turned the corner and Lizia reacted to his move, maneuvering the *Corsair* into position.

Tytus hefted his shotgun up as he rounded the corner and swiftly pointed it straight into thin air.

There was no one there.

Not a single thing other than the sides of the Malïos ships.

"What the hell?" He said, lowering his gun a few inches, baffled at what we were looking at, or rather, what we weren't looking at. "We saw him take cover here. Where'd he go?"

Just then I heard a blood curdling wail and felt a rush of air as the Malïos warrior seemed to explode out of nowhere right between Tytus and me. He swiftly swung his blade at me, and despite lunging backward I felt the charge it emanated as it just missed my chest.

In a frighteningly fast double kick, he knocked my pistol from my hands and planted his thick heeled boot directly in my chest, bashing me down and stealing the air from my lungs.

In response Tytus quickly leveled his shotgun, but it was instantly knocked out of his hands with the warrior's reverse swinging kick.

The Malïos warrior then stopped for a moment, looking Tytus over. Tytus was defiantly standing his ground though couldn't hide his concern. The Malïos warrior then turned around briefly back to me still reeling from his kick to my chest. He looked us both over as though he'd never seen anything like us before.

Our garments were Gaïan, but they were charred, torn, faded, and partially missing, from our escape, and he was no doubt puzzled by our features more than our attire; for there were several differences varying from size, to skin tone, to hair, and more.

The warrior was taller than any of my companions and any Gaïos I'd seen so far. He looked Gaïan though was far stronger and meaner. His skin was remarkably pale, emphasizing his fierce black eyes and tattooed face.

His hair was easily a meter long, jet black, and pulled back into ponytail. His plated armor was far more complete than the others we'd yet seen as it covered his shoulders, torso, and legs.

He wore a spiked wrist gauntlet on his right arm and his left arm was bare, save for wild and other-worldly tattoos and a spiked bangle on his left wrist.

The blade he carried was menacing and slightly bent like a scimitar and glowed with a malevolent violet hue, and for the moment I was hap-

-py that it was resting down at his side; though I would have been far happier if it was sheathed, or better yet nowhere in sight, or still better yet if it were on its way to the planet surface after his body was blasted off the platform by my friends up in the *Corsair*—a feat I quickly realized was impossible since Tytus and I were well within their line of fire.

For a moment we three seemed frozen in an unlockable trance; the warrior was looking at Tytus and me, and the two of us back at him; none of us knowing what was going on in the others' mind.

He then surprised us as he slowly and methodically pointed at me and hissed rather than spoke the words, "Thisss one I know, for he carriesss the blood of the ancient enemy," he then directed his attention to Tytus, "thisss one I do not… what… are you?" He was clearly unfamiliar with Tytus' ancestry.

Before either of us could respond, Brandu landed softly on the ground behind me, having just jumped from the *Corsair*.

He stood exposing a blade that looked just like the katana used by ancient samurai warriors from the early ages.

"Friends, heed not the word of the Enemy, for it is full of lies, deceit, and death." Brandu said as he approached.

"It mattersss not… For all of you will share the sssame fate. ZÏZ will claim you all!"

"The Dark One will never quell the Light!" Brandu countered.

At that the Malïos spit and angrily snarled his upper lip, "The Gaïosss are foolish to think that any amount of light can ssstop the darknessss that isss coming for you. Your Arcosss friend here certainly can't help you. Look at how he recoilsss. He isss no warrior. I will claim him long before the darkness doesss."

Immediately he jumped several meters up into the air and came rushing down at me, blade first. I rolled to my left but was stopped mid-roll as the sword had firmly imbedded in the loose material of what was left of my tunic.

As I gazed up into his dead black eyes I could see death so pure and malicious that I was paralyzed until my gaze was broken when the Malïos warrior suddenly staggered back, withdrawing his sword from my robe.

Brandu had intervened, first parrying the warrior's sword — releasing it from the ground where it'd stabbed through the excesses of my tunic — then firmly kicking him back.

Brandu's intervention only seemed to anger the warrior though as he spit blue-violet blood from his mouth, licked his lips, and snarled exposing razor sharpened teeth, "You will die like all of your kind, wretched Gaïosss filth!"

"You first." I heard a familiar voice say before the distinct blast of a shotgun rang out.

The Malïos warrior staggered forward a step or two as blood now began to dribble from his mouth. I looked past his wavering figure to see Tytus stepping forward, smoke dissipating from the barrel of his shotgun which he still had trained on the wavering Malïos.

"Guess I'm the first Terran you've ever met,

huh? I guess I'll be the last too." He said, firing the shotgun again, shooting out the Malïos leg. He'd clearly used the distraction of Brandu's arrival to his advantage and retrieved his weapon before using it to catch the warrior off guard.

"Te-te-terran?" the Malïos warrior coughed, more blood spilling from his mouth and the scatter-shot wounds in his back and leg. "The Ordained?... You are... foolish to think, such a weapon from such an inferior speciesss can kill me. I... am... Tar'thak of Shakrah! I am... Malïosss! I... am the darknessss! The... the weapon of ZÏZ!"

"Well I am Tytus Hyaeger of Terra. And you just messed with the wrong species." Tytus replied in pure defiance, cocking his shotgun and readying it for a killing shot.

"Wait Tytus!" Brandu exclaimed before turning his attention to the Malïos warrior, "Where is the Prïm'ella? What have you done with Réa?"

"She is on her way to *Her* now. Where she belongsss." He said, spitting out more blood and grinning, again bearing his razor sharp bloodstained smile, "And there isss nothing you can do to ssstop it!"

He suddenly roared as he rose to his feet, frantically swinging his sword toward Tytus, who was quick to dodge the surprisingly quick moves of the wounded warrior. In an instant Tar'thak suddenly stopped where he was.

Before I knew what happened, Brandu was standing behind Tar'thak with his blade sticking through his chest, "She will *never* make it. We will stop you and your precious ZÏZ. And I shall grant you the Darkness you love so much."

Brandu said this as he removed the blade and in a flourishing motion, severed Tar'thak's head from his body.

Tytus and I stood stunned in disbelief at what Brandu had just done—neither of us expected something so violent to come from such a seemingly refined people or individual.

It took me a moment to remember that the Gaïos did have some warriors, and we didn't yet know everything there was to know about Brandu. I wondered what type of life he'd lived on the surface before coming up to the High Citadel.

"The third ship," Brandu spoke, "we must track it down before it leaves the planet."

He said this as he retracted the blade and concealed it within his sleeve. I wasn't sure but the blade's handle seemed to resemble the instrument he'd played on the rooftop the night before.

"We should get back to the others then. We can catch up to them faster on *ZANZABAR*." I said urgently.

"Very well. Let's go." He concluded and turned to approach the *Corsair*.

I looked at Tytus, who stood staring at the body of Tar'thak. He had a look on his face that seemed to say, 'I'm going to kill every last Malïos, or die trying.'

"Hey," I started to say, "you coming?"

"Yeah." He nodded, as he looked away from the body. "Let's get these bastards." With that we turned and headed for the *Corsair*.

Lizia had dropped the *Corsair* to a minimum

hover just above the platforms and we quickly made our way back aboard. I for one was grateful that the incursion was done and over with.

The Malïos were certainly a ferocious enemy, one which I would have to steel myself to fight again; especially after watching them kill Kaitoh and nearly kill me.

"Where to?" Lizia asked, looking back to the hold as we boarded.

"Get us back to ZANZABAR. We have to find that last Malïos raider." I shouted as soon as I was aboard. At that Lizia lifted off before the hatch could even be closed.

"Best deal with those first." I heard Cephus say just before Lizia maneuvered the *Corsair* into a slightly higher hover. "Don't want them causing any trouble for us or the Gaïos later on." Not a moment later I watched as two missiles flew out from the *Corsair's* winglet pylons and impacted on the Malïos raiding crafts, blasting them to pieces.

Looking away from the explosions I watched as Shelyse sat with Tytus, expressing her simultaneous gratitude at his and my return, and continued grief at the loss of Kai. Tytus slumped down next to her near the rear of the compartment and despite the steeliness with which we left the platform; the previous events were beginning to pile up.

I quickly turned away and faced the console in the hold; giving them what little privacy I could and began thinking about the previous events.

Despite the significance of losing my friend of so many years, I couldn't help but ponder the words that Tar'thak and Brandu exchanged; *she is on her way to* Her *now, where she belongs.* Tar'thak truly believed the words he said, as all men do just before they die. So what did he mean then? *Where she belongs?*

We shot off like a rocket back above the city as we were pressed for time to catch up to the last Malïos raider. As I continued to think about Tar'thak's words I looked at Brandu. He was sitting and meditating in one of the other seats aboard the *Corsair.*

"Brandu, what did —" I started to say before Zan called over the com to report that we were about to dock with *ZANZABAR.*

"Jonos is ready to receive us." She spoke for all to hear.

"Already? That was fast." I then remembered that Jonos and the others had gone straight for *ZANZABAR* while we pursued Réa so were already ready to depart.

"Everyone brace yourselves, this is gonna' be an interesting landing." Lizia called out.

Chapter 15: Pursuit

Docking with *ZANZABAR* was a rather jarring experience as we hastily completed our rendezvous, rather pressed for time, but Lizia and Jonos managed to pull it off without fault. We needed to rendezvous with Jonos, Zan, and the others in order to pursue the final Malïos marauding craft; so in a rather scrambled fashion, we pulled off a hasty landing in the main cargo bay rather than an orderly landing in one of the launch tubes.

Lizia carefully positioned the *Corsair* on a matching trajectory along *ZANZABAR's* flight path and we waited for a brief moment of uncertainty as Jonos then quite literally scooped us out of the sky in rapid pursuit of the remaining Malïos.

According to Cephus, Zan had been quite busy while she broadcast to us on the *Corsair*. She had been aboard *ZANZABAR* monitoring the space around Gaïa using its superior navigation systems. She'd picked up the signal of a large vessel that was no doubt the acting "mother-ship" for the two Malïos raiding crafts we'd just dealt with and the one we were now pursuing.

After Lizia successfully landed the *Corsair* in the main hangar, she let out a hefty sigh of relief that fully expressed her newfound sense of ease now that we were safely aboard, "Whoa, now that was a wild ride."

"You did great. Thanks Lizia." I said, leaning into the front compartment.

Cephus then bent over his console to pat her

shoulders, "Great flying."

"I'm heading up to the bridge. You guys take care of getting things secured down here, if I know Jonos, we're probably in for a bumpy ride. Cephus, meet me up on the bridge when you're done."

"Roger." He curtly replied.

I activated the door switch for the left side hatch and briefly looked back at Tytus for a moment. Despite the need for urgency, I left him to mourn while Shelyse comforted him and I quickly disembarked the *Corsair* with Brandu following on my heels.

Brandu and I rushed to the hangar's front access hatch that led to the main corridor and bounded up the stairs in strides of four and five. Arriving at the hatch itself, I tapped the access key and quickly found myself in the main corridor.

Behind us was the way to the ship's aft med bay, machine shop, and engine room; and in front lay the way to the crew compartments, galley, and the bridge. I quickly sealed the hatch behind us before leading the way to the bridge.

When we got there I was surprised to see the lone figure of Jonos sitting in the pilot's chair. "Where is everyone?" I asked as Brandu and I approached him.

"Battle stations." Jonos replied in a serious and somber manner. "Davriel and Jimian are manning two of the dorsal gun turrets, Pria is in the engine room prepping for orbital flight, and Ander and Ayla are in med bay treating Devian. Welcome aboard Brandu." He tacked on, noticing him just behind me.

"Is he…" I started to say, but hesitated, thinking about Kai.

"He's fine, just got knocked in the head by some falling debris. Probably just a concussion. Where's your half?"

"They're fine. They're securing the *Corsair*. But…" I hesitated again, "Kai… he… he didn't make it. He sacrificed himself to save me. Those fiends… they got him and tore into him like it was nothing."

I stopped myself as I remembered the barbarity of the image in my mind.

"The Malïos are truly vile and vicious foes." Brandu interjected, "Your friend's sacrifice was truly noble, but we must not let it be in vain. There will be time for mourning later, but for now we must save Réa, she must not make it to Shakrah."

"If what I heard about her going there is true, no, she most certainly cannot." Jonos added

Brandu and Jonos then shared a quizzical look, as if they both knew something about the intentions of the Malïos but I didn't have time to question them before Zan appeared on the dais of the main console.

"Hello Savos," She greeted, "Welcome aboard Brandu. Please excuse my brevity, but I've found them. They're moving off-planet. Fast."

"We've got to follow them!" I urged.

"On it." Jonos said and immediately he returned his attention to *ZANZABAR* and the ship lurched upward, hurling my innards to the very bottom of my being. "Everyone, strap in and brace yourselves, we're going for orbit in 20 seconds."

Twenty seconds felt like two seconds and I rushed to strap myself into one of the chairs.

Despite *ZANZABAR's* impressive gravitational feats—counterproofs to the physics I'd grown to understand—we would still need to be secured to avoid injury.

ZANZABAR pitched up in a strong thrusting fashion and not for the first time, nor the last, I felt as though I was holding on for my life as Jonos piloted us into infinity.

We broke atmosphere moments later and as we did so the ship felt noticeably lighter and we all felt a brief sense of release without the confines of Gaïa's full gravitational pull.

Our relief was short lived as Zan suddenly broke back over the ship's comm. "Incoming! Enemy fighters inbound!"

"They must be escorts for the main ship." Jonos concluded, "Jimian, Davriel, take 'em down!"

As we closed in on the Malïos Raider we realized it was going to reach the mother ship before we could catch it, especially now that we faced escort fighters.

"Wait, what if we engaged them with the Interceptors?" I suggested, watching as the enemy crafts approached.

"I wouldn't recommend that." Zan replied, "I'm picking up increasing energy readings from the Malïos mother ship. It's amassing power for warp travel."

"No!" Brandu exclaimed, "We must not lose them!"

"I'm not terribly familiar with their systems and can't get a traceable signal." Zan stressed.

Moments later we could see the first outlines of the enemy escorts and the first flares of laser blasts coming from our dorsal mounted turrets. Cephus and Lizia suddenly appeared on deck.

"What's the sitch?" Cephus shouted.

"Inbound enemy fighters!" I barked out.

"Cephus," Zan interjected, "I need you to get nav systems ready for jump. Keep a steady plot of the enemy ship." He immediately took to his station, strapped himself in, and began tapping away at the console's controls.

"What can I do?" Lizia offered up, always ready to act.

"We could use you on the third dorsal laser turret." Zan added.

She took off back down the main corridor to man the third laser turret and aid in the defense of the ship. And just as soon as she entered the bridge, she'd left it. Just after she left there was an immediate explosion off ZANZABAR's nose as the enemy fighters opened fire and scored their first hits.

"I've angled the forward shield with as much power as I can spare, but it won't last long against prolonged direct fire!" Zan then turned her attention to Pria back in engineering, "Pria, I need you and the Tech-Mechs to physically divert power from the launch tubes to the warp drive to accelerate its charge, then lock in auxiliary power for an ignition level blast in the main engines."

"Uh... okay, got it." Pria's voice came over the ship's com and it seemed like there was hesitation in her voice. "Gimmie a minute."

I prayed that she knew what she was doing, and was glad that she at least had the assistance of the Tech-Mechs as I returned my attention to the approaching fighters.

As the Malïos attack crafts loomed in front of us and Jonos barreled down on them, the Marauder came into view.

Though we only saw its rear and it was still quite a ways away, not only was it more menacing than the previous Raiders we'd seen; it seemed all the deadlier.

Large blades and spikes adorning its hull seemed to emerge from every possible surface, save for the areas occupied by the two large cylindrically-curved engines mounted on its sides, and a huge empty wheel-like structure that took up most of the stern of the craft.

On top of the wheel-like mounting there was a menacing twin-linked turret that slowly took aim directly at us.

"We must subdue the mother-ship." Brandu encouraged. "Go for the engines!" I looked back at him skeptically before refocusing on the enemy attack craft and the turret that just bore down on us.

"Working on it." Jonos replied, ever focused on flying.

As he finished speaking I noticed the Malïos turret aim directly at us. As it took aim, it fired almost simultaneously as Jonos keyed a few controls and maneuvered the control yolk to pitch us down, before suddenly executing an impressive barrel-roll that not only tested the ship's capabilities, but the sto-

-machs of the crew as well.

Jorah dammit I hope everyone was strapped in.

As he maneuvered the Malïos fighters continued to open fire as they advanced on our position and overtook us before breaking off to engage in individual attack runs.

"Track targets. Fire at will!" I ordered our gunners before following up, "Jonos, get us as close as you can to that Malïos ship."

After Jonos completed the barrel-roll I refocused my attention on the radar monitor located on the center dais on the bridge. I was able to see a full three dimensional display of ZANZABAR, the Malïos fighters, the Raider we were still pursuing, and the Marauder.

"Zan, if you and Cephus can't track their jump, is there a way we can at least use the hole they'll split in normal space to enter the Galaxia and follow them in?"

She took a second to compute before replying, "It's theoretically possible, but we'd have to be directly behind it and on the exact same trajectory in order to be successfully pulled in with their warp-mass."

"Jonos, get us there!" I shouted to him over the chaos of battle. Moments later I checked the command console once more and noticed one of the attacking fighters disappear from the visual.

"Woo-hoo! Got one!" I heard Lizia's voice over the ship's open comm.

"Great Lizia, don't get cocky!" Jimian replied over the tumult of battle.

"Keep at 'em guys!" Jonos encouraged, not

flinching for a moment as he continued to maneuver *ZANZABAR* toward the enemy ship.

Despite the taxing situation we found ourselves in, I realized for a brief moment that I'd suddenly felt a kind of stillness; my senses were fully attuned — and from that came a new confidence — though I wasn't sure where it had come from.

My mind could suddenly see the full picture of what was happening.

As if in a dream, my consciousness seemed to depart from my body, from the bridge, from *ZANZABAR* itself, and ascend high in the depths of space.

I could see *ZANZABAR* in hot pursuit of the Malïos Raider and Marauder; Jonos, myself and Cephus and Brandu all aboard the bridge; Davriel, Jimian, and Lizia on the individual dorsal turrets; Pria desperately working in the engine room; Ayla and Ander treating Devian back in medical; and Tytus and Shelyse now making their way up from the *Corsair*.

I could see each and every one of them.

Their pain, their bravery, their sense of purpose and drive; I could see and feel it all.

Beyond my friends and family, I could also see the Malïos ships that we had engaged. I easily felt the malicious taint of Darkness that the Malïos vessels exuded, but amidst their malevolence there was a light. A light that burned bright, searing away the darkness around it and combating it; it acted as a beacon to all that are engulfed in the darkness of fear and uncertainty.

As my consciousness focused on the light I

barely noticed the small violet and orange explosions of another Malïos ship attacking *ZANZABAR* but ultimately being destroyed by yet another one of my companion's handiwork.

I looked on in wonder as the light I noticed advanced into the growing darkness before it was ultimately consumed by it. My body then began to tremble.

Despite my previous ease and the prolonged moments that I was truly calm, I instantly snapped to reality.

Several explosions and a violent lurch in our ship, mixed with various shouting from my brothers, friends, and Zan brought me from my reverie as more calamitous hits could be felt throughout *ZANZABAR.*

"They made it to the Marauder! We're running out of time!" Cephus yelled.

"Hits on the left side! We're venting oxygen from the left side launch tube!" Zan shouted.

"Scratch one more bogey!" Davriel called over the comm.

Jonos then announced that we were coming up on the Malïos Marauder while Jimian called in yet another kill.

"Shit! Zan what the hell is that?" Jonos suddenly yelled rather excitedly.

Something was happening to the space around the Malïos ship.

A menacing storm of vicious mauve energy slowly erupted in front of the Malïos ship. Fierce jolts of white hot lighting began to emit from its prow and the malicious light rapidly grew in intensity.

I could see a similar glow emitting from the empty wheel shape on the rear of the ship, though it was no longer empty but also emitting the similar purple and white lightning.

That must be its warp propulsion system.

I then noticed the final Malïos attack craft retreat back toward the Marauder, and the topside turret no longer targeted us.

"They're jumping." Brandu said in grave astonishment reminding us all, that he was in fact still present. "We must move in, now!"

"Savos, Jonos, you're on your own." Zan blurted out.

"What?" I exclaimed, "You can't be serious!"

"If we're going into the warp now I have to divert all my available capacity to keeping the ship's warp regulating shield active."

"But our coordinates aren't locked in." Cephus protested.

"I have to!" She shouted in response. "I'm closing down my processes. I don't have much time. Just follow them as close as you can!"

Her figure then started to dissolve, it seemed as though horizontal lines of her were disappearing one at a time. I watched on in anxious bewilderment before I heard Jonos bark out over the com, "Pria, do I have full auxiliary power on the engines?"

"Affirmative. You are go!" She yelled back.

"Everyone, hold on to your butts." Jonos shouted.

Jonos hurtled us off toward the Malïos ship in a final effort to catch up to it before we'd lost it for good.

"We'll see you on the other side Zan!" I managed to say despite being thrust backward by the continued force of our acceleration.

"No promises." She said as her final lines disappeared and she vanished from the display altogether.

The storm of lightning and crackling energy had grown in intensity and I began to see space bend all around us. The Malïos vessel seemed to shrink and contort in front of us as the space around it seemed to cave in.

"May AÏA's light protect us from the darkness that is to come." I could hear Brandu say before he broke off into his Gaïan tongue.

I looked and saw him floating in a cross-legged position several feet above the deck as he recited what I thought was a prayer. My astonishment was short lived as our own surroundings began to encroach on us and space seemed to become denser.

"Here goes nothing!" Jonos shouted one last time as we approached to within meters of the Malïos ship.

A fraction of a second later we were sucked into nothing as we flew directly toward the spot where it had just been. We followed the Malïos ship into the nothingness that lies on the other side of everything.

May AÏA's Light shine on you, even in the darkest of places.

We entered "normal space" with the same sizzling, ear-popping crackle as before, though this time with far more sirens and claxons of all sorts blaring.

Having experienced the sensation before, I was far more lucid upon entering normal space this time around.

"What's our situation?" I asked.

"Expect incoming enemy fire!" Cephus shouted.

"They were waiting for us!" Jonos shouted over the blaring of another claxon. "We got a few shots of on 'em as soon as we entered normal space. But Zan's still offline and we're going down hard!"

"Going down? Don't you generally need somewhere to go *down*, in order to go down?" I replied, slightly confused at our newfound predicament.

"Look," Brandu said, standing in all seriousness beside me, pointing through the forward viewport.

I looked at the planet that now occupied the entirety of the front viewport. The surface was reddish brown, marred with craters and giant mountain ranges; interspersed with dark foreboding patches of greens and browns of forest and jungles, and black bracken-infested waters.

Despite it taking up the majority of our view I could also make out the image of the Malïos Marauder. It too was losing altitude and aimed at the planet's surface. It was breaking atmosphere.

It was noticeably damaged and for a moment I was grateful that we could cripple it and force it to crash, but was also fearful of our own impending crash landing on the unknown planet before us.

"Where... are we?" I asked.

Brandu breathed in heavily, looked at the floor, and closed his eyes before dismally sighing and saying, "Macra."

www.ingramcontent.com/pod-product-compliance
Lightning Source LLC
Chambersburg PA
CBHW05085825O626
47155CB00001B/9